THE DEBT

TC PARKER

PUBLISHED BY NEFARIOUS BAT PRESS
2022

THE DEBT
Second Paperback Edition

Published by Nefarious Bat Press

THE

DEBT

ALSO BY T. C. PARKER

Saltblood
Hummingbird
A Press of Feathers
Salvation Spring
Maiden (with Ward Nerdlo)
The Long Con: An El Gardener Omnibus

THE EL GARDENER TRILOGY
The Debt (Book 1)
The Push (Book 2)
The Remembrance (Book 3)

For Alex & Zachary

LEICESTER

1976

The first thing he smelled was grass - wet grass, fresh and earthy. Not around him but nearby, somewhere.

The next thing he smelled was himself: stale alcohol, and vomit, and something even ranker and more acrid besides. Eyes closed against the sunlight he could feel even through the pink gauze of his eyelids, he reached a hand down to his trousers, feeling thighs, then groin, then arse through the worn fabric, and his fears were confirmed. He'd shat himself again. Slept in it too, most likely.

The ground under him was hard and unyielding. Concrete, he thought. Damp concrete, watered with the sweat and piss that had no doubt seeped out of him overnight.

There was something propping him up from behind - keeping his top half upright even as his legs flopped out in front of him, limp and crumpled as a pile of old laundry. He groped at his back with a moist hand, and felt the knots and grains of old wood on his fingers.

A doorway. He'd fallen asleep in a doorway.

He concentrated, trying to summon up some recollection of whatever had led him there the night before, but there was nothing, no *there* there, no sense-impression or narrative trajectory where memory should have been, just a ribbon of blankness, stretching from the ride on the bus he'd taken yesterday to stock up on cream sherry at the Co-op to the second that he'd woken, cold and shaking and stinking like a public toilet - not on his kitchen floor or draped over the porcelain rim of his bathtub, but *outside*, in the world, his humiliation on display for anyone and everyone who might walk past to see.

He didn't *want* to know where he'd ended up, where his body had steered him while his mind was absent. But he knew he *ought* to know - if only so he could begin to understand what he might have done, and who might have seen him do it.

He opened his eyes, squinting to protect himself from the unwanted morning sun.

Straight ahead were gravestones - old ones, grey slabs and crosses furry with moss, the grass around them wild and overgrown. Behind them was a path, curving down a slope to an old stone wall.

A churchyard, then. Making the door behind him, he deduced, the entrance to the church itself.

He looked down at himself, at his splayed body. His trousers were muddy, a new tear exposing the fishbelly-white skin of his left knee. There was vomit on the hems; a telltale dark stain around the crotch. One of his shoes was missing.

With great effort, he turned his head.

There was someone next to him - another person in the doorway. A woman.

She was propped up in a sitting position, just as he was, her face turned away from him and covered by a veil of bottle-blonde hair. Her black skirt was short, very short, riding all the way up to the top of her legs; her breasts barely contained by a red tube top. The boots were the real giveaway - high and spiky, the patent leather covering most of her pale calf.

What had he done? Gone into town, picked up a working girl and taken her to a cemetery, then got so drunk with her afterwards that the both of them had passed out?

He scanned her body, hunting for clues. It took him a few seconds to see the bruises; a few more to understand what he was seeing.

They ran all the way along her neck - a scattering of purple welts and blue-black thumbprints that reminded him, to his horror, of a china pattern. There were more on her legs, more again on the thin flesh of her upper arms.

He inched across the doorway towards her, a primitive part of his brain already knowing what he'd find. When he was close enough, he reached out to her, brushing back her hair to touch her cheek with the back of his hand.

She was cold.

FROM THE LEICESTER HERALD

September 1978

CHURCHYARD STRANGLER JAILED FOR LIFE

George Young, known as the Churchyard Strangler, has been sentenced to life imprisonment at the Old Bailey for the murder of Tessa Gardener.

The judge, Mr Justice Penny, imposed a minimum sentence of 25 years, describing Young, an unemployed factory worker from Wells Court, Loughborough, as "a grave danger to the public."

The jury returned a unanimous verdict on one count of murder and a related count of sexual assault.

Mother of one Miss Gardener, 37, who was working as a prostitute at the time of her death, had been beaten and strangled, her body left in the graveyard of St. Matthew's Church in Leicester city centre.

Young, who denied all charges, cried as the verdict was announced, while women's rights campaigners were heard cheering from outside the court.

An alcoholic with a history of violence and a previous conviction for assault, Young, 48, was caught by police at a Dover ferry port while trying to flee for Calais. His ex-wife Amanda, a nurse, was not in court, but in an interview with the Herald told reporters that she "wasn't surprised" to learn about his involvement in the murder.

"He was brutal to me while we were married," she said. "I always said he'd end up killing someone."

Detective Superintendent Martin Sanderson, of Leicestershire Police, termed Young "vicious" and "remorseless."

"I am extremely happy that Young has been convicted of this horrifying crime," he added.

He said there was no evidence at this stage to link Young to other unsolved murders in the East Midlands region, but would be in contact with other forces across the country to "see if we can connect any dots."

FROM THE EVENING REVIEW

March 1993

GREENWICH ARSON ATTACK: MOTHER & DAUGHTER KILLED IN HOUSE FIRE IDENTIFIED

A mother and daughter who died in a suspected arson attack at a property in South East London have been named by police.

Unemployed Heidi Simpson, 31, and her daughter Jade Simpson, 5, were pronounced dead at the scene of the blaze at their home in Greenwich last week.

Police, fire and ambulance crews attended their address in St John's Mews around 2.30am on Thursday morning.

A postmortem conducted on Monday established smoke inhalation as the cause of death of both mother and daughter.

No suspects have been named, but police identified arson as the cause of the fire. A murder investigation is underway.

Detective Chief Inspector Laurel Duncan said: "We have reason to believe that the fire was started deliberately and are treating it as an arson attack.

We are working around the clock to understand the series of events leading up to the starting of the fire. Our thoughts are with the family of Heidi and Jade at this time."

DCI Duncan appealed to anyone who may have been in the area of St John's Mews in the early hours of Thursday to come forward.

If you have any information, please contact the incident room number on 0171 333 4872 quoting Operation Hornet.

SOUTHBANK

1996

The cafe at the National Film Theatre was quietest on a Tuesday afternoon - the preserve of elderly couples, students and cinema historians, their heads buried in academic texts on soundtrack, mise-en-scène and the glory of the edit. El had chosen it for precisely this reason. In an environment like this, she was sure, neither she nor the guest she'd be entertaining would be recognised. The NFT's just wasn't that kind of audience.

She arrived at twelve minutes past the hour, late by design. He was tucked away in a corner, stirring sugar into a teacup. Had anyone around him been paying him any attention at all, his college tie and pinstripe jacket would have marked him out as a banker at 100 feet.

He stood up, clumsily, as she approached his table, knocking the spoon against the cup with a metallic clatter. When she failed to greet him, he flustered, his bewilderment playing out in uppercase across his wide red face.

"Alison?" he asked, uncertainly.

El nodded, firm but curt.

"Bernard Croft," he said, extending a hand towards her. She ignored it, leaving it hanging in the air between them, and lowered herself into the seat opposite his, crossing one leg crisply over the other through the confines of her skirt.

"This isn't how I do things, Mr Croft," she said eventually.

She'd pitched the voice just right - layering the haughty south-east vowels with boardroom impatience and just a hint of chiding matron. He quaked.

"I know," he said, "and I'm so sorry, Alison. Ms Miller. You must believe me - this isn't how I'd normally go about things either."

He looked down at his tea nervously.

"I'm not used to being... summoned," she said. "Especially not by secretaries whom I imagine would struggle to spell the word 'discretion.'"

"I'm so sorry," said Croft again. "That was Ailsa. She's new. She just assumed you'd come to the office. Everyone does."

"I'm not everyone, Mr Croft."

"No. No. I realise that."

"Notwithstanding this summoning," she continued, spitting out the word, "I don't take on new clients cold. I work on an introduction-only basis. And to the best of my knowledge, we don't have a single soul in common. I don't even know how you came to hear of me."

His face reddened further, the lines of his lips drawn down in embarrassment. No, she thought; more than embarrassment. Shame. He was ashamed.

"I... overheard," he said slowly, the admission seeming to cause him physical pain. "At the theatre. The Donmar. Hedda Gabler, you know? With the wife. She loves Ibsen, can't get enough."

"You *overheard*?"

She thought she might have overplayed her hand on that last phrase; come off just a little too Lady Bracknell. Fortunately, it seemed the tone was lost on him.

"The people in front of us," he said, staccato with mortification. "They were talking. About you. How you'd... helped them."

"I see."

"We tracked them down. At the interval."

"And they gave you my name."

It wasn't a question, but he answered anyway, sending a rapid-fire bullet spray of self-justification flying at her from across the table.

"Just your name," he said. "And the phone number, obviously. But only when Judy pushed, really pushed them for it. I tried to get her to tone it down, to leave those poor women alone, but she can be something of a steamroller when she has a mind to, and with Jonathan's exams coming up in May..."

"Jonathan," said El. "Your son?"

"Yes," he said, breathing out. "My son. He's 17. At City of London, just across the way."

He gestured vaguely to the glass separating the cafe from the Southbank and beyond it, the river.

"17," she said, appearing to give the number some thought. "Sitting A Levels this year?"

He nodded, relaxing another inch, evidently hoping this revelation would help steer the conversation in the necessary direction.

"He's a good boy," he said. "Very sporty, always has been. Hockey captain, rugby first XV. Eight tries last season."

She stared expressionlessly back at him, impassive in the face of Jonathan's athletic accomplishments.

"He just... isn't much of a bookworm," Croft finished weakly.

She left him hanging half a minute longer before picking up the thread.

"And so you called me," she said.

"Yes. I thought you might be able to... help. With his exams."

Inside, a part of her smiled, satisfied. It was so much easier when they begged; when you didn't even have to try.

"Help, Mr Croft?" she said.

He was burning up now, the tips of his ears and the bridge of his nose catching fire with humiliation at the request he was steeling himself to make.

He loosened his tie; turned the thick rose gold circle on his ring finger back and forth with his thumb.

The shame surprised her, given his chosen profession and the level of success he'd manage to achieve in it. Maybe, she thought, the papers were right, and he really was the last honest man left in the City.

Or had been, until now.

"He's failing everything," said Croft bluntly. "Ds and Es in all his subjects."

"I see," she said.

"Judy's spoken to the school, and they've not pushed him to apply for university. But I'm a Peterhouse man, and Judy was at Girton, so we always assumed..."

"That he'd go to Cambridge."

"Yes," he said. He sounded small, broken; the antithesis of the confident industry titan she'd seen sparring with Jon Snow on the six o'clock news.

She reached into her shoulder bag; made a show of retrieving a leather-bound notebook and a heavy blue fountain pen. She placed both on the table, but made no move to write. Not yet.

"Before we take this discussion any further," she said, "I need to be absolutely certain that we're on the same page, and that you're clear on - and of course I'm speaking hypothetically - how I might support Jonathan's academic performance this term. How I might be able to ease him through the admissions process. I'd hate for there to be any misunderstanding between us."

He looked furtively from side to side, once over his shoulder, then leaned in conspiratorially towards her. If this was his best crack at guile, she thought, it was probably for the best that she kept her own accounts offshore, safe in the hands of the genuinely unscrupulous.

"The ladies at the Donmar said," he whispered, "that you got them papers. Exam papers. I'd hoped - that is, Judy and I were hoping - that you could do the same for us. For Jonathan."

And there it was; he'd said it. He'd made his move. He sat back in his chair, relieved but deflated.

She allowed herself an outward smile now, though not so broad that it might crack the foundation layered across the muscles of her mouth, and imagined how she must look to him: serpentine, calculating. Weighing up the risks of exposing herself to him against the rewards offered by his deep, deep pockets.

She steepled her fingers together, thoughtfully.

"It's possible," she said, "that I might be able to help you."

The answer sank into him, and gratitude leaked out in response, trickling down from his forehead to his lips. He beamed back at her.

"Thank you," he said. "Thank you. I can't tell you..."

A high-pitched trill chirruped from her handbag, stopping him in his tracks. She held up a finger and reached down again below the table, reentering his line of sight with a mobile phone clamped to her ear. There was, of course, no call; nobody on the other end of the line. But it never hurt to seem in demand.

"I'm sorry," she said softly, one hand covering the bottom of the phone, "I really must take this."

He nodded, reaching reflexively out to brush his fingers against the right breast pocket of his jacket where, she imagined, his own phone was stashed.

"Of course," he said. "Can I get you a...?"

He nodded towards the elaborate silver coffee machine at the counter; the line of glistening pastries in the glass case below it.

She shook her head, rose to her feet and took off purposefully towards the bathroom without a glance back at Croft - bag over her shoulder, the dead weight of the phone still clasped against one side of her face.

Keep them waiting, she thought. Always leave them wanting more.

The yellow fluorescence of the bathroom's strip lighting was harsh, unflattering; seemingly designed to deter all but the most determined from lingering too long. She crouched for five minutes in a cubicle, reviewing the pulse points of Croft's confession and planning her follow-up, the right word in the right moment that would seal the deal. Two more minutes, and she made her exit, shoulders back and chin jutting, sweeping imperiously through the swinging bathroom door and back into the cafe towards Croft.

He wasn't alone. There was someone else at the table with him - opposite him, body spread across the chair El had just vacated.

She was old - that was the first thing El noticed. Couldn't help *but* notice. Her back was hunched, drawing the loose skin of her jaw down into her chest, which was covered by a dirty green shawl pinned in place by a dusty brooch. Her hair was long and grey, unexpectedly thick for her age, breaking free of its bun and falling in strands across the deep-cut lines of her face. Her mouth sagged, saliva visible at its corners; her eyes were blue but unfocused, her expression glazed. She smelled, even from a distance, of dried lavender and stale urine.

She spun around in her chair - *El's* chair - as El drew closer, and looked up at her mistily.

"Have *you* seen my Graham?" she asked, her voice a dry, creaking Cockney vibrato.

El glanced over the woman's head at Croft, who shrugged helplessly.

I don't know where she came from, he mouthed. *She just sat down.*

"I'm afraid I don't know any Graham," said El, not unkindly.

"He went out for a pint of milk this morning, and he's not been back since," said the old woman. "I've got his supper on the table but it won't keep warm."

"Perhaps we ought to... find someone," said Croft to El, studiously avoiding the old woman's gaze.

"It won't keep warm!" said the old woman, more loudly this time. "What's he going to have for his supper if his pie goes cold?"

"Find someone?" said El to Croft.

"To help her," he said. "Take her home."

"We don't know where 'home' is," said El.

Croft nodded.

"Where. Do. You. Live?" he asked the old woman, enunciating carefully.

"I live next door," said the old woman more sharply. "Number 65. Why, where do *you* live?"

"I very much doubt it," said El. "We're on the Southbank."

"What does that mean when it's at home?" said the old woman.

"It means," said El, "that there *is* no number 65. At least not in any residential sense. 'Next door' is the Royal Festival Hall."

The old woman's face crumpled. Tears formed in her eyes.

"I want to go home!" she said, even louder than before. She banged one gnarled fist onto the tabletop, attracting stares from a trio of black-haired teenagers in heavy boots and combat trousers slumped over textbooks at the other end of the cafe.

"I should go and see…," Croft began, pushing himself up into to a squatting position behind the table like a sprinter waiting for the starting pistol.

"No," said El, with such authority that he sat immediately down again, tailored thighs slapping dully against the varnished wood of his seat. "You stay with her. I'll go and find someone to help."

She glanced back at the old woman.

"I daresay she'll have a carer around here somewhere," she added, the back of her hand brushing lightly against the hump of the old woman's back. "She probably just wandered off on her own, poor thing."

The old woman's eyes met hers; they dripped acid.

"You get away!" she hissed, enraged. She lashed out at El with the toe of an orthopaedic shoe. "Don't you touch me!"

El took a step back.

"Are you sure I ought to…?" said Croft, alarmed.

"Stay with her," El repeated. "I'll be back."

She pulled her jacket free of the old woman's substantial buttocks and, ignoring the low-pitched growl she received in return, carried herself away from the table.

She didn't go for help.

She left the NFT through the back entrance, circling half a mile of brutalist concrete before emerging back onto the Southbank. From there she headed towards Waterloo, hailing a black cab just shy of the station and making polite, unmemorable conversation with the driver until they reached the Finchley Road. She directed him to a side street around the corner from the Golders Green underground, then asked him to stop; tipped him an equally polite but unmemorable £5, and stepped out onto the street.

There, sandwiched between a kosher sushi bar and a run-down discount bookshop, stood a Greek restaurant, recognisable as such only from its blue and white awning and the faded script that advertised meze and souvlaki from the window.

The neon Open sign was unlit, but the door was unlocked. She turned the handle and walked inside.

Ignoring the stacked chairs and the raised eyebrow of the lone waiter perched on a stool behind the bar, she made a beeline for the bathroom.

Unlike the NFT's, it had neither fluorescent lights nor cubicles - was in fact a single room separated from the restaurant floor by a broken lock and furnished with a bare lightbulb that illuminated a toilet, a small cupboard built to house toilet roll and urinal cakes, a cracked sink and a mirror spotted with fingerprints of every size. It reeked, as always, of cheap disinfectant and old-fashioned greasepaint - the stink of a fastidious clown's dressing room.

She thrust her face forward, six inches from the mirror, and began to change.

First came the makeup: a few handfuls of water, a scrub of soap and a careful reapplication of eyeliner, and her face was her own again, two shades darker than before as the olive of Alison Miller gave way to the light brown of her own skin.

Then the clothes. She quickly unbuckled the heels; untucked the white blouse, unbuttoned it at the neck until it could pass for a shirt and stepped fluidly out of the pencil skirt, pulling the black tights to the ground with it. She thrust an arm into the cupboard, retrieved blue jeans and a pair of canvas trainers and stepped happily into them, throwing the discarded fabrics and the redundant shoes into her open bag.

She brushed her teeth, trading the residual traces of Alison's Christian Dior for fresh mint and eucalyptus - then, satisfied she was herself again, she walked back out into the restaurant.

In the absence of adequately-arranged chairs and any cutlery or tablecloths, she settled for a seat at the bar. The waiter stepped down from his stool, poured gin and tonic water into a glass and handed it across to her, unbidden. She took a sip and nodded her thanks.

Ten minutes passed; fifteen. She leafed through the pages of a tabloid someone had left open on the bartop, taking in updates on the royal divorce, the tragic breakup of a boyband, the scandal surrounding another cabinet minister discovered in bed with the au pair at the family holiday cottage. She lit a cigarette, finished her drink and was considering asking the waiter for another when she heard the door open behind her.

She looked down into her empty glass. Waited.

A few seconds later, a woman sidled up onto the stool beside her, grey-haired and familiar. Her face was as lined as it been an hour earlier, but her posture was straight, her blue eyes were clear, and she seemed to have shed two decades between the NFT cafe and the restaurant. The dirty shawl was gone too, replaced by a denim jacket and silk scarf. Even the urine-and-lavender smell had dissipated.

"You took your time," said El.

"Couldn't find a parking space," said the woman. Her voice was different too, now: still identifiably East London, but husky rather than creaking, and no quaver in it at all. "You know what it's like when the schools come out round here. It's bloody carnage."

El knew. The bar was where they always met, when they needed somewhere quiet to talk that wasn't either of their homes; where they *knew* to meet, without it needing to be said.

The woman beckoned over the waiter, who slid down from his seat again with a resigned sigh.

"Orange juice and lemonade, love," she said. "And a Coca-Cola for my girl here. I'm going to need her firing on all cylinders later."

"You know I was on the job before?" said El, with no small amount of recrimination.

The waiter turned his back to them, busying himself with the drinks and pointedly not listening to their exchange.

"I sort of got that from the clothes and the accent," said the woman. "Spanish Prisoner? He looked the avaricious type to me."

"Exam papers," said El. "For his son."

"Ah," said the woman dismissively. "One of *them*."

The waiter placed two over-full glasses on the bartop - one dark brown and fizzy, the other a vivid orange.

"I'm going out the back," he mumbled.

"Good boy," said the woman. "We'll call you if we need you."

"You didn't have to come barging in like that," said El as the waiter slunk away. "You could have waited 'til I'd wrapped up with him."

"And miss all the fun? You should have seen the look on that great lump's face when you left him alone with me. Priceless."

El smiled and lit another cigarette.

"Them things'll kill you," chided the woman.

"What were you doing round there, anyway?" El asked, keen to keep her on topic. "Were *you* on a job?"

The woman chuckled.

"I had a spot of business down in Pimlico," she said. "Went for a walk along the river once I'd finished to clear my head. I needed to talk to you anyway, and when I saw you through that window... well, I couldn't help myself."

"And the shawl? Where did *that* come from?"

"Bought it off a beggar by the bridge. Best £10 I've spent this week. Though it didn't half pong - I had to spritz it with half a bottle of eau de toilette before I could bring myself to put it round my neck."

"I hope you found a good home for it after."

"I left it with your friend in the cafe. Thought I ought to give him something for taking care of a little old lady in her hour of need."

This time El laughed.

"So what did you need to see me about?" she asked, when the image of Croft cradling the shawl had finally left her. "What was so important you couldn't say it over the phone? I've got one of these now, you know," she added, pulling her mobile phone from her bag.

The smile evaporated from the woman's face.

"You're not going to like it," she said sombrely.

El stared, waiting for her to elaborate.

"I've got... Bloody hell, girl, there ain't an easy way to say this..."

"Just say it," said El, immediately fearing the worst. Cancer. Heart disease. A death in the family.

The woman paused; threw back her orange juice and lemonade like a whiskey sour.

"The truth is," she said, and paused. "The truth is... I've been done over. *Really* done over."

"How much?" said El, suddenly aware of where all the talk was heading.

"A lot," said the woman quietly. "100 grand. And, look - you know I wouldn't ask if I weren't desperate, absolutely desperate. But I need you to get it back for me."

EDGWARE

1978

El raised the hammer above her head and brought it down onto the bag. There was a crack, mostly muffled by the cloth, a soft baize the colour and texture of a snooker table. She pulled the bag open by its drawstring; peered inside. The glass had broken, she saw - not shattered completely, the way she'd hoped it would, but definitely in pieces, the thick pane now sectioned into half a dozen rainbow shards.

A bit more effort, she told herself; that was all it needed. Steeling herself, she closed the bag, raised the hammer higher, and brought it down again onto the cloth. Harder, this time.

Fifteen feet above her, a woman in high-waisted flares and holding (though El couldn't have known it at the time) a very expensive pair of Francois Pinton glasses stared quizzically down at the courtyard from her balcony, watching the skinny kid with the toffee hammer and the Scrabble bag and the determined look in her eye with a curiosity that was half-personal, half-professional. She watched her go at the glass over and over with the hammer until it was nothing but tiny slivers; watched her pour the slivers into a flat brown presentation case sitting next to her on the bench and secure a glossy red bow to the case's front. Watched her leave the courtyard and head purposefully out towards the main road, case in hand - the hammer and the bag stowed away in what looked to the woman very much like an old school satchel. Then she pushed the sunglasses up onto the bridge of her nose, tied a lightweight sweater loosely over her shoulders and went downstairs into the courtyard, where the girl had been.

Outside the train station, the street was busy, the pavement packed with tired-looking white men in raincoats, all slicked-down hair and briefcases. Commuters, El's Uncle called them; men - and the occasional woman - who worked in London but lived in Edgware and beyond it, scurrying out from Northern Line carriages every night at 6 o'clock in the race home to their wives, their children and a chilli con carne on the dinner table.

More than a few looked likely candidates to her: almost all of them had that pinched, anxious look that said they'd do anything to get through the last leg of their journey uninterrupted. That they were absolutely frantic to shake themselves out of the raincoats, pull their exhausted feet out of the tightly-laced shoes that had imprisoned them all day and settle down by the fire with the paper and a mug of something hot and strong.

One stood out to her, though. He looked even more tired than the rest, more ground-down. About her Uncle's age, but stooped, as if the weight of the world was too much for him. His face was grey; his hair stuck up in sad clumps at the back of his head, exposing a circular bald patch he'd tried, unsuccessfully, to cover.

He took a left out of the station exit. She followed him, the box clamped tightly between her fingers; close enough to keep him in view, but not so close that she'd arouse suspicion. He turned off the main road, towards the leafiness of Penshurst Gardens; she turned with him, closing the distance between them. On Penshurst Gardens she crossed the street, accelerating her pace until she was a few feet ahead of him on the other side of the road. Then she crossed back, still moving quickly, putting herself directly in his path.

They collided on the pavement. As her shoulder met his chest, she let the box fall from her hands. It made a satisfyingly loud crunching sound as it hit the pavement.

He froze. She dropped to her knees, picked up the box from the pavement and shook it, gently. The shards inside rattled. Gingerly, she lifted the lid, revealing the tiny, shattered pieces of coloured glass inside.

The man looked down at the box in horror.

"It's broken!" she said loudly.

"It's... what?" said the man, dazed.

"The jug," she said, injecting a bass note of sorrow into the words along with the initial alarm. "It's broken."

She looked up at him; wrinkled her nose to allow teardrops to form, thick and heavy, in her eyes.

The man bent down beside her, one knee scraping the paving slab. He peered into the open box.

"What... was it?" he asked. He had a stutter, she noticed. A posh accent and a stutter. She wondered whether he was always this nervous, or whether the stutter was a consequence of the strange girl barrelling into him out of nowhere in the street.

She wiped a tear away with one finger.

"It was my Gran's," she said. "She left it to me when she..."

She let her voice catch.

"We had the funeral this morning," she said, sniffling. "We all went back to her house after, and I was looking at it on the shelf, and Dad said Gran had always wanted me to have it, because I'd always thought it was pretty, so she wrapped it up and put it in a box for me..."

She trailed off into a barely-suppressed sob.

"It was made of special glass, Dad said," she added. "From Venice."

The man looked so distraught, she almost regretted what she'd done - what she was about to do. But not quite enough to stop, not now she'd started.

"Perhaps we can... fix it," he said. He moved a slow hand towards the shattered pieces - then, realising the futility of the gesture, withdrew it again.

"I don't think we can," said El, quietly.

"Is there anything I can... do?" he asked.

"Like what?" she said. "It's all broken."

"We could... replace it," he suggested. "I know it won't be the same, but..."

El glared at him.

"It was *Gran's*," she said, with venom. "You can't just replace it. Besides," she added, "it cost twenty pounds, Dad said. Where am I supposed to get twenty pounds from?"

The man blinked. Something twitched at the corner of his mouth. He'd seen a way out, El realised - a possible solution to this unexpected problem, one that might yet lead him back to the dinner table with a clear conscience before dusk.

"I understand it must have had... sentimental value," he said slowly, "and that you can't just... replace something like that. But if money's the problem..."

"What do you mean?" she said, quickly. Too quickly, she thought. She'd need to sort that out, next time. If there *was* a next time.

The man reached into the folds of his overcoat and withdrew a fat black wallet.

"I could... give you the money," he said, unbuckling the wallet. El saw notes inside - a wad of them, more money than she'd ever seen in one place. "For a replacement. It was... my fault, after all. That it got broken."

"It won't be the same," she said, parroting his words back at him. Repeating things like that built trust, she'd read; made people open up to you.

He laid a consolatory palm on her back. She glared at him again, and he quickly removed it.

"Not a replacement, then," he said. "But you could use the money to... buy something else. Perhaps some flowers. For your Grandmother's... resting place."

A twenty quid bouquet? El thought. What world is he living in?

She felt better, after that, about choosing him. It certainly didn't seem like he'd miss the cash.

She cupped her chin as if weighing up the possibility.

"I suppose I could buy her some china frogs for her headstone," she said. "She always liked frogs."

The man brightened, an end to it all in sight.

"You could," he agreed. "Lots of frogs."

She paused.

"Except..." she said.

The man stopped her before she could carry on - before the prospect of escape could disappear from view. He stood up, dug a thumb and forefinger into his wallet, pulled out four five pound notes and thrust them into her hand, which she'd left conveniently open, the palm turned upwards.

"Please," he said. "For your Grandmother."

She stood up next to him, preparing to protest. Never let the mark just *give* you money, the book had said. Not straight away. But he was already putting away his wallet, tightening the belt of his coat, getting ready to make a run for it.

"Are you sure?" she asked, the notes soft and rich as calfskin under her fingertips.

"Absolutely," he said, half-stumbling in his rush to get away from her. "It's my... pleasure. Now I'm afraid I really must..."

He staggered off, looking back at her over his shoulder as he lurched up the road. After a couple of hundred feet he turned and gave her a small, clumsy salute, before disappearing behind the gate of a big detached house, neat and whitewashed and decorated with what looked to El like a turret on one side of it.

She bent down to the ground again; picked up the box with the glass inside, and headed back towards the station.

At the top of Penshurst Gardens, where the pavement spilled out onto the Station Road roundabout, she became aware of someone watching her from across the road - a short white woman with a shock of salt and pepper hair, staring out at her from behind an enormous pair of Jackie O. sunglasses that half-covered her face. She saw El notice her, smiled, and waved back at her cheerfully.

El frowned, tucked the notes deep into the pocket of her jeans, and stalked away.

She didn't spend the money.

There was nothing in the shops she wanted to buy - her Auntie and Uncle were pretty generous with pocket money, if only to convince themselves they were doing *something* for the poor little orphan they'd been lumbered with, and the library had all the books she could ever hope to read. She was too old for toys, wasn't into music or clothes, and her Uncle was sufficiently lax with his cigarettes that she could acquire even those for free with the barest minimum of effort.

In any case, she thought, she hadn't done it for the money. She'd done it to see if she could; if the things she'd read about would actually work, out in the world. The money was just... proof.

She knew, when she'd done it once - once it *had* worked, and that proof was in her hand, then in her pocket, then safely stowed away between the pages of a dictionary under her bed - that she'd do it again. She'd liked it - had felt a fizzing energy coursing through her afterwards like lightning, like a dab of speed on her tongue. And more than that, she thought, she'd been good at it - the money was proof of that, too.

So, the following Wednesday, just before rush hour, she did it again.

She'd needed a fresh piece of coloured glass - the initial shards having fractured beyond recognition after the hammer blows, the crash to the pavement and the innumerable accidental drops to her bedroom floor that had followed. But a replacement was easy enough to come by. She swiped it, as she had the first one, from the resistant materials cupboard in the school art room, wrapped it in the same cloth bag that had held its predecessor and carried it out of the school gates in her satchel, along with the hammer and the now-empty presentation box - through the streets of Burnt Oak and into the courtyard of the quiet block of flats opposite the Greater Barnet Library.

She perched on the same bench she'd sat on the first time, driven by an irrational but unshakeable worry that changing her pattern, changing the ritual surrounding the con would somehow alter its outcome. She raised the hammer above her head, as before; brought it down, as hard as she could, on the drawstring bag.

A shadow fell over the bench. She looked up; saw a woman standing over her, watching. Smiling.

She'd have recognised her anyway, from the smile and the dandelion perm, but as it happened the woman was still wearing her enormous sunglasses, now pushed up against the frizz of her hairline. Her eyes were vividly blue, crow's feet gathering at their edges. El got the definite impression that the woman was laughing at her; having some private joke at El's expense.

"I know you," El said, not smiling back. "You were there the other day, up the road."

"And I know you," said the woman genially. "Or at least I know what you're up to. You want to be careful - you'll get your collar felt if you keep on with all this."

The woman cast a glance down at El's props: the bag of glass, the hammer, the presentation box.

If you're ever questioned, the book said; if anyone ever suspects you're up to something, or accuses you outright - deny everything. Then go on the offensive. They'll quickly forget what they thought they knew once you have them on the back foot.

"I don't know what you're talking about," El said. "And what do you want with me, anyway? You make a habit of following young girls about?"

The woman chuckled, still amused.

"I say something funny?" El asked, papering bravado over her growing unease.

The woman didn't reply. Instead, she stuck a hand out towards El's, and waited. After a moment, to her own surprise, El shook it. The woman's grip was firm and certain; what her Uncle would have called an honest handshake.

"Ruby Redfearn," said the woman. "I live just up there."

She pointed upwards, to the flats overhead.

"You got a name?" she asked El.

"El," said El, then kicked herself for replying.

"El?" said Ruby Redfearn. "What's that short for, then? Eleanor?"

"Epsilon," said El. "You got a problem with that?"

"Epsilon," said Ruby Redfearn, rolling the name around her mouth experimentally. "Interesting. Your mother Greek, is she?"

El fell silent. Two years on, the memory of her Mum still smarted, as painfully as it ever had. Even the word "mother" stung; even when tossed carelessly, as now, from the lips of a stranger.

If Ruby Redfearn noticed, though, she didn't react.

"Here's the thing, El," she said instead, shuffling onto the bench so that they were hip-to-hip, shoulder-to-shoulder. "Your little game with that box over there... you can't keep doing it, at least not round here. Especially not if you live round here, which I'm guessing you do. Once, maybe twice you can pull it off without anyone talking or putting two and two together. But any more than that and you'll be landing yourself in it. And then one day you'll go home, and you'll find an angry mob on your doorstep or the Old Bill sat in your kitchen. You don't want that, believe me."

El could feel her cheeks burning, her stomach knotting and clenching. It was too late to go on the offensive. She *knew*. Whoever Ruby Redfearn was, she knew everything. Might even have *seen* everything.

"Here," said Ruby, not unkindly. "Don't look like that. I ain't going to say anything. There's no benefit to either of us of me running my gob off about it. It's just... if you do a job, you need to be clever about it. Careful. You need to cover your arse."

Something about the way she spoke - the way she said "job" - caught El's attention.

"How did you know what I was doing?" she asked.

Ruby chuckled again - a rich, throaty laugh that made her eyes sparkle.

"Christ, gel," she said. "You think you're the first one round here who ever tried the Marchioness's Gravy Boat? Do me a favour."

El wrinkled her brows involuntarily, confused.

"What's the Marchioness's Gravy Boat?" she asked.

Ruby looked aghast.

"You're doing it, and you don't even know its name?" she said.

"The book called it a Melon Drop," said El, embarrassed.

"Book? What book?"

El considered telling her - what she'd read, where she'd read it, the advice it had given her. Then thought better of it.

"Oh, I get it," said Ruby. "You found one of them old instructional manuals, is that about the size of it? The Boy's Own Book of Short Cons, that sort of thing?"

El stayed quiet.

"And you thought you'd try it out for yourself? See whether you could pull it off?"

It was close enough to the truth to be uncomfortable. El nodded, her earlier bluster now entirely evaporated.

"The trouble with books like that," Ruby said, "is they don't tell you the truth of it. They talk about the setup, and the logistics, the cold hard facts of the job and them bloody daft American names that make it sound like something from The Sting. But they don't tell you the bits that matter."

"Like what?" asked El.

"Like... that hungry look you see a mark get when he thinks he's about to get one over on you - bit like a dog who's just smelled the meat on next door's stove. Like... you should never go to them, you should always get them to come to you, because they'll want it more, and if you tell them no they'll want it so bad they'll never leave you alone until you give it to them. Like, and this one's really important: you don't ever shit where you eat, because the mark and you have both got to live there, and the last thing you want when you nip out to Woolworths is to see him staring at you with his mouth open down the pick 'n' mix aisle."

El replayed this advice in her head - plucking out the salient bits, teasing out the implications. She felt a little of her confidence returning - and, more importantly, felt the first, embryonic cells of an idea begin to form.

"Sounds like you know what you're talking about," she said eventually.

"More than that book of yours, anyway," Ruby replied.

And here we go, El thought. You don't ask, you don't get.

"Think you might want to show me?" she asked.

Ruby pivoted around on the bench and fixed her eyes on El's, holding her gaze just long and steady enough to give El a hint of the core of hardness that might lie underneath the geniality, a sense of what it might feel like to cross her and to have her *know* that you'd crossed her.

And then she smacked her thigh, and snorted, and grinned widely enough to show the metal of her fillings.

"Bloody hell," she said, laughter in her voice. "I walked into that one, didn't I?"

GOLDERS GREEN
1996

The waiter slunk back behind the bar. Ruby glanced across at him through the thickening haze of El's cigarette smoke - making a show of wafting the smoke away with one liver-spotted hand, and causing the bracelets on the corresponding wrist to jangle together in a symphony of copper and gold.

"Them optics of yours look like they could do with a polish," she said casually.

He took the hint - picked up a cloth from under the counter and, turning his back to them, moved to the other end of the bar and began wiping down the already-clean spirits bottles with furious intensity.

"100 grand?" said El, when he was out of earshot. "How did that happen?"

Ruby exhaled, the deep put-upon sigh of the world-weary diva.

"It weren't my fault," she said.

"I didn't say it was," said El.

"I was just trying to do something nice. For the boys. You know they've got their birthday coming up?"

El nodded.

"The boys" were Ruby's twin sons, Michael and Dexter - 35, 6'3" and Savile

Row-tailored, both long qualified as solicitors but still, for El, the gawky 17 year olds they'd been when she'd first stumbled her way into their living room. Dexter was glib and playful, all fast cars and ridiculous jokes, where Michael was serious and career-minded, as driven as his brother was irresponsible. Both treated El like a wayward little sister, warning her away from trouble and offering to have words with anyone who ever broke her heart. Both, she knew, would do anything for their mother - even, in Michael's case, where it meant overlooking any professional codes of conduct and stretching his own ethics to breaking point.

"And you know they used to like the superhero in that comic - that Cloud Cheetah, or whatever its name is?"

El nodded again. The Cloud Cheetah, Dexter had once told her, had been his and Michael's idol through the whole of junior school: a blue-skinned, Island Of Doctor Moreau-ish cat-man of uncertain origins, dedicated to fighting crime, upholding justice and foiling the nefarious plots of all and sundry villains in the London and Thames Valley areas. The Cloud Cheetah and his crab-like sidekick Five Eyes came alive in the pages of the Unimaginable! comic series in the late 60s and early 70s, before its publisher went bust - the quirky Britishness of its characters and settings, and the small budgets of its producer, no match for the glamorous Americana or the deeper pockets of its Marvel and DC rivals.

"Well," said Ruby, "I was shopping round for something to get them, something really special. And then I saw two of them old comics come up at auction..."

Unimaginable!, as it turned out, was considered a bit of a rarity, even by the standards of comic book aficionados. Copies were scarce, pristine copies scarcer. To compound its appeal to the discerning collector, the Cloud Cheetah character had been identified a year earlier as the early, pseudonymously-produced handiwork of Brian Dennison, AKA Big Delta - a Pop Artist of some repute, whose accidental heroin overdose in 1993 had taken him permanently out of circulation.

The comics were expensive, with a guide price of £70,000 for the two, and interest was high - higher, anyway, than Ruby would have expected of something she used to buy with a bag of jelly babies and the Daily Mirror at the Deans Lane paper shop. But she, perhaps more than anyone, knew that the value of a thing - any thing - was as arbitrary as it was changeable, and so along she went to the auction house one evening, cheque-book in hand.

"I did it straight, as well," she told El, leaning over the bartop to help herself to another lemonade. "Totally legit."

She shook her head, disgusted with herself.

The auction was well-attended, the room peopled with the younger, male comic book enthusiasts she could have predicted as well as a few less obvious entries: a man her age with a flat cap and a cane, a teenage girl who could have been one of the young men's girlfriends but wasn't, and a woman in pearls, a feathered fascinator and a salmon-pink two-piece.

"Dressed like she was off to Ascot," said Ruby.

Bidding for the comics started low, but quickly accelerated. The bids rose to £50,000, then £60,000, then £65,000. Ruby hadn't set herself a limit - whatever they went for, she'd reasoned, she could afford to pay it - but she was startled by just how *much* competition there turned out to be. At £70,000, some of the interest fell away - the would-be bidders, she assumed, having reached their own upper limits.

By £80,000, there were just three of them left: Ruby, the man with the cane and the woman in the fascinator. The man dropped out of the race at £85,000, but the woman showed no sign of giving up.

"She kept pushing," Ruby said. "Higher and higher. £86,000, 87, 88. She wouldn't give up."

At £100,000, to Ruby's surprise, the woman abruptly stopped bidding, and the auctioneer declared Ruby the buyer.

"I think I thought she'd reached *her* limit then, too," Ruby said. "I craned my neck round her way. Partly to get a look at her, but also so I could say, you know... no hard feelings. Better luck next time. But she just *glared* at me, like I'd kicked her cat or done my business on her carpet, then flounced right out of the auction room."

"Sounds like a bitch," El observed.

"You don't know the half of it," said Ruby.

She'd paid for the comics upfront, and they arrived at her flat three days later, sealed in transparent polythene.

"I put them in the spare room, in a drawer," she said. "Probably less fancy than they deserved, for that price, but it was dry and safe, and I knew that way the boys wouldn't catch sight of them before I'd had the chance to wrap them up."

They'd stayed there for a week, the polythene gathering dust. Until she'd gone out for dinner in Covent Garden one evening with Michael and his girlfriend, and come home to find them gone.

"The drawer was wide open," she said. "Empty."

But nothing else was missing.

"Oh, they'd turned the place over," she said. "Thrown a few cushions about, pulled some of the ornaments out of the cabinets. But they hadn't busted the front door or put the windows in. It was a professional job."

She said this last part with a kind of grudging admiration.

"Why didn't you call me?" El said. It didn't even occur to her to ask why Ruby hadn't called the police. You just *didn't*.

("It's like them vampires," Ruby used to say in the early days. "You never invite them in."

And some of the other things she kept lying around in that spare room would have raised a few questions, too. The Monet on the wall, for one).

"I didn't want you telling the boys," she answered. "Last thing I need is them thinking I'm some defenceless old dear who can't look after herself on her own."

El saw her point, though she didn't concede it: Michael, she knew, had been pressuring his mother to pack up the Edgware flat and move south of the river, closer to him in Balham and Dexter in Battersea. She'd been resisting, but he was stubborn, persistent. Of course he was, El thought - he was *her* son.

"I'm assuming you know who took them?" El asked. Ruby's intel network spanned the length and breadth of the city. If she wanted something - especially information - then, generally, she found it.

"Took me 2 days," said Ruby. "None of my usual lot had anything to give me. Then Jim Duggan got a tip-off over in Ladbroke Grove. You remember him? He'd got talking to the O'Connell brothers down the Portobello market, and they said *they'd* been talking to this bloke in the pub the night before. A new face, not a bloke they recognised - and they know *everyone* out west."

It's like Chinese bloody whispers sometimes, El thought. Or like gossip in the playground: *he* said, and then *she* said, and so *I* said...

"And what did he say?" she asked. "This bloke in the pub?"

"By all accounts," said Ruby, "he was bragging..."

"Three grand!" the bloke had said, five pints in. "Three grand to do over some old lady's flat! And she wasn't even in. Easiest money I ever made, I tell you."

"And did you know who she was, the old lady?" asked Mark O'Connell, thinking of his 95 year old grandmother in Sligo and wondering, idly, who'd be the first of the Swan & Rushes regulars to lay the bastard out on the cobbles when they heard him congratulating himself for doing over a pensioner.

"How should I know?" the bloke had said. "That posh cow didn't pay me to ask questions, did she? All I had to do was go in, get the package and let myself out again before the old bird came back."

The package? Mark O'Connell had asked.

Yeah, the bloke had said. And this was where it got a bit peculiar. Because the bloke had sworn - not that the sworn word of a dirty, granny-robbing gobshite meant much to Mark O'Connell, you understand - that the package wasn't really a package at all. It was a kid's comic book.

"*Two* comics," the bloke had added, correcting himself. "All tied up together in plastic. Fucking weird, mate, I tell you. Must have been worth a bit, mind, because that posh cow, she was *desperate* to get hold of them..."

The bloke, Mark O'Connell had been delighted to report, had left the pub that night two teeth shorter than he'd gone in, and with a lovely pair of bruises on one side of his face that, with any luck, would stay with him for at least a fortnight.

"And the posh cow was...?" El asked, already knowing the answer.

"The woman from the auction," Ruby said. "Lady Muck with the pearl necklace."

Who, she'd quickly discovered, really *was* a Lady: Lady Rose Winchester, wife of Sir Sebastian, a low-level aristocrat and, until his premature death 3 years earlier, wildly successful and exorbitantly wealthy media entrepreneur. Lady Rose was 40, worth just north of £200 million, and lived alone with her 12 year old daughter, dividing their time between a house in Highgate and an apartment in the 16th arrondissement of Paris.

Beyond her daughter, Lady Rose was known to enjoy two things: rock-climbing, and Pop Art. The former she exercised through annual expeditions to Red River Gorge and Yosemite National Park; the latter through an ever-expanding private collection of Lichtensteins, Blakes and Rauschenbergs.

"And old comics?" said El.

"And old comics," said Ruby.

On the London art scene, at least, Lady Rose had a reputation for ruthlessness that bordered on cruelty - and for getting what she wanted, always, regardless of the cost. She was considered, Ruby had learned, substantially more knowledgeable than the average high-society dilettante; unlike the CEOs's wives and retired rock stars she would regularly bid against, she could more than hold her own with dealers, curators, appraisers. She was also more fastidious than most about security: her Highgate home, the temperature-controlled basement of which housed the largest of her collections, was protected by electronic gates, CCTV cameras and, rumour had it, an armed guard at the entrance.

"So you want me to get in and get the comics back," said El.

"No!" said Ruby quickly. "Not yet. It's too soon. She's sharp - she'd put two and two together easy and work out who it was that did it. And she knows where I live, remember?"

"What, then?" El asked. She lit another cigarette - reasoning that, if Ruby was going to drag her in to whatever this was, then she could stand to suffer a lungful of smoke in the process.

"Something better than a smash and grab job," Ruby said. "Something a bit more sophisticated. She was in my *house*, girl. I want to hit her where it hurts."

"And where's that?"

Ruby didn't answer. El waited, familiar enough with the older woman's style of back-and-forth to know she wouldn't be rushed.

Eventually, Ruby spoke.

"What do you know," she said, "about Keith Haring?"

LEICESTERSHIRE
1996

There were streaks in El's hair - two jagged lines of purple, radiating out from her parting to just below her ears. She was a decade too old for them, at least, and the supermarket dye she'd used to achieve them was so cheap it made her scalp itch, but they fitted. Claire Brandon, whose life she'd be inhabiting for the next few hours, couldn't afford a decent hairdresser, and was - as the streaks, the 'ethnic' wooden jewellery and the dark nail polish all indicated - still clinging to the precipice of her adolescence by her fingertips, in defiance of her chronological age.

She wore black-framed glasses with clear lenses, a loose-fitting skirt made of soft green fabric, a long flowing shirt tied loosely at the midriff and brown hiking boots laced up to the ankle. Now, in the full-body mirror mounted for exactly this purpose in her hallway, she rearranged her features into the right configuration, settling on an expression that said "my PhD is worth more than any money you could offer me," but also, simultaneously, "without this job, I'm going to struggle to pay my rent this month."

Claire Brandon - *Dr* Claire Brandon, as El was sure she'd be likely to remind people at any opportunity - was an early-career academic and specialist in contemporary Anglo-American art. El was especially proud of her thesis, the title of which (*Making Inroads: Street Art and Queer Culture in New York and San Francisco, 1977-1990*) was inspired by the innumerable monographs and art history journals she'd devoured since Ruby had proposed the con three weeks before. The colon, she thought, was a particularly nice touch.

The books and journals now occupied a dedicated shelf in her reading room, sandwiched between equally dense texts on mineralogy and Southeast Asian trade routes, a testament to the thoroughness of her prep work. El had finished her own modern languages degree in her mid-20s after 6 stop-and-start years of enrolment, but had declined to progress to further study, on the basis that the particular line of work she'd chosen offered more than ample opportunity for ongoing professional and cognitive development, in addition to the more practical skill set it conferred. She'd never regretted the decision - and had, she suspected, acquired a broader and more diverse knowledge base over the years than she'd ever have picked up in a classroom.

Ruby, conversely, was aggrieved by her decision to give up the higher education ghost at what she deemed the first hurdle. She'd left school herself at 14, going immediately to work on the production line of a ball-bearing factory in Bethnal Green, but was an avowed advocate of education in others - regarding the string of letters both her sons had amassed after their names as not only a point of pride, but a clear vindication of the transformative power of maternal nagging.

In the mirror, El added to her eyelids a few brushes of purple shadow - an almost-match for the streaks in her hair - and to her lips a smear of Superdrug strawberry lip gloss. She stepped across to the coat-rack by the door, thought for a moment, then picked from the dozen or so accessories hanging there an oversized canvas bag, beaded and furred and decorated with animal print. Into the bag she slipped a piece of paper, neatly word-processed on both sides and sheathed in a transparent acetate wallet, and her house keys - a three-inch silicone likeness of the head of Michel Foucault, purchased especially for the occasion, grinning obscenely from the keyring.

And with that, she was ready.

She locked the front door, activated both sets of burglar alarms and walked up the path to the driveway where she kept her car parked, fortifying herself for the two hour drive into London.

Ruby, whose internal compass identified any point beyond St Albans as The North, had initially questioned El's judgement in buying the house, a 16th century cottage with a thatched roof and three acres of garden. And, indeed, in moving back to Leicestershire at all.

"What you going to do with yourself all the way up there?" she'd asked when El had first shown her the place in the estate agents' brochure - aghast at the prospect of anyone willingly exchanging the civilised pleasures of the city for the wilds of the East Midlands. "Your life's here. Your *work's* here. When was the last time you even did a job outside the M25?"

El had argued her case with conviction - pointing to the transport links, the proximity to nature, the cleaner air and greater availability of land. Eventually, exasperated, she'd thrown Ruby's own advice back at her.

"I'm trying not to shit where I eat," she'd said - and this, at least, Ruby had seemed to understand.

But none of these reasons, valid though all of them were, were the whole of the truth.

The journey south was uneventful, the motorway clear, and she pulled off the M1 into Barnet earlier than she'd anticipated. She parked the car in a side street by the Totteridge and Whetstone station and took the tube the rest of the way to Highgate. Claire Brandon didn't drive; couldn't stretch to a car on her salary.

The house was a four storey Victorian red-brick off Hampstead Lane, gated and detached, set apart from the human and vehicular traffic of the main road. There was no guardhouse out front that El could see, but there was room for one; what had once been the front garden was paved and levelled, creating so much open space that El's own cottage could have fitted comfortably in the gap between the gate and the front door.

She pressed the buzzer by the gatepost, and waited. A minute or so later, a voice rang out over the intercom, buried under layers of static but recognisably young and female.

"Claire Brandon," said El, slipping into the soft Yorkshire vowels left over from Brandon's early years in Halifax. "Here to see Rose Winchester."

Brandon, she'd decided, wouldn't recognise titles; wouldn't kowtow to an antiquated class system and its hierarchies. If this came off as arrogant, it could only help her cause.

A gap appeared in the gates, silently guiding El inside.

Before she'd made it halfway down the driveway, the enormous double doors set under the porch flew open, revealing a girl in the doorway: mid 20s at El's best guess, with loose black curls pulled back from her face in a ponytail, and skin a half-shade darker than El's. She was short but defined, the compact muscles of her calves and biceps straining behind a black silk shirt and leggings. She wore no jewellery, and carried a walkie-talkie in one hand.

"Karen Baxter," she said, reaching out with the other to shake El's hand. "Lady Rose's PA."

And her security detail, El thought.

"She's waiting for you in the war room," Karen added, her accent pure South London.

"The war room?" El asked, with a hesitation that wasn't entirely feigned.

"It's what she calls the conference room," Karen said, but didn't elaborate further.

She led El inside and into the hall, past the artfully-minimalist walls and the thickly-carpeted stairs leading up to the first floor and through to the room in question. There, she found an oblong table, old and solid and varnished, fringed by six incongruously-modern office chairs.

At back of the room, standing poker-straight next to an unused flip-chart, was Lady Rose.

Static, she looked very much as she had in the handful of paparazzi photos El had seen of her: lean and angular, her bright red hair styled into a Princess Diana cut, both earlobes decorated with round pearl earrings. She was more casually dressed than El had expected, in jeans and unpolished brogues, but was still, somehow, archetypically patrician.

She looked El up and down appraisingly as she entered the room.

"Dr Brandon," she said, in exactly the clipped tone El had expected. "A pleasure to meet you."

There was no handshake.

She gestured down at the table meaningfully. El wheeled one of the chairs a few inches free of the table and took a seat. Karen took the seat beside her, Lady Rose a chair at the head of the table.

El dug into her furred and beaded bag, now sitting unobtrusively at her feet, and pulled out the acetate wallet. She slid it slowly across the table to Lady Rose, who picked it up by its edges with a look of bemusement.

"My CV," El said. "I thought you might want to have a look? Or we could talk through it?"

Lady Rose extracted the densely-typed sheet of paper from the wallet and looked down at the words on the page.

"You were at The Slade?" she asked as she read.

"For my PhD," said El. "I did my masters and my undergrad at York."

"And Frank Morrison was your supervisor?"

"That's right."

Lady Rose finally raised her head, and looked El directly in the eye.

"Funny," she said. "I thought he was strictly Art Nouveau. I had no idea he had an interest in anything more contemporary than the Edwardians."

"He's been diversifying," said El, maintaining eye contact.

"So it seems. I'll have to give him a call. I haven't seen him since the show at the V&A last year."

If this was the first hurdle, El thought, then it was an easy one to jump.

"He's on leave this term," El said. "In Sumatra. He should be back in September."

And this, as far as she knew, was true. She'd spent a long, instructive afternoon in the Wilkins Building at the Slade, chatting with postgrads and departmental admin staff and identifying, through a succession of circuitous conversations, the sabbatical calendars of some of its more senior lecturers. Morrison - Professor Francis Morrison, leading expert on the work of Louis Comfort Tiffany - gave her what she needed. A hardened old technophobe close to retirement who refused to acknowledge the presence of his departmental email address, he'd departed for Indonesia in early April with neither his wife nor a telephone in tow, making clear to anyone who asked that he'd be *on leave* and explicitly *out of contact* until late summer.

"I see," said Lady Rose.

She glanced down again at the paper.

"You looked at Keith Haring, for your thesis?" she said.

"And Basquiat, and Kenny Scharf," said El. "But Haring primarily. I'm interested in the relationship between street art and sexual politics, sexual citizenship. How alternative sexual identities have been mediated and constructed in US public space through appropriation of some of the stylistic motifs of pop-culture imagery."

"Sounds like a riot," said Karen drily.

Lady Rose raised a single, arch eyebrow. Karen drew her thumb and forefinger across her mouth in a zipping gesture.

"You're teaching at St Martins currently?" Lady Rose asked.

"Part-time," said El. "I also lecture at Birkbeck, and run evening classes at St. Crispin's College in Notting HIll."

"That must keep you busy," Lady Rose said.

"It does," said El. "But I'm always looking for other opportunities."

"And you have experience, I assume, in authentication?"

"I have," El replied pompously. "I trained at Christie's before my PhD. And I took on a number of ad-hoc consulting projects during my research, before I started teaching."

Karen yawned.

"Sorry," she said quickly. "It's the air conditioning, makes me sleepy. Carry on."

Lady Rose put down the paper.

"Have you ever worked with private clients?" she asked.

"Yes," said El.

"And so you understand that their needs can sometimes be... different than the needs of an auction house?"

El looked her in the eye again.

"I do," she said. "I was told this might be a particularly complex valuation. That there might be some... ambiguity to resolve."

"And you're confident you're able to resolve it?"

"I would hope so," said El steadily, maintaining the eye contact. "I've had similar issues present themselves before, with some of my previous clients. I've always been able to help them achieve a positive outcome. They were much smaller projects, of course. Less.. complex than yours."

Lady Rose looked back at her, still weighing her up.

"I won't go higher than 7 percent of the total," she said eventually.

Here we go, thought El. She's on the hook.

"She's got this painting," Ruby had said. "Rare. Massive great cartoon thing, looks like something off a can of 7 Up. Not my cup of tea at all. But she paid big money for it in New York last year. It was a closed auction, private seller, so it didn't get reported on the way it would've if she'd bought it any other way. But big money, definitely. 1.3 million quid was what I heard."

"Must be a hell of a painting," El had said, taking another drag of her cigarette.

"It's a fake," said Ruby.

Behind the bar, the waiter had stopped cleaning the bottles. They'd fallen quiet abruptly; waited for him to begin again.

"She got taken?" said El, when he resumed his cleaning.

"Don't know how it happened," said Ruby. "She don't sound the type to *let* it happen. But yeah, she did. 1.3 million. Must have stung, eh?"

She'd smiled to herself, relishing the other woman's discomfort.

"What are you thinking?" El asked.

"I ain't *thinking* anything," said Ruby. "It's already started. I've got it all lined up already, got people in place. I just need someone on the inside, someone I can trust."

"Like me."

"Like you."

"To do what, exactly?"

Ruby's smiled had broadened, smoothing out the wrinkles of her cheeks.

"What do you know about Pop Art?" she'd asked.

"At the moment, about as much as I know about molecular gastronomy," El had said. "But I can learn. Why?"

"That painting," Ruby had said. "I need you to help her sell it."

"I want 8," El told Lady Rose, thinking of Claire Brandon's credit card debts, her loan repayments, the two-bed flat in Southwark she'd buy with her boyfriend just as soon as they had the deposit.

"No," said Lady Rose, with her own first hint of a smile.

El glanced over at Karen, who was playing with her walkie-talkie and giving every impression of boredom, then back across at Lady Rose.

"I was told," she said, with a confidence Claire Brandon didn't feel, "that the Haring you have in your collection is a replica. A counterfeit. If that's the case, then whoever agrees to authenticate it will be taking the same risks as you are in passing it off as an original. They'd be risking their career, their reputation. Their freedom, if the police were ever to get involved. £104,000 seems relatively small potatoes for a risk like that. Don't you think?"

Karen laughed.

"Brilliant!" she said through the laughter. "You know, when I saw you coming up the drive, I thought you'd be some timid little mouse with a begging bowl. And just listen to you! I love it. *Love* it."

Lady Rose held up a hand, silencing her. The sleeve of her blouse fell open at the wrist, revealing the flesh of her forearm. It was scarred, El saw - cut or burned, thin ropes of dark pink tissue criss-crossing the skin all the way to the elbow.

She saw El looking; pulled the sleeve down firmly, and buttoned it, concealing the scars under the fabric.

"So you'll do it," she said. "For 8 percent, you'll do it."

"Do you have a buyer?" asked El.

"I have two," said Lady Rose. "Or rather, two potentials. Only one of them, I suspect, will come to anything."

"Who?"

"Is it significant?"

"No. But I'm curious."

Karen snorted, evidently tickled by Claire Brandon's performance and the look it brought to her boss's face.

Lady Rose ignored her. Then she smiled at El - a wide, delighted smile that reminded El for one strange second of Ruby's.

"I'll tell you what, Dr Brandon," she said. "Why not meet her for yourself?"

"Alright," said El uncertainly.

"Wonderful," she said, still smiling.

She glanced down at the thin silver watch that decorated her other, unmarked wrist.

"But I should put on your game face quickly, if I were you," she added. "She'll be here with us in half an hour."

FROM THE DAILY BUGLE

April 1981

MR S. J. L. WINCHESTER AND MISS R. K. ACKROYD

The marriage took place on Saturday, February 18, 1981 in Redbourn, Hertfordshire, between Sebastian, eldest son of Sir Henry Winchester, Bt. and Mrs Lucinda Winchester, of Silverdale House, Oakham, Rutland and Rosemary, only daughter of Mr and Mrs Arthur Ackroyd of Rotherham, South Yorkshire. The Rev Charles Foster officiated. A reception was held at the family home of the groom.

FROM HERE! MAGAZINE

September 1990

EXCLUSIVE: SEBASTIAN WINCHESTER OPENS UP ABOUT HIS FAIRYTALE MARRIAGE TO WIFE ROSE - AFTER 15 YEARS TOGETHER

Businessman Sebastian Winchester has revealed the secrets of his successful marriage - and the reason for his wife's camera-shyness.

The media boss, 35, has exclusively shared what keeps him and wife Rose close, even when his job takes him overseas and away from her and their six year old daughter for weeks at a time.

Welcoming Here! into the family home in North London, Sebastian couldn't stop himself enthusing about Rose, and her recent ventures into fine art collecting.

"She's always had a wonderful eye," he said, pointing to the colourful prints that line the walls of their living room. "An absolute passion for design and layout, for the right look in the right place. It's a real shared interest - one of the things that first brought us together."

Sebastian and Rose, 34, met for the first time as History students at Oxford University. But it was several months before their relationship took a turn for the romantic.

"We were friends first," he said. "Best friends. Everything else evolved from there."

"It's because of that, having that firm foundation of friendship, that we've managed to stay so happy together for so long. We already knew everything about each other before we tied the knot. So there were no surprises."

Discussing the work trips that can often sweep him away to New York, San Francisco and Miami - and away from Rose and Sophie - at a moment's notice, Sebastian said:

"We talk every night on the phone. That's very important to us both - that we keep the lines of communication open. We're both very big talkers!"

Though out at the park with Sophie during our interview, Rose was a constant presence in our conversation.

"I count myself extremely lucky to have her," said Sebastian. "There aren't many men whose wives would put up with the kind of schedules I keep to. But she's a very unusual woman, quite exceptional. And terribly independent. Most women in her position would insist on bringing in at the very least a nanny and a housekeeper. But she's always been determined to do absolutely everything herself, to change every nappy and do every school-run, and I adore that about her, that commitment."

About Rose's infamous aversion to the camera lens, Sebastian said, "She's a very private person. Neither of us were expecting the business to do as well as it has, and she's still adjusting to the attention it's brought us. She's still finding her feet. But obviously we're both delighted with the way it's all taken off, even if she doesn't show it quite as much as I do!"

Despite their obvious happiness, though, Sebastian stayed tight-lipped on whether he and Rose would be adding a little brother or sister for Sophie to their family.

"You'll have to ask Rose!" he laughed. "She makes the decisions in our house!"

Looks like Here! readers will just have to wait and see...

FROM THE EXAMINER

June 1993

OBITUARY: SIR SEBASTIAN WINCHESTER

Sebastian Winchester, 3rd Baronet was the founder and Chief Executive of Fairlight Media, a charismatic leader whose vision and dynamic management style helped steer the organisation to dominance of the UK publishing landscape over the last decade.

Winchester, who has died suddenly of an undiagnosed heart condition aged 38, drew on his early experience as Editor of Oxford University's Cherwell magazine to turn Fairlight's earliest publication, women's magazine Femme, into a near-overnight success in the late 1970s. The subsequent launch of titles like Hot Stuff, On The Box, Metal Machine and Gamer between 1980 and 1985 only consolidated his reputation, while the acquisition of Britain's New Wireless Holdings in 1986 and the American broadcast network SNT in 1988 saw him and Fairlight move into radio and, latterly, television.

Outside of his commercial interests, Winchester was a dedicated outdoorsman and rock-climber who had scaled the summits of both California's El Capitán and Argentina's Aconcagua, the second with his wife Rose. So enthusiastic was he about climbing that he and Rose honeymooned in the mountain ranges of Denali, Alaska in early 1982, in the company of his best man, barrister John Richmond, and her bridesmaid, writer Susan Hayes.

Winchester was born in Amersham in 1955, the eldest of three children. His father was Sir Henry Winchester, founder of the Basildon Group and one-time Conservative MP for Henton; his mother was Lucinda Pell, daughter of the industrialist Sir Hubert Pell. A voracious reader and cinephile, Winchester attended Charterhouse School, where he excelled academically, taking up a place to read History at Wadham College, Oxford in 1973. He founded Fairlight soon after graduating in 1976.

He is survived by Rose, their daughter Sophie and his sisters, Barbara and Camilla.

FROM DOLLY'S DARK DISCLOSURES

August 1993

Fair warning, poppets: this week's Disclosure is a Dark one, even for Dolly...

Which recently-widowed society wife might be mourning less than you'd think for her better-known dearly departed?

Official reports put her on the scene the evening of hubby's untimely - and oh so unexpected - demise. But Dolly's sources say she crept home late that night to find him already cold in bed - after enjoying a discreet (but apparently not *that* discreet) candlelight dinner with a certain square-jawed legal eagle of their mutual acquaintance.

Could this be the *real* reason for all those trips abroad?

FROM LUXE LIVING MAGAZINE (US EDITION)

July 1995

FEATURE: 5 FEMALE COLLECTORS YOU NEED TO KNOW ABOUT

NUMBER 5: LADY ROSE WINCHESTER

It's hard to tell you much about our last collector, England's Lady Rose Winchester. We don't know much ourselves.

Unlike the other women on our list, Lady Rose keeps a consciously-low profile, refusing all interviews and eschewing the celebrity-and-canapes circuit you might think would be par for the course for someone with her (at last count) two hundred million pound fortune.

What we do know about Lady Rose is this: her private gallery houses the largest collection of Hockneys on either side of the Atlantic, and her wider portfolio (of Warhols, Rothkos, Blakes and Hamiltons, among others) was valued, according to rumour, at upward of $50m.

4 other things we know:

- She wasn't always a Lady. British newspaper reports have her father as a maintenance man, her mother as a housewife - and her hometown as Rotherham, a run-down former mining town in the British northeast.
- She married up. Her late husband was a bona fide Baronet, as well as a publishing legend. His company, Fairlight Media, is worth an estimated $1.2b today.
- She's smart. After graduating Oxford University with a double first (the British version of *magna cum laude*), she was instrumental in establishing Fairlight as a key player in the media industry - first in England, then across the world. According to public listings, she still holds significant stock in the company.
- She gets around. When she's out of London, it isn't just the East Coast auction houses she's stalking: in the last year, she's spent serious money in Paris, Cologne, Stockholm and Cape Town.

And one last thing, of course: we'd kill to get a look at her collection.

HIGHGATE

1996

K aren led El down the ground-floor hallway, past a sparsely-furnished sitting room and a cavernous, white-tiled kitchen-diner, so pristine and professionally kitted-out that it could have passed for one of the kitchens at The Ivy. The latter looked to El like the domain of a professional chef, a Raymond Blanc or a Marco Pierre White - an appearance entirely at odds with Lady Rose's apparent reluctance to engage domestic help. Perhaps, El thought, she'd changed her tune since her husband's death; perhaps these days she was more keen to have company around, to hear voices in the house instead of echoing silence. If she was, it would explain the presence of Karen. Or partially explain it.

She took a right turn, passing under a grey marble archway and down a long, winding flight of stairs that opened out into a surprisingly airy, high-ceilinged basement room spanning what felt, to El, like the entire length and breadth of the house.

There was no furniture here; nowhere to sit or relax. The floor was a stark polished hardwood, the walls whitewashed. It was a room - if, El thought, the word "room" could be used to describe a space the size of a bowling alley - dedicated to a single function: the exhibition of Lady Rose's vast art collection.

There were photographs, all monochrome: a Man Ray-style closeup of a woman's face, a Mapplethorpe-like boot-heel crushing the stem of a lily, an androgynous tattooed head and torso that El thought might have been a Diane Arbus. There were Cubist collages, framed comic book pages, vivid snatches of graffiti suspended in Perspex boxes. But mostly there were paintings, Pop Art and neo-expressionist: Lichtensteins and Hamiltons, Patrick Caulfield stills and Julian Schnabel plates and more obscure pieces that El didn't recognise, their colours bright and cartoonish against the austere whitewash.

"Must be your idea of heaven down here," said Karen, watching her take in the space.

"Hmm," said El noncommittally.

There was CCTV too, she noticed, and a lot of it: boxy, wide-lensed cameras, pointing down towards the ground and covering, she estimated, almost every square inch of it.

In the centre of the room, mounted on an easel, was another painting, or what El took to be another painting - two feet long and three feet wide, the canvas concealed entirely by a yellow dust-sheet.

"Is this it?" she asked, pointing to the dust-sheet.

"What 'it'?" said Karen, apparently enjoying playing dumb.

"The Haring," said El testily.

"Oh," said Karen. "*That*. Couldn't say. You'll have to ask Her Majesty."

There was disdain there, El thought - but also affection. She wondered, momentarily, what kind of relationship Karen had with Lady Rose; how their paths might ever have crossed in the first place. Karen didn't seem the type to respond to a job ad in the paper.

"How long have you worked here?" she said.

"Not long," said Karen.

It wasn't an answer that invited any follow-up questions or comments. But Claire Brandon, El thought, would press on with the conversation regardless; wouldn't be comfortable with awkward silence. Besides, she was curious.

"How did you get into it?" she asked. "PA-ing?"

Karen smirked.

"Thinking about a career change, are you?" she said.

The walkie-talkie in her hand crackled. She pressed a button in the middle of the handset, and Lady Rose's voice rang out across the room.

"Visitors," said Lady Rose through the crackle of the speaker.

"On it," said Karen.

She tucked the walkie-talkie into her back pocket, the muscles of her arms flexing involuntarily as she shifted her weight.

"I'm going upstairs," she said to El. "Be back in a minute."

"Okay," said El.

"Try not to nick anything while I'm gone," she added, and disappeared up the stairs, leaving El alone in the gallery.

The first thing she did, before she took a breath or moved an inch, was look up at the cameras.

They were operational, she saw - a pinprick of infrared light blinking in the centre of each.

She took a step to the right, then another. The camera closest to her moved too, swivelling on its bracket to follow her as she stepped.

The question, she thought, was whether anyone was watching - whether there was a security guard out there somewhere monitoring the camera feeds, scrutinising every screen in their bank of monitors for anything untoward or out of place.

Not that it mattered if there was, of course. Her recent forays into fine art fraud notwithstanding, Claire Brandon was an honest, upright, law-abiding citizen. She wasn't a thief or a con-artist, and if she was curious about the painting lying under the dust-sheet, tantalisingly hidden from view, then it was a curiosity driven by professional interest, nothing more. She wanted to see what was under that dust-sheet, yes - but only to look, not to touch or take.

El walked across to the easel, and the camera followed her, whirring slightly, straining at the hinges to keep her in view.

She gripped the dust-sheet by its corners, and lifted - first gingerly, Claire Brandon's hesitation playing out for the benefit of any possible audience, and then more assertively, until the painting underneath was uncovered.

It was remarkable - all the more so, El thought, because it was a fake. All of the hallmarks she'd come to recognise from her crash-course in Keith Haring and the world of '80s street art were there, and in technicolour: the thick, bold strokes that could have come from a marker pen; the fluid, contorted figures, dancing across the frame like a string of energetic hieroglyphs; the sound waves and the love hearts. It was simple, stylistically, verging on simplistic - but there was something captivating about the innocence of the it, the sincerity, and she found it hard to look away. She could understand completely, having seen it, why Lady Rose might have wanted to believe that it was real when she bought it.

She stared at the canvas for a solid minute, mentally constructing the arguments she'd use to convince whoever she needed to of its authenticity, when she heard footsteps on the staircase above her.

She pulled the dust-sheet back over the painting, and stepped quickly away from the easel just as Karen reemerged on the bottom stairs.

"Everything alright down here?" she asked.

"Fine," said El. "Just, you know... looking around."

Karen eyed her suspiciously.

"I should get yourself ready," she said, after a pause.

"Ready?"

"To do whatever it is you do. Talk about art, or whatever."

"The buyer's here?"

"Yeah. Coming down now."

More footsteps echoed above their heads, and Lady's Rose's brogues appeared on the stairs, followed by Lady Rose herself and, behind her, an older woman, sixtysomething and caked in makeup so heavy that her skin appeared to be cracking. Her hair was jet-black, artificially so, highlighted with streaks of ash-blonde at odds with her South Asian appearance. She was heavy, double-chinned and round-hipped, her fingers short and stubby, and the waft of perfume she brought with her was loud, intrusive. She wore dark, coordinated colours from neck to toe - her upper body sheathed by a navy blue pashmina, her legs by charcoal trousers that tapered at the ankle. There was, El estimated, at least £50,000 of gold jewellery hanging from her neck and earlobes.

"And here we are," said Lady Rose, extending a grandiose arm around the room.

"Oh, I love it!" said the older woman, her voice speaking simultaneously of the Middle East and the US East Coast. "And it's all yours?"

"I can't help myself," said Lady Rose, mock-bashfully. "I see something I like, and I have to have it. You know how it is."

"You know I do!" said the woman with a throaty laugh.

The two of them paced the room slowly, taking in the artwork and ignoring El and Karen entirely. When they'd completed a full circuit, Lady Rose led her guest to the covered easel.

"We haven't met," said the woman, finally acknowledging El's presence by thrusting out a hand in her direction. "Maryam Qureshi."

"Dr Claire Brandon," said El, squeezing the hand in hers. It was dry and rough, thick with callouses.

"Dr Brandon is an expert in American neo-expressionism," said Lady Rose, in lieu of a proper introduction. "She'll be authenticating the Haring."

"And she's on your payroll?" said Qureshi to Lady Rose, sceptically.

"Technically, she's on yours," said Lady Rose. "Her fee will be deducted from the price of the painting, should you decide to move ahead with the purchase."

"So she gets paid only if I buy your painting," said Qureshi. "Hardly makes for an objective witness, eh?"

"You're more than welcome to have someone of your own do a valuation," said Lady Rose smoothly. "You know that. But I doubt you'll find anyone more qualified than Dr Brandon."

"Is she from one of the auction houses?" said Qureshi. "Sotheby's, Bonhams, something like that?"

"She's an independent," said Lady Rose. "A freelancer."

"I'm based at the Slade," said El, piping up to verify her qualifications unasked in exactly the way she suspected Claire Brandon might.

"Dr Brandon is primarily an academic," said Lady Rose. "So very much impartial."

Maryam Qureshi snorted.

"If you say so," she said.

She lifted the hem of the dust-sheet with the tip of her foot.

"Is this it?" she asked.

Lady Rose nodded to Karen, who whipped the dust-sheet off the easel with an entirely unnecessary flourish, revealing the painting.

Qureshi examined it, carefully.

"You have all the paperwork for it?" she asked Lady Rose. "The documentation?"

"All of it," said Lady Rose. "The sale receipt, the certificate of authenticity... everything."

"Then why did you bring her in?" said Qureshi, indicating El. "If it's already authenticated - why is she here?"

"Because it never hurts to have some extra peace of mind," said Lady Rose. "That extra layer of reassurance. The paperwork can tell you its provenance, its value - can tell you what it is, and how much it might be worth. But Dr Brandon can tell you *why* it's worth that. She can... bring it to life for you."

She's good, thought El. I almost believe her myself.

Qureshi looked at El, then at the canvas, and then back at El.

"Tell me, then, Dr Brandon," she said, laying down the challenge. "Why should I buy this painting? And why on earth should I pay such an obscene amount of money for it?"

El thought back to her research, to the sheaves of notes she'd made on Haring and his contemporaries. The speech virtually wrote itself.

"Aside from the obvious value inherent in a work considered lost for the last decade and a half," she began, as if addressing a packed lecture hall, "and assuming that its initial authentication date is accurate, which I have no reason to doubt - this piece contains the first use of Haring's signature figures on a canvas background. All recorded uses of the same figures prior this one appeared as street art - as chalk or spray-paint outlines on walls and New York subways."

"This is significant for two reasons," she continued. "One, it represents a substantial stylistic development - the first step in Haring's evolution from experimental street kid to studio artist. Two, and for me more interestingly: it gives us much greater insight into the meaning of the figures. By pinning their first use down to a specific time and date, and cross-referencing this date with documented incidents from Haring's life and the environments he was immersed in at that time, we can begin to understand with much more certainty why he began using the figures, and what he intended to communicate through them."

"I don't know about you, but I'm sold," said Karen to the room at large.

"You say you have no reason to doubt the date of the painting," said Qureshi to El, as if Karen hadn't spoken. "But is there any reason to doubt its origin? Taking the initial authentication out of the equation for a moment: is there any cause to imagine that it might be, for example, a convincing replica, or a homage to Haring's style by another artist of the same period?"

El had been expecting this; had prepared for it.

"Absolutely none," she said, with all the certainty Claire Brandon would have channelled into the defence of her PhD thesis. "There's at least one clear marker here that points unequivocally to Haring as the artist, rather than an imitator."

"Which is what?" said Qureshi.

"The lines," said El. "Haring both drew and painted his figures in clean, unbroken lines - the same kind of lines you see here." She gestured towards the painting. "He'd take a pencil, or a paintbrush, or a piece of chalk or whatever he happened to be working with, and pull it from one side of the canvas - or the wall, or the paper - to the other without ever lifting the pencil, or the brush, or the chalk. He was a master of not breaking the line. The imitators, conversely, and I've seen a few... the lines on the figures are broken, or they've been rubbed out. So when we're looking at a real Haring, an original - it's a very clear signature."

El paused to catch her breath. Karen, she noticed out of the corner of her eye, was watching her, amusement drawing her lips up into a barely-concealed grin.

Qureshi studied the painting.

"I have to say," she said finally, turning to Lady Rose, "this tallies with what I know of Haring. It's possible I may want to get a second opinion on the valuation before finalising the purchase. But at this stage, certainly, I think I'd like to proceed."

"Wonderful," said Lady Rose, beaming.

"Could we perhaps discuss it upstairs?" said Qureshi, with a glance at El and Karen.

Not in front of the help, thought El. Never in front of the help.

"Absolutely," said Lady Rose. "Let's."

She ushered Qureshi up the staircase, following closely behind without so much as a look over her shoulder.

"Nice one," said Karen when they'd gone, a note of respect in her voice that hadn't been there previously.

"Did I do alright?" asked El, some of Claire Brandon's residual uncertainty colouring her words as the adrenaline ebbed out of her.

"Like I said," said Karen. "I was sold."

Karen walked her up the stairs and back through the house, leaving her to find her own way out of the driveway.

"She'll call you," she said, then closed the door in El's face.

There was a car on the driveway, El saw, that hadn't been previously - a Bentley, gold and gaudy, the back windows blacked out and a uniformed driver humming to himself at the wheel. She approached the electronic gates, and they opened automatically - urging her out onto the street just as they'd urged her inside.

She walked to the end of road, where the cul-de-sac met the traffic of Hampstead Lane, and lit a cigarette. Claire Brandon, she'd decided as she'd packed her bag that morning, was a smoker, like El - albeit one with less demanding and firmly entrenched a habit than El's own.

She turned the corner into Hampstead Lane, and paused, deep in thought. She finished the cigarette in short order, and immediately lit another - the smoke filling her lungs and drowning out the taste of strawberry lip-gloss and the White Musk body spray Claire Brandon's mother had got her for her last birthday.

Three cigarettes later, the hideous gold Bentley pulled out of the cul-de-sac and onto the road in her direction, where it slowed to a crawl. She took one final drag, stubbed out the cigarette with the toe of one hiking boot and walked towards it.

The Bentley stopped abruptly. The driver, visible in the front, wound down his window, stuck one hand and a crab-red face outside and beckoned her over.

"Hop in," he said. "She wants a word."

El opened the back door tentatively and slipped into the back of the Bentley. Maryam Qureshi was waiting inside - a long black cigarette-holder of her own clenched between her teeth.

She leaned in towards El, smiled, transferred the cigarette from mouth to ashtray and ran two fingers along El's cheek with maternal tenderness.

"Darling," she said before El could speak, in a cut-glass, English-accented voice that was nothing at all like the one she'd used earlier. "You were *marvellous* in there."

EDGWARE

1978

The Ruby who emerged into the courtyard was an entirely different woman than the one that El had met the day before.

Her hair had changed, for one thing - the salt-and-pepper now a smooth mousy blonde, pinned back with a wooden clip and what looked to El like chopsticks. The Jackie O. shades were gone, replaced by a pair of tortoiseshell glasses connected to her neck by a string. Behind the glasses, her makeup-less eyes were wide and owlish - the eyes of a dazed librarian taking her first steps out of the stacks and into the sunlight. Her blouse was moss-green and sensible, buttoned to the neck and half-hidden behind a heavy waxed jacket. There were clogs on her feet.

Under one arm she held a porcelain doll - old-looking and slightly dirty, traces of dust clinging to its bonnet and petticoats. Its skin was inhumanly white; its cheeks were rouged, its yellow ringlets curling down into the thick fronds of its eyelashes. It was undeniably sinister.

"Here," she said, thrusting the doll at El. "This is for you."

El looked down at the doll, disgusted. What was she supposed to do with it, exactly?

"I'm 14," she said in response, pointedly not touching it.

"Well, you look younger," said Ruby impatiently. "So use it. In fact... here's your first lesson for you: everything you've *got*, use it. You look young, play young. You look old, play old. You look like a gormless village idiot... you let people think you *are* a village idiot. Other people's misperceptions are the best friend you've got in this game."

She adjusted her jacket. There were tweed patches on the sleeves.

"Now," she added, "take the bloody doll. We've got work to do."

They caught the bus to Oxford Circus, neither of them saying much as they climbed the stairs and took their seats at the back of the upper deck. After five minutes of watching the green-grey scenery of the North London suburbs pass by them, El dipped into her satchel and withdrew a box of matches and a Silk Cut, freshly stolen from her Uncle's packet.

Ruby snatched them both from her hand and stowed them away in her jacket.

"Give them back!" El protested. "They're mine!"

'You're too young to be smoking," Ruby said.

"Not for you to say, is it?" snapped El.

"It is today," Ruby snapped back. "You want to learn, then you do as I say. And I'm not having you walk in there reeking of fag smoke. You'll give the whole thing away like *that*."

She snapped her fingers for emphasis.

"Walk in *where*?" said El. "You haven't told me where we're going yet."

"The *where* ain't important. It's the *who* and the *how* that matters, for this one."

"And are you planning on letting me know what *they* are, then?"

The bus pulled into a stop in Hendon, conveniently dislodging the only two other passengers on the top deck down the stairs and out onto the pavement.

"Probably should, shouldn't I?" said Ruby.

And told her.

They got off at Baker Street, by Madame Tussauds. There were tourists everywhere, taking pictures and biting into sandwiches and ambling along slowly enough to clog up the whole of the road. Ruby fell into step behind a cluster of them, El pressed into her side like a baby duckling.

They broke away from the crowd at Allsop Place and turned right into York Terrace, where Ruby stopped. She took El by the shoulder and spun her around so they were face to face.

"You remember what to do?" she said.

"Yes," said El, rolling her eyes. "It didn't sink in the first three times you went over it, but now? Definitely."

"I take back what I said before," said Ruby. "You *are* a teenager. You sounded just like one of my boys then. Still got the doll, have you?"

"In my bag," said El, shaking the strap of her satchel.

"Good," said Ruby. "Right, then. Off you go."

She turned El back around by her triceps and gave her a light shove in the small of her back, propelling her off down the street.

Without turning around to look behind her, El walked on, eyes straight ahead - all the way along to where York Terrace became York Gate. There, by the crossroad, was the place she was looking for: a squat pink birthday cake of a building, its long windows flanked on either side by Greco-Roman pillars. The sign above the open door advertised it as the Cafe Italia, while the menu on the glass and the cooking smells emanating from the doorway billed it as a purveyor of bacon, egg and a fried slice for less than 80p.

She went inside, the bell over the door jingling as she entered.

The decor was exactly what she might have expected had she thought about it, all red vinyl chairs, Formica tables and bottles of tomato sauce on the tabletops. Despite the density of the crowds two streets away, it wasn't busy; there was, as far as she could tell, only one other person in there, an old white man picking listlessly at a plate of baked beans on toast with the tip of his fork. By the counter, a younger white man in an apron - she supposed the manager - was slurping at a mug of coffee, his lips smacking at the rim of the mug whenever he took a sip.

She walked slowly across to the counter, stomach turning with nerves.

"Can I help you?" said the maybe-manager, warily. She wondered what part of her was responsible for his wariness - her age, the scruffiness of her jeans and sweater, her unwashed hair, the suspicious light-brownness of her skin.

She looked up at the chalkboard menu above his head, ostensibly studying the myriad combinations of sausage, egg, bacon, chips and beans with great interest.

"Full English, please," she said, in the meekest voice she could manage. "And a tin of Tizer."

"Have a seat," he said, with no trace of friendliness. "I'll bring it over."

She sidled over to the table furthest away from the old man and sank nonchalantly down into the vinyl. She pulled a book from her bag - a new one from the library, Philip K. Dick's A Scanner Darkly, the pages still crisp and unthumbed - and settled down to read.

She was barely five pages in when the manager brought over the food, dropping the can of pop and the warm plate down so gracelessly that two of the mushrooms spilled out onto the tabletop.

"Thank you," she said, all politeness.

He grunted something she couldn't make out, and strode away without looking at her.

The food was good: hot and greasy and filling, the bacon cut thick and the bread a satisfying mix of sweet and salty. She finished it all, clearing the plate with a crust fried crisp, and washed it down with the Tizer, thirsty enough by then to drain the can in a half dozen gulps.

She crossed her knife and fork over the plate and pushed it to one side, and before long the manager was back, looming over the table like a raincloud.

"Got the bill," he said, handing it over.

She took it and smiled up at him; made a show of digging into the pocket of her jeans. When she failed to find what she was looking for in there, she let her forehead crease in confusion. She plunged a hand into the other pocket, fingers pressing down into the lining of the denim - but there was nothing. Her hand came up empty.

"I'm so sorry," she said, mortified. "My Auntie gave me two pounds for my lunch, and I thought I'd put it in my pocket but I must have left it at home..."

The manager's small eyes narrowed, his lips tightening in disgust.

"I ought to call the police," he said, his voice low and dangerous, and for a minute she worried that he might - that she'd leave the cafe in the back of a Panda car.

"Please," she said, willing herself to tears. "She only lives round the corner - I can run back and get it. It won't take me 5 minutes."

"Run off, you mean," said the man. He muttered something under his breath, something she couldn't quite hear.

"I won't!" she said. "I promise! She's in Marylebone, Balcombe Street. I'd be there and back before you know it. Just... don't call the police on me. Please."

"The hell you would," he said.

"Please!" she said desperately. "You've got to believe me. I'll... I'll leave something here with you. For you to look after. Something to keep, so you know I'll come back."

She glanced down at her open satchel, and his eyes followed hers, scanning the contents. The book. A pencil, worn down to a stub. A rubber band ball. And the doll.

"Like what?" he said. "What have you got that's worth coming back for?"

She looked at the doll, quickly, furtively - just long enough for him to see her looking - then looked away, keeping her focus fixed on the table in front of her.

"What's that you got there?" he asked, pointing down at the doll with the tip of one finger. "Aren't you a bit old for playing dolls?"

"It was my Granny's," she said quietly. "She left it me when she..."

She let her voice trail off.

"What are you carrying it around with you for?" he said - but he was softening at bit, she could tell.

"I'm not carrying it round," she said. "I'm taking it home. That's why I was round at my Auntie's this morning, picking it up."

He looked at the doll again; stared at it.

"Leave it here," he said. "Leave it here with me, and then I'll know you'll come back."

Her lip wobbled, the picture of heartbreak.

"Leave it here?" she asked.

"Yeah," he said. "I mean, you *are* coming back, aren't you?"

She nodded, vigorously.

"Alright, then," he said. "So here's what we'll do: you leave the doll with me, and I'll keep it behind the counter for you until you come back to pay your bill. Safe as houses."

She hesitated, her face broadcasting her train of thought with the volume up. She didn't want to part with the doll, it said; not even for 5 minutes. But she owed him money, and he'd threatened to call the police, and what would her Auntie say...?

She extracted the doll from the satchel by its arm, gently, and handed it over to the manager.

"You *will* look after it, won't you?" she asked.

"Cross my heart and hope to die," he said.

She bit her trembling lip; stood up from her chair, pulling the satchel over her chest.

"I'll be quick," she said.

She shot out of the cafe like a rocket, racing down York Gate and slowing to a walk when she made it to Regent's Park. She stopped just before the Jubilee Gates; sat down on a bench, took A Scanner Darkly from the satchel and settled down to read.

An hour and four chapters passed. When she judged the time was right, she put away the book and jogged back to the cafe - through the park, and back up York Gate.

At the cafe's door, she pulled two pound notes from the back pocket of her jeans, rubbed both against the sweating palms of her hands - *it's the little details*, Ruby had told her, *it's them that really sell it* - and stepped back inside.

The manager was waiting for her behind the counter.

"I'm sorry it took me so long!" she said breathlessly. "My Auntie was out at the shops, and I had to wait for her to get back so she could let me in, and then she couldn't find her purse..."

She threw the now-damp notes onto the counter.

The manager smiled at her - a half-moon wrinkling of the jaw that made him look, she thought, not unlike a frog.

"Not to worry!" he said magnanimously. "You're back now, that's the main thing."

There was a pause, long and - to El at least - painful.

"Do you have...?" she began.

"Oh, yes!" he said, as if remembering. "The doll! Of course, I've got it here."

He kneeled down behind the counter, then stood up again, the doll tucked under his armpit.

He made no move, she observed, to hand it over.

"The thing is," he said, "while you were gone... my little girl came over to see me. She's younger than you, only seven. Still plays with dolls - not like you. And she... well, she took a shine to this doll of yours here. Couldn't stop playing with it."

El said nothing. *Let him do the talking*, Ruby had said. *The more he talks, the less you have to try.*

"She said to me," he continued, "'Daddy, can I keep her?' And I told her no, that she belonged to another little girl - well, a big girl, really - and so we had to give her back. But she got herself worked up about it, wouldn't stop bawling, just kept saying, 'but I love her, Daddy! Why can't I keep her?' And I didn't know what to say. So I told her: that girl's coming back in in a minute to pay for her lunch, so when she gets here I'll tell her about you and tell her how much you love that doll, and we'll see if we can't work something out between us. And you should have seen the look on her face! I'd never seen her so happy."

"I don't understand," said El, understanding perfectly.

"This doll," said the manager. "I know you got her from your Granny. And I know she must mean a lot to you. But let's be honest - you're not going to play with her, are you? Not the way my little girl would."

"I don't know," said El uncertainly. "Probably not?"

"Of course you're not," said the man, pressing his advantage. "She'd just be sitting in a box at home somewhere, gathering dust until you've forgotten all about her. But my little girl... well, having something like that would make her day."

El let her mouth drop open a little - just enough to seem perplexed by the situation.

"What about this, then?" he said, opening the till and ostentatiously rifling around inside. "I've got... let's see... nearly ten quid here. It's probably a fair bit more than she's worth - but I know you must be attached to her. And my daughter, I can't tell you how much she loved that doll, and I'd do just about anything to make her smile. So how about it?"

"You want to give me money for Gran's doll?" El asked.

The manager pulled a handful of notes and coins out from the till - £9.85, she counted, mostly in ones and 50 pence pieces.

"Take it," he said, pressing the money into her hand. "You'd be doing us both a favour."

She stared at the money; at the two other, crumpled pound notes on the counter.

"But... I need to pay *you*," she said. "What I owe you. For lunch."

He pushed the two notes back at her.

"It's on the house," he said.

"About two minutes after you leave to get the money off your 'Auntie'," Ruby had told her on the bus to Baker Street, "I'll make my entrance."

She'd walk over to the counter; order a cup of hot chocolate, extra milky; make polite chitchat with the manager, her accent shifting effortlessly into a crisp RP. In the course of that conversation, she'd have cause to peer over the counter, where - if she was any judge of character - the man would have stashed the doll.

Balancing her tortoiseshell glasses on the bridge of her nose to examine it more closely, she'd ask a string of unanticipated questions - who it belonged to, where it came from. Whether it was his.

"Why'd you want to know?" he'd say, interrupting her.

She'd apologise for her rudeness, for overstepping, but could offer in her defence only that she was tremendously excited - she ran a small antiques shop on the Marylebone High Street and, though she and her partner specialised in children's toys, she'd never seen a Baby Henrietta up close before, not in the flesh.

"A what?" the man would say.

"A Baby Henrietta," Ruby would say, surprised at his ignorance. And then, slowly understanding that he had no clue what she was talking about - that he *didn't know* what he had - she'd explain:

The Baby Henrietta collection of lifelike dolls, modelled after real children, was manufactured by Switzerland's Arnholdt Company between 1921 and 1924. At the time, the dolls were considered commercial failures, their too-realistic appearance judged off-putting for the real-world children to whom they were marketed. Their comparative rarity, though, meant that their value had increased significantly over time - to the extent that the thirty or so Baby Henrietta dolls remaining were now changing hands, among those in the know, for some fairly substantial sums, at least by the standards of the antique toy trade.

"What kind of sums are we talking?" the manager would ask.

"Oh, £2000 or more, at the higher end," Ruby would answer.

Dollar signs would appear in the manager's eyes.

"Two grand?" he'd say, seeking confirmation that he hadn't misheard, that the dirty-looking doll he'd shoved under the stack of Coke cans below the counter could really go for more than the price of a new car.

"At least," Ruby would say airily.

The man would be speechless - initially, anyway.

"If you don't mind me asking," Ruby would add, "where did you get her? I assume you're not a collector yourself."

"She's... my daughter's," the man would reply.

"I don't suppose..." Ruby would begin.

"What?" the man would say.

"I don't suppose you'd ever consider *selling* her?"

The man would fall back into silence, dumbfounded, leaving Ruby embarrassed.

"I'm so sorry," she'd stutter. "I shouldn't have asked. Terribly presumptuous of me."

Seeing the new car drive away from him at speed before he'd even put the key in the ignition, the man would spring into action.

"It's fine!" he'd say, spluttering in his haste to get the words out. "No need to apologise. I just had no idea she'd be worth that much. I mean, obviously I knew she was valuable, you've only got to look at her to know that - but not, you know... *that* valuable."

"Perhaps," Ruby would say slyly, "I could give you my card? I'm on my way to a valuation just now, but as I say, my shop is only on the High Street. You could call in one day this week, and we could have a little chat."

She'd fish a card from her handbag, a sharp-edged matte rectangle that felt denser and more expensive than traditional cardboard, and would pass it across the counter to him.

He'd stare at it for a moment, still processing the information.

"We'll see," he'd say, and tuck the card in his wallet for safekeeping.

On Baker Street, El slipped the banknotes between the pages of her book, the coins into her pocket.

Following Ruby's instructions, she walked through Fitzrovia to Oxford Circus, then took the tube from there to Tottenham Court Road, proceeding on foot for the rest of the journey. The place she wanted, Ruby had said, was just off Endell Street - another greasy spoon very like the one she'd just left, this one going by the slightly grandiose name of The Cavendish.

She found it easily enough. Ruby was there already, positioned at a table with a clear view of the door. She didn't react at all as El came in, though she'd clearly seen her.

El responded in kind, walking over to the till and ordering a cup of tea from the middle-aged Indian woman behind the counter. *Then* she crossed the room to Ruby; slid down into the seat opposite her, nonchalantly.

Wordlessly, she withdrew the notes from the book and the coins from her pocket, and placed both on the table between them.

"How much?" Ruby asked quietly.

"Nearly a tenner," said El, dropping her own voice in response.

"Good girl," said Ruby. She took four notes from the pile, folded them and secreted them inside her waxed jacket.

"You can keep the rest," she added.

El shoved the rest of the money back into her pocket, before Ruby could change her mind.

The Indian woman brought over El's tea. Somehow, in the moment of transferring it across to the table, the cup slipped from her hand, falling onto the floor and shattering, loudly – spilling six inches of copper-coloured water onto the linoleum in the process.

"Sorry, very sorry," she said in broken English, getting down on her knees beside the table to collect the cracked pieces of ceramic and mop up the liquid with a cloth.

The woman's boss, a bearded white man with an enormous belly, stepped out from behind the beaded curtain that separated the cafe from the kitchen and half-ran over to them.

"What have you done now?" he said angrily, his belly pulsing rapidly in and out like a fontanelle.

"She's alright," said Ruby. "Just a little accident. No harm done."

"I don't call this 'little,'" said the man. "What's wrong with you?" he added to the Indian woman, half-shouting, contempt flaring his nostrils. "Can you not even be trusted to make a cup of tea properly?"

The three other diners in the cafe - workmen, two of them still wearing hard-hats - paused, mid-conversation, and turned to look at them.

"Sorry, so sorry," said the woman again, head down, still scrubbing at the floor.

"That cup's coming out of your wages," said the man. He paused, El thought most likely for dramatic effect, then flounced back behind the curtain, belly first.

"Here, love," Ruby said to the woman kindly, her voice loud enough to carry. "You come and sit down a minute, get your breath back."

She moved across to the seat next to her, creating room for the woman to join them.

"Thank you," said the woman gratefully, smoothing down her checked apron and lowering herself onto the vinyl. "Thank you."

The workmen, sensing that the entertainment had drawn to a close, turned back to their fry-ups, a low hum of renewed dialogue drifting over from their table.

"He seems like a prince, that one," said Ruby to the woman beside her, even more quietly than before.

"He's an absolute *oaf*," said the woman, equally quietly. "How anyone thought a man like that could be trusted to wash money for the Cypriots, I'll never know."

El was so absorbed in trying to decipher the meaning of the woman's words that it took her a second longer than it should have done to register the change in her accent, the apparently instantaneous transition from faltering to precisely-enunciated public school English.

"I did *say* you should have started with that bloke in Harrow instead," said Ruby.

"I know, I know," said the woman wearily. "But I do so hate going too far north of the river. It's a *wasteland* up there, I don't know how you stand it."

Ruby glared at her - but affectionately, El thought.

"And who is this?" the woman asked, gesturing almost imperceptibly towards El.

"This is El," said Ruby.

"Another one?" said the woman, raising an eyebrow at Ruby - an eyebrow that was, El saw now that she was closer, perfectly plucked and shaped.

Ruby sighed.

"El," she said, leaning in towards her over the table, "meet Sita. Actress, roper extraordinaire and all-round international woman of mystery. Though apparently her table-waiting leaves something to be desired."

"It's an improvement on your bartending, if memory serves," said the woman - Sita. "I can't imagine *what* that woman at the Gateways was thinking, when she took you on."

"Got you a foot in the door, didn't it?" said Ruby. "And in a few other places too, as I recall."

"That was a wonderful year, wasn't it?" said Sita, a nostalgic smile temporarily lighting up her face.

El cleared her throat, only half-deliberately, and Sita snapped back to the present.

"So," she said, her eyes on El but the question directed at Ruby. "What is it you're teaching *this* one?"

HIGHGATE
1998

The back of the Bentley was less sumptuous than its extravagant exterior suggested.

"It's dreadfully Spartan, isn't it?" said Sita, reading El's mind. "And yet somehow also... tasteless. I mean, really: *cream* leather? It beggars belief."

"I take it it's not yours?" said El.

"Good *Lord*, no! I borrowed it from a friend. A gentleman friend."

Only Sita, El thought, could utter the phrase "gentleman friend" with a straight face.

"It's certainly in character," El said.

"Isn't it? It strikes me as *exactly* right for a woman like Qureshi. Do you know, she's sold me into this as an interior designer? And an amateur one, at that. A *dilettante*."

The "she," El knew, meant Ruby.

"She didn't mention it was you she'd brought in as the buyer," El said.

"Of course she didn't. You know what she's like - she *adores* the element of surprise. I imagine she thought that springing me on you would elicit a more authentic reaction."

She took a long, slow pull on her cigarette holder, closing her eyes in pleasure, then exhaled through her nose, releasing dragon-like plumes of smoke into the confined air of the car.

"Now," she said, taking El's hand and squeezing, "tell me. How *are* you?"

"I'm well," said El awkwardly. "Busy."

"You work too hard."

"I'm trying to slow down."

"You must. Why do we do all this," she threw her hands up in the air theatrically, "if not to luxuriate in the benefits it affords us? The work is the means, after all, not the end."

"I will," said El. "Definitely."

"And are you seeing anyone?" asked Sita, going for the jugular.

She should have expected this, El thought. It was a short leap from Sita quizzing her about work to interrogating her about her sex life.

"Not at the moment," El said.

"What happened to that girl?" said Sita. "The architect?"

The same thing that always happens, El thought. We had a few nice dinners, spent a few long weekends in bed, and then she started asking why she'd never seen my house, or met my friends, and why I never talked about where I grew up or what I did for a living. And *then* she stopped calling.

"It fizzled out," she said.

Sita squeezed her hand again.

"Dear child," she said, "you can't stay on your own forever. It's unnatural."

"I'm not on my own," said El weakly. "I have people."

"And what about me and Auntie Ruby?" Sita continued, as if El hadn't spoken. "We need grandchildren to tend to us in our twilight years."

"You *have* grandchildren," El said.

Sita had been married at least three times, that El knew of. Once at 17, to a Bombay steel merchant fifteen years her senior - an arrangement from which she quickly extricated herself. Then again at 30, to a Danish furniture-maker with a family fortune made in pig-farming, with whom she had two children - one now a stockbroker in New York, the other an engineer in Copenhagen. And finally at 50, to a Lebanese neurologist who'd succumbed, after only two years of marriage, to a fatal haemorrhagic stroke. There'd been an array of other lovers in-between and after, and in some cases (or so Ruby maintained) *during* the marriages - men and women of all ages, shapes, nationalities and dispositions, the only common denominator between them an ardent commitment to pleasing Sita, to accommodating her every whim and desire. Sita, El suspected, wasn't looking for love; she was looking to be worshipped.

"Grandchildren I never see," she said, sadly.

This, El knew, was a lie, since Sita spent at least two months of every year in the US and Denmark in the company of her sons and daughters-in-law.

"Where are you off to now?" asked El, doing her best to change the subject.

Sita took another long pull on the cigarette-holder.

"Now," she said, "I'm going to buy some very, very expensive cocaine from a man in Westbourne Grove. Can I drop you off anywhere on the way?"

El heard nothing for a week from Lady Rose.

When the call came, she was buried in a white paper on educational policy, weighing up the merits of re-engaging with Bernard Croft. She answered the phone, as she always did, in a neutral voice - one that wasn't hers, but wasn't recognisably aligned with anyone she'd recently been, either.

It was Karen, and not Lady Rose, on the line.

"She wants to see you," Karen said, with neither introduction nor explanation. "Come in tomorrow morning at 11. She'll be waiting for you."

Then she hung up.

Early the following morning, El drove back down to Barnet, Claire Brandon's purple streaks and beaded shoulder bag in place - parking in the same spot by Totteridge and Whetstone station as she had before, and taking the tube on to Highgate.

She was surprised, given Lady Rose's security concerns, to find the electronic gates already open when she arrived. She walked through them and up the driveway to the house; knocked on the door with a clenched fist. The door was heavy, antique oak, and it hurt her knuckles.

One long minute later, Karen opened it. She was dressed much the same as before, in black shirt and Lycra leggings, hair pulled back and walkie talkie protruding from her back pocket, but she looked... different, in a way that El couldn't immediately identify. Happy. Pleased with herself, or possibly with El - smiling at El like she was a long-lost relative she'd just spotted in an airport terminal.

"You came, then," she said, still smiling.

"So I did," said El, letting herself be led inside.

They entered the hall, El marvelling again at the thickness of the carpet underfoot – but instead of passing the kitchen to Lady Rose's war room, Karen took a right, heading up the wide, winding stairs to the first floor, and El followed.

The minimalism of the ground floor hallway was absent here, El saw. The walls were white, still, but lined with photographs, almost all of them capturing a young red-headed girl - she assumed Lady Rose's daughter - in landmark stages of development: on horseback outside a stable, grinning from under a riding hat; in a blue-and-white uniform on what must have been a first day of school, straw boater on her head and two front teeth missing from her mouth; on her back in a pinewood crib, chubby hands reaching for the mobile suspended above her. Some showed a man, floppy-haired and athletic, alongside the girl: carrying her on his shoulders in one, cradling her in his arms in another. A handful saw Lady Rose join the man and the girl in the frame, the three of them eating ice cream, unwrapping presents, reaching up to decorate a Christmas tree.

"Bit more human up here, innit?" said Karen, watching El as she studied the photographs. "Less of a show-home."

She guided them into an upstairs room that looked to El like a home cinema - a dark-walled, windowless space lit by overhead spotlights, dominated by two vast black-leather corner sofas turned inwards to face a 60-inch projector screen, a long glass coffee table conveniently positioned between sofas and screen.

On one of the sofas sat Lady Rose, who stood up to greet them as they walked inside.

"Good to see you again," she said, reaching out to shake El's hand. "I really appreciate you coming in."

She was different too, El thought; warmer, friendlier, more casual, in faded jeans and scuffed trainers and a long-sleeved t-shirt, her face less heavily contoured with makeup than it had been the last time El had seen her. Her voice, especially, was different, multi-layered, less crisp and less formal than it had been - the vowels, it seemed to El, now indexing Yorkshire and London as much as European finishing schools and elocution drills.

She was from Rotherham, El remembered, flashing back to the newspaper articles and magazine profiles she'd read as she'd constructed Claire Brandon. Maybe she'd lived in Brixton or Greenwich too, in her younger years - before she'd "married up," as one of the articles had put it.

"Happy to," said El, returning the handshake.

Lady Rose sat back down on the edge of the sofa, and gestured for El to do the same. Karen closed the door, blocking out the natural light from the hallway, and perched on the coffee table, the antenna of her walkie talkie scraping against the glass as she descended.

"I owe you an apology," said Lady Rose.

She's not going to pay up, El thought. She's sold the painting, or she *thinks* she has - but she's not going to give me my cut. Which means I'm going to have to threaten her, try to blackmail the money out of her, security or not. And it's going to get nasty.

And *then* I'll have to tell Ruby, and it'll get even nastier.

"Do you?" said El carefully. "Why?"

"I'm afraid I haven't been entirely honest with you," Lady Rose said. "I imagine you came here expecting a cheque, and I don't have one to give you."

"Did the sale fall through?" El asked - still hoping, faintly, that this might be the case.

"Not quite," said Lady Rose, and paused. She looked hesitant, El thought; uncertain.

"The buyer pulled out?" El said, pushing.

"No," said Lady Rose. "Not that."

She paused again.

"Oh, for fuck's sake!" said Karen impatiently, getting to her feet. "There's no sale, alright? There's no cheque because she's not selling the painting."

"Karen," warned Lady Rose.

"I'm sorry," said Karen, sounding not remotely apologetic, "but you were just sat there *umming* and *ahing*, and it was bloody excruciating to listen to. Just *tell* her."

"Tell me what?" said El angrily, letting Claire Brandon's outrage drown out her own incipient panic. "What's going on here? We had a deal."

"No, you didn't," said Karen slowly, as if explaining a difficult concept to a very small child. "There was never any deal because there was never any sale. Her ladyship here," she pointed towards Lady Rose with one thumb, "was no more selling a painting than your mate Sita was intending to buy one. You with me?"

El swallowed; tried to steady her breath, slow the speed of her racing pulse.

They *know*, she thought. I don't know how, but they know. Whatever else this is, it's a trap.

"I don't know what you're talking about," she said, brazening it out.

"Fucking hell," said Karen, exasperated. "You're as bad as each other, you pair. Watch my lips," she said, looking directly at El. "There. Is. No. Money. Because. There. Is. No. Deal. It weren't real, none of it."

El scanned the room for exits; calculated what it would take to push past Karen and get down the stairs and out of the house. She could move quickly, even with walking boots weighing her down; if she could make it to the front door, she could be out onto the main road and in the back of a cab before either one of them could catch up with her.

"You set me up?" she said, slipping out of Claire Brandon and into her own voice now - not standing up, not yet, but tensing the muscles in her legs and pressing the balls of her feet into the carpet, ready to sprint.

"As if you're one to talk!" said Karen with a snort.

Lady Rose stood up; raised her arms, the palms turned outwards placatingly.

"It wasn't my intention to trick you..." she began.

El sprang upwards, towards the door, but Karen was faster, blocking her path.

"Please, El," said Lady Rose from behind her. "Sit down. There's no need for alarm, I promise."

El froze at the sound of her name.

"You know who I am," she said, turning to face Lady Rose.

"Yes," said Lady Rose gently.

"How?" El asked.

Don't say anything else, she told herself. Don't give her any more than she's got already.

"A friend thought we ought to... meet," Lady Rose said.

"You might know her," said Karen, plonking herself back down on the coffee table. "Old bird, grey hair, big fan of kids's comics?"

Ruby, El thought. Fucking Ruby.

"Ruby set me up?" she asked Lady Rose - if, El thought, Lady Rose was who she actually *was*.

"This isn't a set-up," said Rose.

If it was a practical joke, El thought, then it was a bloody elaborate one, even by Ruby's standards.

"You might want to think of it as an audition," said Karen, smirking.

"And what am I auditioning for?" said El, biting back sarcasm with only moderate success.

"A job," said Rose, entirely seriously. "If you want it. And I very much hope you will."

Rose sent Karen downstairs to make coffee, while El arranged herself on one of the sofas uneasily.

Three weeks, she thought. Three weeks of work, God knows how many art history books and endless hours smelling like a Body Shop perfume counter - and for what?

What the hell was Ruby playing at?

Rose settled down on the sofa across from her, crossing and uncrossing her legs nervously.

"Who did you get to do the mock-up of that painting?" El asked, conversationally.

"What, the Haring?" said Rose. "No-one. It's real - as far as I know, anyway. I picked it up in Tokyo last year."

"Right," said El - more perplexed by the situation with every new revelation. "So, you are who you say you are, then?"

"Who did I say I was?"

"Alright - who *Ruby* said you were. And the press."

"And who is that?"

"A collector. With deep pockets."

And a grade-A bitch, she added silently.

"I have a lot of money and sometimes I spend some of it," said Rose. "Is that what you mean?"

El smiled, warming to her a little.

"So this job," she said, "it's an art gig?"

"No," said Rose. "Nothing like that."

"Then what? What sort of job warrants you and Ruby - and Sita, I suppose? - luring me down here just so you could lasso me into it?"

Rose drummed her fingers on the sofa's leather. Whatever indecent proposal she's about to suggest, El thought, it's making her nervous.

"Can I be honest with you?" Rose said, avoiding eye contact.

You haven't been yet, El thought.

"Okay," she said, warily.

"What I'm trying to do, what I'd like you to *help* me do - it's personal for me. It isn't about money."

And I don't work for free, El thought.

"I don't know what Ruby's told you," she said, "but I'm not a contractor. People don't hire me. The jobs I do - I do them for myself."

"Then why do this one?" said Rose. "Why try to work *me* over? I know you weren't doing it for the cheque."

"It was a favour. To Ruby. Before I found out the two of you were playing me, obviously."

"So it isn't always about money for *you*, either."

El hesitated, feeling the threads of the conversation she'd anticipated beginning to unravel.

"What I'm saying," she said, "is that I'm not for hire. So whatever job you're trying to recruit for, I'm not the one to do it."

"I disagree," said Rose firmly. "Ruby tells me you're the best inside woman she knows. And having seen you in action, I have to concur. This... *thing* I'd like to do - it needs someone like you to even get it off the ground. Someone exactly as good as you are."

"I think you might be deliberately misunderstanding me here. I don't work for other people, and I don't do other people's cons."

Rose looked up at her, making eye contact for the first time since Karen had left the room.

"And I think *you* might feel differently," she said, "when I tell you who the mark is."

"Why? Who is he?"

Rose inhaled deeply, her fingertips stilling on the leather.

"James Marchant," she said quietly.

El paused; thought back to a name she'd occasionally glanced over, or so she thought, in the columns of the FT and the Economist.

"The property guy?" she said. "Marchant Holdings?"

"Property," Rose agreed, "and shipping, and publishing, and steel. He has a lot of interests."

"Sounds like he'll be very lucrative for whoever does the job for you. But I'm not sure why you think dropping his name would change my mind."

"He's... not a good person."

El laughed.

"Are any of us?" she said.

"He's worse," Rose said. "Whatever your understanding of bad or corrupt or immoral might be, I can absolutely assure you that he's worse."

"Should make him an easy one to fleece, then," said El. "The unethical ones are always the greediest."

People say you can't con an honest man, Ruby had told her once. *Now, between you and me, that's bollocks. You can con anyone. But the bent ones, the greedy ones - they're always looking for more. They're waiting for someone to give them something, or they've got an eye out for something they think they can take off you without you knowing. And it makes them easier pickings than some normal bloke just going about his day.*

More satisfying, too.

"I don't want to fleece him," Rose said. "I want to destroy him. I'd kill him if I thought I'd be able to get away with it. But I suspect I wouldn't, and since I don't relish the prospect of languishing in a prison cell for thirty or forty years, destroying his life is what I'll have to settle for."

El was shocked - as much by the calmness of Rose's delivery as by the sentiment.

"Why?" she said. "What did he do?"

Rose shook her head.

"It isn't important," she said. "Or rather, it isn't something you need to know. Not for the purposes of what I'm planning."

The hell it isn't, El thought.

"I wish I could help you," she said, as politely as she could, "but like I said, I'm not the person you want here. Have another chat with Ruby - I'm sure she's got some other names she can pull out for you. Although," she added with a smile, "you might want to think about revisiting your recruitment process."

She stood up from the sofa, ready to leave - already planning the talk she'd be having with Ruby and Sita herself that evening.

"It has to be you," Rose said.

"There are other people out there, I promise," said El, stretching her legs. "Good ones."

"This isn't just about *good*," said Rose, urgently. "I told you - this is personal. I don't just want someone who can do the job, they're ten a penny, even if they don't have your panache. I want someone who *cares*. Someone who wants to bring Marchant down as much as I do."

"All the more reason to get someone else," said El, feeling herself bristle at Rose's tone. "It's not that I don't believe you when you say he's a bastard, but

I'd barely heard of him before just now. I really don't have much invested in doing him over."

"You would have," said Rose, "if you knew who he was. What he'd done."

"I don't *care* who he is," El said, hackles rising higher. "And I'm sorry, but I'm leaving now. Good luck with the job."

She was halfway to the door before Rose spoke again.

"He killed your mother," she said softly. "And she wasn't his first."

LEICESTER

1976

The babysitter was rowing with her boyfriend.

It wasn't the first time El had heard her fighting with him over the phone, or the first time she'd heard her shouting. But it was the first time she'd felt personally implicated in the argument.

"I can't just leave her here on her own," the babysitter - Debra - was saying angrily into the receiver. "She's a kid, Dave. What if she hurts herself on the stove?"

I can cook better than *you* can, El thought. I'm not the one who had to make cheese on toast for dinner because I burned the omelette.

"*No*, Dave," Debra said, the words carrying up the stairs and into the hallway, where El was crouched behind the bannister, listening. "You can do what you like, but I'm stopping here until her Mam gets back. I'll ring for a taxi if I need one."

It was already midnight, a half-hour later than Debra usually stayed, and El's Mum still wasn't back from work.

"*I* don't know where she's got to, do I?" said Debra self-righteously. "I rang that pub she's supposed to work at and they said they hadn't seen her for a month, so Christ if I can tell you where she's been going."

This was new information to El. Her Mum, as far as she knew, had been working as a barmaid at the Cow & Calf in town since just after Christmas. It was the reason she'd got Debra in in the first place, to keep an eye on El until she could get away after last orders.

If she wasn't there, El didn't know where she might have gone. She hadn't had a boyfriend, that El knew of, for over a year, not since she chucked Steve The Mechanic (who might just as easily have been Steve The Train Driver or Steve The Chicken Farmer, but who always seemed to be covered in motor oil) for slapping El's face when she talked back to him. And she didn't have any friends, not really - never had, unless you counted Mrs Biggs in the maisonette above, who'd lost her hearing in the war when the Germans dropped a bomb on the munitions factory she worked in. And El's Mum didn't know any sign language, so it wasn't as if the two of them could talk to each other anyway, not properly.

"I'm going now," Debra said, cutting Dave off in the middle of whatever he'd been saying. "I'll speak to you tomorrow."

She slammed down the phone with more force than El thought was probably necessary. El stayed where she was, hoping her breathing wasn't loud enough that Debra would know she wasn't in bed.

"You alright up there?" Debra shouted up the stairs.

El slid on her stomach across the carpet to her bedroom.

"Fine!" she called back from the doorway. "Reading."

"You want to go bed soon," said Debra. "You got school tomorrow."

"Just finishing this chapter," El promised.

"Make sure you turn that light off when you're done," Debra said, and - from the sound of her platforms hitting the floorboards - trudged off into the living room, El assumed to watch late-night telly or flick through a magazine.

El crept into bed, mindful of her own feet on the ceiling, and returned to the Shirley Jackson collection she'd stolen the week before from the book shop up near the university. It was good, and definitely as creepy as the cover promised, but she couldn't settle, couldn't concentrate, not after what she'd just heard.

Why, she wondered, would her Mum *say* she'd been working at the pub if she hadn't been? What had she been doing instead? It made no sense.

She turned the problem over in her brain, chewing on it, breaking it down into chunks that might prove more digestible.

Could she have got another job - a job she didn't want anyone to know about? Or a new boyfriend she wanted to keep secret?

The second seemed unlikely. She'd told El very firmly, after the business with Steve The Mechanic, that she was finished with men - that it would be just the two of them from then on, her and El, and no belligerent Neanderthals getting in their way.

(El had looked up "belligerent" and "Neanderthal" in the dictionary that night, and had to agree that both described The Mechanic to a T).

As she thought, she listened out for signs of movement downstairs, for the sound of a key in the lock or the phone ringing or a damp coat being shaken out and hung up by the door. But there was nothing.

By 1.30, she'd fallen asleep.

Sometime around dawn, weak sunlight streaming in through the gap in the curtains, Debra shook her awake. She looked rumpled, El thought, eye-makeup running and lipstick smudged, as if she'd only just woken up herself.

"Your Mam isn't back," she said, flustered, unsure. "Is there someone I can ring?"

"Like who?" El said, still semi-dazed.

"I dunno. An Auntie, an Uncle? Has your Mam got any brothers or sisters?"

"She's got a sister," El said. "My Auntie Annie. She's in London, though."

"There's not anybody closer? What about your Granny, your Granddad?"

"They died," said El. "When I was little."

Debra bit her lip; seemed to weigh up her options.

"What's your Auntie's number?" she said eventually.

"It's in the address book," El said. "By the phone. She'll be under A for Anne. Or F for Frederick, that's her surname."

"Alright," said Debra, nodding. "Alright. You wait here. I'll be back up in a minute."

She was more than half an hour. When she finally came back into El's room, her face was softer, kinder. She smelled like toothpaste, and El's Mum's perfume.

"I've rang your Auntie Annie," she said gently. "She's coming up now. Should be here before lunch."

"Was she alright about it?" said El.

Auntie Annie was El's Mum's sister - four years older and miles richer, her husband Alan an accountant for a soap and shampoo-maker with a headquarters, El's Mum had told her, somewhere near St. Paul's Cathedral. She had no children, dressed like a Sunday school teacher and talked like a Radio 4 newsreader, though El knew she'd grown up on the same council estate in Leicester that her Mum had. El saw her twice a year - at Christmas, when she and Uncle Alan came to drop off presents on the way to his parents's house in Derbyshire, and at Easter, when she and El's Mum went together to Gilroes Cemetery, to put flowers on El's Grandma's grave.

"She was fine," Debra said, and though she couldn't say why, El knew she was lying. "Are you alright to get yourself up and ready for school?"

El said she was, and Debra left her to get dressed, looking relieved.

They left the maisonette together, El locking up after them with her key, but parted ways at the bus stop by the post office. Deliberately blocking out any thought, any sensation but the sound of the traffic and the rhythm of her own footsteps on the pavement, El carried on along the main road and into town, not to school but to the central library on Belvoir Street. She'd been there more often than she'd been in lessons lately - losing herself in novels and story collections and reference books for hours at a time, no-one bothering or demanding anything of her in the cool, partitioned quiet of the carrels.

It was early enough when she arrived for there to be only a handful of other people around, all elderly - the regulars, the ones who came in to read the paper in the morning for want of something better to do. She made a beeline for the ground-floor stacks, and the copy of Logan's Run she'd been steadily working through - which, she saw, was exactly where she'd left it on the shelf two days before.

Book in hand, she settled into a desk, far away from the old men and their newspapers, and allowed herself, finally, to think.

There were two things she thought she knew:

1: Her Mum wasn't given to disappearing overnight without a word. She had what Auntie Annie would probably have called A Reputation - the kids at school had hammered that home to El, even before she'd worked out for herself what it meant to have an Unmarried Mother dropping her off at the gates - but she wasn't flighty, wasn't irresponsible. Whenever she was out late, or got held up at one of the jobs she was working that month, she found a way to let El know, always - to make sure she wasn't worried, and wasn't, more importantly, ever on her own in the maisonette after dark. She didn't just *vanish*.

2: She didn't lie to El. She made a point of it - of telling El the truth about things, even when it was awkward or made both of them feel uncomfortable. Like when Uncle Alan had given them some pâté in a hamper, and El had taken a bit and then, curious, had asked what it was, and her Mum had told her, with Uncle Alan and Auntie Annie right there at the table, that it was made out of smashed-up liver, from ducks that had been force-fed corn until they'd nearly burst. Or when Peter Menzies had made fun of her for not having a Dad, and she'd gone and asked her Mum about him, and her Mum had sat her down on the settee and given her a hug and said that, honestly, she didn't know much, but what she did know - that he was very tall, and very gentle, and had a head of thick black hair and a moustache like Omar Sharif, and before he went back home to Ahmedabad he'd brought El's Gran a lovely set of curtains for her front room... well, El was welcome to know it, too. So if she was lying now, about where she was or where she going when she was meant to be working at the Cow & Calf, then there had to be a reason for it - a really *good* reason.

Neither fact did anything to make her feel better.

She read until lunchtime, emerging into the midday sunshine just after 12.30 and winding her way back across town and through the stubby tower blocks and flat-roofed four-storeys of the estate. She let herself into the maisonette and, anticipating nothing but silence inside, was surprised to find Auntie Annie standing in the hallway, waiting.

She looked annoyed, El thought - eyes narrowed and lips pursed like she was sucking a lemon, though her white-blonde helmet of hair was as perfect as ever, sprayed and teased into an immovable Dusty Springfield beehive.

"You're here," she said, seeming surprised herself to see El there.

"Mum lets me come home for lunch," El said.

Truthfully, her Mum was rarely awake early enough to notice El sneaking in to make herself a sandwich and a glass of milk in between library stints - or, less frequently, between lessons. But it didn't seem the time to split hairs.

"You'd better come in, then," said Auntie Annie irritably.

She led El inside and into the kitchen - where, to El's further surprise, she took a tub of margarine from the fridge and two slices of Mother's Pride from the half-loaf in the bread-bin, and began to butter them, furiously, on the chopping board.

"What do you want on them?" she asked El as she buttered.

"Cheese," said El dumbly. "There's a block of Cheddar in the egg tray."

Auntie Annie opened the fridge again and took out the cheese; unwrapped it, sliced two thin squares from the thickest edge with the knife and sandwiched it between the buttered bread. She took a plate from the cupboard over the sink, placed the bread onto it and cut it into 4 triangles, then placed the finished sandwich on the table in front of where El was sitting.

"Thanks," said El.

Auntie Annie pulled out a chair of her own, which separated from the table with a drawn-out squeak, and sat down opposite her.

"Your Mum didn't come home last night," she said, with no preamble.

"I know," El said.

She picked up one of the sandwich triangles and bit into it, leaving impressions in the bread with her teeth.

"Has she done this sort of thing before?" Auntie Annie asked. "Stopped out all night without telling you?"

El could hear the Midlands creeping back into Auntie Annie's voice; wondered if it was worry that was doing it, or just the act of coming back to Leicester unexpectedly.

"No," she said emphatically. "Never."

"Right, then," said Auntie Annie.

She stood up from the table suddenly, and walked over to the kitchen door, her back rigid.

"Where are you going?" said El, startled.

"To fetch the police," said Auntie Annie.

HIGHGATE

1996

El stayed very still.

"Whatever information you think you're giving me, it's wrong," she said eventually, struggling to keep her voice even, to stay unreadable. "It's bad intel. I know who killed my mother, and it wasn't James Marchant."

"You believe it was George Young," said Rose, levelly.

She's done her homework, El thought. I'll give her that.

"I know it was," she said. "And if you've been reading about my mother, then you know it too. They found his fingerprints all over her body."

"Because he touched her," said Rose. "Afterwards, in the graveyard. Not because he killed her."

El flinched before she could stop herself; swallowed down the sudden pain in her gut, the ghost of bile in the back of her throat.

"I don't appreciate being manipulated," she said slowly, letting a note of toughness into her voice, an edge of threat. "So whatever you're trying to do, you want to stop it, now. Before you really piss me off."

"I'm not trying to manipulate you," said Rose, still calm. "What I'm telling you is the truth."

"Says the woman trying to rope me into her con."

"Says a video confession from the man who disposed of her body. Would you like to see it?"

She gestured to the projector screen.

El wanted to shout; to rage at Rose for the stunt, for the set-up, for all of it. To storm out of the room, out of the *house*, past the artwork and the marble fittings and the picture-perfect family portraits. To ring Ruby from the back of the nearest taxi and demand to know what the *fuck* she thought she was doing, hooking her up with a woman who'd use George Young - who'd use El's *mother* - to get what she wanted.

But she didn't. Instead, she let herself acquiesce - collapsing back onto the sofa her without so much as a word of protest.

Because it *was* her mother - and how was she supposed to say no to that? Rose was playing things just right. It was exactly the carrot to dangle.

Rose picked up a large remote control from the arm of her own sofa. She pressed a button, and the lights above them dimmed.

A paused image filled the screen: a bald white man lying in a hospital-style bed with side rails, a transparent tube running from a cannula on his hand to a saline drip to his left. It was clear even with a sheet covering him from feet to chest that he was absolutely enormous, a barrel-chested giant with the thick neck, gnarled hands and fabric-ripping musculature of a bare-knuckle boxer. His skin was yellow, his eyes bloodshot, and there were deep lines etched into his forehead. He looked very, very ill.

"This is Ricky Lomax," said Rose. "Until last year, he was Marchant's head of security. His chief fixer."

"What's wrong with him?" El asked.

"Lung cancer," said Rose, with no trace of compassion. "Stage 4, metastasised to his bones. He died a week or so after this video was shot."

"He looks terrible."

"Yes, I imagine he was in a great deal of pain. Not enough, but a lot."

She pressed another button on the remote control. The video played, and Lomax started to speak.

"It was a weeknight, summertime," he said, in a low-pitched growl that was faintly intimidating, even given how incapacitated he seemed. "1976. He'd gone up to do an overnight for a meeting he couldn't get out of. Some town past Kettering, Market something. He didn't want me or any of the lads to go with him, which meant he had plans for the evening, you know what I mean? So we'd arranged to pick him up the next morning from his hotel. But then it gets to 11.30, 12 o'clock at night, and I'm in with the missus when the phone goes..."

Lomax paused as a coughing fit took hold of him, turning his mouth into the crease of his elbow while his vast body shook.

"He rang you?" said a voice off-screen that sounded to El like Rose.

"Yeah," croaked Lomax, his vocal chords straining. "Tells me to get out of bed and get my arse up the motorway, pronto. Says we've got a situation."

Marchant was staying, Lomax said, in a hotel in the centre of Leicester, a neo-classical place near the station stuffed with cornices and Greco-Roman statues, red velvet drapes and doormen in full top hats and tails. As per Marchant's instructions, Lomax had brought luggage - an empty Dominion suitcase, brown and well-polished, measuring 30 inches long and 12 inches deep.

He'd parked around the back of the hotel, studying the building for a few minutes from his car before slipping in, unseen, through a fire escape. Marchant was on the fifth floor, he remembered; room 507. He'd knocked on the door twice before Marchant answered, smoking a cigarette and wrapped in a silk Noel Coward dressing gown, cool as a cucumber.

"She's through here," he'd told Lomax as he let him inside.

"She" was a woman; a Tom, he'd found out later, naked and battered and sprawled out on top of the bedsheets, the bruises already starting to rise to the surface of her milky skin. She was Marchant's type, Lomax had thought: blonde and skinny, clean-looking, though a few years older than he normally went for. It was obvious, from her contorted arms and legs as much as from her injuries, that she was dead.

"Can you take care of it?" Marchant had asked him, and Lomax had sprung into action - rinsing the body with a washcloth to get rid of any obvious physical evidence, drying and re-dressing her in the short skirt and heels he presumed she'd arrived in. She was even lighter than she looked, and short; he'd got her into the suitcase easily, closing the lid with no effort at all.

Then, while the boss took a bath, he'd stuck on his driving gloves and taken the suitcase down into the lobby.

("You didn't ask what had happened?" said the off-screen voice, incredulous. "You weren't even a little curious about how she'd died? Or who she was?"

Lomax coughed again, this time bent double in his bed with the effort of it. When he raised his head, there were flecks of blood on his lips.

"She was a Tom, and she was in his room," he said indifferently. "What else was there to know?"

El curled her fingers into fists as she listened; dug her nails into the palms of her hands. Hoped he'd suffered as he died).

He'd carried the suitcase to the car with the same ease with which he'd loaded the body inside; had locked it away in the boot and, after downing a lukewarm cup of tea from the flask he'd brought for the journey up the M1, had settled down in the driving seat with a map of the city.

Graveyards, he knew from past experience, were good for body dumps, especially if you could find a fresh grave to piggyback onto. And he didn't want to be driving round for long with 8-odd stone of dead girl in the back of the motor. So he scoured the map for churches, burial plots - the nearer the better.

He'd settled on one a quarter of a mile west - one that was, he'd thought as he'd pulled up in the side street that ran alongside it, just about exactly what he needed. There were no lampposts there, no street lights; the block was all commercial - full of offices, not pubs or restaurants - and looked as if it was deserted after five, once the white-collar drones had gone home for the night. The odds of anyone seeing him, he'd thought, were pretty slim.

He'd carried the suitcase through the empty street and into the churchyard. It had taken him a minute, in the almost full dark, to make out the figure slumped in the doorway - to see that it was a person, not a pile of rags or a bag of rubbish. He'd been ready to run, to chuck the suitcase back in the boot and find another place to dump it, when an idea had occurred to him.

He'd crept closer to the figure, then closer again, then so close he could see its chest rising and falling as it breathed. It was a bloke, an old pisshead passed out cold on the steps, red-faced and open-mouthed, a sour stink of booze-drenched shit coming off him in waves.

He'd tested the water first - stamped his feet on the ground, loudly, then again on the concrete next to the alkie's ear. The alkie hadn't stirred; hadn't even twitched.

It was perfect.

He'd worked quickly, unlocking the suitcase and pulling the Tom's body out in one movement, still amazed at how light it was, even with the muscles starting to seize up. He'd carried her over to the doorway and put her down next to the alkie, her face turned away from his and towards the wall.

And then there'd been two of them, sat side by side - two lushes, passed out together after a night on the piss. Enough to deter anyone who might walk past from taking a closer look.

He'd taken the alkie's hand and pressed it, for good measure, to the Tom's clothes - her skirt, her top, her knickers. But he'd thought then - and been proved right later - that there was no need. Chances are, the alkie would have a feel for himself as soon as he came to in the morning.

"And you know the best part?" Lomax said, smiling to himself. "He went down for it! The alkie went down for it! I thought it would just muddy the water, throw the filth off the scent. But the alkie went down for it! Young, his name was. Sad bastard."

The video paused again, and Lomax stopped mid-sentence, his wide face filling the screen.

"You filmed this?" asked El.

"Yes," said Rose. "At his house in Wandsworth, earlier this year."

El stopped to think, a hundred questions jostling for primacy.

"Why?" she said.

"Why did I film it, or why did he let me?"

"Both. Either. Why would he tell you this? And why did you want to know in the first place? What's your interest in what happened to my mother?"

Rose raised a hand, stopping her before she could ask more.

"Let me start with the easy one," she said. "He spoke to me, and allowed me to film him, because I paid him a very large sum of money. It wasn't to clear his conscience - as you probably saw, he doesn't have one. I gave him £750,000, in two installments - the first half to secure his time and convince him I was serious, and the second when I was satisfied that he'd told me everything he usefully could about his time with Marchant."

"But he was dying."

"Yes. But like a lot of monsters, he's a sentimentalist about the things he's chosen to love. He has children, three of them, and pitifully little to pass on to them in savings. Apparently his need to bequeath them a legacy outweighed any deathbed loyalty he felt to his old employer."

"Why?" said El again. "Why my mother?"

Rose stared at the frozen screen, impassive.

"What you just saw," she said, "is a 20 minute excerpt taken from nearly 18 hours of footage. It's the part most relevant to you, but what happened to your mother... it wasn't unique, from Lomax's perspective. He was with Marchant for 30 years - there were a lot of messes to clean up. There are a lot of stories like hers on this video."

El felt a prickle in the corner of her eyes, a line of something wet trickle down her nose, and realised she was crying, involuntarily, for the first time in years. She dabbed at her face with the sleeve of Claire Brandon's jacket; swallowed.

"My investigators had been looking into him for a few years now," Rose continued, anticipating El's next question. "Along with a few other of Marchant's key associates. They'd pieced together enough to have at least some sense of the things that Lomax might have been involved with, all the way back to the '60s. None of it was certain, by any means. But it gave me a place to start when I interviewed him."

"There were others?" said El. "Other women like my mother?"

Rose nodded.

"Before her, and after," she said soberly.

"And these other women - they're why you're after Marchant?"

"Yes."

She still wouldn't offer more on her own motivations, El thought; not now, not yet.

"If you know all this," she said instead, "why haven't you taken it to the police? We're talking about murder."

The police wouldn't have been El's first port of call, of course. Not even for this. But Rose was respectable, influential. If *she* spoke up, El thought, someone in a position of authority could be persuaded to act.

"I don't think you fully understand the extent of Marchant's reach," said Rose.

El wasn't buying this.

"Whoever he is," she said, "he doesn't have the whole Met in his pocket. You'd find someone to listen, if you looked."

She was hiding something, El thought. It was there in the downward cast of her eyes, the light flush of blood in her cheeks.

"Perhaps," Rose said cagily, "I'd rather not have the police ask too many questions about the provenance of the information. Or about me. You know how that feels, surely?"

El wondered, again, what kind of skeletons Rose might have lurking in her closet - and under what circumstances she might have found herself moving in the same circles as women like Ruby and Sita.

"And what if *I* want him to go down for it?" said El, testing her. "She was my mother."

"Do you?"

"I don't know. You've just... thrown all of this at me. I don't know what I think yet."

The early *shape* of what she wanted, she thought, was something like justice. Not the kind the police delivered, not the kind that everyone told her had been served when George Young was led, snivelling and whimpering, down from the dock at his sentencing. And not the eye-for-an-eye, Old Testament kind that the tabloids crowed about when Young was stabbed to death with a sharpened toothbrush by his cell mate three years later, though the feeling she'd had then was closest to the one growing in her now.

Below the nausea that had spread from her chest to her stomach at the mention of her mother, below the septic wave of renewed grief that had flooded over her at Lomax's confession, she was beginning to think that what she wanted was a kind of justice that looked more like retribution than the administration of law. Something dark and hateful – the extraction of a blood debt, reparations for the loss of her childhood paid in pain, in distress. She wanted Marchant to suffer the way Lomax had suffered, and worse.

She remembered what Rose had said, about wanting the hit on him to be personal, and realised that she wanted that, too. She didn't just want him to hurt - she wanted to be the one to hurt him.

"It wouldn't stick," Rose admitted. "I've spoken to my investigators already about the possibility. And a solicitor friend, off the record. Even if we were able to persuade someone to bring charges against Marchant, a halfway competent brief could have them dismissed in a heartbeat. There's no evidence there that isn't circumstantial. Most of the cases they pertain to have been closed for years, like your mother's. And a confession from a dying man, a confession that the most cursory probing would show that I paid for... well, you can see how it would look."

El saw her point. Even in the absence of the money and power and influence a man like Marchant was bound to wield, it was a non-starter - however persuasive Lomax's testimony had seemed.

"How sure are you that Marchant really *is* guilty?" she said. "How do you know Lomax didn't just take the money and tell you what you wanted to hear?"

She had to ask - it was due diligence. But she'd known as soon as she'd heard Lomax talking that he'd done what he said he'd done, and done it with the same detached professionalism he'd applied to the other "problems" Rose said he'd solved for Marchant. She'd known men like Lomax before, and they didn't lie. They rarely needed to, when brute force and a sociopathic disregard for moral convention could get them where they needed to go.

"I'm absolutely certain," said Rose, and El believed her.

"And Ruby," said El, voicing another of the questions worrying away at her. "She told you about my mother, before she set me up with you and that painting?"

"In a way," said Rose. "She'd mentioned you before, as someone I ought to meet - someone who was very good at what she did, someone I might find interesting. And as one of her girls - someone she'd trained up as a child."

It was probably irrational, she thought, but the idea of Ruby talking to other people about her, even in the vaguest terms, made her uneasy. It wasn't a betrayal - *she* knew Ruby too, and she knew exactly what she might have said, and the benign way she'd likely have said it. And even if Ruby had never mentioned Rose to her before last month, the fact that she knew her at all - and apparently had known her for quite a while - made El think that Rose was, probably, someone worth trusting. Ruby was pretty discerning when it came to the people she let in.

But still, it made her feel unsettled. More exposed than she'd like.

"You *what*, then?" she said, more accusingly than she'd intended. "Got your investigators to look into me, too? Just on the off-chance I might have some sort of secret buried?"

"Absolutely not," said Rose adamantly. "Why would I? But Ruby had used your name when she'd talked about you, you see. Your *full* name. And you must agree, it's unusual. Distinctive. So when my team followed up on what Lomax had said, when they tracked down your mother's case and your name cropped up... well, I put two and two together."

"So you're saying it's a coincidence? Ruby tells you about an inside woman you just *have* to meet, and the same woman turns out to be connected to exactly the bloke you're planning to do over?"

"Of course not. When I saw your name in the reports, I rang her immediately to ask if she'd... broker an introduction. I wanted to make sure you were as good as she'd said, just to be absolutely certain that you'd be able to do the job - hence Sita's bit of embellishment, and the business with the Haring. But I knew the moment I heard who you were and what Marchant had done to you that you were the person I needed. And that if I could just show you a little of what I know about him, you'd agree. He needs to be dealt with. Surely you think so too, after what you just heard?"

"I don't know," said El. "I honestly don't. I don't even know what it is you're planning. What it is you want to do to him."

"Let me tell you, then," said Rose, urgently. "Let me tell you, and you can make up your mind."

El hesitated. Thought about all the other questions she had that needed answers, still.

"Alright," she said. "Tell me."

EDGWARE

1996

uby's flat had barely changed in 20 years. There were fewer plates on the sideboard since Dexter and Michael had moved out; fewer boxes of cereal out on the dinner table and piles of laundered boxer shorts stacked up neatly on top of the ironing board. But it *felt* the same, El thought. Just as welcoming and homely now as it ever had when she was a kid.

It could have been the furnishings. Though the sofas had been upgraded half a dozen times over the last two decades - a set of Harvest Gold loveseats traded in for a bright red three-piece suite, an avocado Chesterfield for the burnt orange sectional that currently dominated the living room - they still privileged comfort above aesthetics. The windows were still high and wide, flooding every room and corridor with outdoor light. Photographs still dominated almost every conceivable shelf and wall-space: the boys, blowing out the candles of birthday cakes and clutching diplomas, mortarboards secured to their heads, at their university and law school graduation ceremonies; Winston, Ruby's beloved husband, dead since 1988 but immortalised in posed family portraits and more naturalistic shots at home, down the pub and at the allotment; Sita, and El, and a few other of Ruby's protégés besides, hugging and chinking glasses and smiling for the camera. Though there were none, El noted, of Rose - however well the two of them might know each other.

There were a handful of paintings, too, scattered haphazardly across the walls among the photographs: a Degas ballerina, a Toulouse-Lautrec can-can, a Seurat landscape, a villa by Cézanne. They could easily have been prints - replicas bought for five quid a go at Spitalfields Market or a little stall off Camden Lock. Except El knew they weren't; knew, at least in the case of the Degas and the Seurat, *exactly* where they'd come from.

Ruby herself sat, high and regal, on a padded yellow wingback, a cushion tucked behind her, another underneath her, and her feet supported by a fluffy gold footstool, warming her hands on a steaming cup of something hot and non-specifically herbal that made El want to gag, even from 6 feet away.

"She weren't lying," she began, in response to El's questions. "We go back a long way, me and Rose. I've known her since she was... well, about the same age you were when I first met you."

"Younger," Sita interjected from an equally stuffed armchair equidistant from Ruby's and the velour bean bag on which El was reluctantly perched. "She was 10, if you remember?"

Was she like me? El wondered. Another little Artful Dodger drawn into the fold?

"Do you know, you're right," said Ruby, thoughtfully.

"It's been a long time," said Sita, with what seemed to El a trace of sadness.

"30 years," agreed Ruby.

There was a drawn-out silence, the two older women swapping coded looks over their teacups. There's another conversation going on here, El thought; one she definitely wasn't party to.

"And you never thought to tell me about her before?" she said, deliberately breaking the silence.

"She's a very private person," said Ruby. "Likes to keep herself to herself."

So do I, El thought. But you still told *her* about *me*, didn't you?

"I'm sure that Auntie Ruby only mentioned you in passing," said Sita, sensing the ticking of El's displeasure and aiming to defuse it before it could detonate. "Perhaps she thought the two of you might hit it off."

There was another rapid-fire exchange of unreadable glances across the room; another round of lip-pursing, eyebrow-furrowing and quizzical head-tilting. They may as well be winking at each other, El thought.

"I need to know," she said, trying to keep a lid on her anger and the sense of betrayal that accompanied it. "Was the video your idea? Because it was a bloody low blow, if it was. You could have just told me what you knew, instead of letting me find out like that."

"What video?" said Ruby, seeming genuinely puzzled.

"You know what video," said El. "Don't try to put one over on me now, alright? I know you know what I'm talking about."

"And I'm telling you, I don't know what you're on about," said Ruby. "*What* video?"

"I'm afraid you have us at a disadvantage, darling," said Sita carefully. "I haven't a clue what this *video* is, and I'm not sure that Auntie Ruby does, either."

They're professional liars, El thought. Faking sincerity is what they do - what *we* do.

But they had their own set of ethics, didn't they? Their own rules that they played by, labyrinthine and endlessly malleable though those rules could be. And they looked after her, always had. The idea that they'd set her up to be hurt like that - it wasn't *like* them. Wasn't commensurate with anything they'd ever done, at least as far as she was concerned.

"Cross my heart, sweetheart," said Ruby, softening her tone, "I've not had nothing to do with any video. Showed you something, did she? Something you didn't like?"

She really *doesn't* know, El decided. Neither of them do.

She felt a flash of relief, so sharp she could taste it. They hadn't been in on it; hadn't known, and kept it from her.

And if they didn't know, then those clandestine looks weren't about guilt or pity. It wasn't them feeling bad for her - or any worse than they'd felt before.

"It doesn't matter," she said. "Not important."

Ruby squinted at her, a mix of curiosity and concern playing out across her face - then glanced back down at the herbal concoction in her hands, apparently willing to let the issue slide for now, if El was.

"So what did you make," asked Sita, "of Rose's proposition?"

"The con the two of you had me audition for, you mean?" said El.

"Oh, come now, darling," said Sita. "You can't begrudge us our little fun, surely? You know there was no malice intended. We only wanted to... show her what you could do. We couldn't expect her to take our *word* for it that you were so prodigiously talented. She had to see you in action for herself."

"You did a bang-up job, from what I heard," said Ruby.

"And all it took was three solid weeks of unpaid prep work," said El, rolling her eyes.

"As if you need the money," said Ruby, ignoring the eye-roll. "What do you reckon, then? Are you in?"

I've been in since the moment I saw that video, El thought. Since the second I heard Lomax reminisce about loading my mother's body into the boot of his car like a roll of old carpet.

"Provisionally? Yes," she said.

"How absolutely *wonderful*," said Sita ebulliently - then, more sombrely, added, "I can't think of a woman better qualified to drag that monster into the light of day."

Ruby flashed Sita another look - this time one that El interpreted as a warning, as meaning something along the lines of "shut it, now." Sita saw the look, and pressed one hand to her mouth in response, a gesture of embarrassed penitence that El wasn't sure Sita even knew she was making.

They know him, she thought. They know Marchant. And well enough to know what kind of monster he is, even if they don't know what he did to my mother.

"Monster?" she said.

"He's... not a nice bloke, that one," said Ruby guardedly.

"So I've heard," said El, equally careful not to show her hand. "You've met him, then?"

"Once or twice," said Ruby. "Years ago."

And that *was* a lie, El thought.

"You find you've come to meet an awful lot of people, when you get to our advanced age," said Sita.

"All sorts," Ruby agreed. "Even the high and mighty," she added, wrinkling her nose.

Try as Ruby might to keep her reaction under wraps, she couldn't hide the contempt. And something else too, something El had rarely heard from her: hatred. Ruby, generally speaking, didn't hate marks, not even the really despicable ones - the Gordon Gekkos and the Peter Rachmans, the ones who probably deserved it. Hers was much more of a live by the sword, die by the sword philosophy: if, she'd told El once, you were going to go around behaving like a grade-A bastard, kicking families out of their houses or snatching pension books out of little old ladies's handbags, figuratively speaking, then you shouldn't be surprised when a bit of payback comes round to bite you on the arse. It was the game you played.

The Marchant job, though - it wasn't about playing, not for Ruby, and apparently not for Sita either. Whatever he'd done to them, whatever they'd seen him do to someone else, it was enough to burrow under their skins and set up home there, over however many years it had been. And for them as for Rose - as for *her*, if only they'd known it - it was personal.

"What do I need to know about him?" El asked - conscious of all three of them skating over paper-thin conversational ice, and as keen as either of them to avoid sticking a foot through into the dark water underneath.

"Ah," said Ruby, smiling for the first time. "Thought you'd never ask."

She reached under the cushion behind her and withdrew a pink plastic ring-binder. One of Ruby's pre-reads - the background dossiers she liked to pull together on suspected marks ahead of any serious job beginning.

She dropped it to the floor and kicked it across the carpet towards El.

"Have a read of this," she said.

Here, El thought, they were on safer ground. As long as they could all at least pretend that Marchant was a mark like any other they'd dealt with - and not, in fact, a monster - then they could pretend, too, that this *wasn't* personal, that it wasn't retribution or a settling of scores. It was business - just another job.

She picked up the folder, opened it and began to leaf through the photos, print-outs, handwritten notes and press cuttings inside.

"Can you run me through it?" she asked.

"My pleasure," said Ruby. "First few pages are historical - date of birth, education, all the usual. Main things you need to know there are: he's an old bastard, nearly as old as me and your Auntie Sita, but he's got no plans to retire. Born in Bristol in '32, son of a moderately-successful shipbuilder and a mother who died in childbirth. No brothers or sisters. Left school at 14 with no qualifications to set up a business selling second-hand kettles to housewives, though that one lasted all of five minutes, then tried his hand at nylons, penny sweets, transistor radios and chess sets, all with about the same degree of success."

"It's as if he had no business acumen at all," said Sita drily.

El looked down at the first photograph, obviously clipped from an old newspaper: a black and white head-and-shoulders shot of a good-looking teenage boy with a prominent nose and piercing Gary Cooper eyes, his hair slicked down and parted to the side and a cigarette dangling, Bogart-like, from his full lips.

"His luck changed in 1950," Ruby continued, "when he met a girl named Elizabeth Bellman - now better known as Mrs James Marchant. She was 17, he was 18, and they got married within a month of him sweeping her off her feet down the local dance hall. Young love, eh? All very romantic. Course, it couldn't have hurt when he found out who her dad was."

"Who was he?" asked El, glancing down at a second photo, another black and white clipping, showing the same boy standing outside a church in a dark wool suit and tie, a flower in his lapel, next to a plainer, slightly chubby girl in a floor-length wedding dress.

"Saul Bellman," said Ruby. "Bloke who founded Handsworth's."

"The department store chain?" said El, thinking of the green-liveried, faded-looking shop fronts she'd passed without a second glance on Edgware Road, High Holborn, the High Street in Leicester town centre.

"One and the same," said Ruby. "Worth a few quid, as you can imagine."

"A terribly nice man," said Sita, distantly. "If a little too fond of the horses for his own good."

"And absolutely devoted to his daughter," said Ruby. "Would've done just about anything to make her happy, the way I heard it. Which could explain the fifteen grand he bunged Marchant's way to help him buy his first block of flats the following year, over in Slough. That's about a quarter of a mil in today's money, in case you were curious."

"They're still married?" El asked - wondering what kind of woman would tether herself to a man like Marchant. Whether the former Elizabeth Bellman knew - whether she even suspected - what her husband did on his nights away.

"45 years last October," said Ruby. "Three kids: Oscar, Harriet and James Junior. There are pictures of them at the back, if you want to have a look."

El flicked to the last page in the file, and a recent colour photograph of what had to be the full Marchant clan: the older Marchant, thicker in the waist but with the same nose and piercing eyes and a head of silver hair, still parted to the side; Elizabeth, thinner and more carefully-groomed than she had been in the 50s, her hair now expensively highlighted and her makeup skilfully contoured to accentuate her cheekbones; two smiling, blandly-attractive men in their late 30s or early 40s, both in dark roll-neck sweaters and tailored blazers, whom El assumed to be Oscar and James Junior; and a younger woman, no older than 30, in jeans and a faded Sisters Of Mercy t-shirt, seeming awkward and out of place in the company of her immediate family.

"I expect you know the rest already," said Ruby. "One tower block turns into two, then five, then a big hotel and load of office space over in South Kensington. By the early '60s he's Marchant Holdings, not just Marchant Properties, and he's started branching out into broadcasting and publishing, buying up dying magazines and a couple of radio stations on their last legs and bringing them miraculously back to life. Fast forward to the '70s, and he's got a hand in shipping and logistics too – cargo boats, freight transport, that kind of thing. As of last year, he's worth about 2 billion quid - or Marchant Holdings is, I should say."

"Not bad going for a guy who couldn't flog a kettle," said El.

"Quite," said Sita. "Though back then, of course, he didn't have the benefit of *Mrs* Marchant as a helpmeet."

"She's involved in the business?" El asked.

"Not officially," said Ruby. "She owns 17% of the company in shares, which is more than he does, but that's more of a formality - a hangover from when her old man first got him set up. He loved his daughter, enough to put up with Marchant as a son-in-law, but he was no fool, that one. We think he must have made the shares a condition of the initial loan. Not that *that* matters - she's never actually cast a vote that counted. No, it's more that she's..."

"The brains of the outfit," finished Sita. "Very gently, and very surreptitiously - more of an advisor than the power behind the throne. But if I were to hazard a guess as to which of them were responsible for some of the more successful deals Marchant Holdings has negotiated these last few decades...."

"It wouldn't be him," said Ruby. "He's a cunning bastard, don't get me wrong. But he's not a strategic thinker, you know what I mean? Not a long-term planner. He doesn't have the impulse-control."

He doesn't need it, El thought. Not when there's someone else around to clean up his messes.

"But he's into politics?" she asked.

On that, Rose had been clear. Marchant, despite his corporate successes, had one, deep-seated ambition that remained thus far unfulfilled: he wanted to get into office. Not buy his way to a peerage or sit on the non-exec board of a policy institute, but actually get elected - to have people *want* to vote for him.

It wasn't even really about power, Rose had said - he had more than enough of that already. It was about ego. He had a narcissist's appetite for veneration - and the kind of sociopathic self-belief that had him convinced the public *would* adore him, if only they knew enough about him. The relatively nominal power of the MP post he coveted was really just a bonus, a sweetener.

"What he's *into* is adoration," said Sita, who knew more than a little about that herself.

"Which is where you come in, eh?" said Ruby.

"Give a man a taste of what he thinks he wants," said Sita, as if quoting Shakespeare, "and he'll follow you into the very bowels of hell. I don't care *who* he is."

The political ambitions were the leverage, Rose said - the crowbar, prying open Marchant's inner world enough for El to slip inside and put Rose's idea into action. To ruin him; to bring him down.

"I think you'll like the crew," said Ruby, changing tack. "They're all women, the ones Rose has got lined up. Just your cup of tea."

"You know them?" El asked.

"Couple of 'em, yeah," said Ruby. "Little Karen Baxter - I've known her since she was in Pampers. Think you've met her already?"

El considered the sardonic, imposingly-muscled girl who'd first greeted her on the doorstep of Rose's Highgate house - and then, briefly, what she might possibly have been like as a toddler.

"And the rest?" El said.

"Couldn't say," said Ruby. "But if Rose trusts them enough to bring 'em in, then they must be halfway decent. One of them's straight, if you can believe it."

"A *journalist*," said Sita, evidently amused.

"Former," said Rose quickly. "She's not doing a story on us for The Times, before you ask."

"How straight can she be, if she's caught in all this?" said El, holding the open folder up for emphasis.

And how much of a liability is she going to be, if she's green? she thought, less convinced of Rose's impeccable judgement than Ruby and Sita seemed to be.

"Couldn't say," said Ruby again.

There was a muffled thud from the direction of the front door, followed immediately by the soft rattle of a key turning in a lock. El slammed the folder shut. And then, before she'd even had time to conceal it in the folds of the beanbag, Dexter was standing in the middle of the room, a burgundy briefcase in his hand.

"Don't stop what you're doing on my account," he said, grinning at her through straight-capped teeth, his eyes on the folder.

"Didn't your mother ever teach you to knock?" she asked.

"If she'd wanted to know I was coming," he said, bending down to kiss Ruby on the cheek, "she wouldn't have given me a key, would she?"

He covered the room in three strides, kissing Sita on one already-outstretched hand before bounding over to El and wrapping her up in a hug. He smelled, as always, like expensive aftershave - sandalwood and pepper and vanilla.

"You look good," she said, making a show of scanning him up and down - taking in the Savile Row suit and pocket-square, the discreetly-patterned socks just visible above the handmade shoes, the tight black curls cropped down to a respectable number 2. All overlaid onto the tall, long-limbed frame she'd once forced into a jujitsu hold on an earlier incarnation of the same living room carpet when, one dull-skied afternoon in the late '70s, Ruby had decided that a little self-defence practice would be a useful addition to the teenage El's developing skillset.

Physically, Dexter was a perfect amalgam of his parents - lighter than Winston but darker than Ruby, with Winston's broad shoulders and Ruby's bright-eyed look of perennial amusement. But where Michael had inherited Winston's earnestness and keenly-felt sense of responsibility, Dexter's personality was nearly all Ruby's: her easygoing humour, her softheartedness, her flexibility around any moral, legal and societal rules she perceived as unhelpful.

"Don't I always?" he said, feigning hurt.

"Shouldn't you be at work?" said Ruby. "I thought you weren't coming round 'til later."

'Work,' for Dexter, was a tiny two-room office off the Strand - a legal practice just large enough to accommodate him, as the most senior and only partner; a junior solicitor named Sandra whose sole purpose, as far as El could ascertain, was to field the dull, mainstream cases that Dexter couldn't be bothered to engage with; and finally Mrs Day, a ferociously competent middle-aged secretary so circumspect that El had never discovered her first name.

"I've got a meeting in Elstree," he said, undoing the heavy brass buckle of his briefcase. "Thought I'd drop your stuff off on the way."

He delved into the briefcase and extracted a folder of his own - a Manila file, unlabelled.

"Best give that straight to this one," said Ruby, pointing to El. "She's the one who'll be needing it."

Dexter pivoted away from his mother and back to El.

"I didn't give you this, obviously," he said, handing her the file with a wink.

"It'd be a lot less incriminating if you didn't wink whenever you said that," said El, taking the file.

There were two pieces of paper and three smaller, rectangular pieces of laminated plastic inside: a birth certificate, a credit card and a National Insurance card, a utility bill and a driving licence, all in the name of Alison Miller. A paler, more imperious variant on El's face stared back at her from the driving licence.

"Alison Miller?" she said.

"That was the one you were using for that posh twat on the Southbank, weren't it?" said Ruby. "It's what he kept calling you."

"While I was on *another job*," said El emphatically.

"You'd hardly started," said Ruby, waving away the objection. "And the way you were playing it with him, it's perfect for Marchant. Just the right amount of haughty."

"I don't recycle," El said.

"Oh, *please*, darling," said Sita. "Do you know how many times I've been a Priya Patel or an Asha Kaur? There's no benefit to reinventing the wheel."

El studied the documents in the folder. They were good, very good: whoever Dex was using these days, they were a perfectionist.

"Has Rose signed off on this?" she asked.

"Signed off on it?" said Ruby. "She's the one who *paid* for it."

NOTTING HILL
1996

They met next not at the Highgate house but at another of Rose's properties, a three-storey Georgian terrace on Ledbury Road. It was, Rose had explained over the phone, her *real* home - the one she actually lived in most of the time with her daughter, one that had never been photographed for the pages of a glossy magazine or profiled along with her husband for an industry publication. Very few people who knew of her or Sebastian or her collections, she'd said, were even aware that it existed - making it an ideal place for her and El and their band of merry cons to get together, and work, and strategise.

From the outside, at least, it was unremarkable by the standards of its more ostentatious neighbours, with their ivy-rich trellises and underground car ports - or as unremarkable, El thought, as a Notting Hill house worth upwards of 2 million quid could feasibly be considered. It was plain and whitewashed, with none of the security fences or CCTV cameras that increasingly characterised the terraces in the area. The ornate metal curlicues around the windows were beginning to rust; the mint green paintwork on the front door was beginning, in places, to peel. If she'd ever been asked to identify the primary residence of a globally-renowned art connoisseur and dealer, she probably wouldn't have picked it out of a line-up.

Inside was another story. Where the Highgate house was, for the most part, a triumph of cold monochrome and minimalist sterility, this one exploded with colour and character, from the Boyzone annual on the stairs (which El assumed belonged to the daughter) to the polka dot wallpaper and the Ed Ruscha screenprint over the telephone stand that, she thought, was probably an original.

"Sorry about the mess," said Rose, as El stepped around a Game Boy left to die on the stripped pine floorboards of the hallway. "I haven't had much time for cleaning lately."

"Totally fine," said El. There were other hazards up ahead: a grey school backpack, unzipped, the exercise books and pens inside spilling out onto the floor; a red-framed bike, propped up against the wall; a Buzz Lightyear toy that El thought the daughter had probably outgrown. She navigated them with caution, following Rose's lead into an open-plan kitchen-diner-lounge with the kind of wipe-clean tiled floors and oatmeal sofas that could only appeal to a parent.

There were people in there already, reclining on the sofas and milling around the coffeemaker - Ruby and Sita and Karen, her security guard outfit swapped for blue dungarees and a plain white t-shirt, and two white women she didn't recognise who sat physically apart from the other three. One looked around El's age, blonde and fresh-faced, her big blue eyes framed by two thick plaits and large gold hoop earrings; the other was older, El guessed mid-40s, in a navy Chanel suit with an auburn Anna Wintour bob and bright red lipstick, looking as fashionably wealthy as Rose had the first time El had laid eyes on her. If the way she was gnawing at her bottom lip and wringing her expensively-manicured hands together was any indication, El thought, she was also very, very nervous.

All of them turned to look at El as she and Rose walked in.

El smiled, tight and awkward, in response, and sat down on the sofa next to Sita, who gave her thigh a silent squeeze in greeting.

"Shall we do introductions, now everyone's here?" said Rose, more dinner party host than criminal mastermind.

"Not on my account, sweetheart," said Ruby, pouring molten coffee and seven cubes of sugar into a mug. "I know half of this shower already, and what's that they say? A stranger's just a friend you haven't met?"

"I'd quite like to know who it is I'm supposed to be working with, if it's all the same to you," said the blonde woman, in a soft Welsh accent that El could imagine getting stronger whenever she was angry, or tired, or drunk.

For a moment, nobody responded.

"I'll start then, shall I?" said Karen, apparently bemused by the set-up. "Karen Baxter. Can't sing, can't dance, can act a little if it's on the job. And I hate all this introducing yourself bollocks, so don't ask me to talk about my dream holiday or tell you what kind of animal I'd want to come back as, alright? I had enough of that when I did telesales."

"You'd be a squirrel, I reckon," said Ruby, manoeuvring herself onto a high stool next to the kitchen counter. "Cheeky little bugger like you. Robbing nuts off all the other squirrels in the forest to take back to your nest."

The blonde woman laughed.

"Drey," said Karen. "Where a squirrel lives - it's called a drey. Not a nest."

"See what I mean?" said Ruby to the others. "A cheeky bugger."

Karen grinned and blew her a kiss.

***

"She mostly works the short game now, does Karen," Ruby had told her, back at the Edgware flat after Dexter had left for his meeting. "Pig in a poke, wallet dips, that sort of thing. But she's a demon with a lockpick. An absolute genius."

"You'd expect so, with a father like that," said Sita. "It's in the blood."

"Who's her father?" El asked.

"Leon Baxter," said Ruby. "Bit before your time, but a hell of a tea-leaf back in his day. Never met a safe he couldn't pop or a bolted drum he couldn't squeeze through."

"Until he vanished, anyway," said Sita.

"He vanished?"

"Like a puff of smoke," said Ruby. "When Karen was all of a year old. I got to know her Mum not long after - his missus. Word was he'd stitched up the crew on his last job and done a runner with the takings, but she wasn't having it. She seemed to think something had, you know... happened to him."

"*Someone*, you mean," said Sita darkly.

"Did she say who she thought had done it?" said El.

"No names, nothing like that," said Ruby. "But she said he'd told her that the bloke who'd hired him and his mates for that last job was a proper hard bastard. Type who'd shoot you soon as look at you. Scared the shit out of him, she said - and he didn't frighten easy, Leon Baxter."

"What was the job?" El asked. She remembered how badly Rose had wanted Marchant to feel *personal* for El; wondered whether she was looking for the same personal connection - the same hate, the same sense of needing to settle a score - in all the women she brought in. And whether the hard bastard who'd commissioned Baxter might have been the same one she'd seen coughing up a blackened lung in the video Rose had shown her.

"Something up north, was all she'd tell me," Ruby said. "Wouldn't even say *where* up north. Could have been Glasgow or Gateshead for all I know. Whatever scared him, she'd caught a bit of it too - that was the impression I got."

That's worth digging into, El thought. When the opportunity presents itself.

"Me next, then, is it?" said the blonde woman, when no-one took the baton from Karen.

"Knock yourself out, love," said Ruby, raising her mug towards the woman in a *cheers!* gesture. She tipped the syrupy coffee inside into her mouth and smacked her lips in appreciation.

"Of course, if someone else'd rather..." said the blonde woman, glowering at Ruby, who drained the last dregs of caffeinated sugar from the bottom of her mug obliviously.

"This is Kat," said Rose, stepping into the space between them.

"Kat Morgan," Ruby had said. "She's an actress. Classically trained - RADA and all that bollocks."

"Oh, *spare* me," said Sita, who'd harboured theatrical aspirations of her own before surrendering wholesale to the allure of the con. "A drama diploma and a couple of student productions of Miss Julie is hardly the RSC, now is it?"

"She's been on Casualty, I heard," said Ruby, whose entertainment tastes ran more to prime time BBC than the West End.

"Oh, well, in *that* case..." said Sita acidly.

"She's the straight one?" El asked.

"Nah," said Ruby. "The acting doesn't exactly pay the bills, if you know what I mean. She works a sort of one-woman badger game out of the casinos round Mayfair and Park Lane. Hangs around the roulette wheel in a little black dress until she catches the eye of some pissed-up foreigner with a stack of chips burning a hole in his pocket, gets him hammered, goes back with him to his hotel and then sneaks off with his wallet and his chips once he's passed out on her."

"And the casinos let her back in?" said El. She generally avoided gambling scenarios - there was too much security, too much risk. And too much paranoia: even would-be marks were forever looking over their shoulder, expecting to get fleeced.

"They love her!" laughed Ruby. "She goes back and spends half the chips at the blackjack table after!"

Rose introduced Ruby and Sita - as a double-act, El noticed - then turned to the woman with the Anna Wintour bob, who avoided Rose's eyes, looking down instead at her own clasped hands.

"This is Hannah," she said, when the woman failed to speak on her own initiative.

The woman - Hannah - raised her head, took in the others, and nodded.

"Lovely to meet you," she said, her voice stronger and steadier than El would have anticipated. "It's a pleasure to be working with you all."

"The journalist," Ruby had said, "her name's D'Amboise. Hannah D'Amboise."

"Should that ring a bell?" El said.

"Depends where you're getting up to speed on your current affairs these days," said Ruby. "She used to do the Nine O'Clock News."

"She was *on* the Nine O'Clock News," Sita corrected her. "As a political correspondent, not a presenter. She's not Moira Stuart."

"Okay," said El, confused. "So what's she doing mixed up with Rose?"

"Wouldn't like to say for sure," said Ruby. "But if I had to guess, I'd say it had something to do with Marchant arranging to have her old man done in."

"That animal," spat Sita. "That *fucking* animal."

El, who'd rarely heard Sita swear - in English, or Hindi, or any of the seven other languages El knew she used on a semi-regular basis - was momentarily surprised. And wondered again what Marchant had done, to Sita specifically, to warrant the reaction.

"What happened?" El asked.

"I've never met the woman," Ruby said, "so this is second-hand information. But what I heard off Rose is: the husband was working at Marchant Holdings, up at the head office over on Bankside, doing something senior in finance. And one day he finds something he shouldn't in the ledgers - some serious cooking of the books. He goes home and tells his missus, who tells him he needs to do his duty and alert all the right people, the big boss included. So the next morning, he gets up and marches off to work, telling her he's all set for a bit of a confrontation with Marchant before he rings the old Bill."

"Now, I don't know if he ever had that confrontation, or if he did how the conversation played out – and I don't know that anyone else does neither, except Marchant and the money man himself - but what I *do* know, what everyone and his dog knows, is that by the time his secretary comes in to bring him his mid-morning coffee, the bloke was dead. Hanging from a coat hook on his office door."

"The Bill weren't sure what they were seeing at first, according to Rose. Until some helpful little worker bee at Marchant HQ shows them the discrepancies in the books. Then they add two and two together, get 15, and before you know it, they've ruled his death a suicide. Said it was guilt over nicking the money - or worry he was going to get found out."

"But Hannah D'Amboise knows otherwise?" said El.

"Exactly. Rose says she did her best to tell the Bill what her old man told her before he pegged it, but nobody listened. Thought she was just trying to protect his reputation - protect herself from a scandal."

"She resigned from the BBC last year," added Sita. "Apparently she's been spending all of her time since then putting together a case against Marchant, trying to assemble enough evidence to prove his culpability."

"Not sure she's made much headway, mind," said Ruby. "He knows how to cover his tracks, that one."

So now she's making her own justice instead, El thought. Like the rest of us.

"And she's never done anything like this before?" she asked.

"Not as far as we know," said Sita. "Though I'd think that what she lacks in experience, she's likely to make up for in commitment. Wouldn't you?"

"And this is El," said Rose finally.

"The famous inside woman," said Kat.

"I don't know about that," said El uncomfortably.

"Karen will also be working the inside," Rose clarified. "In fact, she's already secured a position at Marchant Holdings."

"Starting Monday," said Karen with mock-pride. "The catering department won't know what hit them."

"Since when do you cook, girl?" said Ruby. "I never seen you so much as boil an egg."

"Oi!" said Karen. "I cook. Not starved yet, have I?"

"I'll give you that. But Christ knows what'll happen if they ever stop making them Pot Noodles."

"Karen will be delivering the food, rather than making it," said Rose. "So she'll be out and about in the building, not down in the kitchen."

"And for this may we be forever thankful," said Ruby.

Kat wrinkled her nose, apparently disgruntled.

"What'll *she* be doing, then?" she asked, indicating El. "If we've got someone on the inside already, what's the *point* of her, exactly?"

"You know," said Ruby, pouring more coffee into her mug with the exaggerated slowness of a Bond villain, "I thought you'd never ask..."

Two hours later, Ruby and Rose had laid out between them the bare bones of the plan - and specifically of the role El would be playing in it. Kat had relaxed a little by then, laughing and joking with Karen and Ruby over biscuits and hot chocolate while Sita and Rose talked quietly through logistics. Hannah, conversely, barely spoke at all - was perfectly polite, even friendly when one of the women asked her a direct question, but kept otherwise to herself, writing copious - but from where El was sitting, unreadable - notes into a spiral-bound pad with a fountain pen.

Just after 3.30, the kitchen door opened and a child spilled through it - Rose's daughter, the same red-headed girl El had seen in the photos at the Highgate house. Though older now, almost a teenager, her ears pierced and school uniform lightly modified to project a nascent aesthetic identity: the tie loosened, the shirt untucked, the black trousers tailored tight at the calf and flared at the ankle.

She threw her bag down onto the floor and then, seeing the roomful of women for the first time, froze.

"Who are you?" she said, warily, in the kind of posh-girl London accent that used to grate on El like fingernails down a blackboard when she'd first moved to the city as a kid.

"Sophie," said Rose mildly, "that isn't how you speak to people. Especially not people who are guests in our house."

"Sorry," said Sophie, chastened.

"I thought you were at Alice's for dinner tonight?" Rose said, sweeping the documents she and Sita had been poring over on the counter into a pile and under a broadsheet with what struck El as impressive subtlety.

"She's going to her Dad's instead," said Sophie. Her interest in the strange women who'd invaded her home apparently lost, she wandered past them, opened the fridge-freezer and pulled out a tub of ice cream.

"Nice of her mother to let me know," said Rose with a sigh. She sped over to the cutlery drawer Sophie had begun to root around in - El assumed for a spoon to accompany the ice cream - and swiped the tub from her daughter's hand.

"That's for after dinner," she said, her voice for a moment more Rotherham than Kensington. "Have a bag of crisps if you're hungry."

"But I'm starving!" Sophie whined.

"It's a hard life, isn't it?" said Rose, planting a kiss on Sophie's forehead, a gesture so tender - so instinctively maternal - that it made something in El's stomach crack, so sharply she thought it might have been audible to the others. She remembered, again, why she was there; what had induced her to throw in with these women, in this room. Then saw, so vividly that it could have been a memory, her mother's body, naked and broken on the bed in Marchant's hotel room.

She needed air, she thought. Air and tobacco.

"I'm just going outside," she said, to anyone who might have been listening.

Without waiting for a reply, she jogged out of the kitchen, down the hallway and out of the door, letting it close behind her. On the doorstep she lit a cigarette, smoked it down to the butt in a dozen drags, threw it to the ground and immediately lit another.

The door opened, then closed again behind her.

"You alright, girl?" said Ruby, suddenly standing next to her. "You ran out of there pretty sharpish."

"Fine," said El, watching the tip of the cigarette flare and cool with her breath.

"The hell you are," said Ruby. "Look at me."

She took hold of El's chin with one hand; turned El's face towards her.

"Marchant," El said, and suddenly it was spilling out, all of it, and there was nothing she could do. "He did it. He killed my Mum."

"You what?" said Ruby, frowning.

"It wasn't George Young," she said. "That's what Rose was telling me the other day. It was him, Marchant. He did it."

And then the second cigarette was on the ground and she was crying, uncontrollably, for the second time that week, and Ruby was holding her, arms around El's waist and shoulders and El's face buried in her neck.

"It's alright, sweetheart," she said. "It's alright."

"I don't think it is," said El. "I really don't."

She couldn't breathe; could barely get the words out.

"No," said Ruby, rubbing her back. "No, you're right. It ain't. But we're going to get him, girl. We're going to get the bastard. And then... maybe it will be, eh? Maybe it will be."

SOHO

1996

El had never had cause to step inside Chestnut House, Soho's answer to the private members's clubs that seemed to line the streets of Mayfair and St James's, but Kat assured her that she wouldn't regret visiting, were she ever inclined - that the visual spectacle alone made it worth the effort she'd expend leapfrogging the waiting list and conjuring up the necessary references its membership committee demanded. It was, at least as Kat described it, a fin-de-siècle monstrosity: an uneasy patchwork of velvet drapes, dusty Gothic Revival furniture and dead-eyed taxidermy spanning two subterranean bars and a boutique hotel on the upper floors, its lighting low and its cocktails poured from copper samovars by moustachioed waiters in frocked coats and monocles. Its members were a diverse bunch: CEOs and media magnates, A-list actors and old-money gentry, united by a desire to drink, snort and occasionally - in the privacy of the Chestnut's mirrored bathroom stalls - inject as much as they wanted, without worrying that they might appear on the front page of the tabloids the following day.

It was Marchant's favourite watering hole.

Kat had been hanging out there for a week, she said, before she saw him.

She'd ignored him that first time, though had made a point of walking past his table and directing a smile his way as she walked to the bar for a refill, hiking her dress up her thighs to show them off to their best advantage. He hadn't returned the smile, or seemed to react at all, but then, she hadn't expected him to - nothing that Rose had told them had suggested he was a man who enjoyed a sexually assertive woman. All she'd hoped for, at that stage, was to make a very minor impression - the kind he might recall later, when he met her again.

The next time she saw him, she made her move.

He was sitting alone, as he'd been the first time - sipping at a tumbler of whisky in a wingback chair, his nose buried in the Wall Street Journal. She retired to the toilets before he could notice her; smudged her makeup in the mirror and spritzed her dress with a small perfume bottle of vodka from her handbag, sprayed a little into her mouth, then staggered back into the bar, letting herself weave left and then right. She walked straight to the bar, ordered a double Absolut and soda, loudly, and - suppressing her gag reflex - downed it in one.

She ordered another and nursed it, leaning against the bar on her elbows. And waited. Fifteen minutes later, Marchant appeared at bar beside her and beckoned the waiter over with a crooked finger.

Kat turned her head to look at him, deliberately slowly, as he ordered another whisky. Flashed another, sloppy smile his way.

He saw but ignored it, as before.

Undeterred, she sidled closer to him along the bar.

"What are you drinking?" she asked him, in what she promised El was a pitch-perfect if inebriated Home Counties drawl.

Again, he ignored her.

"What's he drinking?" she bellowed at the waiter.

"Umm... Dalwhinnie?" said the young waiter behind the bar, nervously.

Marchant glared at him, obviously irritated.

"It's on me," said Kat, and passed a banknote across to the waiter, who took it but avoided looking both her and Marchant in the eyes.

The waiter poured the whisky and slid it across to Marchant, who tipped the glass towards Kat and graced her, finally, with a tight-lipped smile of his own.

"Much obliged," he said, and took a sip.

"Now that we've met," she said, dropping her voice to a breathy Marilyn Monroe whisper, "I don't suppose you'd like to come and keep me company?"

"We *haven't* met," said Marchant.

"Then let's do something about that," she said, sidling even closer towards him, close enough that the tops of their legs were touching under the bar. "Jasmine Philips."

"A pleasure," said Marchant curtly, and, still holding the whisky, stepped away from the bar and back to his seat.

She followed him, plonking herself down into the chair opposite his with the confident gracelessness of the lunchtime drunk.

"I'm afraid I'm rather busy," said Marchant before she could speak.

"I'll be direct, in that case," she said, slurring her words a little. "I have a room upstairs. Would you like to join me there?"

Marchant looked her over appraisingly.

"Much as I appreciate the offer," he said, "I believe I'll have to decline."

He picked up the Journal, opened it at the page he'd left open on the table and began, pointedly, to read.

"Well that's just perfect, isn't it?" she muttered as the rejection sank in. "A stellar end to the morning, just stellar. Can't run my story, can't go home because my boyfriend's bitch of an ex-wife is there, and now I can't even give it away to a stranger. Wonderful. Thank you, universe. And thank *you*, Seymour bloody Henderson. Thank you."

She swore to El that she could *see* Marchant's ears prick up at the name, at the word "story."

"Seymour Henderson?" he said. "The MP? *That* Seymour Henderson?"

"What?" said Kat, as if realising belatedly what she'd let slip. "No. No. Different one. Totally different."

She stood up on legs she allowed just the smallest tremor of unsteadiness - but he'd reached out already to grab her arm, stopping her.

"Sit down," he said. "Join me. Please."

"I thought you weren't interested?" she said suspiciously.

"It's not that I'm not *interested*," he said, suddenly apologetic, attentive. "I mean, look at you - what man wouldn't be interested? But, you see..."

He held up his left hand, and pointed to his wedding band.

"Unfortunately," he added, "I'm one of that rare breed that still cares about trifling things like lifelong vows and promises before God."

Rose had snorted humourlessly at this when Kat recounted it, not bothering to hide her contempt. El had found herself again swallowing down bile.

"Married long?" said Kat, sitting back down.

"Longer than you've been alive," Marchant laughed.

"Nice for some," said Kat bitterly.

Marchant signalled to the nervous young waiter, who sped over to their table, and without asking her what she might fancy, ordered them another round of drinks. Less than a minute later the waiter returned with two whiskys, both neat.

"Let's see if we can't improve your day," he said, urging her to drink.

"Thanks," said Kat, still wary.

"Now," he said, "why don't you tell me what happened? It sounds like you've had quite a morning."

"Don't even ask," she said, sipping at the whisky.

"You said something about a story being pulled. Should I assume from that that you're a reporter?"

"You can assume whatever you want."

"Come on. A stranger at a bar just asked you about your troubles. You're *supposed* to bare your soul, are you not? There's a tradition to uphold here."

He was a bastard, Kat said. No doubt about that. But a charismatic bastard, once he'd switched it on - leaning in and smiling, all warmth and attention. You could see why he'd done as well as he had.

"You really want to know?" she said.

"I really want to know."

So she told him.

She *was* a journalist, she admitted - but freelance, not affiliated to any one paper. She had - she said, with a blush of embarrassment - a little money of her own, inheritance money, and it meant that she could be a bit more choosy than your everyday writer about the stories she pursued and the jobs she took on.

"And why not, if you can afford to be?" said Marchant. "Better that than having to forever dance to some editor in chief's tune."

True, she agreed. And she'd always enjoyed her autonomy.

"But wait," she said, as if remembering something even through the haze of alcohol. "You're not in the industry, are you?"

"Couldn't be further from it," he replied, smiling. "I'm in shipping. A total civilian."

She'd smiled back, relieved, and visibly relaxed.

So, a few weeks ago, she told him, she'd caught wind of a story. A big one. She couldn't tell him *where* she'd heard it, but the source was reliable - one she trusted.

"Something about Seymour Henderson?" he asked, innocently.

"You promise this is just between us?" she said.

"Cross my heart."

"Yes, then. About Seymour Henderson."

"And what about him?"

"About the kind of stuff he's into. Sexual stuff."

"*Sexual* stuff?"

"You know... call girls, and bondage, and dominatrixes. Dominatrices? And more. Worse."

She'd managed, she told him, to track down a couple of the girls she'd heard that Henderson had hired: one a full-time domme with a private dungeon in Surbiton, the other a student who went moonlighting as an escort when she struggled to buy textbooks or to pay the rent. Both eventually acquiesced to her requests for an interview, on the record, albeit for a price; both reported first-hand experience of his taste for coke, domination and rough, degrading sex.

Both, moreover, knew exactly who he was - the domme in fact had once lived in his constituency, and made a point of catching him on Question Time whenever he appeared. Though a Lib Dem voter herself, she had nothing but praise for the diligence and genuine concern for local issues he'd demonstrated as an MP.

"Not bad at all, for a Tory," the domme had said. "Though I do wish he'd lay off all that family values crap."

The story had written itself: sitting MP, illicit sex and illegal drugs, prostitutes and emasculation and hypocrisy. Another bit of Cabinet sleaze guaranteed, Jasmine had thought, to make the front page of at least one of the red-tops.

Except that nobody would run it.

"It made no sense," she said, shaking her head, "no sense at all."

Until a guy she knew from one of the Sundays, a friend from university, had agreed to meet her for a coffee that morning, and had told her in no uncertain terms that neither his paper, nor in all probability any of its rivals, would *ever* run the story, and that she should do herself a favour and let it go.

"But why?" said Marchant, feigning shock.

"It's this bloody *fixer* Henderson's got working for him," she spat. "Alison Miller. One of those spin doctors, you know?"

"Never heard of her," said Marchant.

"You wouldn't have. She's super low-profile, or so my friend says. Not some Alastair Campbell type out doing press conferences - she likes to stay hidden. But she's got some serious clout. Enough to put the thumbscrews on half of Fleet Street."

"She sounds... effective," said Marchant.

"Oh, yeah," said Kat, bitterly. "*Very* fucking effective. I'm sitting on a story that'd get anyone else recalled, or at the very least humiliated into a resignation... and no commissioning editor will touch it, because Henderson's got his own personal Machiavelli on the case. Bloody politics, eh?"

She downed the rest of her whisky and placed the empty tumbler onto its cocktail napkin with a trembling hand.

"Interesting," said Marchant thoughtfully. "Very interesting. Another drink?"

"Sounds like he really took the bait," El had said, when Kat finished relaying the encounter in the kitchen of the Ledbury Road house that evening.

"Oh, yeah," said Kat. "Took my number, too. Never called it, mind."

"He didn't need to," Karen had said, rifling through the biscuit tin on the other side of the kitchen. "As soon as he left you at the Chestnut, he went straight back to his office and started calling up every newspaper contact in his little black book, asking if anyone had heard of an Alison Miller. They all told him no, never heard of her. And that *really* pissed him off, I can tell you. He thought they were straight-up lying to him - that she was this great big boogeyman who had 'em so scared they wouldn't even admit to knowing who she was."

Karen's skillset, El had discovered, extended not only to lockpicking and larceny, but to the manipulation of technology. Within a day of starting her contract with the catering team at the Marchant Holdings HQ, she'd squirrelled away listening devices in any office Marchant himself was likely to occupy, acquired a wallet full of duplicate keycards giving her access to every locked door in the building and done something complicated to the phone lines in Marchant's office that meant she could redirect his calls to the number of her choice at the push of a button - and listen in on every call he made and took using an earbud that nested in her left ear and connected via a thin black wire to a Walkman-like device fastened to her left biceps by a Velcro strap.

"I'd tell you how it works," she'd said, when El had asked, "but you wouldn't understand, so why waste both our time?"

The number of her choice had turned out to be for Sita's mobile. Or, as Marchant understood it, the direct line of Harry Fox, editor of the London Herald - a paper Marchant Holdings had tried but failed to purchase from its parent company three years earlier.

Fox was the ideal candidate for the redirect, Karen and Rose had explained, in that Marchant knew *of* him but didn't know him personally. They moved, Rose said, in very different circles - and so were unlikely to bump into each other at the club, or over dinner. Most importantly, Fox knew Rose (and had once known her husband) socially - well enough, apparently, for her to be certain that he'd be out of the country for at least the next month.

So when Marchant's PA called Fox's direct line, she got Sita instead, or rather another of Sita's alter egos: Sheila McAdams, a formidable Scottish woman tasked, she'd told the PA and then Marchant himself, with standing in for Fox during his leave of absence.

Her response to Marchant's questioning had been less than friendly.

"What do you want to know that for?" she'd demanded, when he asked her if she knew of a PR consultant named Alison Miller - and if so, if she'd mind handing over her contact details.

"I'd like to get in touch with her," he replied smoothly. "There was something I was hoping she'd be able to help me with. Do you happen to have a phone number for her?"

"If Alison wanted you to have her number," said McAdams, "she'd have given it to you herself, wouldn't she? If you knew anything about her, you'd know that much. So, sorry - can't help you."

And she'd hung up on him.

But Marchant was nothing if not persistent. Everyone else he'd spoken to, Karen reported, had denied ever having met or even heard of Alison Miller - whereas McAdams at least indicated that there *was* an Alison Miller, and that the two of them were on first name terms.

He rang her back immediately, this time bypassing the PA.

"What do you want now?" growled McAdams, after he'd identified himself.

He'd led in with an enticement - a carrot, not a stick. If she could see her way to helping him, he said, he'd be happy to help her in turn - to give her a leg-up, perhaps even see about getting her an interview for a senior post at one of his own publications. Did she know who he was?

Yes, she'd said - she knew exactly who he was. And the answer was still no.

At which point, he'd fallen back on his more usual approach: outright threat. If she knew who he was, he'd said, then she knew that he could bring her down just as easily as he could help her up. He was very good friends with the brothers who owned her paper - did she know *that*? And with the family who owned all three of its immediate competitors. So how keen was she, exactly, to go back to reporting on school fetes and traffic offences in the Highlands?

And at that, McAdams' bluster had faded, and she'd caved; had handed over Alison Miller's number, followed by a plea that Marchant not mention her name to Miller, if he could help it.

He'd said he couldn't promise anything, and hung up on *her* with what El imagined was a victorious smirk.

That had been yesterday. Today the five of them - El, Kat, Karen, Rose and Sita - were back in Rose's kitchen, huddled around the dining table, sipping coffee and watching the brand-new mobile El had bought on Alison Miller's credit card with the intensity of focus of a bomb-disposal unit scrutinising an unexploded IED.

"Shouldn't he have called by now?" asked Kat.

"Patience, darling," said Sita, the most sanguine of the quintet. "He'll have other things to do, no matter how keen he is to track down our Alison here. But he'll call, I promise you that. You've seen for yourself how much he wants what we're offering."

"She's right," said Karen. "You should've heard him on the phone with all the people he was ringing. He was properly desperate to get hold of her."

"And what if he doesn't?" said Kat. "What are we supposed to do then, just walk away and leave him to it?"

She's a short-game artist, El reminded herself. The results she gets are instant - she's not used to having to wait.

"We're not walking away," said Rose, firmly. "He's going to call."

Kat rolled her eyes.

"I'm going out for a fag," she said. "I can't be doing with all this anticipation."

She pushed her chair back from the table - but before she could stand, Karen raised a finger, silently instructing her to wait. She pressed another finger to the earbud, pushing it further into her ear, and tilted her head in concentration - apparently listening intently to whatever was being said in Marchant's office.

"He's gonna call," she said quietly. "Right now."

A second later the mobile rang, the ringtone shrill and echoing in the tiled silence of the room.

El let it ring - once, twice, three times - before answering.

"Yes?" she said, falling back with surprising ease into Alison Miller's stern schoolmistress tone.

"Am I speaking with Alison Miller?" asked Marchant from the other end of the line.

She nodded at the other women around the table by way of affirmation; made a thumbs-up gesture with the hand not holding tight to the mobile. Yes, it was him; yes, he wanted to talk to her.

"You are," she said into the handset. "How can I help you?"

TUFNELL PARK

1996

They met, at her insistence, at an anonymous chain pub on Fortess Road. He'd queried the choice of venue at first, no doubt irked by the thought of abandoning the city proper for the quasi-suburban hinterlands of Zone 2.

Why not meet at his office? he'd asked. But she'd pushed back, citing privacy concerns.

"I'd rather not be seen going into your building," she said bluntly - and had made it very clear that if he wanted to meet with her, he'd be doing so on her terms. He'd conceded with surprising alacrity.

She landed at the pub half an hour early and settled herself into a booth with a glass of lemonade. Her heart was racing; sweat prickled on the back of her neck and under her arms, stinging the skin and threatening the set of Alison Miller's thickly-applied face and body makeup. She'd run through the scenario a hundred times since arranging the meeting, pre-empting and unpicking - or so she thought - all the ways she might possibly react on coming face to face with Marchant: panic, fury, grief, even fear.

But where ordinarily preparation allayed her concerns, helped her centre herself and focus on getting the job done, here it seemed only to have heightened her anxiety. And the more she thought about Marchant - about who he was, what he'd done, how she'd feel when she looked at him over the table - the more nervous she became.

So she thought instead about Alison Miller, and how *she'd* react to a man like Marchant, allowing the persona to harden over her like a protective carapace, and Miller's thoughts and feelings - a mix of curiosity and irritation at being contacted out of the blue by a high-profile stranger - to subsume her own. Slowly, she let herself fade as the edges of Miller sharpened, until there was barely a *her* at all.

And then she was ready.

He arrived exactly at the time they'd agreed - imagining, she thought, that she'd be late, and that he'd get the drop on her. He looked disheartened, even a little aggrieved when he saw her already in the booth, clocking the cherry-red attaché case by her feet that she'd told him - when he'd asked how to recognise her - that she'd have with her. Though he hid it well - quickly rearranging his features into a warm, genuine smile as he caught her eye.

Objectively, she thought, he was an attractive man, even in his 60s - trim and broad-shouldered, his grey hair thick, his teeth white and his cheekbones defined.

"You beat me to it," he said genially, his long legs bowing as he sat down to face her.

Alison Miller, she thought, would be annoyed by the familiarity, the obvious effort to charm her. She'd have no patience for it.

"I'm here solely," she said, "because you told me you had, and I quote, *information I might find useful*. So if we could cut to the chase, I'd appreciate it. I really don't care for the cloak and dagger approach."

"It's like that, is it?" said Marchant, smile still firmly in place.

"What information is it that you have for me, Mr Marchant?"

The smile widened, becoming predatory.

"It's about your client," he said. "The Honourable Member for Silvertown."

"What about him?"

"I know about him. About his... predilections. The whores."

Miller would bluff, she thought; would give nothing away, even when confronted with facts she knew to be true.

"I have no idea what you're talking about," she said.

"Now, we both know *that's* a lie, don't we? Us and half of Fleet Street, by all accounts."

"I don't know where you're getting this *information*, but you're mistaken. Mr Henderson doesn't have so much as a kiss and tell story to his name."

"Because you've quashed them all. Very efficiently, I might add."

She picked up the attaché case and retrieved her jacket from the back of the booth, preparing to leave.

"I don't have time for this," she said, sliding an arm into the jacket.

She'd planned to make her exit then; to play hard to get, and force him to do a little more chasing before she capitulated to whatever he offered. Before she'd even made it to her feet, though, the plan was thrown into chaos.

Bernard Croft - reluctant theatre-goer, Group Chief Executive of the second largest bank in Europe and father of the academically-challenged Jonathan - was standing over their table, an expression of nervous desperation writ large across his pink, porcine face.

"Alison," he said restlessly. "I'm so glad - I was told I might be able to find you here. Do you have a spare minute?"

Bloody Ruby, she thought, drawn momentarily back to herself. It must have been her. Always stirring the pot. Though how she'd even managed to get in touch with Croft...

She took a breath; steeled herself. There was nothing to do but brazen it out.

"Mr Croft," she said, in the clipped schoolmarmish tone that had cowed him so effectively last time, "I'm with someone. This is quite spectacularly inappropriate."

"I know, and I'm so sorry," said Croft, seeming genuinely apologetic. "But you weren't answering my calls, and we've got so little time before, you know... the big day."

Jonathan's A levels, she thought. His mock exam results must have been worse even than the school had anticipated.

"Now," she said, casting a deliberate glance across the table at Marchant, "is *not the time*."

Marchant, she noticed, had been watching the dialogue play out between them with an expression of absorbed, faintly amused interest - a silent spectator at a tennis match unexpectedly invaded by a streaker.

"But..." Croft began.

"I'll call you," she said, interrupting him. "Later today."

"You will?"

"Yes. Now, if you don't mind..."

Croft seemed to notice Marchant's presence for the first time - evidently recognising him, and immediately recoiling in embarrassment as he realised who else had been party to the conversation.

"Yes," he stammered. "Yes. I'll... be going. And you'll... be in touch?"

"This afternoon," she said - the statement somewhere between a promise and a dismissal.

"Good," he said, scrabbling to retrieve the shreds of his dignity. "Good. I'll... expect your call, then, shall I?"

"*Goodbye*, Mr Croft."

Croft looked as if he was about to say more, then thought better off it, nodded, and scuttled, crab-like, away to the door and out of the pub.

"Bernard Croft is one of your clients?" said Marchant, impressed.

Ruby had judged it right, then. A little extra convincer wasn't such a bad move, after all.

"I'm leaving now," she said, buttoning the jacket.

"Before you've heard my offer?"

"What *offer*? You have nothing I want."

"I want you to dump Henderson and whoever else you're working with and come and work with me instead. Exclusively."

She laughed, a derogatory chuckle that caused his lips to tighten and his eyebrows to lower in tightly-controlled anger.

Not many women talk to you like that, do they? she thought. And we can probably guess what happens to the few that do.

"That isn't an offer, Mr Marchant," she said. "It's a request. And I'm inclined to pass."

"How about this, then?" he said. "Come and work with me, and I'll double what Henderson is paying you."

"No."

"Triple it, then."

"Do you think we're *negotiating*? My answer is no."

She stood up, attaché case in hand.

"Henderson's on borrowed time," he said quietly. "You're a clever woman, you must know that. You can lean on every journalist from here to Aberdeen, but eventually the rumours will get enough of a head of steam that you won't be able to stop them spilling out. He's careless, isn't he? With the working girls. And careless men tend to ruin themselves in the end, no matter how capably they're handled from the outside."

"Is that a threat?" she said.

"No, it's a statement of fact. But surely a very good incentive to investigate new opportunities. Especially the lucrative ones that go out of their way to seek you out."

She stared at him, Alison Miller's artificially green eyes meeting his pale blue ones, and, without breaking the gaze, lowered herself back down into the booth.

"Ten thousand a week," she said.

"Done."

"I wonder if you entirely understand what it is that you're buying. Corporate crisis management isn't my area."

"I know. I'm very aware of where your expertise lies."

"And you don't think you might be better served by a more conventional PR firm?"

"Hardly. Not for what I have in mind."

"Which is what?"

He placed his own briefcase up and onto the table; cracked it open, and pulled a sheaf of paper and a black pen from its depths.

"Sign this," he said, pushing the pen her away across the scratched wood, "and I'll explain."

It was a non-disclosure agreement rather than a contract - six pages long and held together in the top-left corner with a paper clip.

She made a point of reading it intently - taking her time, lingering over every clause and restriction. It was watertight but generic; she imagined his solicitor drawing up a dozen of them a week. If anything, it was less constraining than she'd imagined.

But then, perhaps lawyers weren't his first - or his preferred - port of call, when he needed to enforce an obligation or remind his associates of the necessity of keeping their mouths shut.

The thought would have chilled her, in other circumstances. But Alison Miller was tough. She'd dealt with harder bastards than Marchant before, and she would do again.

"This all looks very standard," she said. It wasn't a compliment.

She took the pen, and signed with Miller's signature - a series of looping, unintelligible peaks and troughs in which an A and an M could be discerned, if you squinted.

"Now talk," she said. "Tell me what I'd be getting myself into."

He tucked the signed NDA away into his briefcase.

"I want to stand as an MP," he said. "An independent. And I want you to run my campaign."

She nodded, as if she'd been expecting this. Which she had - albeit not quite in the way that Alison Miller would have been.

"It'll be harder without party backing," she said. "A lot harder. Especially in the absence of any relevant experience."

"I'm aware of that. It's why I need you running the show."

"And you realise there's a limit on campaign spending? You can't just buy your way in."

"Yes. And fortunately I'd rather play things smart than simply throw money around left, right and centre."

She nodded again, approvingly.

"Do you have a particular seat in mind?" she said. "I'm assuming next year's general is the election you have your eye on."

"I do," he said. "Which is another reason I thought you might be the best woman for the job here. The one I have in mind is Silvertown. Seymour Henderson's seat."

Inside, El smiled. Rose really *did* know what she was doing.

He wasn't a patient person, Marchant told her. Waiting wasn't his style. He was much more inclined to *make* things happen, as and when it suited him.

Biding his time until a general election that was a year away just wasn't an option.

What he wanted - what Rose had *known* he'd want - was an election he could fight on his own terms. One he knew was coming; one he'd prepared for in advance.

He wanted a by-election, and soon. And since he couldn't know for sure which if any of the dozens of sitting MPs in the Greater London area were likely to die on the job in the coming months, leaving an empty seat for him to contest, his best bet was a resignation - a seat vacated by someone forced out of office by a personal crisis, or a scandal; a criminal investigation, or a public humiliation. Someone whose position had been made untenable.

And Seymour Henderson, as he saw it, was the man for the job.

HOLLAND PARK
1994

L ines. Two blue lines, intersecting - a little Nordic cross against a grey plastic background.

Pregnant.

Hannah blinked; loosened her grip on the test and shook it, up and down and side to side, then looked again.

Pregnant.

The utter improbability of it was startling, almost ridiculous - a whoopee cushion of a revelation, releasing an unexpected raspberry into the quiet stillness of the life she'd built. The life *they'd* built.

She was 42 years old. 42 years *old*. Solidly middle-aged; fast approaching the point at which menopause, not periods or pregnancy, would prove the bane of her gynaecological life.

(*Except*, said a small voice in her head, *didn't you read somewhere about there being a surge in fertility just* before *you hit menopause? Some sort of last hurrah of your ovaries, before they go gentle into that long good night?*)

They'd *wanted* children - had started trying a year into their marriage 10 years earlier, when he'd still had hair on his head and before she'd begun to find, in a terrible inverse of his baldness, a dozen or so coarse white hairs of her own sprouting up in arbitrary patterns on her chin and neck.

Children, though, hadn't happened for them, and eventually - when their sex life had become another household chore dictated by the rhythms of her ovulation cycle, and they'd both submitted to so many blood tests at so many clinics that the tops of their arms were permanently bruised from the needles - they'd agreed to stop trying.

"At least we'll get to have a lie-in in the mornings, eh?" he'd said gently, wrapping his arms around her as she cried into his chest. "You know what you're like, when you don't get 8 hours."

And she'd laughed, and let him hold her, and then cried again - for the stretch marks that wouldn't settle on her stomach, the cot she'd never keep beside the bed, the home-office that would never be a nursery.

Pregnant.

They'd settled, after that. They'd taken holidays - three a year, at least. Koh Samui. Tasting tours in Napa Valley. Diving in the Maldives. They'd learned to salsa and swing-dance. Eventually they'd acquired a rescue dog - a Norfolk terrier named Horatio who was watching her now from the carpet as she paced the bedroom, waving the testing stick maniacally back and forth.

She needed to tell Justin. But when? Should she ring him at work - ask (no, *tell*) his secretary to pull him out of whatever meeting he was in and call his wife, right now? Should she go to his office in person - greet him in the lobby with a smile and a jewellery box, the positive test tucked away inside like an oversized engagement ring?

Or was it better to wait until later, when he'd finished for the day - to set out candles, dim the lights, press a glass of champagne into his hand as he walked through the door?

No; not champagne. Apple juice. Mineral water. Something non-alcoholic.

She flashed back to the night before, to the two glasses of red she'd had with dinner and the half a joint she'd smoked to wind down before bed, and tried not to feel guilty.

Deciding against an impromptu visit to Marchant Holdings, she spent the afternoon in a frenzy of cleaning and polishing, wiping down surfaces and stacking the dishwasher with the fervour of a '50s sitcom housewife. Just after 4 o'clock, as she was ransacking the kitchen drawers in pursuit of candles, she heard a key turn in the lock; heard the front door opening.

It couldn't be Justin, she thought. She couldn't remember the last time he'd left the office before 6.

Unless... unless he *knew*, somehow? Unless he'd sensed something, felt in his bones that she had something to tell him, something significant - something that required him to be *here, now*?

Was that possible?

She ran towards the door, almost tripping over her own bare feet in her haste to get to him. But when she saw him, she stopped abruptly in her tracks.

He was pale, blanched, the pink blush that usually dusted his cheeks faded to sickly yellow. His shirt collar was loose, his tie missing. And he smelled - smelled *bad*, like old sweat and stale tobacco, and nothing at all like the notes of soap and bergamot that had clung to him when he'd left the house that morning.

"Have you been smoking?" she asked. He'd quit years ago, when he was still in his 30s. She couldn't imagine him smoking these days; couldn't reconcile a burning cigarette end with the fastidious, immaculately-upholstered man who shared her life, the one who took vitamins and watched his weight and jogged four times a week around Kyoto Garden.

"I found something," he said, ignoring her question, staring over her shoulder into the middle distance. His voice was weak, faltering; not a voice she recognised as his.

"Justin?" she said, reaching out for him. "Sweetheart?"

His head snapped around to face hers. His eyes were bloodshot, the pupils dilated to twice their normal size.

Had he *taken* something?

"I found something," he said again. "At work. And I don't... Hannah, I don't think it's something they want me to know."

"I lost the baby," Hannah told El, pouring a second shot of Scotch into first her tumbler, then El's. "After Justin... three days after they found him in his office. The doctor said the two things weren't connected, necessarily. That there were a few possible factors - my age, for one. But you know your own body, don't know? You know how it feels. And I could *feel* it happening, after he died. Feel it... stopping, I suppose you'd call it. All those non-essential functions just shutting down, until I wasn't the right environment for a baby anymore. Wasn't, you know... a viable host."

It was the first real conversation they'd had; the first time El had heard her speak more than a handful of sentences at a time.

"I'm sorry," El said. And she was: though she'd never wanted kids herself, she'd seen enough other women her age and older try for them, and fail, to have some second-hand understanding of the drawn-out pain of it, the never-ending wrench in the gut.

"I'm aware that it happens," Hannah said, pushing the second tumbler in El's direction across Rose's vast dining room table and taking a quick, dainty sip from her own. "I've seen the statistics. But I can't say that they help much."

"No," said El, looking down at her own drink.

"I named him, afterwards. The baby. It makes no sense, I know - at that stage there's barely anything *to* name, just cells, clusters of cells. But it didn't seem right not to call him *something*."

"What did you call him?" El asked, tentatively.

"Joshua."

"That's a good name," said El, feeling a little out of her depth. "Solid."

"It's what we'd always said we'd call him, if we had a boy - and Justin always wanted a boy, I could tell. It's after Joshua Tree - the park, you know, in California? We went there one year, just after we were married. A beautiful place."

She shook herself, sleek head and narrow shoulders, as if shrugging off the memory, and rubbed at her tired-looking eyes with one knuckle. They were dry, El saw.

I guess there's only so much crying you can do before you start to bore yourself, she thought. Disgust yourself, even.

"You must regret asking now," said Hannah, sipping again at the drink.

"Not at all," El said. "I like knowing who I'm working with."

And this extra bit of information, she thought, made sense of another part of the puzzle: why a woman like that, a *respectable* woman, would walk away from a respectable life and a respectable career to throw in with a group as disreputable as theirs.

"When Rose made her offer," Hannah said, "it felt like a gift. Or perhaps not a gift, exactly, given the circumstances... A reprieve? A *break*, finally. I've spent the last year digging and digging, trying to find *something* on Marchant I can make stick... and I've got absolutely nowhere. Then one day there she is, on my doorstep, with a team and a fleshed-out plan and a means of actually *implementing* it..."

And it falls like manna from heaven, El finished silently. So of course you take it; it's exactly what you want, at exactly the moment you want it.

It's the way you want your mark to feel, right before you take them.

"Did you know Rose well?" she asked. "Before?"

"I wouldn't say *well*," said Hannah. "We'd see each other from time to time socially, but I don't remember the two of us ever being alone together. It was Justin who knew her, really - or knew Seb, anyway."

"Her husband?"

"Yes. They were at college together, back in the day. Justin was a couple of years ahead, but their paths crossed, or so I gather, at societies and things. I don't know that they were *close*... but he *liked* Seb, I know that. And he must have known him reasonably well, because he'd always say when we saw the two of them out and about how surprised he was that he'd taken up with Rose. He said he'd always assumed that Seb..."

Laughter broke through the ceiling from one of the rooms upstairs - a cackle, undeniably Ruby's, and a softer chuckle that might have been Kat's.

Hannah jumped at the sound, a full-body shudder that caused the tumbler in her hand to twitch and the liquid inside to spill over the rim and onto the table.

El waited, holding back her questions while Hannah soaked up the Scotch with a napkin, then asked:

"What did he assume, about Seb?"

"What?" said Hannah, rubbing at the wood in tight concentric circles, apparently lost in thought. "Oh. Nothing, really. Just that he hadn't expected him to get together with someone like Rose."

"Someone like Rose?"

The kitchen door opened, and Rose herself stepped through.

"What about me?" she asked, smiling widely at El.

"I was asking how you two knew each other," El said, cutting Hannah off before she could reply.

"*That*?" said Rose. She pulled a chair out from the table, the one closest to El, and sat down next to her. "Not a very interesting story, I'm afraid. Our husbands were friends at Oxford."

"You were there too, weren't you?" said El.

Rose pushed her chair backwards an inch; angled it slightly towards El so they were facing each other.

"I was," she said, still smiling. "But Justin and I ran in different crowds.

And he was older than me, obviously - finishing up his masters while I was in my first year, I believe. So our worlds didn't really overlap."

Hannah drained what remained of her whiskey and got to her feet, still shaking very slightly with what El thought might be the aftershocks of the previous fright.

"I should be going," she said.

"Already?" said Rose. "It's barely 6."

"I need to walk the dog," she said, adjusting her scarf around her neck and pulling her handbag over one shoulder. "Before it gets too dark. I'll be back in the morning."

She scurried away from them and out of the kitchen, the spiked points of her stilettos hitting the tiles trailing sound waves after her.

"Something I said?" Rose asked.

"She's just nervous," El said. "I mean, this isn't exactly her regular scene, is it?"

With Hannah gone, the proximity of Rose's body to hers felt more intrusive than it had. She pushed her own chair away from the table, picked up the empty tumblers and walked them, very deliberately, across to the dishwasher.

"She's tougher than you think. She's had to be."

"I'm sure she is. But it's still a lot, isn't it? *We're* a lot."

She reached a questing hand into the pocket of her jeans; flipped open the lid of the cardboard box she found there with her thumb and closed two fingers around the comforting smoothness of a cigarette filter.

"Where are you on Marchant's contract?" Rose asked, suddenly businesslike.

"I'm calling him tonight to confirm," she said, equally curt.

"Why not do it now?" said Rose. "Before you go outside to smoke that cigarette?"

And *this* is why I don't do other people's dirty work, El thought. You're forever on their clock, dancing to their tune.

"Why the urgency?" she said.

"I want to keep up the momentum. Keep moving forward."

"And *I* don't want to push him. We need to let him come to us."

"Leave him too long and he's apt to get cold feet."

El took a deep, performative breath - as much as an expression of her impatience as to keep her annoyance at bay.

"I know what I'm doing," she said. "This is my area. You have to let me work. Let me do it my way."

"And I *don't* know what I'm doing?" said Rose, her jaw visibly clenched with the effort of keeping her own anger in check.

"I'm not trying to offend you. All I'm saying is, this is my job, and I know how to do it. It's why you brought me in."

"I brought you in..." Rose began, the thread of Rotherham back in her voice as her temper rose, but El stopped her - pointing a finger to her lips, and then to the mobile phone she'd left, face-down and unattended, on the table. It was ringing.

"It's him," she said, without looking at the display.

She picked up the phone; pressed the Answer button.

"Yes?" she said impatiently, slipping back into Alison Miller's skin, her unshakeable confidence. It got easier, she knew; easier every time.

"Alison?" said Marchant.

"Who am I speaking to?"

"James Marchant. We chatted earlier this week - I imagine you remember."

He sounded, to her disappointment, relaxed; louche, even a little amused with himself. She'd hoped to find him more needy, more anxious.

"And how can I help you, Mr Marchant?" she replied, upping the hauteur of Alison Miller's delivery in response.

"I was hoping you might have an answer for me. Given our deadline."

There wasn't a trace of uncertainty there; no concern that she might say no, might put the phone down on him and walk away from the offer. Just reproach, and the mild irritation of a man unaccustomed to waiting.

She glanced away from the phone and up at Rose, who was watching her so intensely that it might, in other circumstances, have frightened her. But Alison Miller didn't *do* frightened.

She tilted her head; raised an eyebrow. *Now?*

Rose nodded.

Now.

"I want 50% of the fee upfront," she said. "And a written agreement specifying services."

"I'll have my solicitor draft it this evening," said Marchant.

"Please don't take what I'm about to say personally, Mr Marchant," she said, "but I'd rather *my* solicitor took care of the contract in this instance."

"Don't you trust me, Ms. Miller?"

"Why should I need to *trust* you? I'm putting you in office, not accepting your hand in marriage."

He chuckled down the line, a good-humoured baritone she was sure other people would find disarming.

"*Your* solicitor, then," he said. "Bring him in tomorrow, and we can get started straight away."

"He'll need a few hours in the morning to sort out the paperwork. We can be with you for 2 o'clock."

"Shouldn't you check in with the man first?"

"If I needed to *check in* with him before I made commitments," she said, the vulgar Americanism leaving a bad taste in Alison Miller's mouth, "then he wouldn't be my solicitor."

Marchant chuckled again.

"I'll see you tomorrow," he said, and ended the call.

She switched off the phone and slid it into her back pocket.

Rose was staring at her from the table - no longer, as far as El could tell, looking for a fight.

"What?" El asked, sloughing off Alison Miller and stepping back into herself.

"You're a very good liar," Rose said. "And I intend that as a compliment, not a criticism."

"It's my job," El repeated, shrugging. She slid the cigarette out of its packet and placed it, unlit, in her mouth. "I'm just going to..." she started, gesturing at the door.

"Wait," said Rose, standing.

El paused; removed the cigarette.

"I'm sorry for snapping at you, just now," Rose said. "I think I just wanted to... push someone to get a reaction."

"Don't worry about it," El said.

"It's been... well, truthfully, it's not been a good day."

"No?"

"No. I've had to send Sophie away."

El was taken aback. They'd seemed very close, in the bit of time she'd spent with them - their easy, knockabout intimacy a kind she'd seen more than once in the dynamic between single parents and their kids. A kind she'd had herself, with her own mother.

Sophie, she'd thought, was Rose's world. The idea of Rose *sending her away*... it didn't compute.

"Not far," Rose added. "She's with Seb's sister, down in Sussex. But, you know... any distance is too far, when it's your own child you've sent packing."

"Why?" El asked, realising immediately afterwards how judgemental she might have seemed, how close the question might have sounded to *what kind of mother* are *you, anyway?*

But if Rose was insulted, she didn't let it show. There was no anger there now, that El could see. She just looked tired; tired and sad.

"To keep her safe," she said quietly.

Safe from who? El wondered. From them - the bunch of cons she'd invited into the family home? From her, and Ruby, and Sita, and Karen with her muscles and her beltful of lockpicks?

No. There was no logic in that; no sense. However it had happened, whatever the backstory, Rose had known Ruby and Sita for years - for decades, by the sound of it. And Karen had been there, embedded in the Highgate house, before El had ever heard of Rose Winchester and her art collection.

Not them, then. They weren't the threat.

Which meant that the threat had to be Marchant.

"You're that frightened of him?" she asked. "Of what he might do?"

Rose dropped her gaze to her own lap; ran a fingernail, El thought probably unconsciously, along the tendrils of scar tissue snaking upwards from her wrist into her shirt-sleeves.

"After everything he's done," she answered, "I'm not sure that I'm frightened enough."

VAUXHALL
1996

Nothing reminded El of Dexter more than the smell of burnt fish.

Ruby's flat had reeked of it, the day she'd met him. Ruby hadn't explained why at the time, though El had gathered afterwards that it connected in some way with a long con she and Sita were running in the kitchen of a West End seafood restaurant.

The boys had seemed immune to it - the two of them stretched out lengthways on the living room carpet, heads buried in biology textbooks, still wearing the maroon blazers and striped ties that identified them to El immediately as students of the rich-boy school in Hampstead, the one with the belfry and the gates so high and spiked you'd likely do yourself an injury trying to sneak in or out.

Ruby had talked about them, long before she'd ever invited El over for tea, so much and in such detail that El felt like she knew them already: knew that, although they were physically identical, they had very different temperaments. That Dexter was the funny one, the joker, and that Michael was more serious, more polite and circumspect.

They were taller than most of the men she'd known; even then, at 17.

They were neat, well-kept and cared-for: their shirts clean and ironed, their trousers pressed, their hair combed and sculpted into short, tidy Afros. And they were good-looking, soft-eyed and long eyelashed in a way she knew a lot of girls her age would find appealing - even if, as she was beginning to suspect, she was unlike a lot of girls her age in at least a couple of quite critical ways.

"This is El," Ruby had said, before she bustled out of the room to put the kettle on. "She's not lived round here long, so you two - get your backsides up off that floor and make her feel at home."

Both boys had obeyed, but one, seeing Ruby disappear through the doorway, had sat immediately back down again, flashing El a crooked smile that she read as half-cheeky and half-apologetic as he returned to his book.

That'll be Dexter, then, she thought.

The other boy stayed standing.

"Very nice to meet you," he said awkwardly, sounding three decades older than he looked; a stiff headmaster, welcoming parents at an open day.

"And you," she answered, unconsciously matching his crisp, clipped delivery with vowels so excessively over-pronounced that she sounded, she thought, like an East End barrow girl auditioning for a Jane Austen adaptation.

"Have you known Mum long?"

"Just a few weeks."

"And she's showing you the ropes?"

El was shocked into speechlessness. Did they *know* what their mother was, what she did?

"At the laundrette," he clarified. "I take it you're one of the new people?"

Ah, she thought. So *that* was Ruby's cover story.

"Yes," she said. "I do weekends," she added. "You know... folding. Unloading."

"How are you finding it so far? It must be very tiring. Quite demanding, physically."

"Very," she said, thinking fast. "I'm on my feet all day. And the machines are very... heavy. To open."

"I'm sure they are. With all those clothes in there, especially. Brassieres and underpants and so on."

The boy on the floor sighed and looked up from his book.

"Must you do this with *all* of them?" he said, addressing his brother. "Ignore him," he said, turning his attention to El. "He plays this game every time Mum brings home someone she works with. He *knows* she's not a laundress, any more than Auntie Sita is the Empress of Rajasthan, or whatever she's pretending to be this week. He just likes to watch you squirm."

The standing boy grinned, showing perfectly white teeth - the teeth of a high-school athlete or a Hollywood actor.

"Sorry," he said to El, his register less formal, less stilted than it had been the moment before. "He's right, I'm just messing with you."

He stuck his arm out towards her, inviting a handshake.

"Dexter Redfearn," he said. "That one down there with a stick up his arse is Michael. And *you* must be the girl Mum's been talking about lately. The mouthy one with the hammer."

The accent was more refined these days, Ruby's rasp and Winston's lilt flattened into a generic South East by mock trials and Law Society dinners, so that he sounded more and more like the chinless Bullingdon Club types he used to parody, even in everyday speech. But the same playfulness was in him now, almost 20 years on - the same sense of delighted amusement in the world as he found it.

"It's not bad," he said, passing the stapled pages of the contract to El over the tablecloth and helping himself to a parcel of her ravioli with his fingers.

"Near on watertight, if I say so myself. If this Alison Miller existed, and any of her services were actually on offer, she'd have herself a *very* sweet deal."

And that was the other thing about Dexter: he wasn't afraid to get his hands dirty or bend the law to breaking point if Ruby - or El, or Sita - asked him to.

Michael was as straight as a die, so squeaky-clean he left the room when his Mum and her friends talked shop, lest he hear something incriminating. He was in the City now, specialising in corporate litigation, the first Black man to be offered a partnership at Fine & Porter, and had plans to set up his own firm within the decade. He was, by any estimation, an upstanding citizen - more his father's son than his mother's, although there was something of Ruby's laser focus, her methodical ferocity, in the way that he attacked a brief.

Dexter, conversely, was a chancer, a wheeler-dealer. Though as materially successful as Michael - his bank balance evident in his suits, his Porsche, his Battersea penthouse - he preferred to operate under the radar. His own two-man firm - ably supported by the redoubtable Mrs Day - was unheard-of by all but a very select client-base; his business came exclusively via word of mouth. Like Michael's, his record was clean, his right to practice absolute; unlike Michael's, his reputation - where it was known at all - was decidedly murky. He was good, every client he'd ever had in his office agreed; there was no one better to solve a complicated problem or resolve a complicated dispute that couldn't be addressed by more conventional means. But, those same clients would add quietly: you wouldn't always want to know *how* he did it, would you?

"Cheers," said El. She scanned it, briefly, and passed it back to him. "I owe you."

"How would you like me today?" he asked, washing down the ravioli with a swig of mineral water. He wasn't much of a drinker; neither twin was. Despite their differences, they both saw value in keeping a clear head. "Lapdog, pitbull? Tenacious legal terrier?"

She considered the question.

"Let's play it by ear," she answered. "Just... follow my lead, alright? No improvising. I know what you're like."

"Epsilon," he said, smirking the way he always did when he had cause to use her real name, knowing it annoyed her, "I wouldn't dream of it."

They settled up and drove together over Southwark Bridge to Hastings House, Marchant Holdings's UK base - a 20-storey glass-box off Bankside modelled after the interwar skyscrapers of Chicago and Manhattan. Marchant's office was, as El had expected, on the top floor, its gargantuan back window treating him and any guests he might entertain to a view of the river, of Victoria Tower and the Palace of Westminster.

Marchant himself was installed behind his desk as one of his assistants led El and Dexter inside - neither rising nor greeting them as they landed.

The other person in the room, a man in his forties stuffed like a factory-packed sausage into a pinstripe shirt a size too small for his body, was more effusive.

"Redfearn!" he barked cheerfully, leaping up from his seat to seize Dexter's arm by the elbow and lock him into an enthusiastic handshake. "Wasn't expecting to see *you* here! Old Hannity let you out for the day, did he?"

"Old Hannity," El thought, was almost certainly *George* Hannity - one of the senior partners at Fine & Porter, and Michael's direct superior.

He thinks Dex is Michael, she realised.

Dexter, returning the handshake with the same broad grin he'd given *her* the day they'd met in Ruby's living room, had evidently reached the same conclusion.

"Lovely to see you again," he told the man, straightening his spine and subtly readjusting his voice until both his posture and his speech were near-perfect replicas of Michael's. "Are you well?"

"Oh, you know," said the man. "Busy, busy."

"This is my brief," said Marchant, interrupting him.

The man, remembering himself and where he was, slumped a little, and let go of Dexter's hand.

"Roderick Creighton," he told El, sounding chastened. "Representing Mr Marchant."

"Can we get started?" El said, addressing Marchant over Creighton's shoulder.

"Let's," said Marchant.

El lowered herself into the chair opposite Marchant's - the chair that had previously been Creighton's - and crossed Alison Miller's legs, leaving the two lawyers to hover, impotently, by the side of the desk.

"We've prepared a draft of the necessary agreement," said Dexter stiffly, still in character. "Rod, would you care to take a look?"

Creighton took a pair of half-moon reading glasses - the kind El had only ever heard described as *spectacles* - from the pocket of his trousers, and placed them, gently, onto the tip of his nose.

"Hand it over, old chap," he said, "and we'll see what's what, eh?"

Dexter removed the stapled contract from the document folio tucked under his arm and lay it out on the edge of the desk, forcing Creighton to hitch up his trousers and bend over, with obvious effort, to examine its contents.

"I assume," said El to Marchant, as Creighton read, "that you intend for us to start work this afternoon, all being well with the paperwork?"

"That's the plan," said Marchant, with a thin smile. "In the meantime - coffee?"

"Love one," said El.

Marchant picked up the phone on his desk and murmured an order into the receiver. Barely a minute later, the assistant who had shown them inside returned with a tray bearing a polished-silver milk jug, a cafetière and two coffee cups.

No drinks for the hired help, El noticed.

The assistant poured the coffee into the cups and promptly vanished again, leaving El and Marchant to sip in silence as Creighton read and Dexter remained, military-straight, by El's side.

"It all seems to be in order," said Creighton after several minutes had elapsed. "No obvious issues, that I can see. If you're sure you're happy with the fee?" he added, casting a nervous look at Marchant.

"Do you think I'd have bothered to make the offer if I weren't?" Marchant snapped.

Creighton wilted in embarrassment.

("If *he'd* been a dog, in that moment," Dexter said later, "that dog would have been an incontinent puppy. The one you take back to the rescue centre when it shits in your shoes").

"Does that mean we can get on and sign the thing?" said El impatiently.

"Ready when you are," said Marchant.

At Creighton's direction, they applied the relevant signatures - the assistant returning, briefly, to act as witness.

"I'll have the copies faxed across to you by end of day," Dexter told Creighton, sweeping the papers back into his folio.

"Marvellous, marvellous," said Creighton - though he sounded, El thought, more subdued than he had previously, ashamed at having been emasculated in the presence of a well-connected colleague.

"Shall we?" El asked Marchant. "We have a lot to do, and I'm conscious of time."

"We certainly do," he said. "Bianca will see you out," he added to the lawyers, not bothering to look at them as he dismissed them.

Her eyes fixed on Marchant's, she couldn't see his face as the two of them turned and exited the office, but El imagined Creighton must have looked forlorn, because she heard what sounded like a consolatory hand clamping down on a meaty shoulder, and Dexter - still wearing a facsimile of Michael's voice - saying, "Drink, old man? You look like you could do with one..."

So very like his Mum, El thought. Always stirring the pot.

"Thank God for that," said Marchant as the door closed and the sound of the lawyers's conversation faded. "Can't *stand* that man. Useless pompous twat."

"I'm afraid they're all like that," El said. "Even mine."

"'The first thing we do, let's kill all the lawyers,'" Marchant said, emphasising the *kill* with a relish that made El shudder and choke and scream even as Alison Miller smiled back in agreement.

Can you take care of it? he'd asked Lomax, that day in the hotel. Like her mother's body was a dining cart; a stack of old room service dishes he'd left to moulder.

She let her eyelids flutter closed, just for a second; pushed the reaction down, into her chest and gut until it was buried under the heat and pressure of Alison Miller's personality, her cut-throat professionalism.

He was watching her, expectantly.

"I should tell you," she said, her voice - Alison Miller's voice - as smooth and unruffled as it might have been had she just paused to contemplate the size of the cheque Marchant was about to write her, "that I don't take notes, and I don't keep records of my assignments. Anything we discuss, and anything we implement as a result of that discussion, will be keep exclusively in *here*."

She tapped, once, lightly, at the side of her head.

"Very wise," he agreed.

"I expect you to honour this approach, and to reciprocate in kind," she continued. "That means nothing typed or written, of course. No notepads or letters or documents. No email, if you use it. But it also means no sound recordings. No Dictaphones."

"Sounds like a very good idea."

"So you're happy to acquiesce?"

"More than happy. It's hardly in my interest to demand a paper trail, is it?"

"Good. Then I think the most sensible thing in the first instance is for me to outline the approach I have in mind for our campaign. *Your* campaign, I should say."

"And I'd love to hear it. Except..."

"Except?"

"Please don't think I'm questioning your methods, Alison. I already have the utmost faith in any strategy you propose. But ought we not to deal with the initial obstacle first? The fly in the ointment?"

"Henderson, you mean?"

"*Yes*, Henderson. We can't very well have me contesting his seat while he's sitting in Parliament, can we?"

He waited - expecting her to back-track, to offer something new - and she let another smile bloom and spread across Alison Miller's borrowed face.

"We certainly can't," she said. "Fortunately, I have good news in that regard."

"You do?"

"I do. This isn't my first spin on the merry-go-round, Mr Marchant. And Seymour Henderson is being dealt with even as speak."

NOTTING HILL

1996 - The Night Before

Collateral damage, El thought. You don't want it; you try to avoid creating it, where you can. But sometimes it's unavoidable.

Sorry, Seymour, she told the man on the screen, silently. *It's nothing personal.*

She and Rose were in the basement of the Ledbury Road house, in what El thought might once have been the family TV room. There was a roll-down projector on the far wall, facing a cluster of mismatched comfy chairs that looked, to El, a lot less expensive - and a lot more worn - than Rose's other furniture. Between two of the chairs was a rickety side-table, the green paint peeling from its stumpy legs; she imagined microwaved popcorn spilling out onto it from plastic bowls on cold Saturday nights, Rose and Sophie reaching for handful after handful as they worked their way through Aladdin, The Lion King, the entire Disney back-catalogue.

This evening, though, the screen showed not Scrooge McDuck or singing warthogs, but a black and white video feed of a naked man - Seymour Henderson, the Honourable Member for Silvertown - spreadeagled on a four-poster bed, his wrists secured to the upper posts by wide leather bondage cuffs, a padlocked chastity cage clamping his penis tight against his swollen scrotum. The lens that captured his predicament was angled in front of and above the bed, giving them a bird's-eye view of his body. The camerawork was raw and imprecise, cinema vérité shaky.

A pair of arms - slim and hairless, probably female - dangled intermittently into close-up view from the left and right sides of the shot. The camera itself, this suggested, was positioned somewhere *between* the arms - somewhere on the person of whoever the arms belonged to.

("And it'll stay on there the whole time, will it?" Ruby had asked earlier, as El helped secure the tiny, button-like spy-cam to one of the breast-cups of Karen's latex corset.

"Yes, it'll stay on," Karen had replied, exasperated. "It's held in place, look. And he'll hardly be able to pull it off himself, will he?"

"Don't look very steady to me, that's all."

"Think you can do better, do you? Fancy trying it on with Henderson yourself?"

"If I were 10 years younger, I'd have a go."

"10 years?" Karen had snorted, the ripple of her amusement causing El's hand to lose its grip and the button-cam to slip down into the cleavage of the corset. "That's optimistic. Just hope I have your confidence, when I get to your age").

An inaudible instruction was issued off-screen, and Henderson wriggled his wrists in their restraints, trying to manoeuvre himself upright.

"Yes, please," he gasped, sounding to El very different - and altogether more compliant - than the man she'd recently seen argue NHS budget cuts with Nicky Campbell on Central Weekend.

"Yes please *what*?" said a voice that was recognisably Karen's - albeit a sterner and more authoritarian Karen than El was used to.

"Yes please, *Mistress*," said Henderson, breathing heavily.

"Not good enough," said Karen.

There was a whoosh of air, a squeaking of resistant materials against flesh, and one of the off-screen arms reappeared in shot - this time to bring the leather tongue of a riding crop down hard on the sensitive skin of Henderson's inner thigh.

He cried out, in obvious pain.

"What do you say?" Karen asked him.

"Sorry, Mistress," he whispered.

"Good," said Karen, and hit him again, harder.

El winced. Rose laughed, sounding more relaxed and unguarded than El had ever heard her.

"She's a natural, isn't she?" Rose said, gesturing to the screen, where an invisible Karen was looming over the supine, whimpering Henderson. "If the grifting doesn't work out, I can see an entirely new vista of opportunity opening up for her."

"I'm not sure it's something she wants to cultivate," said El, and Rose laughed again.

The riding crop flicked back into the shot - this time to caress Henderson's cheek.

"You're doing well," Karen said - changing gears, her tone tender rather than commanding.

"Thank you, Mistress," said Henderson quietly, arching his back and neck to press his face against the leather tongue.

"So well," said Karen, "that I'm going to give you a reward. A little treat. You'd like that, wouldn't you?"

"Yes, Mistress."

"Good boy."

She picked *that* one up from Ruby, El thought.

A hand entered the shot, in extreme close-up, its blurred fingers appearing to reach directly for the camera. Then the hand changed course, vanishing from the frame - only to reappear a second later, an old-fashioned glass vial half-filled with snow-white powder clasped between its thumb and forefinger.

The camera moved closer to the bed, shaking back and forth with every step Karen took, until Henderson's face and upper body filled the screen - beads of sweat discernible on his forehead, his breath erratic.

A finger - Karen's finger - returned to press against the side of his nose, sealing off one nostril. A hand was thrust, palm down, against his upper lip.

The tip of the glass vial came back into view, now uncorked - tilted forward by the unseen camerawoman until its powder contents spilled out in a thick, rough line onto the back of the hand, directly under Henderson's nose.

("It's marvellous stuff," Sita had said, pushing the vial of coke down until it sat snugly in Karen's *other* breast-cup. "The man I bought it from said it was the best he'd ever had. Our Mr Henderson will be seeing stars after you've given it to him. Seeing *galaxies*."

"And you don't think," Karen had replied, shifting her weight from one foot to the other as she struggled to get comfortable under her layer of latex, "that he might have had, you know... an ulterior motive for telling you that? What with you emptying your wallet at him for half a gram?"

"Oh, hush," said Sita, pulling the straps of the corset tighter at the back, until Karen's breasts bulged formidably out in front. "You young people - you're always so *cynical*").

"Time to take your medicine," said Karen offscreen, her second hand snaking back into shot to caress Henderson's damp, greying hair.

He lurched forward, pushing his open nostril as far towards the line as his cuffs would allow, and hoovered it up in two rapid snorts.

"And the rest," Karen ordered.

He pressed his lips to her hand, opened his mouth and licked the remaining powder from her skin hungrily, then leaned back against the bed, muscles taut as wire but a sated, delirious look in his wide, pink eyes.

"Now," she told him, her voice - and El, imagined, her body language -

communicating the absolute impossibility of his disobeying, "I'm going to go next door, and you're going to stay here. Maybe I'll come back, and maybe I won't. Maybe I'll leave you here for the housekeeper to find in the morning. But - and this is very important - you *will not* move from this bed. Do you hear me, Seymour? Are you listening?"

"Yes, Mistress," he answered, teeth chattering - from fear, arousal, the strength of the coke or a combination of all three, El wasn't sure.

("It wasn't all made up, what I told him about Henderson and the girl in Surbiton," Kat had told El, the night she'd come back from Chestnut House after she'd failed to seduce Marchant. "You know - the girl with the dungeon. Rose sent me down to talk to her the other week, before she dragged you into all this."

"She'd already started the con then?" El had asked, surprised.

"Oh, yeah. She's a forward-planner, that one. Always six steps ahead of where you expect her to be").

The camera made a sharp 90-degree turn, so that it faced a second room connected to the first by a whitewashed door, pulled halfway open to reveal a writing desk, a frayed loveseat and a bookcase stacked with Penguin Classics and Jeffrey Archer paperbacks - the sitting room of Henderson's Tower Hill bolthole, the residence he *hadn't* declared to his wife and constituents. Karen stepped inside; the camera swivelled around again as she booted the door shut with a firm front-kick, the ball of her foot almost splintering the cheap wood as it connected, and then settled on a closed sash-window, its dusty blinds drawn.

"Right, you lot," Karen whispered from behind the camera, and she was speaking directly to El now, to Rose and Ruby and the rest of the audience at home, "it's done. And I bloody hope you got all the footage you wanted, because I'm telling you now - I am *not* touching that cage again."

"You sure you don't mind doing this?" El had asked Karen earlier, when the two older women had left and she and Karen had found a coat in Rose's wardrobe that was long enough and dark enough to mask the latex and leather underneath.

"You offering to step in?" Karen had replied, flashing her a grin that reminded her a little bit of Dexter and lot of Ruby.

"Not sure I'd be able to keep a straight face, knowing what he's into."

"Sure you would. I mean, you've got incentive to make this one work, haven't you? We all have."

El paused, playing the last sentence back to herself.

"What do you mean?" she asked warily. Did Karen *know*, about Marchant and her mother? Had Rose told her? Had *Ruby*?

"Don't look so worried," Karen said, catching the change in El's expression. "I just assumed you were like the rest of us, that's all. That you had some sort of history with Marchant that made you want to bring him down."

"Have you been talking to Ruby?"

"About you? No. Didn't ask, and she didn't tell. Whatever beef you've got with that cunt, whatever skeletons of his are rattling round in your closet, she's keeping schtum about 'em. None of my business, is it?"

"I didn't say that," said El, automatically on the defensive.

"You didn't have to. And anyway, like I said - it's none of my business. I've got my own shit to deal with."

A curtain of silence fell between them, heavy and awkward.

"Ruby ever mention my old man?" Karen said eventually, the question sounding casual but evidently - to El's mind - anything but. "Leon Baxter?"

"No," El lied. "Never."

Vanished like a puff of smoke, Ruby had said. *Word was he'd stitched up his crew on his last job and done a runner with the takings.*

"Bullshit," Karen said. "Of course she has. Woman like you wouldn't get into something like this with a bunch of strangers without doing your homework on 'em. And it's not as if it's a secret, is it, what happened to him? I *still* get people asking where he went, when they find out who I am. As if I'll turn round and tell 'em."

"But you think it was something to do with Marchant?"

Karen stared down at the front of the coat; took longer than she needed to tie the belt around her waist. Buying herself time, El thought. Pulling herself together, even if she doesn't want to show it.

"I *know* it was," she said, not looking at El. "I didn't know *him*, Leon - not personally. I was about 18 months when he upped and went. Even when I *think* I can remember something about him, him throwing me up in the air to make me laugh or taking me to look at the giraffes at the zoo, I don't *actually* remember it. I've just seen it in a photo somewhere or had someone tell me it happened. You know what I mean?"

El's own recollections of her mother were, she thought, fairly reliable - or as reliable as any memory ever could be, reconstructed through the distorting prisms of time and distance, grief and nostalgia. But even she was prey to the occasional cognitive misstep, to a flashback felt so vividly she'd imagine, momentarily, that the associated event *must* have been true, *must* have happened, even when she knew, logically, that it couldn't be, couldn't have: the two of them standing in an airport security line, when they'd never been abroad; sitting down together to eat a roast lamb dinner, when her mother hadn't touched red meat since the 60s; rooting through the attic for Christmas decorations, when they'd lived in a maisonette.

"Yeah," she said, "I think I do."

"But *other people* knew him," Karen said. "My uncles, my granny, my mum. People I trust. And I trust what they tell me about him - when they tell me that he weren't the sort of bloke to just do one in the night. Especially not with a baby on the way."

"A baby?"

"My little brother. Mum was five months pregnant with him when the old man vanished."

Karen adjusted the collar of the coat; pulled it up to her ears and over her neck, covering the highest and most visible of the corset's straps.

"That's how I know," she continued. "That it was Marchant - that Marchant did him in. See, Leon was excited about the baby. He was well into kids, especially *his* kids, everyone said so. It was all he talked about, them last few months. And mum getting pregnant again, with me and my sister so little, it made him.... I suppose you'd say *re-evaluate* some of his choices. That's how my Uncle Perce put it - *re-evaluate his choices*. Not about the job, exactly - a man like that doesn't just *stop* robbing, not when he's so good at it it's practically an artform. But about some of the people he'd fallen in with. Some of the people he'd been taking orders from."

"Marchant?"

"Marchant, right. He'd been doing bits and bobs for him for a few years. Nothing heavy - getting round security systems, lifting documents, that sort of thing. Manila folder, industrial espionage bollocks. Then one day the ask changes. Marchant starts telling him to get physical, here and there - rough up a guard, kick a German Shepherd in the head so it won't bark. And Leon doesn't like it. He was a big bloke, a hard bloke, could've been a bouncer from the look of him, and he used to go boxing as a kid, so he was *built*, you know what I mean? But he never used his fists on a job, never wanted to. It wasn't his style."

"So after he's said no to Marchant a couple of times - said he's not up for hurting animals, let alone people - he decides, enough's enough. Or so Perce says. He goes home and talks to my Mum about how to handle it: Marchant had a lot of clout even back then, everyone knew it, and he wasn't someone you said no to if you wanted an easy life. And him and Mum, they decide between them that they'll go away for a while, get out of London. Not forever; just for a little bit, until Marchant loses interest in him and things go back to normal."

"But they both know he can't *go*, just like that. He's got to be clever about it. So between them they say: he'll do one last job for Marchant, to get him off his back, create a bit of breathing space. And *then* they'll go, before Marchant comes back asking for another favour."

"And *was* there a job on the table?" El said.

"Not right then, not 'til about a week later. But here's the thing - the job came, but no-one knew what it *was*. Not Mum, not Perce, not any of them. Leon just gets a call one day from Marchant's head of security, this bastard Lomax, telling him to get up north, pronto. Gives him a time and an address, but fuck all else. No details, nothing."

"Up north?" El thought - her mind's eye picturing Lomax, younger and healthy, driving through Leicester city centre in the middle of the night all those years ago, looking out for somewhere he could dump a body. What did "up north" mean to a Londoner? Were the Midlands "up north"? Was Leicester?

"Where?" she asked, not sure she wanted to know the answer. "What was the address?"

"The exact address?" Karen said. "Fucked if I know. A place called Holt, that was all mum got out of him. You heard of it? It's up by Cheshire – little town near the Welsh border. Might even be *in* Wales, for all I know."

Not the Midlands, then, El thought. Thank Christ for that.

"And he went?" she asked.

"Oh, he went. Takes three of his regular lads with him in the back of the van, and off they go. Lomax asked him to go alone, but that was never Leon's style either - he always liked to have backup with him. It was one of *them* who set the talk going later on, by the way - them rumours about him taking their cut and doing a runner. Ungrateful bastard - he *knew* what actually went down up there, *knew* what must have happened to Leon, and he still talked shit about him."

"See, Perce and one of his brothers, my Uncle Keith - they went and had a word with those lads after, once they'd got back and it looked like Leon had done a disappearing act. And Perce and Keith - they're big blokes too. Not people you want to fuck around with when they're asking questions. So those lads who'd been up north with Leon, it didn't take 'em long to start talking. And what they said..."

Karen paused; took a breath.

"What they *said*," she finished, "was that the job was a doddle - a piece of piss. Just a smash and grab in some factory in the middle of nowhere - not *skilled* work, nothing that needed finessing. They couldn't understand why Marchant needed to send someone all the way up there to do it, when a local boy could have done it just as well. They got in, got the stuff - machine parts, one of them told Perce - and then they were off, back up the motorway. Only, they said, that was when it started to go pear-shaped."

"They'd arranged with Lomax to stop off at one of the services on the M6, Knutsford way, to do the handover - the goods, whatever they were, for the cash. 8 grand - not bad going for the '70s, even split 4 ways. So they pull into the car park, Leon steps outside to make the trade, walks into the cafe with a sports bag full of cogs and spindles over his shoulder... and that's it. He doesn't come back. Leaves them there in the back of the van with the engine running."

"None of them saw anything?"

"They *said* they didn't. And like I said, Perce and Keith, they're hard bastards. But then, so was Lomax. So's Marchant. So who really knows? But doesn't take a genius to work out what happened, does it? It's pretty fucking obvious."

"Is it?"

"Yeah, it is. Leon was valuable - the best cracksman south of the river. Marchant wouldn't have wanted to let him go - definitely wouldn't have wanted him to go running to a competitor. And I'm thinking he heard on the grapevine that Leon was looking for a way out. That's why he had Lomax lure him up there, had him make up some bullshit reason for getting Leon out of London. So he could kill him."

Rose rewound the camera footage, pausing on an unflattering close-up of Henderson - sweating, wild-eyed and straining at the manacles, a light dusting of cocaine still clinging to his philtrum.

"If I had to bet on an image most likely to grace the front page of the News of the World this weekend," Rose said, "it would be this one."

"You've sent them the video already?" El asked. If she had, she really *did* move fast - their first round of viewing had been a live feed, sent as it happened to Rose's home computer, and thereafter to the screen in front of them, from Karen's technologically-augmented lingerie.

Henderson, almost certainly, was still tied to the bed - beginning to wonder, perhaps, if there were release catches built somewhere into his restraints. Karen, meanwhile, would barely have had time to catch the night bus home.

"Not yet," Rose said. "But Hannah should be passing it along to a friend on the news desk first thing tomorrow. And don't worry," she added. "He won't be on his own like that for long. Karen left the front door of the flat unlocked, and I asked to put in a quick call to his wife as she was leaving - there's a phone box just around the corner. I'd be very surprised if Mrs Henderson wasn't in a taxi on her way there now. Although letting him out may not be the first item on her agenda."

At least this way she'll find out first-hand, El thought. And not from the Sunday papers.

"I feel a little bad for the guy," she said, picturing the scene unfolding - Mrs Henderson pacing the room, alternately shouting and crying and demanding answers, while Seymour - bound at the wrists, caged at the crotch, heart pounding a mile a minute from the coke still in his system - cast around for an explanation, *any* explanation, that would rationalise his predicament.

"He claimed £10,000 in expenses last year," Rose said, "and spent nearly all of it on sex workers. Feel sorry for *Mrs* Henderson, if you must - but really, he has no-one to blame but himself."

She looked up at the screen and smiled, her face softening.

"Seb would have found this *hysterical*," she added.

"He didn't like politicians?" El asked, curious. It was one of the few times she'd heard Rose reference her husband directly since they'd started the job; had assumed that, even three years on from his death, she found talking about him distressing, the loss of him an unhealed wound likely to be aggravated by any mention of him at all.

"He didn't like hypocrites," Rose said.

"And he thought Henderson was a hypocrite?"

"He thought men *like* Henderson were hypocrites - Tories especially. Politicians and editors and talking heads who'd sing the virtues of Back To Basics and Victorian Values and then sneak away to pick up strangers on the Heath or pay a teenage rent boy to shove a ball-gag in their mouths. He was at the Tory party conference in '87, up in Blackpool - I forget why now. Something for work, I expect. He heard Thatcher's speech, the one on education and morality and children being taught that they have an inalienable right to be gay. Came back absolutely seething."

This piece of information about Sebastian Winchester – *Sir* Sebastian Winchester – sat uncomfortably alongside the impression El realised she'd already formed of him: of an overgrown public schoolboy, commercially-minded and business-literate but solidly traditional at the core. A natural Thatcher voter; a champion of property rights and unfettered markets, albeit one with only a limited grasp of the ideological nuances of Thatcher*ism*.

"He had a lot of gay friends?" she asked. It seemed the most obvious solution to the misfit; men like Winchester, in her experience - or, at least, Winchester as she'd imagined him - tended not to develop liberal inclinations later in life without a precipitating incident or personal catalyst.

Rose squinted at her; creased her forehead, confused.

"Well... yes," she said slowly. "He *did*, certainly. We both did. But, I mean... that wasn't why it upset him. *Seb* was gay. Didn't Ruby tell you?"

OXFORD

1975

T he Old Moat looked innocuous from the outside - just another steep-
pitched Tudor Revival pub tucked away down a side street, a half-hour
walk from St Hilda's and light years away from the usual student haunts.
Nothing out of the ordinary.

If you didn't know what it was - who it catered for - then you'd have
walked right past it. Maybe even popped inside for a pint after work before
you realised.

It wasn't *obvious*.

Rose didn't go in - not at first. Just stood outside, on the other side of
the narrow road, watching from the doorway of a boarded-up tobacconist as
a steady trickle of men and women - though mostly men - went in and out.
And *they* weren't obvious either, she thought - at least, most of them weren't.
Perhaps some of the men wore shirts a little more fitted than you'd see on
the high street, blue jeans just that bit tighter around the buttocks than the
average, and some of the women had short hair and ties around their necks
- but so did some of the girls at college, even the ones with boyfriends. The
clothes on the own didn't mean anything, necessarily.

After 20 minutes in the doorway, when it was full dark and beginning to rain, she crossed the road and walked inside.

The pub was loud and heaving, every spare inch of space crammed with music and voices, limbs and bodies - bodies standing, talking, dancing, expressing waves of heat and a steady haze of cigarette smoke. By the door, two men were kissing, the back of one pressed up against the wall by the chest of the other - ordinary-looking men, middle-aged and paunchy, still wearing the suits they must have put on to go to the office that morning. She stared at them, then became aware of what she was doing and looked immediately away, blushing, in the opposite direction. Neither man seemed to notice - or if they noticed, to care.

She squeezed herself through the bodies, parting stiff denim and sweat-soaked nylon until she was close to the bar. The queue was three deep, the beer pumps barely visible through the sea of heads blocking her way. She stared down at the ground as she waited her turn to be served, at the sticky burgundy carpet under her boots - determinedly *not* looking up, *not* looking around.

Something - some*one* - tapped her on the shoulder.

She spun around.

A shaggy-haired blond boy stood behind her, smiling good-naturedly.

"We've met before, haven't we?" he said, loudly enough that she could hear him over the competing background noises. He sounded, to her, like every other boy at Oxford: polite, upper-crust, undeniably southern. Soft.

She studied his face, trying to place it but failing.

"Last month," he said helpfully. "At Lance Keaton's party. I was Bowie, you were Liza in Cabaret."

The party, at least, she remembered: a fancy dress thing in a house off-campus, hosted by a braying third year boy done up - appropriately, she'd felt at the time - as a pantomime horse. She'd gone, reluctantly, at the insistence of a girl from her corridor, an anxious social secretary type who couldn't bear the thought of Rose - or anyone - opting out of an invitation, and who'd pressed upon Rose not only the importance of *making an effort* with her costume, but a cane-and-black hat combination that had made Sally Bowles the most straightforward look to achieve at short notice.

Unfortunately, there had been at least three David Bowies at the party, that she'd counted - all of them sporting the same orange wig and lighting bolt makeup.

"You don't remember me at all, do you?" he said. "I should have known, in that get-up. Teach *me* to try to butch it up in a house full of straight boys. Perhaps next time I'll go as Cleopatra."

"Elizabeth Taylor or Amanda Barrie?" asked Rose, and immediately blushed again - understanding a moment too late that a boy like that, with an accent like that, was a more likely audience for Dryden's All For Love than for Carry On Cleo.

The choice of options, though, seemed to delight him.

"Oh, Amanda, absolutely!" he hooted. "Always Amanda. Liz is so *po-faced*, isn't she? So serious. No, I prefer..."

He stopped, mid-sentence, and seemed to take her in, to catalogue and name her - the bright red hair, stylelessly centre-parted and reaching almost to her hips; the patterned ankle-length skirt; the long-sleeved *marinière*, the most considered of her wardrobe choices, modelled after Jean Seberg in *A bout de souffle*.

"You're new, aren't you?" he said.

"I've not been here before, no," she answered, ignoring the obvious subtext of the question and sounding, to her ears, more conspicuously northern - more clanging and leaden - than she ever had at home.

"You don't have to be embarrassed," the boy said. "We were all new once. Who brought you?"

Not *who are you here with?*, she thought - *who brought you?* As if you couldn't just *be there*; couldn't just turn up unannounced. No, you had to be "brought," had to be *shown around* - introduced to the regulars like a debutante at a coming-out ball, a new initiate at a secret society.

"Nobody," she said, mustering defiance. "I'm here on my own."

He looked her up and down again, reappraising her.

"Gosh," he said. "You're brave. It took my friend Anthony at least three tries to persuade me to walk through the door. And that was after I'd sunk the best part of a bottle of creme de cacao."

She shrugged, hoping for the appearance of nonchalance; in truth, she couldn't conceive of a single person in her current life who might suggest The Old Moat as an appropriate venue for a night on the town. Nor anyone, unless she'd very much misjudged the impression they had of her, who might think she'd be open to the suggestion.

"Who are *you* here with?" she said.

"Funny you should ask. I'm here alone myself tonight. Well... perhaps not *entirely* alone. But certainly amenable to a change of company."

He leaned in to her until his mouth was almost level with her ear, drowning out the overlapping conversations and the opening chords of Metal Guru.

"That chap to your left," he said, "the one in the grey tank top - *don't look*! He's been following me around all evening, absolutely *desperate* to catch my eye, and just between us, it's starting to make me a touch uneasy."

Her eyes flicked left, as surreptitiously as she could make them, her peripheral vision taking in the man in the tank-top. He was plain, average-looking; hawk-nosed, face slightly rubbery, thinning hair combed unprepossessingly over his crown. And he was *old* - at least 35, maybe closer to 40. Not an obvious match at all for the pretty blond boy.

"I've spent the last hour dodging him," said the boy, "but everywhere I go, there he is, watching! It's positively *sinister*."

He mock-shuddered.

"I don't suppose," he said, as if the idea had suddenly occurred to him, though Rose wondered later if he'd been planning to suggest it since he saw her queuing at the bar, "you'd like to be my bodyguard for the night, to help fend him off? Since *you're* not here with anyone, and *I'm* not here with anyone... And who knows?" he added, an impish twinkle in his bright blue eyes. "Maybe he'll think you're my girlfriend."

The spent the remainder of the night wedged together into a corner by the toilets, Rose leaning for support against a drinks-shelf as sticky as the carpet underfoot. Over the course of three hours of long and meandering discussion, she discovered that the boy, Seb - *Sebastian Winchester, Baronet-in-waiting*, as he'd dubbed himself with a faux-pompous flourish after his fourth pint - was a second year at Wadham and, like her, was reading History.

"Not that I could tell you anything *about* History," he said. "I expect the barman knows more about Bismarck than I do. I wanted to do English, or go to New York to make films, but the paterfamilias had his own ideas."

Seb's father, Rose understood, had been some kind of newspaper man before his retirement, an influential Citizen Kane type with a substantial inheritance and an aristocratic title regarded as worthless by anyone who actually cared about the peerage. From Seb's description, he swung to the right of Enoch Powell politically, vehemently and vocally decrying everything from Commonwealth immigration to the necessity of levying taxes.

"I think it might kill him, if he ever found out about me," Seb said. "Or *he'd* kill *me*. Either way, you can be certain only one of us would come out alive."

Once, he told her, during his morning constitutional around his Hertfordshire estate, Winchester Senior had stumbled upon the head gardener - incidentally Seb's first crush - naked from the waist up and locked in a passionate, Lady Chatterley-style embrace with a male houseguest in the groundskeeper's cottage. Sir Henry had banished the guest from his home, and immediately thereafter dismissed the gardener, without pay and without a reference - but not before he'd beaten the man almost into unconsciousness with the metal end of his walking stick.

"Do your parents know about you?" he asked Rose.

She'd expected the question; had prepared her response in advance.

"No," she answered. "But I don't think they'd mind much. I think they might've known a few people, you know... like us."

"Gay people," said Seb. "You can say it, you know. The *word* won't bite. So if they wouldn't mind, why haven't you told them?"

"I don't want to give them any more to worry about," she said honestly.

She changed the subject, and Seb let her.

By closing time, she could have written his biography - schools, boyfriends, the mountain-climbing holiday he was booked to go on over the Christmas break - and they'd made plans to meet for breakfast the following morning.

"He adopted me as his best friend more or less thereafter," Rose told El, pouring them both a second glass of Pinot Noir. "I barely had a say in the matter."

They'd moved from the TV room to the kitchen, and something, it seemed to El, had changed between them - or changed in Rose - somewhere along the way. Maybe it was that she was talking about something other than work, El thought; something personal, something other than Marchant. Maybe this was what Rose was actually like, when she wasn't running a crew.

She'd even put an ashtray on the table so that El could smoke.

"Everyone thought we were a couple, of course," she continued. "Not close friends or any of the people who *really* knew Seb, but everyone else. And we played along with it, it has to be said - let them all think that we were going out for a candlelit dinner the nights we went to the Moat, or that one of us had stayed over in the other's room when he'd gone home with a boy, or I'd met a girl. He used to say it was hilarious, the assumptions that people made - that he enjoyed watching them get it all so wrong. But also, I think, we did it because it was easier for both of us to pretend. He wouldn't have to risk the wrath of Sir Henry with a girlfriend on the scene, and I wouldn't have anyone asking any intrusive questions or poking around in my private life."

"Sure," El said neutrally. She'd heard variations on Rose's story a dozen times, a hundred: from women she'd dated, women she'd slept with, women she'd met on the job who'd elected to see her, or the *her* she'd been that day - the vet, the calligrapher, the wedding planner - as their confessor.

She hadn't been expecting to hear it from *Rose*, admittedly. But she couldn't say that it had shocked her, either - even if the revelation of her lavender marriage raised yet more questions, added yet another layer of mystery to *this* job, *this* setup.

And if Ruby *knew*, why hadn't she said anything - especially when she'd been happy to tell El about Justin D'Amboise's murder, Leon Baxter's disappearance, Kat's stolen casino chips? What made *Rose's* secrets so different from anyone else's?

"I expect you think Seb was no better than Seymour Henderson," said Rose. "Saying one thing and doing another. But I can promise you, he wasn't a hypocrite. He never lied to anyone directly, especially not after he left college and Sir Henry's grip on him loosened. Everyone who mattered knew about us."

"But you stayed married? To each other?"

"We did. And we were mostly happy together, I think. Obviously it wasn't a conventional marriage, in the way that word tends to be understood. But I'm sure you know yourself - there's more than one way to be married to someone. When he asked me, all those years ago... It really wasn't so hard to say yes."

She hadn't seen the proposal coming.

They'd been living together for a year when he asked - splitting the rent on a two-bed flat in Chalk Farm while he got Fairlight Media off the ground and she ran the back-office of a gallery in Bethnal Green. Sir Henry, true to form, was outraged at the cohabitation - though not, as Rose pointed out on the rare occasions the old man had come to visit, as outraged as he *would* have been, had he been privy to the reality of the arrangement.

("I suppose we should count ourselves lucky that *your* parents never make it down to London," he'd say in response.

"I suppose so," she'd reply, vaguely).

Seb had just split up with a boyfriend, a theatrical agent with a burgeoning barbiturate problem; she hadn't had sex, let alone any kind of meaningful relationship, since her final year of university.

"We should just get married," he said. They were cooking, chopping vegetables for a salad; she was only half-listening to him talk, her attention instead on the radio, where a stoic-sounding woman was reporting on a suspicious fire at a Stepney tower-block.

"What?" she asked.

"I *said*, we should get married. Make all this official."

She pulled herself out of the trance the news report had lulled her into; snapped back to the here and now.

"It wouldn't work," she said, deadpan. "A man like you could never stay pinned down to just one woman."

"I'm serious."

She put down the knife she'd been using to dice the onions.

"Then you've lost your mind. What you've just suggested is completely insane."

"Is it, though?" he said, with some of the firmness of conviction he adopted in negotiations with the magazine's backers. "We're practically married already - look at us."

"And you don't think there might be a flaw or two in your plan?"

"I'm not asking for *fidelity*. Or that we *sleep* together."

"Oh, well, in *that* case..."

"I want security, Rosie. I want someone to come home to."

"You already come home to me. We are, right this second, at home together."

"For now. Until you meet some... I don't know, some tortured artist who makes her own jewellery and keeps her own chickens, and the two of you run off to Brighton together to open a bookshop."

"She sounds very busy. Will she even have time for me? Or does she need someone to help her feed the chickens?"

"I told you, I'm *serious*! I want to settle down with someone, and you're the best person I know. The only person I can actually imagine myself growing old with."

He *was* serious, she thought.

She put her hand on his, gently.

"Seb, darling," she said, "you'll meet someone. I promise. And he'll be handsome, and kind, and funny, and he'll love you to death and you'll love him to death. *He'll* be the one you go home to. And I'll feel like a very poor substitute by comparison."

"He won't be you, though, will he? *You're* kind and funny, and I *already* love you to death. And I know you're going to bring it up again, that we don't have sex. But how many married couples *do*, with each other? And I'd never ask you to hide *your* mistresses. I'll invite them over for dinner myself."

"And if one of us were to meet someone we wanted to be with, be with properly? Not whatever hypothetical poultry-farming silversmith you've already paired me off with - a *real* person."

"Then we'd cross that bridge when we came to it. Perhaps we'd have them move in with us, if they wanted to. And we could always get divorced, if we absolutely had to."

"You make it sound so reasonable."

"Isn't it, though? People marry for far more mercenary reasons than genuine affection. I'm fairly sure my mother only married my father for his money. Which reminds me - there's another incentive, too. A more material one. I didn't mention it before, because... well, frankly I wasn't sure how you'd react. But you know I had lunch with Father last week?"

"Vaguely."

"Right. Well, he... that is, he made me an offer. Said he'd give me a leg-up, plough a bit of capital into Fairlight. Enough to get us on a really even keel."

"Oh, Seb! That's wonderful."

"Hold your horses. It is, and it isn't. It wasn't a gift - there's a condition, strings attached. He'll give me the money - but only if I, and I quote, 'make an honest woman of you.' I don't think he can bear the thought of his son and heir living in sin."

She couldn't think of a single thing to say.

"We wouldn't have to lie to anyone," he continued, filling the silence. "I mean, we'd have to lie to *him*, obviously - but when has it ever mattered what *he* thinks? And to your parents too, I suppose. Although... don't they already think we're a couple?"

They did, and he knew it.

"But as for everyone else, our friends - we'd just tell them we were doing it to keep the old man sweet. They know what he's like - it's not as if they'd judge us for it. And in any case - I *want* to be married to you. I love you. I want you to be my wife."

"I don't want his money," she said abruptly.

"And I don't blame you in the slightest. But what about *my* money? Would you take *that*? The amount he's talking about - it would make an enormous difference to the business. It would take us to another league - me and you, not just Fairlight. We could buy somewhere better than *this* place, somewhere much more liveable. You could leave the gallery and do something you actually enjoy - I know you hate it there, don't even try to deny it. And all we'd have to do is slip into our ballgowns and turn up to a party in our honour."

"I hate parties."

"I know you do. So how about this? Say you'll marry me, ditch plain old Rosemary Ackroyd for *Lady Sebastian Winchester* - and you have my word, I'll never ask you to go to another. You can spend your every waking moment until the day you die buying Old Masters and cataloguing them down in the cellar of your mansion, and I promise you, as a gentleman and a scholar - I'll never say a *thing*."

***

"The wedding was the following February, 1981," Rose told El. "Sir Henry came through with the money almost as soon as we'd announced the engagement, so by the time we got married, Fairlight was doing well, and we'd bought ourselves a house. *This* house, in fact. And how's this for irony? When the wedding actually happened, Seb had already met John, and I'd started seeing Suzie..."

"John and Suzie?" El asked, recalling the obituary she'd read in the paper: *he and Rose honeymooned in the mountain ranges of Denali, Alaska in early 1982, in the company of his best man, barrister John Richmond, and her bridesmaid, the writer Susan Hayes.*

"John was Seb's partner," Rose said. "They got together just before the wedding; they were still together when Seb died, though neither of them cared very much for monogamy. And to pre-empt the obvious question: yes, he was fine with the arrangement. He was a junior barrister - a QC, eventually - and he didn't feel able to come out in chambers. This was the early 80s, remember: the real AIDS crisis hadn't hit then, it wasn't really being talked about in this country, but the law was - still is - a very conservative world. He'd have lost clients; possibly lost his job. It was very much in his interests for his lover to be some woman's devoted husband, rather than a known gay man; it let them hide in plain sight. And we got on famously, which was a lovely bonus. It meant things weren't too excruciating when he and Seb and I - and Suzie, back then - would all go out for supper, and I'd slip away and leave them to it after the main course."

"And Suzie?"

Rose shook her head.

"She and I didn't last," she said. "Again: not because of Seb. There were no issues *there*. Suzie was a semi-public figure herself, a children's author - you'll have seen her books in the shops, even if you've never had cause to buy one. She always said she couldn't be a lesbian and write the kind of stories she did, for the audiences she did. The press would have eviscerated her. So it suited her very well to be a close friend of the family, or whatever it was they called her."

"Here's another layer of irony for you: children were exactly the reason we separated. Seb and I were always clear that we wanted a child, and John was perfectly happy to be involved in raising Sophie at a remove, as a godfather or an unofficial uncle - we'd always intended to tell her the truth about us all, or some version of it, once she was old enough to grasp the complexities. But Suzie..."

"Didn't want kids?"

"Didn't even want to be *around* them. Rather unexpected, given her genre of choice, but there you are. She was fine when Sophie was just an *idea*; I'm not sure she took it very seriously to begin with. But when we started to talk about clinics and cycles and blood tests... then, I'm afraid, it all became a little too real for her, and she bolted."

"But John stayed?"

"To the very end. He and I had dinner together the night Seb... the night we found him. Seb had stayed in with Sophie - he'd been feeling ill all day, complaining about dizziness and heart palpitations, but quite honestly, both John and I had been inclined to think he was being a drama queen. He was *terrible* at being unwell; he was very fit, physically, so it didn't happen often, but any time he had a cold or a stomach upset, he'd behave as if he'd been stricken with TB or cholera. An absolute Camille of a patient."

She smiled again, affectionately, at the thought of him.

"It was the first night out I'd had in ages - it's so incredibly difficult to go anywhere when you have children - so I relished it. I had three courses, coffee, a cheese-plate, everything. It was after midnight when we got home. John popped out for a cigarette while I went to check on Sophie, and then the two of us crept up the stairs together to look in on Seb. We'd been drinking with dinner; not an enormous amount, but enough to make us silly, to make us think it would be a *scream* to sneak up and surprise him in his sickbed. We didn't even turn on the light as we were creeping into the bedroom. I really wish we had."

His skin was cool. Not cold, exactly, but *chilled*, reminding her - to her horror and disgust - of the feel of a plate of deli meat, left out on the side for guests to pick over at a buffet.

He was mostly naked - he always slept naked - but there were socks on his feet, preposterously, as if he hadn't quite been able to muster the energy to take them off before he fell into bed. No amount of shaking roused him.

John seemed to understand the truth of it before she did - pulling her away from Seb, away from Seb's *body*, as soon as it was obvious that no amount of shaking would help.

"He's dead, Rose," John said, voice flat. "He's dead. Please, stop."

They stood over the body for what felt like hours, clutching at each other like frightened schoolkids.

"You have to leave," she told John eventually, when she began to come back to herself.

"What?"

"Leave. You have to. I'll need to call the police, and they mustn't find you here when they arrive."

He didn't answer - knowing, she thought, that she was right, but not wanting to acknowledge the fact. Not wanting to be *that* man - the kind of man who would crawl away like a coward to save his own career, who would leave a woman on her own to deal with the aftermath of a death. Her husband's - *their* husband's - death.

"Go now," she said, surprising herself with her composure, the clarity of her thinking, "and there'll be no questions. No one turning up at your chambers to ask what you were doing in the bedroom of a married couple in the middle of the night. No one wondering to themselves why they've never seen you with a woman, why you've never been married yourself. Stay, and it will come out, all of it. Everything about us, about our lives. You know it will. And with Seb's name, and yours - I wouldn't be surprised if it made the papers, too. The gossip columns."

"I can't just... go," he said quietly.

"Yes, you can. I'll tell anyone who asks that you dropped me at the door after dinner and went straight home."

"Rose..."

"Please, John. Now. Before we wake Sophie. I don't want her to see this." He nodded, ashamed.

"Please call me," he said as he left. "As soon as you can."

She promised him that she would. Wondered, as she heard the front door click closed behind her, whose reputation she was really protecting. Whose privacy.

"Hypertrophic cardiomyopathy," Rose said. "That was what I was told, afterwards. An enlarged heart. Hereditary, and sudden-onset. Seb would have had no idea he had it - it's the type of thing you usually see in young marathon runners or football players, boys who collapse on the pitch in the middle of a match."

She pushed the ashtray, now half-full, back towards El - a cigarette still burning in her own hand. To El's surprise, she'd smoked at least three of her own as she'd talked - Gauloises, dark and tarry, taken from a packet she evidently kept hidden from Sophie on the highest shelf of a cupboard.

"It was all so absurd," she said softly. "A heart attack at 38, for God's sake. He tomcats his way around New York and San Francisco in the middle of a bloody plague, climbs Kilimanjaro at the weekends - and it's a *heart attack* that gets him."

"John's never recovered - Seb was the love of his life. I wonder sometimes if he was the love of *mine*. Having him there, he and Sophie - I think perhaps it kept me grounded. *Tethered* to something, you know? And when he was gone..."

She took a long drag on her cigarette; pulled the smoke deep into her lungs.

"When he was gone," she said, "there was nothing to stop me; no one to tell me I ought not to do something. And the plans I had, the... darker impulses - there was less and less reason *not* to act on them. Which is how, I suppose, we've ended up here."

BANKSIDE

1996

W hat you are," El told Marchant, in Alison Miller's voice, "is a clean slate. You're James Marchant, entrepreneur - but you're also *not* Seymour Henderson. You're *not* affiliated with the Tories, with sleaze or corruption. You have no baggage. And the reputation you *do* have, as a concerned citizen with no obvious Westminster connections, is a distinct advantage here. You're successful. You're independently wealthy. There's no question of you entering politics to line your own pockets, because those pockets are already straining at the seams with the money that you earned with your own two hands."

"And that's our tagline, is it?" asked Marchant.

He's playing his cards close to his chest, El thought. He likes the idea. He doesn't want me to *know* he likes the idea - but that's a Duchenne smile in the corners of his eyes, and he can't quite keep his mouth from turning up at the edges. He's excited.

"It's our *position*," she said. "The essential proposition at the heart of your campaign. Everything we do strategically stems therefrom."

"And how does that look, in practice?"

"As a first step, a soft launch. A very intimate press conference announcing your candidacy - small, just a handful of trusted journalists. I have a few lined up for us, once the Henderson story breaks. I've also pre-emptively drafted an announcement speech for the event. It's succinct, but given the context, I think brevity will work in our favour. We need you assertive - confident, but not loquacious. Chatty men make voters suspicious - at best they see them as apologetic and effeminate, and at worst as habitual liars. Which reminds me: we'll also need to talk about speech tags and hedging."

"Hedging? And what the hell are speech tags?"

"Unnecessary rhetorical questions tacked on to statements - a way of asking your audience for confirmation. Don't you...? and Isn't it...? - that kind of thing. They make you seem weak, so we'll need you to avoid them - although you don't strike me as a man who looks to others for assurance, so perhaps we needn't worry. And you can take "hedging" as a proxy for any sort of conditional language - all those little modifiers and self-deprecations and uncertainties that tell other people we're not sure about whatever it is that we're saying. Whenever you speak, hereafter, you speak authoritatively. The public won't trust you if you sound like you don't trust yourself."

"This is all just style. What about content? What's the substance of this speech?"

"The style *is* the substance, at this stage of the game. Policies come later, if they become necessary. Do you think anyone wants to hear, once Henderson resigns, how you propose to mend potholes or keep the library open on a Thursday afternoon? No. They want to see that you're not a deviant, and they want to believe that you care - about them and about Silvertown. They want reassurance that you won't squander their money on prostitutes or appear on the cover of the Telegraph with a bin bag over your head and an orange in your mouth. And they want to know that you'll listen to them - that you'll be there to receive them when they come to your surgery to complain about the construction work next door, about the care assistant they suspect is stealing from their elderly mother. They want the appearance of sincerity."

"I'm sure I can manage that."

"I'm sure you can," said El, with feeling.

She hadn't wanted to watch the rest of Ricky Lomax's video testimony - to wade through hour upon hour more of the horrors Marchant had committed and Lomax had willingly concealed, recollected with the same bloodless detachment the big man had applied to the disposal of her mother's broken body. But she had to know: not because of any need to satisfy a curiosity of her own, but because preventing herself from knowing, consciously avoiding information about the mark would have been idiocy on any job. Dangerous, even. You didn't go into a con blind; you read, and you learned, and you tried to understand the mark's buttons and levers and pressure points, however personally repugnant you found them. You did the homework.

Rose had started chronologically, helpfully for El's purposes - beginning the interview with questions about Lomax's early days with Marchant, his first exposure to the true nature of his employer and the real demands of the position he'd accepted.

"The first time?" Lomax said, responding to a query asked offscreen. "'67 - July '67. Month or two after I started with him. She was one of his girlfriends. He always had two or three on the go at once, you learned that quick - always out in the suburbs, away from Liz and the kids. Away from Saul too - Saul Bellman, Liz's old man. He was still going then. Cantankerous old bastard. But it was his money in the business, one of his houses they were living in, so the boss had to keep him sweet, keep him on-side. Wouldn't have been surprised if he was a bit afraid of him, too. Or at least afraid of the power old

Saul had over him. The boss never liked feeling beholden to anyone, know what I mean?"

"Anyway, this girl - Katie something. I'd had her in the car with me once or twice before, driven her up west to go shopping. Nice kid, pretty. I was 20 then, and she couldn't have been no older, not from the way she talked."

"One Tuesday lunchtime, he tells me to drive out to check on her, make sure she's alright. Doesn't say why. He's got her stashed in a ground-floor bedsit out Ealing way. Perivale, up near the Hoover Building. I ask if I need to take one of the lads with me, if there's gonna be any trouble. Not from her, she's about six stone soaking wet in her drawers, but sometimes there's brothers or angry boyfriends or an old girl with a rolling pin to think about. But no, he says; don't take no-one with you. Go, but go on your own."

He rang the doorbell to the girl's bedsit, but there was no answer - not at first. On the second ring he heard footsteps in the entrance hall, and then the front door opened a few inches, a whey-faced old man in a long white coat crouching behind it.

"I'm here for Katie," Lomax said, without preamble.

"Did Mr Marchant send you?" the old man asked, voice tissue-paper thin.

Lomax didn't bother to answer; just brushed the old man aside by his frail shoulders and pushed his way in. The door to the girl's bedsit was unlocked.

"Please, before you go in there..." said the old man, but Lomax ignored him; stepped into the flat.

He was almost sick when he saw her.

He'd seen bodies crushed before - as a kid in Borstal, then in the ring and out on the cobbles, boys and men with busted teeth, split ears, ivory bone jutting up through torn skin. But never women; never girls.

She was alive, just - he could see her chest moving, *up-down-up*, with every breath she struggled for. But the blood was everywhere, permeating everything: the sheet that half-covered her, the mattress underneath her, the air he was breathing. And it didn't smell the way blood ought to - wasn't sharp or penny-copper like a smashed nose or a shredded lip but rich and meaty like an abattoir, like a butcher's shop in summer.

There was blood in other places, too. On the dining table, the white sheet on top drenched brown from it; spattered in drops and smears across the lino floor in such a way as to suggest that she'd been moved *from* the table to the bed.

By the old bloke? Lomax thought. It didn't seem possible. He had to be 70 if he was a day.

"What the fuck have you done to her?" he said, turning to face him. The man shuddered; mouth trembling and hands shaking, as if the very fact of Lomax was a physical threat.

"An accident," he said, almost crying. "Only an accident. She was sedated, but she jerked upright when the scalpel went in, and I lost my grip..."

"He was a doctor," Lomax told the camera. "Or he'd *been* a doctor, way back when. By the time I met him, he'd been struck off 10 years. Got a bit too fond of his own prescription pad was what I heard. That's when he started working with the girls, the ones who'd got themselves in trouble."

"He performed terminations?" Rose asked, audible but unseen.

"You didn't hear the word said," he replied, through another round of coughing. "Nobody talked about "terminations" or "abortions" or what have you the way they do now. But yeah, that was him, the old geezer. An abortion doctor."

"And Marchant paid him to work on this girl - on Katie?" said Rose, seeming to make a point of using the girl's name, of humanising her.

"He must've, mustn't he?" said Lomax, wiping his lips on his sleeve. "I mean, I didn't exactly *ask* him afterwards, but it was pretty bleeding obvious from the setup what had happened. He wouldn't have wanted her walking around carrying his kid if he'd knocked her up, would he? He'd got too much to lose. He'd have had to have dealt with the problem, even if it meant throwing a bit of Saul Bellman's money at it."

"So what happened next? After you found her?"

"Not a hell of a lot, at first. The old bloke was running round like a headless chicken, saying it was an accident, wasn't his fault, his hand slipped - all that. And meanwhile the girl's just lying there on the bed, bleeding to death."

"You didn't try to help her?"

"What do you take me for? Of course I fucking did. I gave her water, tried to get her to eat something. Got her to hold a towel between her legs to try to stop the blood. But I couldn't exactly call for an ambulance, could I? Not without landing myself back inside, and the boss with me."

Rose muttered something, the words lost in a crackle of static.

"It took about an hour," Lomax said, voice fainter than it had been. "For a while she was sweating and shivering, then her lips and her fingers lost their colour, starting turning blue. Then she just... stopped moving. Stopped breathing."

"It was an accident," the old man repeated, dazed. "Only an accident."

Lomax didn't panic. He was paid to *not* panic - to keep a clear head, assess the situation, decide what needed doing and do it, quickly.

"She got a phone?" he asked the old man.

"I think I saw one in the corridor," said the man automatically. "But you can't ring for the police!" he added. "Please, don't ring for the police."

Lomax stepped into the man's space; grabbed the lapels of his white coat and pulled, so that their faces were almost touching and the man's feet were raised an inch off the ground.

"Do I look like I want the police here, you stupid cunt?" he growled. "Do I?"

The old man didn't respond. Lomax let his clenched fists open, letting go of his lapels, and the man crumpled to a heap on the blood-streaked floor.

Lomax took off his shoes and walked softly out into the entrance hall, feet making barely a sound as they struck the carpet. He closed the door to the bedsit behind him; considered using one of the picks in his workbag to lock the man inside, then thought better of it. The last thing he needed was attention, and the old man seemed the type to scream and shout and work himself into a state, to bang on the walls and bring the neighbours calling.

He scanned the corridor. Saw the man was right - there was a phone there, right in the corner, balanced on a dusty stack of old newspapers.

He called Marchant at the office.

"Deal with it," Marchant told him, after Lomax had updated him - very briefly, and very quietly - on the situation in the bedsit.

"How?" Lomax asked - not familiar, then, with Marchant's foibles, with the gap between what he said and what he expected you to infer. With his obsessive compulsion to tidy up loose ends; to minimise risks to himself, his family life and standing, by systematically removing the evidence of his sins and peccadillos, his mistakes.

"By getting rid of them," he said. "How else?"

Lomax was startled; thought maybe he'd misunderstood something, somewhere down the line.

"Both of them?" he asked, not expecting the answer to be yes. "Him *and* her?"

"Yes," said Marchant, irritated at having to clarify. "Both of them."

"What did you do with them?" Rose asked.

"*She* was easy," said Lomax, fiddling with the cannula in his hand. "All I had to do with her was wait 'til it got dark, wrap her up in a bin-bag and drive her out to Uxbridge Hospital. It's closed down now, but there was a medical waste incinerator on site. I used that one more than once."

"And the doctor?"

"Bit more challenging. See, I'd made a name for myself before I started with Marchant - served a bit of time, got a bit of a reputation as a bad lad, a hard man. It's why they took me on. But I'd never *done* anyone, you know what I mean? Never killed no one. And I tell you, it ain't as easy as you think it'll be, that first time."

He had to do it, he knew that. It was part of the job. People had expectations. And it wasn't as if he had any *moral* objection to doing him, was it? A bloke who stuck knives up young girls for money, so old he was probably close to pegging it anyway?

But the reality of it - the feel of the old man's chicken-neck on his thumb pads, the squawking sounds he made as the rope tightened round his throat, the piss streaming down onto Lomax's socks when the man's bladder gave... none of that was fun. He wasn't sure he wanted to do it again.

And all the boss said, when Lomax rang him that night to tell him it was done, it was sorted, was: *good. That's one less thing to worry about, isn't it?*

Is that how he thinks of me, El wondered - as someone he'll eventually need to worry about, a loose end he'll eventually need to tie up?

"The best thing you can do for now," she told Marchant, with all of Alison Miller's self-assurance, "is prepare for the press conference. When Henderson resigns - and it will be soon - we'll have to move very quickly. I'll need you to be ready."

Marchant smiled - faintly, humourlessly.

"I'm sure I've told you," he said, "that I don't have much of an appetite for waiting."

"And as I'm sure you've heard many times in return," she replied sharply, "some things take time to come to fruition. This is one of those things. You aren't *really* going to tell me that a few days is too long for you to keep your powder dry?"

It was a response she knew would antagonise him, just condescending and borderline-emasculating enough to put him on edge.

"Do you always speak this way to the people paying your salary?" he asked, the pitch of his speech dropping an octave in suppressed anger.

"Only when they're paying me to *give them advice*," she said, not rising to him.

He stood up from his chair, getting ready to shout, or admonish her, or end her contract altogether - and then, his eyes fixing on something over her shoulder, sat down again, silently.

"Have I come in in the middle of something?" said a voice behind her - a woman's voice, dry and steeped in money.

"Not at all," said Marchant, changing gear to shift with no apparent effort into his usual tone of good-humoured superiority. "We were just finishing up."

El turned around. Behind her, in the same severe eye-makeup she'd worn in the photo El had seen but with a t-shirt now advertising Nirvana rather than the Sisters of Mercy, was Marchant's youngest child - his daughter, Harriet.

She looked from El to her father - scrutinising them both, weighing up the dynamic between them with undisguised interest.

"Should I wait, in that case?" she asked him.

"No need," said El, standing. "I'm on my way out. Let's catch up later, shall we?" she added, addressing Marchant but walking to the door and out into the corridor without waiting to hear his reply.

She felt Harriet's eyes on her - curious, appraising - until the moment she stepped into the lift.

ST LUKE'S HOSPITAL, ISLINGTON

1996

T he waiting area was uncomfortable, a shabby, humid testament to poor design: plastic chairs hard and ergonomically unsound, flakes of sickly pink paint peeling from the walls, thermostat turned up feverishly high. Its unpleasantness felt to El deliberate, engineered - a way, perhaps, to deter visitors from camping out there any longer than was absolutely necessary.

If it *was* deliberate, she thought, then the strategy was working. Besides her and Rose, only three other people occupied the twenty or so seats available: a crying boy, barely school-aged, held tight in the arms of a red-eyed man with a shaved head, and ten feet away, by the automatic doors, an old woman in a headscarf, staring blankly at the vending machine on the opposite side of the room.

"How much longer, do you think?" Rose asked, scratching nervously at her wrist. She'd covered her hair with one of Karen's wool caps and borrowed a pair of Ruby's sunglasses, but had made few concessions otherwise to modifying her appearance. El, conversely, was unrecognisable, every last vestige of herself - and of Alison Miller - buried under foundation, heavy biker boots, a short auburn wig and a grey zip-up top with a hood, shapeless enough to give no hint of the type or even the gender of the body inside.

If Marchant or one of his men came to the hospital - and she thought it unlikely, though not impossible that they would - they'd find nothing in her that they recognised.

"You know as much as I do," El replied, keeping her tone carefully neutral to avoid drawing attention.

"You think it's my fault," Rose said. "What happened to her - you think that I'm responsible in some way."

"Now isn't the time for this conversation."

"I would never have told her to go, if I'd had even the slightest sense that something like this would happen."

"You don't have to justify yourself to me."

"Obviously I do, if you're going to sit in judgement of me like this."

"I'm not judging you," El lied.

Rose's shoulders sagged.

"I should have listened to Ruby, shouldn't I?" she said.

"You and me both," said El.

They were back in the kitchen at Ledbury Road, all of them but Karen, when he'd called.

"It's mine," Kat had said, pointing to the mobile Karen had bought her specifically for the job, the one whose number she'd given out to Marchant at Chestnut House.

None of them had expected him to ring it.

"What do I do?" she asked, to nobody in particular, as the little black box beeped and chirruped a digital approximation of a quacking duck - Karen's idea of a joke, El assumed.

"Answer it," said Rose quickly.

Kat didn't hesitate.

"Jasmine Philips," she said to the voice on the line - crisp but breathless, an exaggerated aural picture of well-bred femininity, and entirely unlike herself. "How can I help you?"

She's not bad, El thought. Not bad at all.

The others, she saw, were watching Kat intently, their prior activities on pause - ears pricked, pens left to lie on notepads, coffee cups suspended between hands and mouths.

"Yes," Kat was saying. "Yes, of course I remember. So lovely to hear from you."

"What does he want?" mouthed Ruby.

Kat mimed a circular writing motion in the air with her thumb and forefinger.

Ruby passed her a pen; laid a pad of paper on the table next to her.

He wants to meet, Kat wrote, holding the pad up for the others to see.

Rose picked up a pen of her own.

Meet him, she wrote.

Kat looked at her for confirmation that this was really what she'd meant, what she really wanted Kat to do. Rose nodded; Kat shrugged, a wordless *if you say so* gesture, then nodded back.

"This evening sounds great," she told Marchant. "Where did you have in mind?"

"What the bloody hell are you playing at?" hissed Ruby to Rose. "This wasn't in the plan."

"He thinks she's a journalist," Rose whispered. "He must want her at the press conference. A sympathetic ear for his campaign."

"I don't like it," said Ruby. "El's already told him she's got him a load of them lined up. What does he need more for?"

"Because he likes control?" said Rose. "That shouldn't be new information."

But aren't you the one, El thought, who keeps reminding everyone that he's dangerous, that we need to watch ourselves around him? Maybe a little caution wouldn't be the end of the world?

"I can't say I know the place," Kat was telling Marchant, "but I can certainly find it. What kind of time?"

"I don't like it," said Ruby again.

8pm tonight, Kat wrote on the pad. *His country place - nr Berkhamsted. Still yes?*

Still yes, wrote Rose.

The boy had stopped crying; had fallen asleep on the chest of the red-eyed man, who pulled intermittently at the loose skin of his cheeks to keep himself awake. The old woman in the headscarf kept her vigil by the entrance, barely blinking.

"I thought we'd miss something, if she didn't go," Rose said, somewhere between apologetic and defensive. "Something that we'd need to know."

El couldn't bring herself to reply.

"Have you lost all the sense God gave you, girl?" Ruby had said to Rose, after Kat hung up on Marchant. "He calls her out to his place in the middle of bloody nowhere for no good reason I can make out, and you tell her you'll do her a packed lunch and pay for her petrol?"

"I don't want us kept in the dark," Rose said evenly. "If he has his own agenda for this press conference, one that El isn't privy to, wouldn't you rather we all knew *now*, rather than have it ambush us later?"

"And you reckon he'll tell *her*, do you?" said Ruby, with a nod to Kat. "Some young tart who tried it on with him at his club? No offence," she added.

"None taken," said Kat wryly. "I do a pretty decent tart, if I say so myself."

"I think we'll know more if she meets him than we will if she doesn't," said Rose. "And I think that any information we can gather is potentially valuable to us. Which is why I'm suggesting that she go."

"But darling," said Sita to Rose, speaking for the first time since Marchant's call, "are you not concerned that there might perhaps be an element of risk here, for Katherine if not for the rest of us? She may be the only person able to connect him to Henderson - El's involvement notwithstanding. Might he not conceive of her as another of his... problems to solve?"

His *loose ends*, El had thought. We're all thinking it. Why not just say it?

"It's probably a bloody trap, is what she means," said Ruby. "And you're sending her in like a lamb to the slaughter."

"Oi!" said Kat, indignation hardening the musicality of her accent. "I can look after myself, you know. I'm not some fucking *civilian*, not like that one."

She waved the pen in her hand at Hannah, who said nothing - probably wisely, El thought.

"No one is saying that, darling," said Sita placatingly.

"You know better than anyone what he is," said Ruby, eyes blazing and locked on Rose. "You want to be responsible for putting some other girl in that position?"

"It's *because* I know what he is," said Rose, her own eyes fixed on Ruby, "that I'm saying we ought to do this. I will *not* have us working blind if we can help it. Not on this."

What the hell does *that* mean? El thought - conscious again of a subtext

233

she couldn't decipher, the weight of a different history than hers pressing down on the other women.

"And what about you?" Ruby said, rounding on El. "You've not said a word this whole time. Where do *you* stand on this?"

El considered the question.

"I think," she said, the idea concretising as she formed the words, "that there might be another way. A better way than sending her in on her own."

Time passed. The red-eyed man dozed, his arms still wrapped around the sleeping boy on his lap. The woman with the headscarf remained exactly where she was, still as marble.

Somewhere around what El took, from the faint light streaming in through the windows, to be sunrise, there was a nurse standing over them - a stocky white woman in a blue nylon uniform, bottle-blonde hair pulled back into a ponytail high and tight enough to flatten the lines from her forehead.

"Are you here to see Katherine Morgan?" she asked.

"Yes," said Rose, clearing her throat.

"And you're family, are you?" said the nurse, with the kind of weary scepticism El imagined she'd feel herself at the tail-end of a 12-hour shift.

"She's our sister," El said, sticking to the story they'd agreed upon on their way to the hospital. A wave of exhaustion rippled through her, hot and sickly.

"How is she?" said Rose. "Is she conscious?"

The nurse took in Rose's expression, her palpable anxiety, and softened.

"Why don't the two of you come with me," she said, more kindly, "and we can talk in private?"

"What way is that, then?" Ruby had asked - crossing both arms over her stomach, ready for another confrontation.

El swallowed, suddenly aware of just how long it had been since she'd gone up against Ruby - or against Sita - and walked away the better for it.

"You're worried about Kat going up to see him on her own, right?" she said. "So wouldn't it make sense for one of you to drive her up there, so you're watching out for her?"

A kind of awkwardness settled over the room; a metaphorical shuffling of feet at the suggestion.

"One of *us*?" said Ruby. "Not counting yourself in there, then?"

"I can't chance him seeing me in the car with her, can I?" El said. "He knows me."

"Look..." Ruby began, but Sita stopped her with a hand on the shoulder.

"I'm afraid," Sita said, "that he may know *us*, too. Me and Rose and your Auntie Ruby. Well enough to recognise us, even from a distance."

El thought back to the conversation she'd had with the older women in Ruby's living room; to the specific words they'd used to describe their relationship with Marchant.

"I thought you only met him *once or twice, years ago*?" she said.

The older women exchanged another round of maddeningly uninterpretable looks.

"We did, and we didn't," said Ruby eventually.

"What the hell does *that* mean?" El said.

"It means it was a bloody long time ago, and there's been a lot happened since," said Ruby sharply. "And you watch your mouth, alright? Remember who you're talking to."

"And who's that, exactly?" said El, temper rising. "Because I don't seem to..."

A loud, unlikely banging cut her off mid-sentence; the sound of dull wood striking metal and reverberating.

"*Thank* you," said Kat in the silence that followed - a wooden spoon gripped firmly in one of her hands, and a saucepan lid in another.

"Got something to say, have you?" said Ruby - but some of the fire had gone out of her, some of the fight.

"I do, as it happens," Kat said, putting down the spoon, the makeshift gong. "Very nice of you to ask. What I *wanted* to say, before the four of you got carried away with yourselves, was: why doesn't *Hannah* go with me?"

All four of them turned, almost in unison, to look at Hannah. She'd been sitting quietly at the table as they'd argued, making notes in her neat journalist's shorthand - so quietly El came close to forgetting she was there at all.

"Me?" she said, startled.

"Why not?" asked Kat. "Marchant doesn't know you, does he?"

Hannah lapsed back into quietness. Was she thinking? El wondered. Remembering?

"We met," said Hannah softly. "Only once. At Justin's funeral."

"And would he know you, if he saw you? If we kitted you out a bit - changed your hair, that sort of thing?"

"No. Probably not."

Kat spun around on her heels, looking at each of the women in turn.

"There you go then," she said. "Problem solved."

They followed the nurse out of the waiting room and down the connecting corridor - another pink-walled non-place, this one cluttered with empty trolley-beds and the skeletons of disused wheelchairs.

"Through here," she said, guiding them into a side-room, very small but better-furnished, bookended by twin two-seater sofas and bathed in the glow of an inoffensive floor lamp.

It's the bereavement room, El thought. The Death Room. She's going to tell us Kat's dead.

"What happened?" Rose demanded, evidently thinking something similar. "Is she...?"

"She's out of theatre," said the nurse. "She's still unconscious, but that's very much what we'd expect at this stage."

"Then what are we doing here?" El asked, too tired for politeness. "Isn't this where you bring people to break bad news?"

The nurse sighed.

"She's out of theatre," she repeated, "but she's still in critical condition. The trauma to her head caused what we call an intracranial haemorrhage - bleeding inside the skull. It's put a lot of pressure on her brain. Now, the doctors were able to relieve some of that pressure during surgery through a procedure called decompressive craniectomy," she lingered over the words, drawing them out syllable by syllable, "but we won't be in a position to assess her condition or get a sense of any complications until after she wakes up."

Decompressive craniectomy, El repeated to herself, visualising the process with grotesque clarity. They cut out a piece of her skull.

"So she *will* wake up?" Rose said, pressing the nurse for more - more detail, more understanding, more of anything that might give reassurance.

The nurse grimaced.

"Truthfully," she said, "we don't know."

Karen hadn't been happy either, when she'd eventually made it back to Ledbury Road from Marchant Holdings.

"You let her go and meet him, just like that?" she said, incredulous. "What the fuck did you do that for?"

"He put us on the spot," said Rose. "We had to make a decision."

"And you didn't think to run it past me first?"

"You weren't here. And we couldn't very well have rung you at his office to get your opinion, could we?"

"I could've rigged her up with something. A camera, a wire... something. Anything would have been better than the nothing you gave her."

"Hannah went with her," said El, though it sounded weak even to her.

"Oh, *did* she?" said Karen, spitting sarcasm. "Well, that's all right then, isn't it? As long as you let her have the really *big* guns for backup."

They barely spoke for the next few hours, although none of them seemed inclined to leave the house, or even the kitchen. Rose cleaned and tidied, wiping surfaces and rearranging the contents of drawers; Ruby nursed a cup of tea, while Sita read Kierkegaard in what El thought might have been Danish; Karen did something complicated with a screwdriver and a circuit board, electronic miscellany scattered on the floor around her as she worked. Resentment, agitation and barely-concealed tension hung over them, thick and membranous as a caul.

10 o'clock came, then 11. By midnight, El was debating whether to leave and check in again the morning.

At 12.15 the doorbell rang, and all hell broke loose.

They were allowed to keep the room - to stay in it as long as they needed to compose themselves.

"Just shout when you're ready," the nurse had said.

She'd closed the door behind her as she walked back out into the corridor, giving them the first semblance of privacy they'd had in hours.

"We'll have to speak to her family," said Rose. "There are no parents, not anymore, but she has at least one sister that I know of. She deserves to be told what's going on."

Sisters, El thought. I never even thought to ask if she had sisters. Or brothers, or aunts, or a pet hamster as a kid.

"Is she in London?" she said.

"Wales. In Holt, I believe. Not far from Wrexham - it's where Kat grew up. And it's virtually Manchester, so God knows how long it will take her to get here, even if the roads are clear."

Under the rapidly-accreting layers of tiredness, confusion and blind panic, something in the conscious part of El's mind clicked into place.

Holt - the same place, Karen said, that Marchant sent Leon Baxter on the smash and grab that turned out to be his last.

You heard of it? she'd asked El. *It's on the Welsh border, up by Cheshire. Might even be* in *Wales.*

But Kat would have been a kid then, wouldn't she? 11 or 12 at the oldest.

Unless...

"Her parents," El said slowly, still only half-sure of the question she was asking. "What happened to them?"

There had been blood on Hannah's clothes. On her face - dried around her mouth, smudged across her cheeks, rising up under the skin from the broken vessels under her eyes - and in her hairline, too, gluing the no-longer-immaculate strands of her bob to her scalp in stiffened clumps. But it was the blood on her clothes that El was drawn to: the streaks on her jacket, the splashes on the clouded leather of her shoes, the white piping turned pink on the collar of her blouse.

She was barely standing: slumped against a pillar in the front porchway, knees bent and bowed at the waist.

Ruby got to her first - ducking outside, down and around until Hannah's arm was draped around her shoulder and hauled her bodily upright.

"Someone get her other arm," she shouted to the others.

Karen and Sita sprung forward - though Rose, El noticed, hung back, apparently frozen to the spot.

"The car," Hannah said as Karen lifted her, air whistling through her teeth as she spoke. "She's in the car."

She jerked her neck to one side, towards the pavement behind her, where the BMW they'd taken to Berkhamsted jutted out at an angle from the kerb, its windows smashed and bodywork dented.

El got to it first, sprinting down the path with an urgency that had little to do with rational thought. Ruby and Karen followed, pulling Hannah with them.

"Cover your hand, girl," said Ruby, before El's fingers could reach the door handle. "We don't want to leave no more prints than we have already, if the Old Bill come knocking."

El nodded in acknowledgement; wrapped the sleeve of her sweater around her left fist until it covered all her fingers and tugged at the handle, opening the passenger door.

"Fucking hell," said Karen under her breath.

Where Hannah's clothes and face were smeared with blood, Kat's were saturated with it. The beginnings of bruises were forming at her temples; her lips were parted, exposing broken teeth. Even in the dark of the street, El could see the dent in the back of her skull, gore pooling in the unnatural concave left at the crown.

"They drove us off the road," said Hannah, still struggling for breath, the effort leaving potholes in her words as she tried to explain what had happened, what it was they were seeing. "At Berkhamsted. Near the house. Marchant's house."

"Who, darlin'?" said Ruby gently. "Who drove you off the road?"

"Couldn't see," said Hannah. "Country roads. No streetlights. Two of them, maybe. Men. Pointed a gun at the windscreen when we'd stopped. Told us to open the doors."

She paused for breath, then carried on, gathering steam as she spoke.

"They didn't want me," she said. "It was Kat - they wanted Kat. One of them hit me with the gun, and I must have blacked out, but before... They were beating her with something, both of them. Sticks or batons, I'm not sure. Kept going until they thought she was dead."

"What happened then?" Ruby asked.

"They hit me again. I couldn't stay awake, and then... I don't know. I woke up, and they'd gone, but it was so dark and there was nobody for miles, and all I could think of was getting away. I don't know how I got from there to here. I must have driven. And then we were here, and I could hear her next to me, trying to breathe, and... oh, God. Oh, God."

She stopped speaking as suddenly as she'd started, face immobilised by the memory.

Ruby stared at the scene inside the car - at Kat, at the blood, at the fragments of glass sparking like gemstones across the fabric of the seats.

She's thinking, El thought. Working it out. She's not flying into a tailspin like the rest of us - she's *planning*.

"Take her inside," Ruby told Sita, indicating Hannah. "She'll need looking at."

Sita nodded; gave Karen a moment to disentangle herself, then slipped Hannah's arm around her own neck and led her, slowly, back up the path and into the house.

"You still got that van of yours?" Ruby asked Karen.

"Yeah," said Karen. "Parked it round the corner."

"Then run and get it. I need you to get this one to a hospital, now."

She pointed down at Kat. Karen nodded assent, complying with the order as readily as Sita had, and sped off up the road.

Which left only El.

"Tell me," said Ruby softly, "you bring any of them bags of tricks with you down here? Wigs and makeup and that?"

"In the house," El replied.

"Good. Go inside and get yourself dressed - and take Rose with you. I want you both unrecognisable, understand? Because in about two minutes, Karen's going to be putting one of them epileptic bracelets round this one's wrist," she looked down again at Kat, "and your number's gonna be on it for the doctors to find when she drops her off at A&E. Alright?"

The nurses were changing shift. El could hear them lingering outside the Death Room, talking and laughing; hear their shoes clattering, step on step, as they traversed the corridor.

Rose still hadn't answered her question.

"What happened to Kat's parents?" she asked again. She was pacing now, not quite able to sit still despite the fatigue.

Finally, Rose replied.

"You've been talking to Karen," she said. "About Leon Baxter."

There was no point in denying it, El thought. Not at this stage of the game.

"Yeah," she said. "She told me Marchant sent Leon up north the day he disappeared, to a place on the Welsh border. A place called Holt. Bit of a coincidence, isn't it? Two girls drafted into the same job, wanting to take down the same man - and the father of one of them vanishes on his way back from the same small town in the middle of nowhere that the other one came from."

She waited; let the statement and its implications hang in the air.

"It's not up to me to share the details of other people's personal lives," Rose said. "If Kat had wanted you to know about her family or her motivations for working with us, she'd have told you herself, as Karen did. I'd prefer not to be accused of spreading gossip."

"That's a very noble sentiment, coming from a woman whose plan sent her to intensive care with a brain injury."

It was a low blow, a cheap shot, and El knew it. Rose winced, recoiling from the words as if El had thrown a punch at her - as if she were preparing to land a second.

"I'm sorry," El said, ashamed of herself. "That was a shit thing to say. I shouldn't have said it."

Rose looked up, directly at her; she was crying.

"If it's what you think," she said, "then you should certainly have said it. I can hardly deny it, can I? She *is* in here, and it *is* because of me."

"It's not... I don't think that. She made her own choices, we all did. I'm just... it's been a very long day, you know? I'm running on empty. And this job... sometimes it feels like I only know half the information I'm supposed to know, that I *need* to know to do it properly, and you and Sita and Ruby are leaving me just enough of a trail of breadcrumbs to keep me on the hook without ever actually sharing anything useful. I mean, I'm not a bloody detective. I'd rather people just *told* me things than insist I waste my energy trying to work out the clues for myself."

She tailed off, realising how much *she'd* said, how much *she'd* shared - then, embarrassed, sat down quietly on the sofa opposite Rose.

"What is it you think you don't know?" Rose asked after a while.

El almost laughed at the absurdity of the question.

"Are you serious?" she said. "I know almost nothing. Beyond the video of Lomax and the bits I've picked up from Karen and Hannah, I'm pretty much completely in the dark about why any of you are doing this. I know why *I* want Marchant gone, but the rest of you? No idea. I know you have some kind of history with Ruby and Sita that neither of them will talk about, but I couldn't even take a guess what that might be. And you or your husband obviously have a connection to Marchant, something big enough to make you hate him as much as you do and plough the money you have into planning this job and bringing the rest of us in on it. But what that is? Again, I have no idea. Like I said, I know almost nothing. And that's not something I'm used to."

Another silence.

"*I'm* sorry," Rose said. "I thought... Or rather, I *assumed* it wouldn't matter to you or to the others what *my* motivations were. Not when you all have so many reasons of your own for wanting him stopped."

"Of course it matters. It's another data point, another thing to understand about who he is and what makes him tick. The less I know, the less able I am to do what you need me to do. And the more information you have but hold back," she added, voicing the concern she'd been suppressing since the day before, the week before, the second she'd heard Lomax tell the camera how light her mother's body had felt as he'd bundled it into his suitcase, "the more danger you put me in. Put all of us in."

She'd expected Rose to argue; to fight her corner. But she didn't.

Instead, she got up from her sofa and walked the few steps there were across the room to sit down beside El.

"You're right," she said. "It isn't fair. You're taking an enormous risk at my behest, and I haven't been willing to share even the things that are mine *to* share."

"Don't worry about it," said El awkwardly, looking anywhere but at Rose.

There was a rustle of fabric. El looked to her right, and saw that Rose had rolled up one of the sleeves of her shirt, exposing the arm to the elbow.

Up close, the scarring was worse than it had seemed the few other times El had caught a glimpse of it: angry red lines crosshatched with faded silver, the epidermis scaled, drawn too tight over the muscle and bone.

"He did this," she told El, holding the arm up and close enough that El could see the few faint hairs that remained on its skin. "Marchant. When I was a child."

El was shaken. Not by the scar itself, or the revelation that Marchant was responsible for it, but by the *child* part of the sentence - the suggestion that Rose had known him for the length of time it implied, that her animus might go back not years but decades.

"You knew him then?" she asked. "When you were a kid?"

Rose traced a thumb over her forearm, back and forth across the scar tissue.

"I've known him all my life," she said. "He's my father."

CLAPHAM
1966

S he wasn't Rose, back then; she was Olivia. Not Olivia Marchant, like her father, but Olivia Green, like her mother.

The day of the night he tried to kill her had been, as she remembered it later, a fun one; an adventure. He'd taken them out, her and her little sister Pamela; for ice cream floats at the Italian cafe up the road, then on to the Regal in Streatham to watch Thunderball. They'd been the only ones in the cinema, which she'd found thrilling - the thrill compounded by the presence of her father in the afternoon, and on a school day, when usually she saw him only once or twice a month, and always in the evenings.

That evening had been less fun. He'd gone back with them to the house; not just dropped them off but stayed for dinner, the three of them and her mother huddled up in the dining room with the pie and mash the cleaning lady had heated up for them before she left. It must have *been* the cleaning lady, Olivia had reasoned: her mother didn't cook, if she could possibly help it - she'd choose a glass of Hock over a meal every time - and she'd never seen her father so much as pick up a cheese-grater.

Her mother was already drunk when they arrived home, and became progressively more so as they ate, working steadily through the uncorked bottle on the tablecloth as she picked with no obvious enthusiasm at the food on her plate. Drunk, and combative.

"Are you staying tonight?" she asked Olivia's father, a bellicose edge to the words.

"Not tonight, no," replied her father mildly.

"Because you're going back to *her*?" said her mother.

Her father laid down his knife and fork.

"Girls," he said, addressing Olivia and Pamela, "would you go upstairs and play in your room, please?"

"But I want pudding!" said Pamela, who was six, four years Olivia's junior, and given to whining at the slightest provocation.

Olivia, who knew better than to antagonise their father, grabbed her by the hand and dragged her, complaining, out of her chair and into the hallway.

She also knew, though she wished she didn't, which *her* her mother had been talking about - that the days and nights he spent away from them, neither at the dining table nor in their mother's bedroom, he spent instead with his other family, his *real* family.

Who they were, these phantom almost-relatives - where they lived, how they talked, what they ate - these were things she didn't know. Things she'd rather *not* know.

She moved towards the stairs, then hesitated - torn between wanting to ignore the argument that she knew would be going on in the dining room, to emphatically *not hear* any of the words exchanged, and the necessity of keeping an eye on her mother, in case there came a time later that night that she needed to help her up to bed, or put a cushion under her head where she'd passed out, or roll her over onto her side on the settee to stop her choking.

"Daddy said to go and play," Pamela chided her. "You're not supposed to be *spying*."

"Go up, then," said Olivia. "Nobody's stopping you, are they?"

Pamela harrumphed and stamped her feet - then, failing to get a rise out of Olivia, stomped away upstairs.

Left alone, Olivia pressed an ear to the door and listened.

They *were* arguing - her mother's voice loud and angry, her father's cooler and more measured.

"I refuse to keep having this conversation," he was saying. "Especially with a woman so full of cheap wine she can barely string a sentence together."

"Why do you think I drink?" said her mother, half-shouting. "I'm on my own with your kids every hour God sends while you're off with *her* doing I don't know what."

"And I'll continue to," he said evenly. "You know I have no intention of leaving her, and you know why. Who do you think pays for this house you're living in? For the woman who mops your floors, that very expensive school you were so eager for the girls to attend? It's Liz's money, all of it. Without her, there ceases to *be* any money. She and Saul would take every penny if they ever caught wind that I were anything but a model husband. And what kind of life would either of us have then?"

"Has it never occurred to you that there might be more important things than money? That I might prefer having you around to just having you foot the bill?"

"This is the arrangement we made. And for as long as Liz trusts that I'll come home to her each night, and as long Saul persists in remaining healthy as a damn carthorse, it's the arrangement we will keep."

There was a lull; the sound of liquid sloshing in a glass.

"And what if," said her mother slyly, "someone were to tell old Liz that her boy was playing away? What would you think about that?"

Olivia heard footsteps, heavy shoes echoing on tiles.

"I would think," said her father, "that whoever it was would know better than to toss around idle threats."

"Who says they're idle?"

A sound like a thick whip cracking, sharp but organic, somehow fleshy - an open hand striking a face, an arm.

Olivia bolted up the stairs and into the bathroom. Sat on the edge of the bath with the door locked, waiting for the arguing to stop.

"I can't sleep with the light off," Pamela called up to her from the bottom bunk as she climbed up the ladder to her own. "Turn it back on, Livvy. Please. It's scary with the light off."

Olivia pulled the sheets up over her chest - annoyed and disgusted by her sister's fear, in a way she didn't fully understand. How, she thought, could something like the *dark* be scary, when there were real problems, grown up problems out there worse than anything your imagination could conjure up in the darkness?

"It's staying off," she said. "Go and get in Mum's bed if you don't like it."

Afterwards, when she dreamed of her sister, it was that line she'd hear, that moment she'd replay.

She was already awake when the smell of the smoke hit her, jerked from what must have been deep sleep by a pair of leather-gloved hands on her shoulders - shaking her, dragging her down from her bunk through the gap in the railings.

"Come on, girl!" said a muffled voice - the voice that belonged to the hands that were pulling at her. A woman's voice, one she thought she recognised. "You need to move it, now!"

Olivia rubbed at her eyes, and before the heat from the smoke-clouds crowding the room burned into them and took her sight, she saw her: a lady about her Mum's age but much shorter, not very much taller than Olivia; brown hair cropped like Twiggy's, her own bright blue eyes widened in alarm and a silk scarf wrapped around her face, covering her nose and mouth. The cleaning lady - the one she knew then as Martha, but wouldn't always.

"What are you doing here?" Olivia asked her, coughing and retching as the smoke poured into her open mouth, then her chest. The room was hot, hotter than an oven, scalding her skin from all sides, and under the heat was noise, a low rumbling like a train passing through a station.

"Didn't you hear me?" Martha shouted over the noise, through the fabric of her makeshift mask. "We've got to go!"

She took hold of the sleeve of Olivia's nightdress and pulled again, hard. Olivia didn't fight her. She'd let herself be dragged out onto the upstairs landing when she realised what she *hadn't* seen, *hadn't* heard.

"Pamela," she said, still coughing. "Where's Pamela?"

"Come on!" said Martha, yanking at Olivia's arm, avoiding her question.

"My sister!" Olivia said, almost screaming to be heard. The noise was growing, more roar now than rumble, though she couldn't have said where it was coming from. "Where's my sister?"

Martha's eyes darted left, to the room at the end of the landing: her mother's bedroom.

With a twist of her hips, Olivia broke free of the cleaning lady's grip and ran towards it, mindful of neither the thickening smoke pouring from under the closed door nor the temperature, which rose to boiling point as she neared the room.

"Bloody *stop*!" Martha shouted, tearing after her, but too late: Olivia's elbow was already on the stainless steel handle of the door, the weight of her body pressed into her forearm as she lurched forward into the searing heat of the wood.

She'd never known pain like it - pain so enormous, so absolutely all-encompassing that it was as if not just her arm but her whole body was on fire, the fat and muscle roasting in its own skin, and she could neither speak nor force her thoughts into coherence.

She screamed again, or thought she did, and fell to the floor.

Martha took her by the waist and pulled her upright; picked her up with a strength that Olivia - the thinking, functioning Olivia - wouldn't have expected of a woman that small, and slung her over her shoulder, pressing Olivia's face into the side of her neck.

She carried her down the stairs and out of the house through the back door in the kitchen, the heat and smoke growing less and less the further they travelled from the upstairs bedrooms. At the bottom of the garden, a rusted-iron gate led out onto the road - not a busy main road like the one at front of the house, but a quiet one, facing a few square feet of scrubby common land that she and Pamela and some of the other kids used as a playground, ducking in and out of the thigh-high weeds in summer and pushing each other into the mud the day after a rainstorm. Martha carried her down the path and through it, into the street.

She'd known about the gate, Olivia realised later. Known about it, even though none of the grownups ever used it - even though her mother had forgotten it was there.

"Can you walk?" Martha asked her, placing her down on the pavement. The concrete was icy under her bare feet; the polar opposite of the fire in her arm.

She took her weight in her legs and stood, not quite able to speak. This seemed to be enough for Martha. She took Olivia's hand, her *other* hand, and tugged her - with less force this time - onto the common land, and over it, until they spilled out onto another road, a side-road that was more like an alleyway.

A car was parked there - a little silver Aston Martin, a James Bond car. It looked brand new, sleek and unscratched and polished to a high shine.

She'd have wondered, if she'd been able to think, how it was that a cleaning lady could afford a car like that.

"Get in," Martha said, climbing into the driving seat and pushing open the passenger door from the inside.

Mindlessly, Olivia obeyed.

Martha put a key in the car's ignition, turned on the engine and pulled out into the street. Something about the motion seemed to jump-start Olivia, to bring a part of her back to life, and the tumble of her thoughts hit her one by one and all at once, striking her like the shards of a rockfall.

The smoke. The heat. Her arm on the bedroom door.

Her mother.

Pamela.

She opened her mouth, the beginnings of another scream rising up through her throat from her chest, and the world went dark.

Voices brought her round, close by and unfamiliar.

"Perhaps we should have taken her somewhere," said the first - a woman's voice, so crisp and clear it could have been delivering the Queen's Speech on the television.

"No," said a second, this one deep and male and strangely-accented. "Any hospital, one look at her arm and they'd be asking questions."

"Can't you do nothing for her, Win?" asked another, one that sounded like it could have been Martha.

"I've washed and dressed the area," said the man, with an air of authority Olivia associated with doctors and dentists. "Painkillers would be a good idea, when she wakes up. But she'll need more help than I can give her here if there's any infection."

"We'll just have to hope there's not, then, won't we?" said Martha.

She forced her eyelids open and took in the people around her, standing over her: Martha, soot on her cheek and a strip of leopard print cloth tied around her head; a tall black man with a pencil moustache, one of his hands pressed to the stiff white bandage running from the wrist to the elbow of her damaged arm; another woman, brown skinned and black haired, with a small gold stud in her nose and perhaps the most beautiful face Olivia had ever seen, the face of a film star or a pin-up girl.

Wherever she was, she was lying down on what she took to be a sofa or a chaise longue - her feet extending out in front of her and the back of her head supported by something soft but firm, a pillow or a cushion. She took in the gas fire, the orange rugs, the radio on the sideboard, and decided that it had to be a living room - the living room of someone else's house. There were toys on the floor, she noticed: marbles and Matchbox cars, toy soldiers, a wooden Muffin The Mule.

"You're alright," said Martha, seeing her looking. "You're safe here. It's all alright."

She laid a palm against Olivia's forehead.

"She's burning up still," she said, less to Olivia than to the other two adults in the room.

"It's the heat from the fire," said the man. "It's built up in her system. She needs water, cold water."

The other woman, the beautiful woman, raised a glass to Olivia's mouth. She smelled like night air and jasmine, clove cigarettes and cinnamon.

"Drink," she told Olivia, squeezing her undamaged hand.

Olivia swallowed. The water was lemon-scented, the glass half-filled with ice cubes, and so cold it hurt her teeth. She coughed, and it came right back up, falling in thick droplets onto her nightdress - which was covered, now she noticed, in black powder, dark as coal dust. She wiped her mouth and sunk back onto the maybe-cushion, tired and embarrassed, confused and afraid, and wishing, desperately, that she could remember enough of the preceding hours to understand how she'd ended up here, in a state like this.

"Where am I?" she asked.

She sounded hoarse, scratched. Wondered if they'd know what she was saying, through the croaking.

"You're at my place," said Martha, after an eternity of awkward silence. "*Our* place, I should say." She stepped in closer to the black man; rested a palm on his lower back. "This is my husband, Winston."

"Why am I here?" Olivia said, the words escaping in a frightened whisper. "What happened to me?"

Where's my Mum? she thought, but didn't say. And where's Pamela? Why aren't *they* here?

Another awkward silence.

"Tell her," said the man to the two women, in a low voice he probably thought Olivia couldn't hear. "You can't keep it from her, something like this. It's not fair."

"She's ten years old, Win," said Martha reprovingly.

"And how old were *you*?" said the man cryptically. "Ten is old enough to know."

The woman who wasn't Martha - Sita, she learned later, her name was Sita - hesitated, and then, appearing to reconcile herself to some kind of decision, lowered herself down on the sofa beside Olivia.

She took Olivia's hand between both of hers; rubbed pacifying circles with her thumbs into the thin skin around the joints of Olivia's fingers.

"There was a fire," she began. "At your house. And your father... it looks very much as if he started it."

Many years later, leafing through one of the true crime books Seb devoured during his downtime, she came across a phrase, a descriptor used to categorise a particular genre of man: *family annihilator*. Men who slaughtered their wives and children, suddenly and violently, with carving knives, cans of lighter fluid, showers of bullets; aggrieved men, resentful men, men who'd rather stab their partners with a barbecue fork than fight a custody battle. Men reacting to, or fearing, loss of status; coldly pragmatic men, who saw their families as impediments to their own good fortune, as obstacles to be removed by any means necessary.

Her father, she'd thought, fit the last archetype perfectly.

He'd started the fire at the house, Sita had told her, as she lay that night - or the morning after, she couldn't be sure - on an almost-stranger's sofa, head spinning and pain radiating outward from her ruined arm. Had left after the row with her mother, but then come back; let himself in with his own key, carrying a can of lighter fluid and newspaper for kindling, and gone straight upstairs, to her mother's room.

"We think he set the fire there," Sita said "and then closed the bedroom door behind him before he left. To give him time to slip out through the back garden. His doing that... it would have stopped the flames spreading straight away. It's almost certainly why Ruby was able to get you out in time."

Ruby? she'd thought. Who's Ruby? And then: Pamela.

"My sister," she said, the thought that had been dancing horribly around the edges of her mind crystallising into something like knowledge. "I told her to go and sleep in with Mum. In her bedroom."

Sita and Martha exchanged looks, but it was the man who spoke.

"I'm afraid," he said, slowly and patiently as an undertaker, "that there wasn't time to get to them. Ruby tried, but with the fire and the smoke, she wasn't able to get through. The door was too hot, too heavy. I'm very sorry."

They're dead, she thought. Dead and burned.

And it was him who killed them. Locked them up in a room for the fire to eat them.

If anyone had asked her, before just then, how she thought she'd react to knowing this - to being *told* this - she'd had imagined crying, screaming. Not the numb calm that settled inside her, that landed in her stomach and pushed up and out like an icicle, freezing the parts that should have screamed, should have cried.

(I was in shock, she'd tell herself later. How could I not have been?)

Calmly, she asked: "who's Ruby?"

Ruby was Martha, and Martha was Ruby.

"Martha's a, what do you call it?" Martha/Ruby said, sometime in the long, strange hours of the day and night immediately after the fire. "A stage name. For work."

Olivia didn't ask, then, why a cleaning lady would need a stage name.

Other things she didn't ask: how Martha - *Ruby* - knew that her father had left the house and then come back, when she'd left herself before he did. How she'd come to see him go in, and then out again. How she known what he was doing there.

The pain in her arm was no less intense than it had been - in spite of the cup after cup of milky tea and plate after plate of biscuits Sita insisted that she eat and drink, in spite of the ointment the man called Winston rubbed into the red-raw skin whenever he changed her bandages.

(She'd winced, the first time he'd tried to dress the wound; pulled her arm away sharply, protecting herself from the fresh starbursts of agony created by every dab of the cotton pad.

"Let him get on with it," Ruby had told her, not unkindly. "He was a medic in the war. He knows what he's doing."

"I'll make it as fast as I can," Winston had said. And true to his word, had swiped the rubbing alcohol so quickly and so efficiently over the burn that she barely had time to cry out).

It was impossible to determine, from her position on the sofa, just how much time passed for her in Ruby's living room. The curtains were drawn, and heavy enough to block out any natural light, and the daily lives of Ruby and Sita and Winston seemed to follow no obvious pattern. The children whose toys she saw, whose voices she heard in the rooms outside never materialised; probably, Olivia thought, Ruby was keeping them away deliberately, stopping them from seeing anything that might upset them or encourage them to ask awkward questions.

She found that she couldn't think about Pamela or her mother, even when she wanted to. The part of her brain that usually held the shape of them - the memory of them now, she supposed - wouldn't open up to her; wouldn't spring to life when she tried to access the material inside.

("Trauma," Ruby told her later, when she asked *why* something like that would happened, what was *wrong* with her that she couldn't remember her own family in anything other than the broadest strokes. "Does funny things to your head").

The adults came and went, bustling in and out of the room with their plates and cups and bottles of peroxide. The initial impulse to ask questions, to find answers had ebbed away, and she found she didn't want to talk to them, not then - even when they asked how she was or how she was feeling.

Instead, in the absence of clocks and daylight, she used the rhythms of her body to mark time: the rumbling of her stomach, the throbbing in her arm, the frequency with which she emptied her bladder into the ceramic pot tucked discreetly under her sickbed (and taken away to be emptied, just as discreetly, whenever Sita came in to reclaim the crumb-covered plates and empty teacups. Olivia thought at first that she ought to be embarrassed to have someone who looked like Sita doing *that* for her - but then found that embarrassment, too, was beyond her emotional reach, in that room).

Days, hours, minutes later, Ruby was back beside her, pulling up a footstool beside Olivia and sinking down onto it with a sigh Olivia associated with people much older.

"We need to have a talk," she told Olivia. "I didn't want to have to do this now, and Christ knows you're barely well enough to stand, let alone move about, but I'm not sure it'll keep. The fact is, you can't stay here. Not because we wouldn't have you," she said quickly, pre-empting any possible offence Olivia might have taken. "You could stay here as long as you like, for me. Me *and* Win. But it ain't safe, not here. Not in London."

"Safe?" Olivia said, not following.

"Your old man," Ruby said. "I don't know how much you know about him - not much I reckon, if he had anything to do with it. But he's an influential person, if you know what I mean. Got a lot of connections in a lot of places. And if he were to find out that we got you out of that house, out of the fire... it wouldn't surprise me if he'd try to come looking for you, or get one of his mates to."

And if he did? she thought - memory-images of the man who asked her about her homework and took her out for ice cream colliding dissonantly with the man she'd been told about, the one who'd walk into his own kids's home with an armful of accelerant and walk out again without looking back. If he did find me, what then?

"You could name him, is the problem," Ruby continued. "Tell people who he is - who he is to *you*. Tell his wife. Tell the Old Bill. And he's not gonna want that."

A creak of door hinges, and Winston was in the living room, crouching down next to his wife, looking right at Olivia.

"It's alright, though," he said, speaking softly. "We've found you somewhere, somewhere you can go. Somewhere you'll be safe."

ST LUKE'S HOSPITAL, ISLINGTON
1996

El leaned back against the wall, grateful again for the quiet privacy of the Death Room.

"And they did it?" she asked - fully awake now, her earlier exhaustion banished. "Ghosted you out of London, just like that?"

Rose rested her own head again the same wall, lost in the telling.

"More or less," she said.

They gave her clothes to wear - a skirt and a blouse two sizes too big, a pair of tan tights, brown loafers that fit her feet, just about, but looked like nothing either Ruby or Sita would ever choose to own. She had nothing of her own left to take with her, nothing to pack.

It was morning then - the living room curtains, now opened, giving her a glimpse of the light outside. Only Ruby and Sita went with her, bundling her out of the flat - it *was* a flat she'd been in, she realised, not a house -

and downstairs, straight into the back of a yellow Ford Anglia that was, Olivia thought, the polar opposite of the Aston Martin Ruby had driven. Winston stayed behind, charged with looking after the kids she'd heard but never seen.

"Everything will be alright," he told her sombrely before she left. "We'll make sure of it."

They were going north, Sita had told her - out of the city and up, on to Yorkshire, to somewhere near Sheffield. There'd be people to see there - a man and a woman named Ackroyd, old friends of Ruby's and Sita's.

"They're good folk," Ruby said. "Solid. You'll like them."

"And what are we going to do when we get there?" she asked.

"That's really up to you, darling," said Sita. "You and Arthur and Diane. You must see how you feel, when you meet one another."

The answer, if that was what it was, had left her none the wiser.

Olivia hadn't often been driven to places. Her mother didn't drive a car - *hadn't driven* a car - and her father had always been reluctant to take her and Pamela out in his, and she found herself excited, despite the circumstances; gazing breathlessly out of the windows as Ruby barrelled the Anglia past Elstree, Potters Bar, Luton, the names of each place as alien and exotic as their village greens and old stone churches.

The journey took hours. In the front, the two women spoke amongst themselves in low voices, letting Olivia hear only snippets of their conversation.

"They'll have to move," Ruby said, as they passed Bletchley. "You can't just have a 10 year old kid no-one's ever seen before rock up on your doorstep and not expect the neighbours to ask questions. They'd have child welfare on their backs quick as you can blink. Coppers too, probably."

"They've already told you they're happy to relocate," said Sita. "It's not as if they've put down roots in Barnstaple, or whatever it's called."

"Barnsley," Ruby corrected her.

"*Barnsley*, then. And I've had a chat with Ralph Anderson. He can have the documents ready for them by next week, providing we give him the right information and enough time to work."

"I bet he can. Fourteen quid for a birth certificate! It's a bleedin' crime."

"And you made *how* much from that Henry Moore affair last year? Do remind me."

Ruby fell silent, and didn't speak again until they reached Northampton.

"What do they even know about bringing up a kid, the pair of them?" she asked quietly, as if she'd been mulling the question, chewing it over long before she'd said it aloud.

"What did any of us know, before we had them?" said Sita. "They're prepared to learn, that's what matters."

"It's a hell of a lot to ask."

"Yes, it is. And yet they've agreed to it, wholeheartedly. So would you please bring an end to the... what's that ridiculous expression of yours? Mithering. Stop mithering. You've asked, and they've accepted. It's done. A *fait accompli.*"

"You must mean business, if you're pulling out the Latin on me."

"It's French, as you very well know. Now, would you mind keeping your eyes on the road while you're driving? I'd prefer not to meet my end in the buggy of this horseless hay wagon, if I can possibly help it."

They drove on, past Leicester and Loughborough, Nottingham and Derby, the green space around them giving way to brick-fronted factories and high industrial chimneys.

"Not long now," Sita said, shifting in her seat so she was facing Olivia.

Miles came and went. They passed a sign welcoming them to Sheffield; a sinuous row of high-rise council flats, vast and grey and twisting, looming over them from the top of a vertiginous hill.

"Could we hurry on a little?" asked Sita. "All this Brutalism is giving me a headache."

"It's what you get, when you come out of London," said Ruby.

"Appreciative though I am of your devotion to the city," Sita said, "it's hardly immune to architectural faux pas. I spent half of last summer working that director at the National, if you recall. I've never *needed* so much aspirin."

"Mind what you say, eh?" said Ruby, flashing Sita what Olivia recognised as a *not in front of the children* look. "Loose lips sink ships, and what have you."

To Olivia's surprise, Sita chuckled.

"Given where she's going," she said, "this kind of talk may be something she needs to get used to."

It was early afternoon when they arrived, Ruby drawing the Anglia to a screeching halt outside a line of wide terraced houses, their bay windows protruding out into the street.

"Here we are," she said, grimacing at what Olivia thought must be the northernness, the *not-London-ness* of their surroundings. "Sunny Barnsley."

"Oh, do be quiet," said Sita, detaching herself gracefully from the passenger seat and pushing it down to free Olivia from the back.

"Is this where they live?" Olivia asked. "The Ackroyds?"

"For now," said Ruby.

She locked the door of the Anglia, to Sita's amusement ("is there really any need? It's hardly a magnet for criminals") and the three of them walked together to the front door of one of the houses - a neatly-kept two-up two-down with a scrubbed step and a hanging basket fixed to the brickwork.

The door opened before they could knock, swinging back to reveal a staircase, an expanse of green carpet and, immediately in front of them, a woman. She was older than Ruby and Sita, and somehow more old-fashioned - her curly hair grey and backcombed, her dress protected by a spotted pinafore. There were lines around her green eyes; deep grooves in the corners of her mouth.

She froze on the spot for a moment, seeing them, then stepped forward - not towards Sita or Ruby, but to Olivia.

"Hello," she said gently - the way, Olivia thought, you'd speak to a big dog or a colt, soothing and tentative, so it didn't bolt or bite you as you stretched out your hand to stroke it. "I'm Diane. And you must be Olivia. I'm so sorry for your loss. But it's very, very nice to meet you."

"They couldn't have children," Rose told El. "Diane had a hysterectomy in the '50s, and Arthur had been in prison, so they were never able to legally adopt. They'd been desperate for a child, though, and Ruby knew it. Which I suppose is why it was them she approached in the first place."

"Good to see you, Di," Ruby said.

"And you," said Diane, half her attention still fixed on Olivia. "Now get in here, quick, before someone sees you hanging round my doorstep."

She didn't sound northern, in the way Olivia understood northern accents to sound; nor anything like Ruby, nor as refined as Sita.

("She's from Grantham," Ruby told her. "Lincolnshire way. It's a bit of a nothing accent, that one").

The house was as neat inside as it was outside, uncluttered and immaculate. In the front room sat a ginger-haired man, apparently waiting for them, his fingers fiddling nervously with the bowl of a pipe.

Arthur, Olivia thought.

Even sitting down he was short - small and wiry and compactly-muscled, his simian body built for climbing trees or swinging from the rafters of a big top.

He was a steeplejack, she found out later; a steeplejack and a thief, adept at roof repairs, construction work and, occasionally, the acquisition and redistribution of fine art, precious stones and high-end automobiles. When she was older, old enough to understand what it was he did and to want to know more, he agreed to take her out with him on a job – choosing for the occasion a low-risk, low-stakes break-in at the top floor of a five-storey museum in Manchester. She'd liked it, so much that, having proved herself a help rather than a liability that first time, she went back with him again and again, learning more each time about pitons and carabiners, about when to wear gloves and when to trust the feel of the ropes under her bare hands. Learning so much that Seb would struggle to understand, during the many mountaineering holidays that punctuated their marriage, how a girl from Rotherham could possibly be so good at scrambling up cliff-faces without even a harness to hold her in place - just as he never quite understood the strange closeness she seemed to share with the two eccentric middle-aged women, her "family friends," who would materialise in their kitchen from time to time before whisking her away for drinks or dinner.

Arthur stood up when he saw her, putting his pipe away in his trouser pocket and brushing the residues of tobacco off his palms. He was looking at her, she realised, in the same way that Diane had: anxiously, as if she might run out of the door at any moment.

"Alright, love?" he asked her, by way of greeting. He *did* sound northern, she thought; like one of the characters from This Sporting Life.

Diane settled them into armchairs, then perched herself on Arthur's wingback, knees pressed together - trying to take up, Olivia thought, as little space as possible. He wrapped a sinewy arm around her; squeezed her shoulder.

Everyone was tense; Olivia could feel it, the pressure of it gathering over them like storm clouds.

"Right, then," said Ruby, when Olivia was just about ready to implode from the weight of it all. "Let's get down to it, shall we?"

"I knew I couldn't go home," Rose said. "Even before they told me, I knew. The house was gone, and my mother and Pamela. My Mother had no family, so I'd never had grandparents to speak of, and since my father - since Marchant - had... done what he did, there was no-one left. Nothing to go back to."

"The Ackroyds wanted to take me in - that was the gist of what Ruby told us. Told *me*. They knew about the fire, about my situation, and they wanted to help. To... foster me, I suppose you'd call it. There'd need to be paperwork in place - a forged birth certificate from one of Sita's contacts in the *demimonde*, a handful of other records falsified. But that was easily achieved, or so she said. The plan was to pass me off as Arthur and Diane's daughter to anyone who asked - schools and doctor's surgeries and so on."

"The issue for them, of course, was that they couldn't stay in Barnsley. It was a small community, then; small and claustrophobic, or at least what *I* would find claustrophobic. Everyone intimately familiar with what everyone else is doing. To have a child appear out of nowhere, an unknown child, and to claim that child as your own - it just wasn't feasible."

"What neither Ruby nor Sita had known, but what we'd all discovered that day in their sitting room, was that they'd already started the process of moving. Had started it the day Ruby had first called them from London. Arthur had resigned from his job with the council, and Diane had taken a lease on a new house a handful of miles away, closer to Sheffield. Rotherham wasn't far, but it was far enough, in those days. Far enough to afford them - afford *us* - some measure of anonymity."

"And people in the new place bought the story?" El asked. "They thought you *were* their daughter?"

"As far as I know," said Rose. "Arthur's looks helped, I think. People see a man and a young girl both with a shock of red hair, and they tend not to look too closely at their finer features. And as for the rest..."

"Me and Sita are going to be sticking around here a couple of weeks," Ruby said. "Not *here* here," she clarified, in response to Diane's look of horror, "but *around* here. In the general area, up north. We'll most likely get a B&B in Sheffield or somewhere."

"Or a hotel room, like civilised people," Sita added.

"Why?" said Diane - looking, Olivia thought, slightly panicked, as if a gift she'd been given were about to be taken away.

"You're going to need help getting her settled in," Ruby told her. "She's had a hell of a rough ride this last week, and that sort of thing don't just disappear. It stays with you. It ain't going to be easy, the three of you learning how to live together. That's not all of it, neither. Have you heard the girl talk? She's a walking elocution lesson. You can tell people you sent her away to boarding school, or what have you, and that'll go some of the way to explaining it, but we'll have to at least *try* to roughen her out a bit round the edges if we're saying she's sprung from the two of you. And then there's her name..."

"I couldn't stay Olivia," Rose said. "If I was going to stay hidden, have all this new paperwork to protect me from anyone who might come looking for me, then my name, the name my mother had given me... it would have to go. And rationally that made sense to me, of course it did. I was a child, but I wasn't stupid. I knew I'd be putting myself at risk, if I didn't listen to Ruby and Sita. But you get rather attached to your name, don't you? It's a sort of anchor for your sense of self. With everything else I'd lost, I found the thought of relinquishing mine a little distressing."

El, who couldn't remember a time she hadn't traded names and identities as easily as lighting a cigarette, nodded.

"Why Rose?" she asked.

"It's my Mum's middle name," she told the room, not meeting anyone's eye.

Ruby looked concerned.

"I don't know about that," she said. "Ain't it a bit risky, choosing one that close to home?"

She'd gone along with everything they'd suggested so far. Had let them decide for her where she'd live, who she'd be, how she'd speak.

But on this, she was immovable.

"It's the name I want," she said, challenging Ruby to argue, to fight her on it. "Are you going to stop me from choosing my own name?"

Ruby stared at her; seemed to consider the costs and benefits of picking this particular battle.

"Alright," she said. "Fair enough. Rose it is."

Rose looked down at her arm, at the wrist she'd been cradling.

"I stayed with Arthur and Diane until I left for university," she told El. "They never treated me as anything but their daughter. I *was* their daughter, I suppose, in all but blood."

"Arthur died in 1983. Stomach cancer. Diane lived long enough to meet Sophie, but she'd had two strokes already by then, and she wasn't able to get around without help. We paid for two nurses to live with her when she refused to move down to London, but I think she resented their presence - she was fanatically independent. *She* died in '88. And then there was just me and Sophie and Seb."

"But Ruby and Sita stuck around?"

"God, yes. I'm not sure I could have shaken them off if I'd tried. You know what they're like."

There was a question El hadn't asked; an answer she felt she needed.

"What happened after the fire?" she said. "To the house and... everyone. I assume the police got involved?"

Rose nodded.

"It was years before I heard the details," she said. "There was coverage of the fire on the news, so I knew in very broad strokes what they'd found there. That there were bodies - a woman and at least one girl, possibly more. I found out later that Sita had spoken to one of her friends at the Met, not quite a Commissioner but almost, and he'd fudged some of the information they gave to the press. Suggested that there were *two* girls in the house, but that one of them was so badly burned that they weren't able to identify her definitively."

"No-one made the connection to Marchant, even when our names were released to the public. I assume he paid the rent in cash. Or gave the cash directly to my mother to pass to the landlord, which feels to me more likely, in light of what we know of him. And nobody ever came looking for me. To all intents and purposes, and certainly for Marchant's purposes, Olivia Green burned to death in a house fire in 1966."

Something else was nagging at her, El realised; not so much an unanswered question as the vestige of a memory, an echo of something she'd seen or heard, but that hadn't registered as significant at the time. An analogue of Rose's story, but more recent, and nearer.

And then she remembered.

"There was another fire," she said, trying to call the specifics of the incident to mind as she spoke. "Last year, in Greenwich. Two people died - a woman and a little girl, mother and daughter. They said it was arson, but they never caught whoever did it."

Rose smiled, joylessly.

"Yes," she said. "That was him. Marchant - my father. His handiwork."

"You know that for sure?"

"My investigators were certain of it. That case was the reason I hired them, in fact - I'd read about it, too, and had the same thought you did just now. That it was too great a coincidence, too similar a set of circumstances. A single parent, a rented house in the suburbs, no obvious leads. It was exactly Marchant's style. I needed to know."

"But you didn't tell the police?"

"There was nothing to tell. The investigators only made the connection definitively when they interviewed the next door neighbour - showed her pictures of Marchant and asked her if she'd ever met him, ever seen him go into the house. She said she had, that first time - but then when they went back again for more details, she wouldn't speak to them. Wouldn't answer the doorbell."

"You think Marchant got to her?"

"We all assumed so. But regardless of whether he did or didn't - she was hardly a reliable witness. Getting the Met to scrutinise the comings and goings of one of the richest men in London, a man who also happens to sit on the board of several of the better-known police charities, on the word of a woman who probably wouldn't have opened the door if they came knocking... well. None of us thought it very likely."

"But didn't Ricky Lomax mention it, when you interviewed him? Wouldn't that have been something, something your detectives or whatever could have worked with?"

"Lomax?" Rose said, snorting derisively. "He denied all knowledge of it, absolutely and categorically. Said whole thing sounded like the work of an angry ex-boyfriend. But that if Marchant *was* behind it - *if* - then he hadn't delegated; that he must have done it himself. With his own two hands, the way he had before."

SOHO

1996

Seymour Henderson was sweating again. Beads of perspiration gathered on his nose and forehead; wet the furrows of his widow's peak in the glare and flash of the camera lights.

"I want to apologise," he said, bending his head towards the microphone bank in front of him but avoiding eye contact with the cameras, "for the errors of judgement I've shown in recent times and the embarrassment I have caused. This apology I extend to my constituents, who put their faith in me and whom I have so terribly let down. To the government with whom I have been lucky enough to work, and the Prime Minister under whom I have been privileged to serve. Above all, I must apologise to my wife Kim, whose love and support over the last 18 years I have so badly abused."

He paused to take a sip of water; wiped his damp forehead with a handkerchief.

"While I have no one but myself to blame for the situation in which I now find myself," he continued, "it is with great sadness and regret I announce today that I will be stepping down as Member of Parliament for Silvertown. To those who have contacted me to let me know how terribly

I have disappointed them with my actions, I again apologise profusely. To those who have offered their kind words and understanding these last few days, I am profoundly grateful. I am grateful too to my staff, supporters and the network of volunteers who have worked and campaigned so tirelessly on my behalf over the course of three elections. I only wish I could have been more deserving of the faith you have placed in me."

"Pathetic," said Marchant. "Gets caught with his hand in the tin and crumbs all over his mouth and he can't even admit to enjoying the biscuit. Absolutely pathetic."

He pressed a button on the remote control in his hand, and the screen - jutting, improbably, from the antique oak-panelled walls - faded to black.

If Chestnut House was baroque, a cornucopia of carved wood and gilt edging, brass cornices and glasswork that El had to admit was every bit as immoderate as Kat had described, then the private basement room that Marchant had reserved for their meeting was more so. Their sole light source, three storeys underground, was a set of cast-iron candelabra, dripping hot wax at either end of the banquet table they'd appropriated as a work desk; stuffed badgers, teeth bared and eyes like gimlets, peered out at her from every corner. The widescreen television until a second ago projecting the final death spiral of Seymour Henderson's political career from three feet above their heads was the room's sole concession to modernity.

"You wouldn't have apologised?" she asked, with Alison Miller's politely-feigned interest.

"Weren't you the one who told me that an admission of weakness wouldn't be expedient, politically?"

"In most circumstances it wouldn't. But occasionally a *mea culpa* is the only avenue left."

"On that," he said, baring his own teeth in a vulpine grin, "I have to disagree. Even if nobody wants to be heard admitting it these days, everyone knows what men are and what they like. We fight and we fuck, and we'll happily die doing both if we have to, because that's how we're built. It's encoded in us. There's no point feeling embarrassed about it, much less denying it to ourselves. People may *say* they want a New Man, a reconstructed man, but actually what they want is a *real* man, one who isn't ashamed of what he is. Take my word for it: things would have gone better for Henderson there if he'd just come out and said, *I like whores. I can't help it, and why should I have to? And by the way, it has no bearing at all on my ability to get your laws passed and your drains unblocked.* Oh, perhaps you'd get some blowback at first - from talking heads, and feminists, and the media morality police. But I absolutely guarantee you: you'd have the understanding of almost every man in this country. And some of the women, too."

You don't actually believe that, though, do you? El thought. You're trying to goad me into arguing, to see how much objectionable commentary I'll take before I bite back. And I'd put money on you doing the same with everyone you've got on the payroll.

The longer she spent in Marchant's company, the more convinced she became that nothing of what he said was true - or rather, that nothing of what he said reflected an essential self, a *quiddity* that she could deconstruct or begin to understand. She'd gone into the job expecting a monster - and certainly what she'd found *was* monstrous, but not entirely in the way that she'd anticipated. The crimes he'd committed, the violence he'd enacted had suggested a degree of complexity, from a distance; had built a picture in her mind of a multifaceted Hannibal Lecter of a man, one struggling to reconcile the darkness of his fantasies with the demands of his public life.

What she'd found instead, at least up to now, was a kind of void - an absence. There was still margin for error, for having entirely misjudged him - and she knew better than most the impossibility of ever *really* getting inside someone's head - but it increasingly seemed to her that he, and by extension his actions, were motivated not by sadism or any pleasure taken in the kill, but by convenience. Where other people proved themselves roadblocks, he removed them - it was that simple. It wasn't that he *hated* or *wanted*, she thought; more that he didn't care for much of anything beyond his own self-interest.

She didn't know which idea was harder to bear: her mother beaten and strangled and buried by an out and out misogynist, one who'd actively enjoyed her suffering; by a man who'd kill her because she'd irritated him, or asked the wrong question at the wrong moment, or - and this, she thought, was perhaps the worst option of all - by one who'd chosen her to indulge his morbid curiosity, his *interest* in killing because, from his perspective, she really didn't matter at all.

And why would she have done, to him? To someone who'd burn his own kids to a cinder to protect himself from fallout?

"Can I assume that won't be your *first* public statement on the matter?" she said calmly - denying him, she hoped, the satisfaction of whatever rise he'd expected to get from her.

He laughed, but it rang false, the way so many of his reactions seemed to.

That's because they *are* false, she told herself. There's nothing authentic about them. They're a performance of humanity; a simulacrum, not the real thing.

"We should talk about the video," he said.

They'd agreed on a short campaign video as the best means of introducing Marchant at his debut press conference. Two minutes long and modelled after the multimedia efforts of campaigning American congressmen, it would communicate, as succinctly as possible, the myriad accomplishments of Brand Marchant before the man himself took to the stage: the wealth, the power, the glory.

I don't *have* to do this, it would say. I have everything I could ever need already. But I *want* to do it. For you, and for Britain.

What they *hadn't* agreed, but what El - and Rose, and Ruby and Sita and the others - had already decided, was that Karen would be the one to make it.

"This ends now," Ruby had said, when El and Rose had gone back to Ledbury Road from the hospital, heavy-limbed and almost delirious from lack of sleep. The atmosphere in the house was thicker than treacle, the air in the kitchen where the remaining women sat a fug of stale coffee and exhaustion. Before Ruby's pronouncement, none of them had spoken a word; only cradled their hot drinks and empty mugs, avoiding one another's eyes. Sita wasn't even pretending to read.

"And you've just decided that for everyone?" El had replied belligerently - objecting more to Ruby's tone than to the sentiment itself. Because they probably *should* stop, she thought. Stop, and back away, before any more of them got hurt.

"You think different, do you?" Ruby said, raising her voice. "Even after seeing your mate's head stoved in with a tyre iron?"

Hannah had winced at the words; pulled the blue wool blanket she had wrapped around her tighter against her body.

She'd changed her clothes - exchanging the gore-spattered blouse and jacket for a baggy yellow t-shirt that had probably belonged to Seb, once. But she hadn't washed or showered, and her hair was still matted with blood, her face still streaked with it. She looked haunted, paler than she ever had.

She must know as well as the others how bad things look, El thought; how much damage whatever weapon Marchant's men had used on Kat had done. How easily it could have been *her* wheeled into the operating theatre; *her* in intensive car, hooked up to a ventilator in the bed next to Kat's.

"I think," El said slowly, reining in her anger, "that all of us should have a say in where we go next. We all signed up; we should all get a chance to decide whether we stop or change tack or keep going the way we planned."

"I ain't having any more of you lot hurt," Ruby said. "Not for him."

The unexpected softness of her tone made El hesitate, and she saw, for a second, not the tough-but-protective old lady she was used to - the mother-hen with a sharp tongue and a steel-trap of a mind who'd sat her down one day in a courtyard in Edgware and showed her how to work, how to *think* - but shades of someone else, someone more vulnerable: of the woman, El's own age or younger, who'd run headlong into a burning house with nothing between her and the smoke but a scarf pulled over her face to drag a kid she barely knew to safety. Who'd had no choice but to let another kid be taken by the fire.

"We won't be," said Rose, equally gentle.

She's remembering too, El thought.

"Do we think he knows?" Karen asked.

"Knows what?" said Ruby, rubbing at her temples.

"About us. Who we are, what we're doing."

"There's no reason to think so," said Sita. She took a sip of her tea - masala chai, hot and sweet and smelling of cardamon and ginger. Something she drank, El knew, only when she needed comfort.

"He went after Kat because she gave him Henderson," Rose said, sounding every bit as drained as she looked. "He wanted to make sure there was no connection between Henderson's resignation and his campaign. That's all. Hannah, I'm afraid, was just in the wrong place at the wrong time. And I realise," she added, turning to Hannah, "that I bear much of the blame for that. I'm really very sorry."

"It's alright," said Hannah, pulling the blanket even tighter.

"No point laying blame," said Ruby. "Not now. What we need to be doing now is working out where to go from here. And I'm telling you, we ought to pull out. Let things lie for a bit."

"Should we, though?" said Karen, pensively rolling a screwdriver between her fingers. "I mean - I can only speak for myself here, but Marchant... he's the reason I've never met my old man. Thinking about him is what keeps my mum awake at night, you know what I mean? And I get what you're saying, about what happened to Kat and keeping the rest of us out of harm's way... but if he doesn't *know* about us, then we're still in the clear, right? We're still safe. So if we can still work the job, still bring him down, and it don't hurt nobody else... then I want to. I think I sort of *have* to."

El had never heard her sound so polite; so hesitant.

"And the rest of you?" said Ruby.

El shrugged noncommittally.

"Ask me tomorrow," she said. "Or after I've slept. I can't string a coherent sentence together in this state, let alone make a decision."

"I'm not sure that I can, either," said Rose. "All I know as things stand is that I have no interest in putting the rest of you in the firing line on my behalf. Ruby's right - there's too much risk, too many uncertainties. God knows I want my pound of flesh as much of the rest of you... but Marchant's a killer. And I can't be responsible for exposing you to that, not again. So I suppose what I'm saying for now is: if there *is* a vote, then I abstain. You must make whatever decision you make for yourselves."

"Sita?" asked El.

Sita took another sip of tea - slowly enough, El thought, to buy herself time to compose her thoughts before she gave a definitive answer.

"I'm afraid I'm inclined to agree with Ruby," she said, with none of her usual bite or good humour. "If we can't guarantee your safety, then I don't see that we can justify continuing."

She lowered the cup of tea back down to the table with a thump. Its landing had the finality of a judge's gavel.

"No," said Hannah quietly.

Every one of them turned to look at her.

"Something you want to say, sweetheart?" Ruby asked her.

Hannah drew herself up to her full height, inasmuch as that was possible from a sitting position, and lay one of her hands on top of the other, suddenly composed. There was blood, still, under the nails.

She was a journalist, El remembered. A broadcaster. It probably shouldn't have been a surprise that she knew how to pull herself together under pressure.

"I don't want to stop," Hannah said. "I hear what you're all saying, and I appreciate your concern for my welfare - and for Kat's - but as Karen said: I have to do this. I lost a husband and a child to this man. I've given up my career, my friends, what's left of my mental health to try to drag what he's done into the light of day. So please, please - don't ask me to put the brakes on now. Not when we're so close."

She sank back into her chair and pulled the blanket back around herself, as if the effort of holding court had sapped her strength.

The others, unused to her speaking out on *anything*, took a beat to react.

"You ain't thinking clearly," said Ruby, without judgement. "Makes sense, after what's happened to you. But you'll feel different once you've rested up."

"I'm thinking perfectly clearly," said Hannah. "Do you genuinely believe, after everything, that I don't understand the risks involved? I *choose* to keep going. And if you think you're somehow honouring Kat or paying her respect by pulling back now, I can absolutely tell you that it's not what she would want."

"And how can you be sure what she would want?" said Sita.

"She told me. In the car, before we... On the way to Berkhamsted. We were both a little anxious, after Marchant's phone call and the discussion it generated here. I asked her outright if she thought we were doing the right thing in driving up there, if she ought to be meeting Marchant at all. And she said yes. 100%, yes."

The BMW took the unlit country lanes of south Hertfordshire at a steady, unwavering 30. It was one of Ruby's, clean and well-maintained and stored for the most part in a double-door lockup in Colindale, side-by-side with the half-dozen other cars she kept for the jobs that might need them. More importantly, for Kat's purposes, it was custom-made - the licence plate a mock-up, the VIN number untraceable.

"Are you sure you want to do this?" Hannah asked again, both hands fixed anxiously to the steering wheel.

"Wouldn't have said I was if I wasn't, would I?" said Kat. She pulled down the passenger visor; reapplied her lipstick in the mirror by the murky halogen reflection of the headlamps.

"Aren't you at all nervous, coming to meet him?"

"Oh, give it a rest, would you? You're starting to sound like Violet bloody Kray back there."

Ruby snorted.

"Called me that, did she?" she said. "Cheeky cow."

There was no malice there, El thought. Just amusement and under it, sadness.

The creep of a blush spread across Hannah's cheekbones, joining the darker layer of dried blood that speckled them.

"I'm so sorry," she stammered. "I'm sure she didn't mean..."

"Calm down," said Ruby. "I've been called worse in my time, believe me."

Usually, El realised, Sita would have filled the silence that followed with a quip - something dry and laconic about Ruby's past misadventures that would open the door to the call-and-response bickering that they'd carried on, in one form or another, for thirty years or more.

Instead, she sat quietly at the table, staring down at her teacup.

Kat pursed her lips in the mirror – then, apparently satisfied with what she saw, closed the visor.

"Honestly," she said, "Do you lot think I'm made of glass, or what?"

"They're just concerned," said Hannah. "We all are."

"Well, don't be. I did two years on Commercial Road in Pill before I was 18. I survived that, then I can manage this, thank you very much."

"I'm afraid I'm not familiar with... wherever that is."

"Not spent much time in Newport, then? No, I suppose you wouldn't have. It's not exactly Bond Street, Commercial Road."

She looked out of the window at the shadowy open countryside surrounding them on either side; tapped out the first few notes of The Entertainer on the glove compartment with one long, lacquered nail.

"It's the red light district," she said, after a while. "Wall to wall working girls, morning and night. Bit like King's Cross, if you took away the nightclubs and the stations and it was in the middle of fucking nowhere."

"And you... worked around there?" asked Hannah tentatively, eyes fixed to the empty road ahead of them.

To her surprise, Kat laughed.

"Too bloody English for your own good, you are," she said, a smile in her voice. "Yes, I *worked around there*. And before you kill yourself trying to find a polite way of asking me what it was I did, I'll tell you: I was selling it, the same thing every other girl was doing."

Hannah's reddening cheeks were visible through the darkness.

If El was surprised, it wasn't by the way that Kat had made her money, once upon a time. All of them, she assumed, had done things they'd regretted, through bad luck or circumstance or their own poor judgement. Certainly, *she* had.

No; if anything surprised her, it was Kat's willingness to disclose it so readily. And to Hannah of all people - a woman whose knowledge of the world of prostitution was likely gleaned less from any first-hand experience than from Channel 4 documentaries and purple-prose accounts of Victorian London.

"Did you know?" she asked - to Ruby, and to Rose.

"That she'd been on the game?" Ruby replied. "She might've mentioned it, yeah."

Rose didn't answer. Perhaps, El thought, she'd really meant it in the hospital, when she'd talked about respecting other people's privacy - the secrets they'd shared with her directly, and the ones she'd bought from Lomax.

"She was sixteen," said Hannah. "A child. She didn't choose it."

For a moment, El hated her. Hated the narrow, middle-class parameters of her moral compass, her belief - implicit but louder than bombs - that only two types of women could ever do sex work: the blameless ones, the ones who'd been coerced into it and couldn't get away, and the others, the scarlet women who'd *chosen* it, who'd rather walk the streets than do an honest day's work on an assembly line or stacking shelves in Tesco. Innocent sheep and profligate goats.

Which category, El wondered, would she think El's mother fell into?

"It was Marchant's doing," Hannah continued. "If anyone put her there, it was him."

"My dad was an engineer," Kat had told Hannah, apropos of nothing.

"Alright," Hannah had said, confusion heaping itself on to the embarrassment and awkwardness that had gripped her after Kat's initial revelation.

"Well, I say 'engineer'... He was a bit more senior than that, really. Owned his own company, a couple of factories, that sort of thing. Made vacuum cleaners, blow dryers, food mixers... you name it. Fancied himself as a bit of an inventor too - a bit of a George Stephenson type, you know? Forever tinkering away on something in his workshop."

She paused.

"And I expect you want to know why I'm bringing him up, after what I just told you?" she said.

"Perhaps a little," Hannah replied cautiously.

Kat wound down the window; took a pack of cigarettes from her handbag and lit one, releasing pure white contrails of smoke into the dark air outside.

"It all comes back to Marchant," she said, watching the smoke twist and coil from her open mouth. "Just like bloody everything. He ruined my dad, see. Took everything he had. And when the business was gone, and the house, and they found him hanging in the woods - well, that was when I ended up in Pill."

He rarely used its real name, its *official* name, and he never told them exactly how it worked. But she was a nosy kid, always peering round corners and listening through walls, and she'd picked up enough to know that it was some kind of engine component - but for ships's engines, not cars's. Something to make them move faster through the water, more efficiently.

He'd been working on it for the best part of a year - first in his shed in the garden and then, after a while, in the dedicated workspace he'd carved out in a backroom of the factory over in Holt.

He called it The Prototype, with a capital P and a definite article she'd heard in his voice long before she ever saw it written down.

It didn't look like much to her - just a load of valves and horns and bolts, a little grey elephant of a thing that, even if it *wasn't* an engine, could easily have fitted under the bonnet of a car. Nothing at all like the *other* engines she'd seen in some of her dad's books: the Difference Engine that could have doubled as a church organ, the rocket-sized marine propulsion systems that wouldn't have been out of place in an industrial dairy.

"It's a turbocharger," her sister Jan had told her, when she'd come down for one of her weekend visits. "You put it *on top* of the engine - or *into* it, or something. Makes it go quicker."

Jan was 19 then, living down in Pontypool with an apprentice heating technician named Eoghan who had her convinced of his mechanical genius.

"Why's it so small, then?" Kat had asked.

"Because it's a *prototype*," Jan had told her, disgusted by breadth of the 12 year old Kat's ignorance. "What it *is*, is a model. It's not meant to actually go *in* the ship - just show how it'd work, if it did. For demonstration, like."

"But it *would* work, would it? In real life?"

"You'd best hope so," Jan had said, shrugging. "Sunk just about everything into it, Da has. You know Gareth Price, who works at the building society? I saw him down the pub last night. He said Da's been taking out loans left, right and centre to pay for the parts. On the house, on the business, you name it."

Kat had heard of older siblings who, after the death of a parent, had become protective; had stepped in overnight to play a parental role for their younger brothers and sisters. That wasn't Jan. She'd only got harder, after their Ma had passed - less patient of Kat's naivety, less inclined to shield her from harsh realities. It had been a relief when she'd moved in with Eoghan; more so, when the two of them had moved down south.

"What's he going to do with it, when he's finished it?" said Kat.

"Fucked if I know," said Jan. "Gareth said he'd got a buyer lined up, though. Someone interested, anyway. Some big cheese in shipping and haulage, Gareth said. England's answer to Aristotle Onassis."

Kat hadn't known who Aristotle Onassis was, but had also known better than to say so in front of Jan.

"He'll make the money back, then?" she'd asked instead.

"If he doesn't fuck it up," Jan said, "and if that Prototype works as well as he says it does... then he'll do a lot more than that. You'd be looking at triple, quadruple the amount he's spent on it already. More, even."

"Wow."

"*Wow*'s about right. I just hope he spreads some of it around where it's needed. Not being funny, but some of us could use a bit of a cash injection."

"The Holt factory got broken into about a month after," Kat said, taking a final drag on her cigarette and throwing the butt out of the window. "They didn't take much - a few tools, a bit of money from the safe. And the Prototype."

Hannah, who'd sat through enough interviews with talking heads and politicians to know when it was better to listen and let other people talk, stayed quiet.

"It was obvious what they'd been after," Kat said. "And it was obvious who'd sent them to get it - this shipping bloke, this whoever-he-was Onassis."

"Marchant?" Hannah asked.

"Yep. Not that I could've said then who he was. My dad was a secretive old sod when he wanted to be - he hadn't told anyone the *name* of his buyer, or any sort of, you know... identifying detail. Hadn't even put it in his notebook, he was that paranoid. It wasn't 'til Rose came calling with that video of hers that I knew enough to say who for certain who it was who'd done it."

That was it, El thought, another piece of the wider picture sliding into place. That was the break-in up north that Karen had talked about. And getting hold of the Prototype, whatever it was - that was Leon Baxter's last job.

She studied Karen's face; watched her grimace, and then pull the muscles in her face back into blankness with impressive self-control as the implications of Kat's story hit her. Sita looked down into her teacup, still steadfastly refusing to make eye contact. Ruby was impassive, but there was a crease between her eyebrows deep enough to suggest that this last bit of information had taken even her by surprise.

All these women's lives, tangled up together like fishhooks, El thought. And none of them knew how much, until we got started.

None of them but Rose.

"The bank took the factories first," Kat told Hannah, spraying her wrists and neck with heavy vanilla perfume and popping a stick of peppermint gum in her mouth. "It took them a while to come for the house - it wasn't quick, you know? More this sort of long, drawn-out parade of red bills and bailiffs and the electric getting cut off. We were staying in a B&B in Llangollen when he topped himself."

"I had to move in with Jan and Eoghan pretty sharpish. Wouldn't have been my first choice, but it was that or the children's home in Wrexham, and we'd all heard the stories about what happened up there. Jan was a fucking chocolate teapot, but Eoghan tried to make me feel at home, bless him. I can't say I made it easy for them, either, bunking off school and smoking weed and what have you. Then I met a boy from Newport - well, a man, really - and ended up more or less living with him. And he turned out to be... well, not so nice, put it that way. Who'd have seen *that* coming, eh? And before you know it, it's midnight and I'm out on Commercial Road with a mini-skirt barely covering my arse giving handjobs to dirty old men in alleyways for three quid a go."

This time, Hannah grimaced. Kat chuckled.

"Offended your sensibilities, have I?" she said. "Sorry about that."

"I wasn't..." Hannah protested, and then stopped. There was another car on the road behind them, its make and colour all but obscured by the blinding brightness of its headlights.

The car accelerated, moving so close behind them that Hannah could keep her vision free of its glare only by turning her head away from the mirrors. It swerved right to overtake them, giving her a momentary glimpse of something long, sleek and black - a Jaguar or an American sedan, its smoked glass obscuring the driver inside.

Then, when it was perhaps 50 feet ahead of them, it swerved again, swinging back horizontally into the left lane - *their* lane - until it was blocking the road ahead with its body.

"Go around it," said Kat, sounding panicked. "Just fucking go around it."

But Hannah, on autopilot, had already slowed the BMW; was already pressing a foot down onto the brake.

"I don't know why I did it," Hannah told them, hanging her head. "I don't know why stopping was my first reaction."

"Bound to be," said Ruby. "It's basic road safety. Sort of thing you get drummed into you as soon as you start driving. You see something stop dead right in front of you, you stop dead yourself before you hit it."

"I should have gone around it," Hannah said. Then: "But it doesn't change the point I've been trying to make. Kat didn't want to stop then. She wouldn't have wanted us to stop now. Marchant hurt her, every bit as much as he hurt all of you."

"And now he's hurt her again, hasn't he?" said Ruby.

"Yes, he has. Which is all the more reason for us to keep going - to finish this. Because if it was worth us doing it before - well, are you really going to tell me that it isn't worth it now?"

Hannah sat up straight; looked right at Ruby. Ruby stared back.

The door opened, and a pair of frock-coated Chestnut House porters, both young and extravagantly bearded, entered the basement room, wheeling between them an antique dining trolley. On the trolley lay half a dozen silver serving dishes, their lids removed to reveal lamb steaks and mint sauce, French beans and new potatoes. Two bottles of wine, one white and one red, sat uncorked beside the dishes.

"I don't remember ordering this," said Marchant.

The taller of the porters, his nostrils and forehead still freckled with teenage blackheads, stepped forward, pre-emptively shielding his colleague from the brunt of Marchant's ire.

"It's lunchtime, sir," he said. "Your assistant told us you'd like to have lunch when she made your booking."

"What I'd *like*," said Marchant, "is a little privacy. Is that too much to ask?"

Another figure appeared in the doorway, behind the porters: a woman, tall and elegant, her make-up a perfectly-applied mask and her suit impossibly well-tailored.

Hannah, in her warpaint.

"How do you do it?" she asked Marchant, ignoring the others. "How do you sit there, eating, after the things that you've done?"

She was good; better than El had expected she would be.

"I'm sorry, who are you?" said Marchant. "Or rather, what the hell are you doing down here? This is a members's club, not Victoria station. You can't just walk in off the street."

He's lying again, El thought. He recognises her. He might not know yet *why* he recognises her, but the way he's looking at her - he's seen her before. She's not a total stranger.

Hannah stepped forward, further into the room.

"You think you can hide from it," she said, her voice steady. "That if you burrow down in your rathole, then nobody will find out. But you're wrong."

"Find out?" said El, planting the smallest seed of concern into Alison Miller's delivery. "Find out what?"

Hannah twisted her body towards her, eyes blazing.

She's *very* good, thought El.

"What he is," Hannah told her. "What he's done. He's a murderer. A murderer, and worse."

"Forgive me for asking," said Marchant to the porters, "but could one of you please *do your fucking job* and remove this woman?"

Hannah raised her hands, palms up.

"No need," she said, "I'm going. But consider this a warning shot," she added to Marchant. "I have proof, you see. Proof of the things you've done. So enjoy your wine and your lunches. Because I don't plan to keep it to myself for long."

She smiled at him, lips curling wide enough to show her gumline - then, as suddenly as she'd entered, turned her back on them and walked out into the passageway, the click of her heels echoing along the flagstones.

A moment later the porters, shell-shocked, took off after her.

Marchant, by contrast, seemed relaxed - entirely unfazed by the incident.

He extended a leg towards the dining trolley; hooked a foot behind one wheel and pulled it towards the table.

Relaxed, El told herself, or just a hell of an actor.

"I've always thought the security here a little lax," he said. "Seems fair to say I was right, doesn't it? There's a mental health facility two streets away, you know. Out-patient, as well as in."

He paused.

"Everything alright, Alison?" he asked.

She probably looked anxious, she thought. But perhaps the appearance of anxiety wasn't so bad, under the circumstances.

"I don't enjoy surprises, James," she said slowly. "Surprises can blindside you. They can derail campaigns. So I'm going to ask you this once, and I have to insist that you're honest with me when you answer: is there something I ought to know, before we go any further? Are there any surprises likely to crawl out of the woodwork between now and the election?"

He snatched a single French bean from the trolley with his fingers; bit into it with apparent relish.

"Absolutely none," he said.

EDGWARE

1996

R uby dropped a custard cream into her coffee, added two more lumps of
sugar and then, when she'd judged the biscuit sufficiently soggy, fished
it out with a tea spoon and ate it.

"I don't know what you wanted to meet here for," she told El, curling up
like a stately housecat in her yellow wingback chair. "Ain't we seeing enough
of each other at Rose's?"

"I imagine she has a few questions for us," said Sita from the sofa, "and
she thought it might be easier to ask them *here* rather than there. Questions
about Rose, perhaps. Isn't that right, darling?"

El was wrong-footed. She'd thought insisting on speaking to them both at
Ruby's flat, urgently - but not telling them *why* - would put her in the driving
seat; would give her a bit of control over the course of the conversation that
ensued. But as Ruby never tired of reminding her, they were clever old birds.
And anything she'd learned, in the past two months - any new data point
she'd collected, any tiny insight she'd unearthed - they seemed to know
already, and to know more besides. The way they did now.

"You mean Olivia?" said El, playing her strongest card first.

Neither of them gave her the reaction she'd been hoping for.

"Told you about that, then, did she?" she Ruby mildly, reaching for another custard cream.

"I must say, I'm glad she felt she could," said Sita. "She doesn't trust easily. Though who would, in her position?"

"And you didn't think to mention it before?" El asked. "Say, when you first roped me into this?"

Ruby chewed at the biscuit contemplatively.

"I've kept it to myself for nigh on 30 years," she said. "Both of us have. We didn't know no other way to keep her safe. So we weren't about to go spreading it around now, were we?"

To her irritation, El found herself agreeing with the logic of the statement, the bubble of her indignation deflating. What other way was there but secrecy and silence to keep Rose out of Marchant's crosshairs?

"I wish you'd told me," she said.

"I wish we could have," said Sita. "I really do."

El took a sip of her own coffee.

"What I don't understand," she said to Ruby, "is what you were doing at her house in the first place. I assume you were running a job on Marchant - but why go to his mistress's place, when he only went there himself once a fortnight? Why not his wife's?"

"Ah," said Sita, catching Ruby's eye.

"She didn't tell you that bit, then?" Ruby asked.

"What bit?" said El.

"Well," said Sita, sounding almost sheepish, "the thing is... we *were* there, you see. With his wife. Or rather, *I* was..."

It started with a chest of drawers.

"Not just *any* chest of drawers," Sita assured her. "A Louis XIV commode - brass and tortoiseshell, absolutely exquisite."

The chest - the commode - sold at Sotheby's in the autumn of 1965 to Mrs Elizabeth Marchant, née Bellman: daughter of retail magnate Saul Bellman, and wife of entrepreneur and property developer James Marchant. Sita read about the sale in the trade press; was immediately captivated by the glossy photograph that accompanied the article, by the intricate Boulle Work that jumped out at her from the page.

"All I could think," she said, "was how utterly *magnificent* it would look in my sitting room. I knew I had to have it."

A few discreet but well-placed enquiries into the habits and foibles of Mrs Marchant later, and Sita settled on a plan for liberating the commode from her clutches: the Fortune Teller.

She'd run it before, more than once. It worked especially well, she'd found, on the very wealthy, who ran as a cohort more superstitious than the average - very likely, she considered, because they had so much to lose, and so much as a consequence to *worry* about losing.

The first time, she'd gone all out, draping herself in bandanas, gold jewellery and flowing skirts - a caricature of a fairground gypsy. She'd quickly realised, though, that many of the props were unnecessary; that the subtle aesthetic suggestion of Eastern mysticism was more effective, a better convincer for the white, middle-aged power brokers of Europe than a crystal ball and a deck of Tarot cards. Thereafter, she'd kept things simpler: a sari here, a hint of henna there, an occasional bindi on her forehead to complement the Delhi sing-song she'd allow into her voice.

Since, as she'd learned, Mrs Marchant was not only an astute businesswoman but a sucker for the esoteric and the uncanny, and a much-seen presence around the occult bookshops of Charing Cross and Fitzrovia - and since Sita's web of connections spanned the length and breadth of the city, up to and including its more arcane corners - it was comparatively little effort to contrive a first meeting. Favours were called in, palms were greased, and in a matter of a fortnight, two booksellers, a clairvoyant and a specialist in astral projection had dropped into their conversations with Mrs Marchant the news that a rare and exceptional talent in the art of divination had settled in the capital: a Madam Raksha Chandravali, late of Gurgaon. One of the booksellers, after no small amount of persuasion on Mrs Marchant's part, had offered up a phone number for Madam Chandravali - and thus Sita's work began.

The first reading took place on a dull Tuesday afternoon in the Marchant family home, at Madam Chandravali's insistence. To accurately predict the fortunes of her clients, as she told Mrs Marchant during their initial telephone exchange, it was necessary to regard them in their natural habitat - to get a sense of the physical objects and more nebulous energies that surrounded them in daily life.

The house had been very much what Sita had expected: a mansion at the nicer end of Elgin Crescent, wide and white-washed on the outside and high-ceilinged and badly insulated within. There were no obvious charms or magical trinkets on display in the hallway or the small library Mrs Marchant settled them into - but perhaps, she'd thought, *Mr* Marchant was less keen than his spouse on the mystical side of life, and his wife felt compelled as a consequence to conceal the evidence of her enthusiasm from view.

The library, in any event, had everything she needed for the reading - a pair of comfortable chairs, a solid teak table to gaze meaningfully across, and little enough natural light that long shadows seem to peer out at them from every corner - and the session progressed without a hitch, if uninspiringly, Sita peppering Madam Chandravali's generic, Eastern-accented pronouncements on the state of Mrs Marchant's health and marriage with more specific facts gleaned from a cold read of her face and body. Mrs Marchant was beside herself - drinking all of it in with a childlike wonder that belied her age and social status.

"I didn't *do* a great deal that first time," Sita said. "It was very much an exercise in scene-setting - in piquing her interest, building her trust. You know how it is, with the Fortune Teller."

In fact, El didn't. She'd never liked the Fortune Teller; had always found it faintly distasteful, avoiding it wherever she could, even where she knew, rationally, that it would be the best tool for the job.

"She called that evening to invite me back for a second reading at her house, for the following morning," said Sita.

"Paid over the odds for it, and all," added Ruby. "She was *that* keen."

The second session, held again in the library, progressed much as the first had, with Mrs Marchant as delighted as she'd been the day before by Madam Chandravali's pearls of prophetic wisdom. This time, however, Madam Chandravali made a request of her host: that she be allowed to view the whole house, or those parts of it into which visitors were usually allowed, in order that she might commune more directly with its psychic life force - and give, in turn, a more accurate and comprehensive reading.

"Oh, gosh, of *course* you may!" Mrs Marchant replied, seemingly horrified that the thought hadn't occurred to her first.

They toured the ground floor first: the austere Georgian interiors of the drawing room, the dining room, the breakfast room, Sita's eyes peeled for any trace of the Boulle commode. Then the first floor: the predictably floral bedrooms of the Marchants and any guests that might come upon them, the felt-lined playrooms of their two young sons, the nursery of their baby daughter.

And then, the study.

She saw the commode immediately - a vision of alloy on ebony, calling out to her from beside an entirely forgettable Edwardian loveseat.

She swooned, only partially for her host's benefit; leaned into cushions of the loveseat for support.

"Are you quite alright?" Mrs Marchant asked, looking anxiously down at her.

Madam Chandravali pressed a palm to her heart; inhaled deeply, as if to compose herself.

"That chest," she said fearfully, pointing to the commode. "It is yours?"

"Yes," said Mrs Marchant, puzzled. "We bought it last week at auction. My cousin Judith saw it in the catalogue. She thought it might go nicely with the sofa."

Your cousin Judith, Sita thought, is a groundling, an utter philistine, and if there were any justice would be barred from every auction house in England.

"The energy," she said, her breath coming in shallow, erratic bursts. "It is... wrong, you know? Dark. Very dark."

"Its... energy?" said Mrs Marchant.

"The vibrations. They are, how do you call it? On a negative frequency. All around it, there is darkness - deep, terrible darkness. Painful darkness. I'm sorry, I cannot..."

She straightened up, pushing down on the loveseat and jettisoning her body away from the commode, feet propelling her backwards until she was very nearly in the doorframe.

"I cannot be here," she said. "I cannot be in this place with a thing so dark as this. I must leave, now."

She swooned again - and allowed her body, this time, to fall all the way to the floor.

"A Cursed Object scam?" said El, incredulously. "Really?"

"People were less clued up in them days," said Ruby, El thought a little wistfully. "You'd tell 'em their mattress had an evil spirit living in it, and they'd *pay* you to get rid of it."

"And send you flowers afterwards," said Sita.

Mrs Marchant helped her up from the ground and walked her, gingerly, to the guest bedroom.

She rallied.

"I'm very sorry," she said, settling down on the end of the bed and cradling her temples in her hands. "My head..."

Mrs Marchant knelt down in front of her, between her legs, and placed her own hands over Sita's.

"The chest," she said. "You said... you said there was something *wrong* with it?"

Take it gently, Sita told herself. Slow and steady wins the race.

"In my country," she said, "we call them *bhoots*. Ghosts, you know? The spirits of the dead. Angry spirits, vengeful spirits, full of evil and hatred. They walk this world, but they become sometimes... tangled in material things. Trapped in them. Like a genie in a lamp."

"Spirits?" said Mrs Marchant, looking as haunted as the commode.

"No-one knows how it happens, how it is that a *bhoot* comes to be made. Some say it is when there is violence at the moment of death - a spirit cannot pass on, because of the strength of his anger at the wrong that has been done to him. Often he will rage and scream and rattle his chains, like the poor sad things that linger in your cemeteries and your haunted houses. But other times, they say, he will bind himself, his very essence, to the object that is nearest to him as his life ebbs away - a weapon, an item of clothing, an ornament. A piece of furniture."

Mrs Marchant squeezed Sita's hands with an urgency that was more panic than comfort.

"And you believe," she asked quietly, "that my cabinet is one of these objects? That it's... possessed, somehow?"

Sita squeezed back, in a show of solidarity.

"There is no *believe* about it," she said. "A *bhoot* has made his home in it - and a bad one, very bad, one that wishes all of us great harm. The only question I am asking now is how we must evict him."

"I knew I had her," Sita said, sighing. "From the moment she asked about the commode, I knew that she'd want to be rid of it, any way she could be. I wonder sometimes why I didn't wrap things up there and then - why I didn't just offer to take it off her hands and walk away."

"But you know this one," Ruby told El, gesturing to Sita. "Never knows when to call it a day, that's her trouble. Especially not when she's got a mark on the hook in a million pound house out west."

"17 million these days," said Sita. "I saw it listed recently. And unfortunately," she added for El's benefit, "your Auntie Ruby is right. I never *do* know when to stop. And I'd be lying if I said that I hadn't wondered more than once at the time whether there were any more treasures like the Boulle hiding up there in plain sight..."

"Before we speak more," Madam Chandravali said, "may I trouble you for a glass of water? And perhaps a headache tablet?"

Mrs Marchant scrambled to her feet. There were, Sita knew, at least three staff below stairs, a nanny, a cook and a maid, the latter of whom would typically perform the task of bringing drinks and analgesics to the Marchants and their guests - but equally, she suspected that, in this moment, the lady of the house would likely seize any opportunity to flee the room and catch her breath.

She only hoped it would take her a while to find the glass.

"I'll get it," Mrs Marchant said, backing out of the room but leaving the door wide, and tantalisingly, open.

When the sound of her host's footsteps grew fainter and further away, Sita sprung from the bed, stepped out of her shoes and crept from the room, quiet as a mouse.

She took the carpeted steps to the second floor two at a time, on tiptoe. The floor plan she'd managed to source from a contact at the council before Madam Chandravali made her entrance had indicated that it comprised three rooms, each of a similar size. Could one of them, she wondered, be a strong-room? A holding place for the Marchants's other acquisitions?

The first room held nothing but musical instruments: a spruce and maple cello, a pedal harp - late 19th century, she thought - and a baby grand piano, a pitch-black Bechstein that might in other circumstances have captured her attention.

The second was evidently intended for use by the children. Here, unlike elsewhere in the house, there was a small television set and a wireless; a stack of dog-eared Beezer, Topper and Dandy comic books piled haphazardly onto an end table.

The third was more interesting.

From outside, she could see perhaps half the space inside: the leg of an armchair, the thick tassels of a Persian rug, the back end of a writing desk that could have been a Mackintosh. What she could *see*, however, was less curious than what she could *hear*: an Englishman's voice, hard-edged and irritated, reciting a string of numbers, and then - after a brief pause - the word *axiom* into what she assumed to be a telephone receiver.

She listened.

"A line of digits and a code word down the phone," said Ruby. "Know what that means, don't you? 9 times out of 10 anyway."

"Swiss bank account?" El replied.

Sita nodded.

She craned her neck towards the door, straining to hear more, not least the password that could be used, in the absence of other identifying information, to gain access to the account remotely – by, for example, a third party with a good memory for numbers, a conversational fluency in French and Italian and a working knowledge of Swiss privacy laws and banking conventions.

But the man behind the door - and it was Mr Marchant, it had to be -

gave her nothing, and eventually, conscious of the imminent return of Mrs Marchant from the bowels of the kitchen, she gave up, retreating downstairs to the guest room whence she came.

"Suffice to say, that weren't the end of it," said Ruby.

"But that it *had* been," said Sita. "The thing is, you see, that numbered account... it lit rather a fire under me. Because if our Mr Marchant had a numbered account - or more than one - then he almost certainly also had something to hide. Something to hide, and a great deal of money he hadn't been declaring."

"The top two things she looks for in a bloke," Ruby added.

"In a *mark*, certainly," said Sita.

"So you switched targets?" El asked. "From Liz Marchant to her husband?"

"Essentially, yes," Sita said. "Though I don't mind telling you, it took the effort of the gods to sacrifice the commode..."

"Still - greater good, eh?" said Ruby.

"Sacrifice?" said El.

"It must be destroyed," she told Mrs Marchant, as the lady of the house handed her the water.

"Destroyed?" Mrs Marchant replied, aghast.

"Destroyed," she repeated. "Immolated, if such a thing is possible. It is the fire, you know? Only the fire can burn away the spirit within."

"You've got to hand it to her," said Ruby. "It was a hell of a convincer. She could have took it away and told her she was doing some sort of private exorcism on it behind closed doors, but no - she stood there with her in the garden, shoulder to shoulder while it burned, saying her incantations and what have you."

"I lit the first bloody match," said Sita ruefully. "And dear God, the *smell* of it when the ebony started to smoulder! It almost bought me to tears."

"Worked though, didn't it?" said Ruby.

"I suppose it did," Sita conceded.

"Tell you what," said Ruby, leaning conspiratorially towards El. "If she trusted *Madam Chandravali* here *before* she rid her house of evil spirits, then afterwards... well, she started looking at her like she'd hung the moon."

"Which was fortunate, really," Sita added. "Given how anxious I was to get to know her. And her family."

Madam Chandravali was a frequent visitor to the Marchant home thereafter, sharing tea and confidences with Mrs Marchant and delivering, where necessary, a psychic reading of such depth and sagacity that it quickly became impossible for Mrs Marchant to imagine how she'd navigate the world without her guidance.

The older Marchant children warmed to her, fascinated first by her exoticism and then, when its appeal threatened to wane, by the boiled sweets she'd hand them as they mobbed her at the door. Saul Bellman was similarly charmed - by her slender neck and the curve of her hips as much as by her knowing good humour.

"You've got to remember," Ruby said, casting an appraising look Sita's way, "she was a proper looker in her day. Could hardly nip down the shops for someone handing her chocolates or asking her out for dinner. I'd probably have tried it on with her myself, if I were that way inclined."

"I'm sorry?" said Sita, arching an eyebrow back at her. "*Was* a looker?"

Only Mr Marchant remained chilly - avoiding her wherever he could, and refusing point-blank his wife's every invitation to join the two of them in the library.

It was obvious from the first that he disliked her - and moreover, that he resented her presence in his house, and the extent to which she monopolised his wife's attention and affections.

"What was he going to do about it, though?" Ruby said. "Couldn't afford to piss Liz off, could he? Not while old Saul was alive and holding the purse-strings, insisting Liz stay on the board and had a say in all the company decisions. He had to keep his mouth shut."

A month of furtive but unprofitable rifling through ledger books and notepads later - her every muscle primed to spring up like a jack in the box and race to Marchant's office whenever his wife left the library to go to the toilet or attend to the children - and Sita was no closer to finding any passwords, or any hint of where such passwords might be.

Surely, she reasoned, he'd written them down somewhere - no man would be so foolish as to rely exclusively on his own recollection when the stakes were so high, particularly not if there were multiple accounts at play. But where?

She was confident by then that she'd explored every inch of the house in which exploration was possible, had peered down every nook and cranny and cracked open every cheaply-made safe inexpertly hidden behind a Renoir print - which forced her to conclude, grudgingly, that he was keeping the records elsewhere, somewhere away from his primary residence.

Probably not at his office, she thought. Old Saul still had a finger in every pie of his business - and were she in Marchant's position, she certainly wouldn't risk an inquisitive father-in-law happening upon sensitive, possibly incriminating documents the next time he popped by. She'd put money, in fact, on no other member of the Marchant household having any inkling that the Swiss account - or accounts - existed; was reasonably certain moreover, from the rumours she'd heard circulating about his less than savoury commercial reputation and apparent absence of professional scruples, that at least some of the deposits Marchant would have made *into* the account would have been siphoned, somehow, from the private funds of either Elizabeth or Saul himself.

If she were Marchant, she thought, she'd keep a second office; a clandestine one, entirely separate from and unknown to his wife and father in law.

The question, again, was: *where?*

"Which is where I came in," said Ruby.

"I needed someone to follow him." Sita said. "To find out where he was going, when he wasn't at home or at the office."

"Someone a bit less conspicuous than Madam Chandravali here," added Ruby.

"Your Auntie Ruby always was a dab hand with a pair of binoculars," said Sita. "And I appreciate you wouldn't immediately think so, but she can blend really quite masterfully into the background when she needs to."

El had seen this unexpected talent of Ruby's for herself, more than once, in the course of a job, and the unlikely marriage of woman and skill had never failed to surprise her. The experience was not dissimilar, she thought, to happening upon an elderly and asthmatic Yorkshire terrier that could, when it wanted to, dance a perfect merengue.

"Weren't easy, I'll tell you that much," Ruby said. "Do you know how many blocks of flats he owned by then, how many houses? And not just in London - all over the bleedin' country. I swear to God, I spent half that October speeding round backroads after him when he went to look in on 'em."

"I don't know *why* you did," said Sita. "I told you he wouldn't be keeping anything in any of them. They were Saul's properties too - he'd never have taken the risk."

"You couldn't've known that for sure, though, could you?" Ruby argued. "It was guesswork."

"I trust my instincts. They've been good to me, so far."

"And I like to have a bit more evidence before I jump to conclusions, thank you very much."

El snorted at the sheer audacity of the lie.

"Anyway," said Ruby, shooting El a look that suggested there'd be significantly fewer custard creams and cups of coffee in her future if she'd didn't watch her manners, "mostly they were short trips. Never more than a minute or two, normally. Checking they were still standing, was my take on it. But there was one place he stopped for longer, the couple of times I seen him go in there. And by longer I mean overnight. Little place in Clapham - nice enough, but nothing special from where I was standing. Unless you count the woman kissing him hello on the doorstep or the two little girls who were hugging him and calling him Daddy."

"Rose and her sister," said El slowly, processing the information.

"Got it in one," said Ruby.

"A second family, a second home," said Sita. "It was the obvious place for him to hide the things he didn't want to be found - and the one place neither Saul nor Elizabeth could ever know about."

"So obviously," said Ruby, "it was the one place we knew we had to be."

They decided on a two-pronged attack, with any profits split between them, 50/50.

Madam Chandravali would continue her visits to the Marchant home, ferreting out whatever nuggets of information she could from Elizabeth, Saul and the family cook – a cheerful and pleasantly talkative woman with whom she was cultivating the beginnings of a friendship.

Ruby, meanwhile, would find a way to insinuate herself into the *second* Marchant house - ideally in such a guise as to allow her easy access to its secrets and, eventually, to the bank passcodes that Sita was sure she'd find there.

As a cleaner, perhaps. Or a housekeeper.

"I was expecting getting in to be more of a challenge, to be quite honest with you," said Ruby. "As it was, I barely had to break a sweat. She was a stroppy one, the mistress - Rose's Mum. And a drinker. But she was a snob, too. Thought she deserved better than what she'd got - you know the sort. Women like that don't need much of a nudge to start believing they ought to have servants."

"What did you do?" asked El.

"Bumped into her down the Co-op," said Ruby. "And I mean *literally* bumped into her - sent her shopping flying. Baked beans and Golden Wonder bloody everywhere. By the time I'd picked everything up and helped her carry it home, good citizen that I am, she'd given me her life story - all except the shacking up with a married man, obviously. She told me *he* was a salesman, something high up in insurance - that he made a lot of money, but wasn't home much."

"Now, I'd love to tell you it was my gift of the gab that got it out of her, but I'm pretty sure from the smell coming off her she was already half-cut by then, even if it *had* just gone lunchtime. And I didn't get the sense she had a lot of people round her willing to just... listen to her."

"I said how hard it had to be for her, raising two girls practically on her own with no-one to help her with the cooking and cleaning and clearing up after them, and she said it was - that she'd do anything for a bit of time to herself now and then."

"So I said to her: this bloke of yours. He might not have much time to give you, but if he's got as much money as you say he has, why don't you get him to spend some of it on a domestic? You know - someone to help you out a bit in the evenings and get the tea ready for the kids when they come home from school?"

"She thought it was a bloody *brilliant* idea, didn't know why she hadn't thought of it before. Asked me if I knew anyone who fit the bill."

"Which was Auntie Ruby's cue, of course," said Sita, "to tell her that, as luck would have it, she had some experience herself in domestic work - and happened, by a further stroke of good fortune, to have very recently vacated her last position..."

It was undemanding work, especially for a woman with two young boys of her own who knew her way around a chip-pan. She did four days a week at the Clapham house, cleaning and tidying in the mornings and cooking dinner for the family in the afternoons. She went by the name Martha, because it tickled her, and hoped Marchant's mistress was no more of a Bible scholar than she looked.

The mistress was a nightmare, vacillating like a lot of drunks Ruby had known between ostentatious displays of gratitude for Ruby's help and unpredictable flares of temper, also directed Ruby's way - one often following so closely behind the other that a single afternoon might reasonably accommodate both a heartfelt proclamation of affection and an accusation of stealing sixpence from the dresser.

The girls, though, were a delight - thoughtful and intelligent and sensitive, the younger girl more playful where the older one was more earnest. Ruby liked both of them enormously; wished more and better for them than the hand they'd been dealt, in spite of the private schools and pony lessons bankrolled by their largely absent father.

From Marchant himself she kept her distance, keeping her head down and her back to him on the rare occasions he'd come to stay - in part as a protective measure, to keep herself from being identified in the future, and in part because, whatever she might say, she trusted her own instincts every bit as much as Sita, and her instincts were telling her loud and clear that he was a man she'd do well to avoid.

Of the promised bank codes, to her frustration, she found nothing.

"I was a month or so into the job when it happened," she told El. "*He* was meant to be round that night, having dinner with the kids, so I plated up the food for the four of them and made myself scarce."

She hadn't planned to follow Marchant anywhere that evening - assuming, as was typically the case when he visited his second family, that he'd be staying the night.

She'd skulked around the overgrown garden, very briefly, after her shift ended, while he and the kids were eating - poking her nose into the tool shed near the rusty gate at the bottom, just in case she'd missed anything the third or fourth time she'd been in to investigate. Then she'd made her way back up, through the tall grass, and tiptoed quietly through the alleyway that ran alongside the house and spilled her back out onto the street by the front door.

There were raised voices, his and the mistress's, drifting out through the open kitchen window as she passed, but she hadn't thought much of it - the mistress had been hammering the Blue Nun all day, getting more and more belligerent with every glass, and Marchant had a short fuse himself, so a slanging match had seemed to her the inevitable consequence of throwing the two of them together in a confined space for any length of time. She couldn't catch many of the words, but the gist of it was clear enough: she wanted him to leave his wife, and he never would.

I shouldn't push your luck, love, she'd thought.

She'd parked the Aston Martin three doors down and across the road from the house - assuming (so far accurately) that neither the mistress nor loverboy would believe that a woman like her could ever own a car like that, even if they saw her approaching it with the keys in her hand. She had the lights on and the engine running already when she realised her glasses weren't where they should have been - that she must have left them inside, neglected to put them back in her handbag after she'd taken them off to clean.

She didn't need them to drive - they were sunglasses, purely decorative - but she didn't fancy leaving them behind, either: they were Oliver Goldsmith, Manhattans, and exactly the sort of thing she could imagine the mistress pocketing if she saw them lying around unattended. She'd likely think they were knock-offs, that Ruby had picked them up down the market rather than direct from the Goldsmith family in Poland Street, but that hardly mattered - real or fake, they'd still be gone.

She had the driving side door half opened and was running through excuses to get herself back in the house and up to the bathroom when Marchant emerged outside - looking shiftily from left to right, like a caricature of a burglar, then striding briskly over to his MG and disappearing inside.

Interesting, she'd thought - the Manhattans suddenly forgotten. He'd never left before, not even after a row.

She ducked down into her seat; waited until he'd pulled out onto the road and then followed him in the Aston as he drove away.

"I was expecting him to head off home," said Ruby. "Back to Liz and Elgin Crescent. But he didn't. He didn't go far at all."

He stopped the MG outside a corner shop in Stockwell. She watched him go inside; kept her binoculars, an army-issue pair Winston had brought back from Italy after the war, trained on him through the shop window as he exchanged a handful of coins for a box of safety matches, two heavy broadsheets and a can of lighter fluid, square and bulky.

He was wearing gloves now, she noticed. Leather gloves and a soft brown homburg, the wide brim pulled low over his face.

Head down and shoulders hunched forward, he darted out of the shop and back into his car - weaving the MG in and out of what felt to Ruby like every backstreet in South London and avoiding all the major arteries.

By the time he pulled back up onto the pavement around the back of his mistress's house - and conspicuously not *in front* of it - Ruby's instincts were baying for attention. When he slipped a key out of his pocket, let himself in without knocking and closed the door very gently behind him, they were screaming.

"I must have known what he was doing, even before I saw the smoke starting to trickle out the back," Ruby said, her eyes clouding over with the effort of the telling. "They were all gas fireplaces in them houses, hers included. There was nothing there you'd need setting alight."

"I couldn't go inside while he was there - I knew that and all. I was starting to get a sense of what kind of character we were dealing with, and I think now the same as I thought back then: if he'd caught sight of me inside and thought I might've been able to finger him for the job... he'd have killed me, there and then. There's no doubt in my mind."

"So I waited, God forgive me. Waited to go in 'til he was out the house and he'd let himself out the back gate. 'Cause I didn't know, then. Didn't know it was that bedroom he'd chose to start the fire. Didn't know the little one had crawled in for a cuddle while her Mum was passed out cold in bed. Didn't know..."

She stopped talking, abruptly, and closed her eyes. She wasn't crying - El had never known her to cry - but her hands were shaking, and she was biting her lip to hold herself together.

You got Rose out, El wanted to tell her, for all the comfort it would have given. You got one of them, even if you couldn't get to the other. At least one of those kids is alive because of what you did.

As suddenly as they'd closed, Ruby's eyes sprang open, looking straight at El.

"When I tell you that man is dangerous and you need to be watching yourself every *second* you're around him," she said, "I need you to listen to me. Really bleedin' listen. Because *I* might not've known that little girl was in there, but *he* did. He must've done. And he set that fire anyway. Set the fire and ran away out that house and back to his wife."

"And I never told Rose this, because she don't need to have it in her head after what she's seen, but I'm telling you now: he didn't just *shut* them in that room. That weren't enough for him. No, he *locked the door.* Locked the door, locked the pair of them in there, and left his own little girl screaming for her Daddy to come and help her while she were burning to death."

EARL'S COURT

1996

T ell me about your family," Alison Miller began.

"My family?" Marchant asked - warily, as if she'd enquired into his medical records or the state of his personal finances.

"Your wife. Your children. Grandchildren, if you have any."

He took a chunk of bread from the basket and dipped it with surprising daintiness into the little plate of oil and vinegar beside his water glass. His head didn't turn, she noticed - nothing so overt - but his eyes flickered momentarily around the restaurant before he chose to respond; took in the rows of unoccupied tables, the absence of hovering, keen-eared waiting staff.

"What about them?" he said.

"I'd like us to make better use of them during the campaign. Raise their profiles."

He spluttered, sending wet pellets of half-chewed sourdough in her direction.

"Absolutely not," he said.

El tucked a strand of lacquered hair behind her ear and adjusted the new, thicker frames of Alison Miller's glasses - conscious of their bulk, and specifically of the pinhole camera embedded in the join between the lenses, where the plastic and titanium met the bridge of her nose.

It was completely secure, Karen had assured her; entirely invisible to the naked eye of the observer. But El was lo-fi - a pen-and-paper planner, analogue in her approach to the job, and Karen's reliance on technology made her uneasy. Other people were variables enough; adding hardware and its potential to malfunction into the mix felt like asking for trouble.

"They're a clear differentiator for voters," she told him, with the calm reserve that was swiftly becoming her fallback in dealing with his objections. "Seymour Henderson is a documented adulterer - a pervert and a whoremonger. You, conversely, are a family man with no known peccadillos and a marriage that's lasted for decades. It's an obvious strength, and we ought to be playing to it. Which means bringing your wife, and ideally the whole family into the spotlight."

He hesitated. She wondered whether, had she known nothing at all about him, she would have been so cognisant of the cost/benefit analysis he seemed to be performing before he replied: the publicity use-value of a well-put-together spouse and clean-cut offspring versus the potential risk presented by inviting press and public interest into his private circumstances. Not to mention the provocative red flag that a publicly-paraded marriage might represent to surviving mistresses and second families, past and present.

"I don't doubt it would play well to the cheap seats," he said. "But you'd have a hard time persuading Elizabeth. She doesn't care for attention, never has."

El considered Elizabeth Marchant as Sita had described her: the bad taste, the naivety that bordered on the gullible, the longing to have someone listen to her so great that she was willing to pay for human company. Had she ever been *offered* much attention, or at least much attention from her husband, over the course of a marriage that had lasted almost all her adult life?

"And the children?" she asked.

The combined background information Rose and Ruby had gathered on Oscar and James Junior had been substantial, and pointed to Oscar, the eldest - settled, solvent and the logical heir to the Marchant empire - as the most attractive candidate to dangle in front of the media. James Junior was dissolute by comparison - a playboy, a gambler and a celebrity hanger-on with no obvious enthusiasm for the family business beyond its capacity to bankroll his competing interests in cocaine and handmade Italian loafers.

Though El had met the youngest, Harriet, in person at Marchant's office, it was Harriet she felt she knew the least. What background they had on *her* was infinitely more sparse, factual but light on detail - which meant, El guessed, that neither Ruby's contact network nor Rose's investigators had succeeded in prising any illuminating personal anecdotes from those that knew her. From her university and work records they knew she was an academic, a social psychologist with a focus on norms and behavioural decision theory who taught part time at King's; they knew she was unmarried, had no children and had lived alone for the last few years in an unexpectedly modest one-bed rental above a charity shop on the Holloway Road. To satisfy her own curiosity, El had sought out one of her most recent journal articles, on antisocial personality characteristics and game theory, and had enjoyed it, though the central speculation - that sociopathy could serve as a useful indicator of rational decision-making - had raised questions for El about what might have led Harriet to settle on *that* topic, *that* hypothesis.

"I'll float it with them," Marchant said noncommittally. "See what they think of the idea. But I can tell you now that it'll be a no from Harriet."

"A no?" said El.

Though she knew it was impossible, she was sure she could *hear* the camera recording - the hiss and whirr of it burrowing into her skin, vibrating through her bones.

"You need to keep your head straight," Karen had told her, "and keep your eyes forward, so they're right on him. No point bothering with any of this if all you end up with is three hours of footage of a blank wall."

She'd pushed the glasses up onto El's nose and hooked the black plastic arms around her ears, fiddling with the hinges until the fit was snug.

El had stayed perfectly still, not daring to move for fear of dislodging some vital component of the device.

"Heard any more about Kat?" Karen asked, as casually as if she'd been enquiring what El had made herself for lunch. El was fairly sure it was a front; that Karen was as worried as the rest of them.

"Not since Ruby's mate called yesterday," she answered, wishing she had something more to share.

Since they'd learned - first through Ruby's old friend Arlena, a staff nurse at St Luke's, then through TV news bulletins and headlines in the Standard - that the police investigation into the assault on Kat was very much ongoing, they'd avoided visiting the hospital or ringing to check on her condition. There was, moreover, no longer any way for the hospital to contact *them*: the phone number Ruby had offered up to the ICU via Kat's supposed epilepsy bracelet had belonged to a burner handset, cheap and untraceable, that El had no hesitation in abandoning to the river. She'd bought another immediately afterwards - issuing the new number to the handful of people she felt would need it and enjoying, despite the circumstances, a brief sensation of pleasure at the knowledge that Bernard Croft would have no means of hounding her about his son's exam results thereafter.

She'd tried, despite the permacloud of anxiety and uncertainty that had hung over the Ledbury Road house since the attack, not to think too much about the night that she and Rose had spent in A&E after Kat had been admitted; about ambitious young constables in back offices, hopped up on black coffee, poring zealously over enlarged CCTV stills of the two of them in the waiting area and competing with one another to match blurred images to known names and faces, to identify the mystery women who'd claimed to be Kat's sisters but - as surely everyone knew by now - weren't. Her one consolation was that there hadn't been, at least as far as she remembered, any cameras in the Death Room - and no way, therefore, for those constables to have heard Rose's story, and to have joined the dots from there.

Arlena's latest update had been, in effect, that there *was* no update. Kat remained stable but unresponsive: still unconscious, still in ICU. Her comatose state meant that no reliable assessment could be made of the damage to her brain and body, nor of how successful the craniectomy had been in mitigating that damage. She was a black box, all but the most basic of her vital signs unknowable. And the longer she stayed a black box, the lower the odds of her coming out whole and unscathed on the other side.

"I'll ring tonight," Karen said.

"You can't," El said. "They'll trace the call."

"Believe me, they won't."

You're kidding yourself if you think they'll tell you anything, El had thought. Even *if* – and it's a big *if* - there's something for them to tell.

"How did you learn to do it?" she asked, casting around for a change of subject.

"Do what?"

El pointed a finger upward to the glasses.

"All this," she said. "The gadgets and the cameras. I thought you were meant to be a thief?"

Unexpectedly, Karen had laughed.

"I've got to be one thing or the other, is that it?" she said. Then, without waiting for El to answer, she added: "I *am* a thief, as it happens. A good one and all - maybe not quite up there with my old man, but pretty fucking close, especially if we're talking security networks. I've also got a BSc in mechanical engineering, a masters in electronics and once we've put this job to bed, I have every intention of getting back to that MPhil in applied cryptography I keep meaning to write. And if you think these things are mutually exclusive, then I'd politely suggest that you might want to find yourself a different vocation than weighing people up for a living."

She flashed a grin at El, one that suggested that this wasn't the first time she'd been underestimated and that she found it, for the time being, more entertaining than insulting. El took her in again - the tightly-packed muscle, the South London accent, the security guard stance - and kicked herself for her misconceptions. Her embarrassment was only amplified later, when Ruby let her in on the fuller story.

Karen, it turned out, wasn't just a wallet dip, a short-con artist or a safecracker, although she was all of these things. She was, or had been, a child prodigy with a particular aptitude for numbers and machines: admitted to Imperial at 15, UMIST at 18 and the Engineering Council at 20. She held patents for 3 different machine vision innovations - one of which, a gait analysis system widely considered in the industry to be at least a decade ahead of its time, generated enough annual licensing revenue to ensure that neither Karen nor any children she might have would ever want for anything material.

("She don't need to work any more than you do," Ruby had told El, sucking on another of her disintegrating custard creams. "But she likes a challenge, same as you. And neither one of you are doing this one for the money, are you?").

"So," said El, returning Karen's grin with an apologetic smile of her own, "I should trust you when you tell me this thing will work?"

She touched the bridge of her nose, in roughly the place she thought the camera might be.

This time Karen's laughter was a roar - amused and forgiving.

"It'll work," she said. "It's not mechanical failure I'm worried about with this one. It's human error."

"Harriet doesn't approve of me," said Marchant. "She finds my work... you might say distasteful. Between us, I suspect she finds the whole idea of *commerce* distasteful. She'd never deign to sully her hands with it. And as for my politics... Suffice to say, my daughter and I are very different people. We have very few things in common beyond the basic biological connection, and our respective political beliefs are not among them. In other circumstances, I'd be exactly the sort of candidate she'd picket. As it is, we restrict our conversation to safe subjects - her mother and brothers and so on."

El privately saluted both Harriet's politics and her sound judgement of character.

"Should we consider her a liability?" she asked.

"Good God, no. Whatever ill she might wish me, she'd never actively work against me. Doing that would only hurt Elizabeth, and Harriet knows it."

She imagined for a moment what life might have been like for the legitimate Marchant children, what flashes of their father's cruelty they might have glimpsed, growing up in his house - especially once Saul Bellman was gone, and with him any reason Marchant might have had to keep himself and his temper in check at home.

A shadow fell across the table. Marchant reached for the menu, readying himself to bark instructions at whichever waiter or sommelier had been assigned to them.

El kept him in her line of sight, the camera capturing every change in his expression as it happened: surprise, at looking up to see not a waiter or a sommelier but an angular woman in Chanel, a blue cardboard folder clasped in her hands where a notepad should have been; annoyance, at being disturbed during dinner by a stranger; recognition, then horror, upon realising that the stranger wasn't really a stranger at all.

Hannah hovered over them - an avenging angel, brandishing her folder like a burning sword.

"You again?" said Marchant, clicking his fingers to attract the attention of the waiting staff. "What do you want?"

Hannah opened her folder and pulled from it a stiff A4 rectangle. She let it drop to the table in front of Marchant, face-up. It was a photograph - a posed black and white studio shot of a young woman, dark-haired and pretty, holding a toddler of indeterminate gender in her arms. Both the woman and the child were smiling.

Marchant pointedly avoided looking at it.

"Heidi Simpson," Hannah said. "And her daughter, Jade."

"That supposed to mean something to me, is it?" said Marchant.

A waiter rushed towards them from the bar, red-faced, still holding the cutlery he'd been polishing a moment before.

"I would hope so," Hannah replied, speaking softly, "since you murdered them."

Marchant froze in place, his face unreadable, then held up a hand to shoo the waiter from the table. The waiter, puzzled but obedient, turned on his heels and sped away, back to his place at the bar.

"I'm not going to ask who you are," Marchant told her, his voice equally quiet, "because I don't care. But if you know who *I* am, and I assume you do, then you'll also know that I have some very, very expensive lawyers on retainer, and that they earn the bulk of their really quite substantial invoices by defending me and my organisation against defamatory claims. They're clever and they're tenacious, and they couldn't care less if I'm being slandered by a bin man or the editor of the Telegraph - they'll go after them just the same. So my advice to you, whoever you are, is to pack away your pictures and your accusations and take yourself somewhere that isn't here. Because the best outcome for you currently, and the only one that doesn't see you bankrupt and begging for scraps in a gutter, is that I never have cause to think of you again."

Hannah ignored him; pressed her thumb down onto the corner of the photograph.

"They died in a house fire 3 years ago," she continued. "Deliberately set. Before that, they lived in a rental property in Greenwich - a mews house, the kind you'd think would be a little out of the price range of a single mother on benefits. It was leased to Heidi through a shell company, Hallett Lettings - one of yours. I'm not sure why the detective investigating the fire didn't find that out - it took *me* all of 5 minutes at Companies House - but there we are. I'm sure she had her own reasons for looking the other way."

"Do you have any idea how many properties I own?" he said, unfazed. "If *this* is what you've seized on as evidence of my involvement in this woman's death..."

"Jade was your daughter," said Hannah. "I assume that's why you killed her and her mother? To keep your wife from finding out about her? You're not listed on her birth certificate, of course, and her body was too badly burned for there to be any reliable physical evidence. But you can never *completely* cover up something like that, can you? Take the kindergarten she went to, for example - again, a very good kindergarten for the daughter of an unemployed hairdresser. Perhaps not quite as expensive as your legal bills, but certainly not cheap. I had a quick chat with the owner not so long ago - a very nice woman, quite loquacious - and she was as surprised as I was that Heidi had been able to afford the fees. She seemed to think that there was a man in the picture, supporting her - paying her bills. She'd never met him, but she remembered seeing him once, waiting in the car outside when Heidi came to collect Jade. An older man, she said - quite a bit older than Heidi. Driving a little red sports car - something vintage, she thought. A Lotus or an MG."

"Tell me, James - what is it that *you* drive?"

The bare bones of the story were true, El knew - one of Rose's investigator's *had* spoken to the kindergarten manager, and she *had* mentioned spotting an older man in an MG in the car park one afternoon. But the information hadn't been given quite so freely as Hannah had suggested: money had changed hands, and the woman was nothing like as certain about what she had or hadn't seen. As evidence went, it was even flimsier than it sounded.

"Have you quite finished?" asked Marchant.

"Almost," Hannah replied. "Now, I know what you must be thinking - that this is all circumstantial, it doesn't prove anything. Doesn't really prove that you knew them, let alone that you had anything to do with their deaths. But bear with me. I have just a little more to tell you, and I think you'll want to hear it."

El leaned in across the table towards Marchant, the glasses still trained on his face. He looked calm, she thought; untroubled.

"Someone saw you set the fire," said Hannah, in a whisper so low that El was afraid the camera wouldn't catch it.

Now his expression changed - his eyes widening a fraction, the skin around his mouth tightening as he sucked in his cheeks. He was afraid, she thought. Hiding it well, but afraid all the same.

"This is absurd," he said. "Utterly absurd."

"Absurd, but true," said Hannah. "This person - he saw you go into the house that night with a can of petrol. And he saw you drive off afterwards, once you'd used it - albeit in something a bit less distinctive than the MG. He doesn't follow the news, and he's certainly not an FT reader, so he hadn't heard of Marchant Holdings - he had no idea who you were. But he's got a fantastic memory for faces, really very impressive. And he knew *exactly* where he'd seen you before, once I showed him your photo."

There was no man, El knew; no convenient bystander who'd borne witness to Marchant's crime. But Hannah sold the lie so beautifully, so convincingly, she could almost believe it.

"The question I'd be asking myself if *I* were you, Jim," Hannah said - and she was wrapping up now, El could feel it, "is this: if he's already talked to me, how long will it be before he talks to someone else?"

Marchant was pale, his jaw clenched, as if he couldn't bring himself to open his mouth.

"What do you want?" he said eventually, each word a bullet spat from between his teeth.

Hannah slid the photograph off the tablecloth and back into her folder.

"Nothing you can give me," she said. "You've taken everything already. But ruining you, the way you've ruined me... if that's my consolation prize, then I suppose I'll have to take it."

She left the restaurant without fanfare; he didn't try to stop her, although El hadn't thought that he would.

For a long time, there was nothing but silence between them.

This is it, El thought. Showtime.

"Her name is Hannah D'Amboise," she told him. "She's a political correspondent, ex-BBC. Don't insult either one of us by telling me you didn't recognise her. Though I imagine you're more familiar with her husband Justin - Justin D'Amboise, your CFO. Your *late* CFO. The one she seems convinced you did away with."

His mouth opened, but she raised a hand, pre-empting his question.

"I do my homework," she said. "And after that incident at your club, I thought it in both our interests to find out who might be invested in causing you harm. As it transpires, there's rather a long list of candidates."

She smiled ruefully; sipped at her sparkling water. It was warm; flat.

"I told you, didn't I, that I dislike surprises? That surprises can derail campaigns, ruin candidacies?"

He nodded, apparently dumbfounded.

"Under ordinary circumstances, this would be exactly the kind of surprise that would see me walk away from a campaign. If a client isn't honest with me about the challenges we're likely to face together, it becomes very difficult for me to represent them successfully. It prevents me, Mr Marchant, from doing my job - which has its own implications for my reputation. And I care very deeply for my reputation."

"Alison..."

"There are, however," she said, not allowing him to speak, to control the course of the conversation, "three factors working in your favour in this particular instance. The first is the effort I've already expended in planning your campaign - which, sunk cost fallacy or not, has been significant. The second is you yourself. Were you able to resolve the particular challenge that now confronts us *before* it becomes public knowledge, then you stand, I believe, a very, *very* good chance of taking the vacated seat in Silvertown. And the third... well, the third is more personal. I will *not* be held hostage - not by anyone, for any reason. If and when I leave a client or abandon a campaign, it's because I've chosen to. Not because my hand has been forced."

"It didn't happen," said Marchant flatly. "What she said - there's no truth to it."

"Whether there is or there isn't is immaterial to me. I'm not your confessor - what you may or may not have done in the past matters to me only inasmuch as it's likely to affect your profile. I won't be pressed into a corner, but nor am I keen to back a losing horse, much less one that may be facing a murder charge in the not too distant future. So answer me this, Mr Marchant: is this a problem that you're able to deal with?"

"What do you mean?" he asked - sounding surly, petulant.

"I mean: can Ms D'Amboise and her vendetta - and any witnesses she claims to have to the crime she says took place - be made to go away?"

He stared at her; seemed to take stock of her. She wondered if she'd shocked him; if he was asking himself whether he'd underestimated her - and if he had, by just how much. The idea pleased her. There was something reassuring, she thought, about the possibility that even monsters could be horrified.

"Yes," he said eventually. "I believe she can."

"You have the resources?"

He swept another gaze around the restaurant, which was now entirely empty but for their table.

"I have a private security team," he said. "My own, not the company's. They're... experienced. And discreet."

"And they're intelligent men? Strategically-minded? This isn't a job for blunt instruments, however well you may be able rely on them to keep their mouths shut. Ms D'Amboise is a journalist - or was, before she took her leave of absence. She'll know how to protect her sources, and she'll know if she's being followed. It won't be enough to stage a bungled break-in or a hit and run. Whichever resource you deploy to extract the requisite information from her and then remove her from the equation... they'll need to be able to *think* as well as *do,* and think quickly. To adapt."

This was a gamble, maybe their biggest. If Rose was right and he'd yet to find a head of security to replace Ricky Lomax, a new right-hand man, then he *didn't* have the resource to carry out the kind of hit she was proposing. He'd have to go looking for it.

His brows creased; he was coming, she suspected, to the same realisation.

"Shit," he said, as much to himself as to El.

Rose *was* right, then, El thought - impressed again by how well she'd calculated the setup and the players involved, how meticulously she'd structured the con.

She took a second, slow drink of her water, making him wait.

"I'll take that as a *no,*" she said.

He bristled. It was beginning to needle him, she thought: both the calmness of her delivery and the way she'd taken the upper hand, made him unexpectedly subordinate. To get under his skin.

"I can deal with it," he said, so abruptly it was nearly a snarl.

She let out a sigh, and reached down into her attaché case for a pen. On the thick white cloth of her napkin she jotted a line of digits; folded it in half, and held it out to Marchant.

He fixed her with the same, faintly worried stare as before - the one that said he knew he'd misjudged her, that perhaps he hadn't quite known what he was buying when he engaged her services. And then he took it.

"Call this number," she said. "The man who answers will ask for a name. Give him mine, and he may be willing to help you. If he is, tell him to bill me directly. I'll add the cost to my final invoice."

Now she was sure she'd wrong-footed him; he looked stunned, utterly lost for words.

"He's reliable, he's efficient and he can think on his feet," she said, when he failed to speak. "If you *must* bring in additional support, and it sounds like you must, then given the delicacy of the situation I'd much rather that support be delivered by someone I'm confident can actually do the job."

He unfolded the napkin; studied the number, then refolded it and put it carefully into his jacket pocket.

"You know," he said, "you're really not at all what I expected."

He was still irritated, she was sure; still resentful of her power over him. But there was something else there too now in the way he looked at her - something like admiration, and something like affinity. He thinks he *knows* me, she thought - or rather, knows Alison Miller. He understands her. He thinks she's just like him.

"Call the number," she repeated. "Neither of us can afford for you to wait."

HERNE HILL

1996

The air in the car was foggy with smoke; clouds of it so dense El felt her eyes stinging in sympathy.

"I wish he'd put that fucking fag out," Karen said, twiddling the resolution button on the projector remote. "It's misting up the lens."

Like the video feed broadcast from Seymour Henderson's flat by way of Karen's corset, this one was live - beamed direct to the basement room at Ledbury Road from a white Audi parked in a quiet cul-de-sac off Coldharbour Lane. The camera in this case was anchored to the wraparound sunglasses worn by the man in the driving seat. The glasses were dark and unremarkable, like everything else about the man: his plain t-shirt and jeans, his manicured hands, his shaved head and neatly-trimmed beard. His appearance was a case-study in anonymity, in social camouflage; once seen, El thought, he'd be immediately forgotten. His sole concession to style was the piercing: an obsidian stud, half the size of a penny but twice as thick, apparently driven into the cartilage of his right ear.

"Can he hear us?" Rose asked.

"I fitted that earpiece myself," said Karen, insulted. "Course he can hear us. Can't you, you lazy twat?"

The man in the Audi twitched.

"You don't have to speak to me like that," he said, in a soft voice that had, El thought, more than a touch of a whine to it. "I'm doing my best here."

"Do better," Karen told him. "And open a window while you're at it. It looks like a fucking hotbox in there."

The man grumbled something inaudible, but opened the door to the Audi a crack, clearing some of the smoke and affording all of them a sharper view of the grey pavement slabs and low-rise council flats outside. Then closed it again, sharply.

"He's coming," he whispered.

The camera swung left, to the empty seat next to him. The unlocked passenger door sprung open, and a second man slipped into the car, long legs first: Marchant, in a navy puffer jacket and an oversized baseball cap that were more casual than anything El had seen him wear before.

"Are you Tony?" Marchant asked, without preamble.

"Depends," the other man replied, sounding cooler and more intimidating than he had previously. "Are you Jim?"

Marchant nodded in the affirmative.

"You recording this?" the man asked him.

Marchant shook his head.

"Prove it," said the man. "Unzip that coat."

Marchant grimaced, appalled by the demand, but complied.

"The shirt too," the man added.

This time Marchant hesitated; parted his lips to object.

"Open the shirt, or get out of the car," the man said. "I ain't telling you twice."

Marchant wrinkled his nose, in anger or disgust, but reached for his top button.

"What now?" he asked testily, when the greying hairs and pink-white flesh of his chest were exposed.

"Now we talk," said the man. "And you tell me what problem it is you want me to solve for you."

The boy El had met in Rose's kitchen a month before had looked markedly different from the man in the Audi.

In his designer jeans and basketball shoes, with a head of short dreadlocks and no hair at all to speak of on his cheeks or chin, she'd taken him for a teenager; 15 or 16 at most. Only when Karen had introduced him as her brother had she done the maths - realised that, if his mother had been pregnant with him when his father disappeared, then he must have been at least 20, maybe older.

He'd stood up politely as El entered the room; even shaken her hand.

"I thought young people were meant to be rude these days?" she'd said, smiling at him.

"Reckons he's smooth, don't you, Theo?" Karen said. "A real ladies's man."

"At least some of us still have manners," Theo replied, returning El's smile.

"Well, you're barking up the wrong tree with this one," Karen told him, gesturing to El. "So sit your arse back down before you embarrass yourself any more than you have already."

If Karen hadn't told El they were siblings, the conversation that had followed would have made it abundantly clear - their bickering reminding her in no small way of Ruby and Sita's.

"Theo's a musician," Karen told her. "A drummer."

"In a band?" El had asked - conjuring mental images of the boy in front of her sweating shirtless over a drum kit behind guitar bands in Camden, neo-soul singers in Hoxton, 12-piece reggae collectives in Brixton.

"The Royal Philharmonic," Theo said. "I'm a percussionist."

"But basically a drummer," Karen added.

He was straight, she told them later; had never had so much as a parking ticket, let alone been arrested, unless you counted the occasional stop-and-search by police who'd seen him hanging around too long outside Southwark Cathedral or the Albert Hall. But he was also Leon Baxter's son, a son who'd been brought up on stories of the father who'd never got to meet him - so when Karen told him about the job and asked him if he'd help them pull it off, he was always going to say yes.

"But *can* you do it?" Rose had asked him, acknowledging the elephant in the room. "I don't intend this as a criticism, but I don't know that I've ever met a more unlikely assassin."

Theo considered this.

"Can I do it?" he asked, mulling each word as if putting the question to himself. "Hmm... *can* I do it? Let's see..."

He drummed his fingers on the table, then looked at Rose and grinned.

It was like magic, El thought; like a spell he'd cast on himself. He seemed to physically change in front of them at will, to age and grow; his posture stiffening, his slim frame widening at the shoulders, the cast of his face toughening until he wasn't a boy anymore but a man - and a hard man at that, the kind who'd pull a blade on you in the pub if you took his stool at the bar or looked at him the wrong way. As transformations went, it was nigh on perfect. She wasn't sure Ruby or Sita could have done better - or, for that matter, that she could have done better herself.

"You know what?" he said, in a cold, rough voice that wasn't his own. "I reckon I can."

Neither she nor Rose spoke.

"Yeah, alright," said Karen, grudgingly. "They've seen you do it; you can stop now."

Theo clicked his fingers theatrically, and his expression changed again, back to its original look of teenage bemusement.

"Little fucker went to *Sylvia Young* before he got into Guildhall," Karen added. "Thinks he's one of the kids from *Fame*."

"You bring what I asked?" said Theo.

Marchant, his shirt now re-buttoned, shoved a hand into the recesses of his jacket and retrieved a thin envelope. He passed it to Theo in silence.

Theo opened it; examined the contents, a single piece of paper on which a name and address were written in finely-drawn uppercase. A passport-sized photo of Hannah's face and upper body was stapled to the corner of the page.

"There's only one name here," he said. "You said on the phone there were two."

"There are," said Marchant. "But the second one is... an unknown quantity."

"What does that mean?"

Marchant sucked in a breath - feeling uncomfortable, El suspected, about having to articulate his requirements so bluntly, after so many years of issuing elliptical orders to lieutenants and having them obeyed.

"I don't know his name, or where you'll find him," he said. He tapped Hannah's photo with one finger. "But *she* does. I'll need you to deal with them both."

"You want me to get it out of her before I do her, is that it?" said Theo.

This time, Marchant's breathing was so loud it sent a crackle of feedback through the video output. *Definitely* uncomfortable, El thought. He hates that he's going to have to say it aloud.

"Alison told me you were able to handle that sort of thing," he said.

"I am. But it'll cost her. Cost her extra."

"Money isn't an issue. Just get it done."

Theo reached over to the glove compartment, his arm brushing Marchant's en route. Marchant flinched, and Theo let out a snigger that came out closer to a growl.

"Calm down," he said, making no effort to conceal his amusement at the old man's alarm. "Nobody's paying me to take *you* out."

He opened the glove box, placed the slip of paper inside and pushed it closed again, still smiling.

El felt herself smile, and realised - slightly belatedly - that Theo, or whichever TV gangster he was imitating, wasn't the only one enjoying Marchant's discomfiture; that she was finding her own pleasure in his fear. She wondered if Rose and Karen felt the same.

"When?" Marchant asked, when he'd recovered himself.

"Soon," said Theo. "Tomorrow or the day after."

"How will I know when it's done?"

"You want proof? Photos?"

"God, no! Just... confirmation."

"Your boss'll get my bill, that's how you'll know. Same as always."

Even through his fear, Marchant bridled at the suggestion.

"She's not my boss," he said. "*She* works for *me*."

"Whatever," said Theo, his interest in Marchant apparently waning. "We done here?"

"Do you have everything you need?"

"I'd've said if I didn't."

"Then I suppose we are."

"Good," Theo said. He pulled out a lighter, a heavy gold brick that could have been raided from the Romanovs, and lit another of his cigarettes, blowing the smoke in Marchant's face. "Out you get, then," he told him. "I got work to do."

"Do *you* have what you need?" Rose asked Karen, when Marchant had exited the Audi and Theo had, with a sigh of relief he didn't bother to disguise, pulled the sunglasses from his face and the pseudo-piercing from his ear.

"More than," said Karen, turning off the projector. "What with this and what we'd got before, we should have a proper sizzle reel ready once I've stitched it all together in the edit."

Karen's studio workspace-cum-editing suite, location undisclosed, had become the stuff of legend at Ledbury Road. El imagined something like a Batcave: an underground fortress bathed in blue phosphorescence, stacked floor to ceiling with complex technologies of unspecified purpose and accessible only through a network of secret tunnels.

"We're on the clock with the video," El reminded her. "You okay with that?"

"It'll be ready for Friday," Karen said. "Sooner, if I can swing it. I'm pretty fucking motivated, believe me."

She packed up and left them to it, hauling her canvas bag of cables and hardware out of the house and off, El presumed, to the Batcave to get started.

El had expected Rose to leave too, to retreat upstairs to the living room and put in a call to her sister-in-law in Sussex - checking in on Sophie before bedtime, the way she had every night since she'd sent her away.

Instead, she ambled over to the old drinks cabinet behind the sofa; grabbed a nearly-full bottle of Malibu and two glasses, and put both on the side table next to her armchair.

"The cupboard isn't very well stocked down here, I'm afraid," she said apologetically. "I have to take what I can get."

She filled both glasses; passed one to El, and kept the other for herself.

"Camilla's taken Sophie out this evening," she said, before El could ask. "Bowling, I believe."

She leaned back against the armchair's headrest, stretched out her legs and rolled up the sleeves of her sweater, exposing the scarred skin of her forearm. She was more relaxed about showing it since their conversation at the hospital, El had noticed; less concerned, maybe, that seeing it would prompt questions she didn't want to answer.

"Sounds fun," El replied absently. Then: "Do you think we're ready?"

"I think we've done as much as we can," said Rose, taking a drink and wincing as it hit her throat.

El wanted, suddenly, to make an apology of her own: to explain that she didn't normally get nervous on the job, or look for eleventh hour reassurance, but this one was different, personal. And then realised that she didn't have to - that Rose almost certainly knew already, and very likely felt the same. It was personal for all of them; every one of them needed the payoff as badly as she did, whatever that payoff might bring. Relief, she hoped; some respite from the memories of her mother, reconstructed and imagined, that had plagued her more and more since the day Ruby had sent her off to Highgate to look at a painting. The blood debt, paid.

"Do you think you'll feel better, after?" she asked Rose.

"No," Rose said - and if El had expected an honest answer, then it wasn't that. "This, what we're doing - it isn't restitution. It's reparation."

"There's a difference?"

"I believe so. There's no bringing them back, is there? Not my sister, not your mother - not any of them. No restoration, no justice to be had - not in any conventional sense. And peace of mind seems too much to hope for."

"Then why do it?"

Rose seemed to hesitate before answering, for so long that El wondered if she was going to answer at all.

"Because it needs to be done," she said finally, small and exhausted - not a warrior on the brink of battle but a just-widowed wife, making sandwiches for the guests the night before a wake. *Because it needs to be done.*

El reached across the side-table and took her hand.

"It will be," she said.

SILVERTOWN

1996

On Alison Miller's advice, Marchant had opted for a modest venue for the campaign lunch: the function room of the Custom House Irish Centre, an echoing church hall-like affair better used to hosting ceilidhs, children's dance classes and live broadcasts of the Six Nations Championship.

There was no stage, but the raised wooden platform at one end of the room had been kitted out with a long rectangular table complete with a microphone and a carafe of water, and a pull-down home cinema screen had been fixed to the wall behind. An arrangement of stackable plastic chairs, five seats wide and five deep, faced the table. On the chairs sat twenty or so journalists, handpicked for their known sympathies for mavericks and independents; at the table sat Marchant, flanked by his eldest son and the most loyal and long serving of his PAs. El herself was in the press pit, in the centre of the front row - a position that afforded her the closest possible view of Marchant's face.

He wore what El - what *Alison* - had advised him to wear: a charcoal suit cut in a 1940s style with a maroon tie, pocket square and patent leather Oxfords. It was a look, she'd told him, that spoke subtly of wartime leadership, of Blitz spirit and Churchillian integrity. He also wore a lapel pin, large enough to fall just the wrong side of subtle. The pin was handmade, polished silver and shaped into a pair of perfectly-balanced Themis scales. If all went well, she'd told him, the scales would become the campaign's trademark - a symbol of his commitment to fairness, justice, transparency and good counsel.

He looked confident, she thought. And that was good. She wanted him confident; unprepared.

Oscar Marchant spoke first, leaning into the microphone with the robust self-assurance of a university debate captain.

"Good afternoon, ladies and gentleman," he said. "And thank you so much for joining us. I realise this may be a little different from some of your standard briefing haunts."

This elicited a hoot of condescending laughter from the assembled press.

"As you're all aware," he continued, "we have a by-election approaching here in Silvertown. I don't think I need to tell you why."

Another burst of laughter, this time at Seymour Henderson's expense.

"The Tories, of course, will put forward one of their own to fill the vacated seat - though it's fair to say their last pick has given us some cause to question their vetting procedures. Labour and the Lib Dems will likely also be fielding candidates, as they should."

"We're here today, though, to ask you and the people of Silvertown a very important question, which is this: do we want to carry on with business as usual in this constituency? Are we really happy with the same parade of faces, the same rehashed promises? Or do we deserve something different - something better?"

It was a fine speech, she thought with a twinge of pride - the lines she'd written fortified by the measured hammer-blow of his delivery. No matter that neither Marchant had ever had cause to set foot in the borough before now; no matter that neither could have cared less what the people of Silvertown did or didn't want. The words had power.

"I believe we do," he said. "I invite you, therefore, to cast your eyes over the brief video presentation we've prepared for you, and to join me thereafter in welcoming the newest independent candidate for Silvertown - my father, Mr James Marchant."

There was a brief round of clapping from the audience. Marchant Senior beamed, and returned the applause with a small, bashful wave.

Oscar Marchant nodded to a colleague at the back of the room. The lights dimmed; behind the table, the screen lit up, and the video El had carefully loaded into the projector began to play.

She held her breath, and waited.

What Karen had made, in her hidden lair with her unknown technologies, had exceeded their expectations.

It ran to barely 10 minutes, but every frame justified its presence - the disparate bits of footage she'd collected knitted together into a damning, cohesive whole.

It opened with an introduction from Ricky Lomax, explaining briefly to the camera how long he'd worked for Marchant, and what his duties had comprised - then cut to a heavily edited description of the backroom abortion he'd witnessed in Perivale, his murder of the abortion doctor and the way he'd disposed, on Marchant's instructions, of the remains not only of him, but of the girl who'd bled to death on her own mattress.

From there it segued to a digitised series of newspaper headlines from the late '70s, sequentially documenting the discovery of El's mother's body, the Leicestershire Constabulary's arrest of their prime suspect and, finally, George Young's conviction at the Old Bailey. The news stories were accompanied by a voice-over offering an alternative take on the official record: Lomax's gravelly, emotionless recounting of what he'd found in Marchant's hotel room, the state of the body, the suitcase he'd used to transport it to the graveyard where he'd left her.

"'Can you take care of it?', that was all he asked me," Lomax said as last headline faded. "But he didn't need to say no more. I knew what he meant."

The next scene was more recent, showing Marchant at the table he'd shared with El in the restaurant in Earl's Court the week before - carefully cut to keep Hannah's face out of shot, even as she laid out the charges before him. Here again Karen had layered on headlines and front page news items - these ones detailing the house fire killings in Greenwich, the arson with no obvious suspects.

Finally, there was Marchant in the passenger seat of the Audi, passing an unseen Theo a sheet of paper - the name and address on it obscured and the photo attached blurred to a series of unrecognisable pixels.

"I'll need you to deal with them both," he said - the sound quality enhanced, the order and the implication loud and clear.

The film closed with a title card, white letters on a plain black background: Vote James Marchant - The Honest Choice For Silvertown.

"He may run, afterwards," Rose had told El, the day she'd outlined the plan she'd had in mind. "Or he may stay and brazen it out. It doesn't matter. Once the press see it, it will be less than a day before every local and national newspaper in the country is baying for his blood. Less than a few hours, possibly. And at least one of the journalists in that room will pass what they've seen and heard along to the police, even before the video itself reaches their newsdesks. He may be well connected, and he may have influence over the upper echelons of the Met - but whatever connections he has are apt to crumble in the face of this kind of evidence going public. None of his friends will be able to protect him, if they have any interest in keeping their pensions."

"And what about me?" El had asked. "What do I do, when all this is happening?"

"You leave," Rose had said. "As quietly and discreetly as you can. While the video is still playing, would be my advice."

Something was off. She knew it within seconds of the film beginning; before she was able to process what she was seeing.

It was a different video, up on the screen; the *wrong* video.

Instead of Lomax and the headlines, there was a family - a woman, a man, a small child riding piggyback on his shoulders and a medium-sized spaniel on a lead, the four of them walking together contently through sunlit parkland.

"I've lived in Silvertown all my life," said the woman, directly to the camera, "and I've seen at least three MPs come and go. They were from different parties, but they all had one thing in common: I didn't believe a word they said."

"We're ready for a change," the man chipped in, his happy pink face filling the screen.

It was an advert, El realised; the American-style campaign ad she'd promised Marchant, the one that would never be allowed on TV or the radio but that could easily do the rounds at meet-and-greet sessions and parish hall stump speeches.

And if it was playing now, that meant that someone had switched the film reel on the projector - exchanging hers for their own.

Which meant, logically, that someone had known in advance what hers had contained.

She lowered her gaze, momentarily, to Marchant; expecting to see his head turned towards the video, to see him basking in the glow of its reflected glory.

He wasn't.

He was watching her. Looking down at her, and smiling.

He knows, she thought. I don't know how, but he knows.

I need to get out. Get out *now*.

She pushed back her chair and ran for the exit, as fast as Alison Miller's feet would carry her.

NEWHAM

1996

She sprinted to Custom House Station, and from there hopped the DLR to Canning Town, looking over her shoulder the whole journey.

At Canning Town, she crossed the main road and strode with as much of an aura of entitlement as she could muster into a mid-range chain hotel - one neither expensive enough to have invested overmuch in door security, nor so low-budget that the reception staff would be on the lookout for non-residents seeking shelter from the elements.

Inside, she made for the disabled bathroom at the end of the lobby; locked the door, hung Alison Miller's lime-green blazer on the coat hook welded to the tiled wall and, with ball after ball of damp paper towel, stripped the other woman's heavy, pale foundation from her face, neck and hands. Skin scrubbed, she loosened the first three buttons of her white blouse and untucked it from her trousers, until she looked more like an off-duty barista than a middle-aged executive. She took her mobile phone and Alison Miller's ID, credit card and the handful of cash in her bill holder from her attaché case and stuffed them into her trouser pockets. The case itself she shoved behind the toilet, out of sight.

Then she sat down on the toilet lid, and let herself think.

Marchant had known about the video; that much was certain. And if he'd known about the video, she reasoned, then he'd very likely also known about *her* - that she wasn't who she'd said she was. That she wasn't Alison Miller.

In which case: did he know her real name - who she was, where she lived?

Did he - and even the idea of it made her breath catch and her heart beat faster - know about the rest of them, about Rose and Ruby and the house at Ledbury Road? And if he did: did he know *why* it was that they'd come after him?

What she didn't ask herself, but would wish later that she had, was: *how* had he come to know any of it at all?

She checked Alison Miller's watch; saw that half an hour had passed since she'd left the Irish Centre.

How far could he get, in half an hour? What kind of resources could he mobilise?

Could he - or more likely, one of his security team - have made it to Ledbury Road already?

She retrieved the mobile phone from her pocket and dialled Rose's home phone number. There was no answer, although she let it ring for a solid minute.

Which didn't mean anything, she told herself. They were probably in the kitchen, waiting, all five of them, Rose and Ruby and Sita and Karen and Hannah. Would they even hear the phone from there, when it rang in the hallway?

She dialled another number from memory: Karen's. It didn't ring at all; the phone, a message told her, had been switched off.

She didn't panic; didn't *let* herself panic. Panic was paralysing - it wouldn't get her anywhere.

Leaving the blazer on the coat hook and the attaché case behind the toilet, she left first the bathroom, then the hotel.

On the street outside she hailed a cab to Rose's. They hit traffic at Blackfriars, a stretch of cars stacked bumper to bumper from the bridge at Victoria Embankment all the way to Charing Cross, and it was another hour before they made it to Westbourne Park. She stopped the cab at the tube station and walked the rest of the way to the house, taking Tavistock Road at a pace so brisk that a light sweat broke out on her back.

She climbed the steps to the front door and rang the doorbell three times in succession, her heart pounding.

Her relief, when Hannah opened the door, was overwhelming.

"What happened?" Hannah said, alarmed.

El tried to speak, and found she couldn't. She pushed past Hannah, almost throwing herself into the hallway, and slammed the door behind her; locked and bolted it, and pulled the chain across. For all the good it would do them, if Marchant or his men came calling.

"Is everyone okay?" she asked. She sounded wild, terrified, even to her own ears; entirely unlike herself.

"They're fine," Hannah replied, now confused as well as concerned.

"Where are they?"

"In the kitchen. What...?"

She ran down the hallway for the kitchen, leaving Hannah in her wake. If the rest of them were there, she could warn them; could get them out and somewhere safer, somewhere out of London. Maybe out of the country.

She saw Ruby first, through the half-open kitchen door; the older woman leaning back against the counter, hands behind her and elbows bent, as if she were preparing herself to perform a triceps dip. Her eyes flashed to El when she saw her coming, but she didn't acknowledge her; didn't wave or bellow a greeting the way she usually would. Just blinked, twice, then looked away.

Sita stood beside the counter, entirely still; her arms held stiffly in the air, palms-up. Her mouth was a tight, straight line; her face expressionless. She gave no indication of having seen El at all.

El was through the door and in the kitchen before she could consider what either of these things might mean.

Which was when she saw the others.

Karen was on the sofa, her head bowed. *Her* hands were hidden; El thought she might have been sitting on them, her thighs flattening them down into the upholstery behind her. The muscles of her arms and legs were tensed, clenched so hard that the fabric of her shirt and cycling shorts seemed in danger of tearing. There was a patch of discolouration just visible on the side of her jaw; it might have been the beginnings of a bruise.

And then there was Rose.

She was standing, like Ruby and Sita, but she wasn't still. Her feet paced the floor by the dining table, moving backwards and forwards and left and right in a tight square - the movements giving El the impression of an animal caught in an enclosure, an electrified fence penning it in on all sides. El thought, at first glance, that she was clutching at her wrists with her fingers - and then realised, with something like dread, that her hands were bound; held together with a length of dark red material, a thin scarf or a tie.

It was seeing Rose that brought home to El what *else* she was seeing: that the women in the kitchen were prisoners. Hostages.

She spun around towards the door, preparing to fight or flee or both.

And saw Marchant, stepping forward into the room from behind the door that had hidden him - a smile on his face and a gun in his hand.

It wasn't *much* of a gun; that was El's first thought. She had no direct experience of firearms, but if she'd ever had cause to give consideration to her own mental model of *gun* as a concept, she'd likely have cited a few basic level attributes: black casing, a rough rectangular grip, a straight blunt muzzle and a cartridge chamber. Marchant's had none of these; had the appearance, rather, of an old-fashioned revolver, its wooden handle and long silver barrel connoting Spaghetti Westerns and Golden Age detective fiction. Visually at least, it was unimpressive.

It'd kill you all the same, though, wouldn't it? said Ruby's voice in her head.

El listened to the voice, and backed away from Marchant and the gun - further into the kitchen, closer to the others.

"El!" he said warmly. "So good to meet you at last. Meet you *properly*, I should say."

She stared - at him, at the gun, at the other women. It was all she could do.

"Don't tell him nothing," snarled Ruby. "Don't give him the satisfaction."

"I'll say it again, Martha," Marchant said, swivelling towards her and aiming the gun in her direction as he turned, "I don't need any of you to *tell* me anything. That's not why I came."

"Then why don't you stop fucking talking?" said Karen, rising up from the sofa. El saw the cut on her lip as she raised her head; she'd been hit or punched, hard enough to draw blood.

"Stay where you are, Miss Baxter," Marchant told her, "or it won't be a slap next time. I'll put a bullet in your kneecap."

But he kept his eyes on Ruby as he spoke, El noticed - almost as if he considered her the greater threat of the two, despite Karen's age, her obviously greater physical capacity. She wondered what had happened in the house before she'd arrived; what Ruby had said or done to him to warrant the reaction.

Which led her, inexorably, to another question.

"*How* are you here?" she asked Marchant. "How did you get in?"

"I should ask *her*, if I were you," said Ruby, pointing a finger past Marchant; towards the hallway beyond.

Between the kitchen and the hall, framed by the solid timber of the door, was Hannah.

"I'm afraid I let him in," she said.

It was another transformation.

The Hannah El had worked with - had virtually *lived* with - in the preceding months had been fragile, vulnerable; a sad porcelain doll of a woman. Elegant but, you could well imagine, easily shattered.

This Hannah was stronger and taller, her demeanour more arrogant than forlorn. There was a cruel quirk to her lips now; a suggestion of amusement taken in the suffering of others, of a joke made at someone else's expense. And something else, too - an echo of another face, another bearing, one that El knew better.

"You let him in," she repeated.

"How could I not, when he knocked so politely?" Hannah said, and there was amusement in her voice, too.

She's laughing at me, El thought; at all of us.

"You sold us out," she said, because it was the only thing that made sense, the only rational explanation for what she was seeing and hearing. "You sold us out to him."

Hannah looked to Marchant, and they exchanged smiles - genuine smiles, laced with mutual affection.

"Guilty as charged," she said, still smiling.

What did he give her? El thought. What could he possibly have offered her, to get her on side? To get her to *like* him - and like him enough to throw us to the wolves?

"Whatever you're asking yourself," said Ruby, who knew what she was thinking - who'd *always* known what she was thinking, "it ain't the right question, believe me."

"Honestly, Ruby," Hannah said. "You can hardly expect her to *guess*."

To guess *what*? El thought. What the fuck is going on here? What am I missing?

"She's *family*," said Rose, revolted. "His daughter."

"And *your* sister," Hannah told her, beaming. "Isn't that *hilarious*?"

HOLLAND PARK
1994

ines. Two blue lines, intersecting - a little Nordic cross against a grey plastic background.

Pregnant.

Hannah blinked; loosened her grip on the test and shook it, up and down and side to side, then looked again.

Pregnant.

The thought frightened and repulsed her every bit as much as she knew it would delight Justin. It was almost unbearable. Not only the pregnancy itself, the 9 months of harbouring the parasitic seed of that milquetoast in her body - although that part alone was horror enough. But the aftermath: the next 18 years or more of parents's evenings and homework and July fortnight holidays to Disneyworld and Mallorca with the parasite in tow, Justin fawning and simpering every step of the way.

She couldn't let it happen.

She rang the clinic that afternoon and booked an appointment for the following week. It was still early, she told herself; she couldn't be more than 8 weeks along. There was still time to get the tablets, to flush the thing out of her with the minimum of inconvenience; she wouldn't have to suffer the indignity of a forceps dilation and an overnight stay at the Portland.

Then, because it soothed her, she set to work on the house, cleaning and tidying and reorganising - finally, when she was finished, settling down on the couch with the dog and a Sonoma Chardonnay that would, she hoped, go some way towards dulling her awareness of the little interloper living inside her, albeit very temporarily.

At around 4pm, to her surprise, Justin dragged himself through the door, looking haggard and dishevelled and reeking of cheap alcohol and cigarettes, eyes red-rimmed and remaining hair sticking up from his scalp in childlike tufts. On another man, the *dishabille* might have been attractive, a signifier of rugged masculinity; on Justin it seemed shabby, pathetic, the physical manifestation of a lack of self-respect.

"I found something," he said, before she could ask him what he thought he was doing leaving the office in the middle of the day. "At work. And I don't... Hannah, I don't think it's something they want me to know."

"What the hell are you talking about?" she said. "And what are you doing home so early?"

He staggered into the lounge and collapsed, to her annoyance, into the space on the couch she'd just vacated.

"Lou applied for a promotion," he began. "She's going for Group Accounting Manager."

She was aware, dimly, that Lou was one of his finance team underlings - a meek, becardiganed woman who'd seemed to Hannah more suited to the secretarial pool than to corporate money management.

"What does that have to do with anything?" she snapped.

"Shut up and I'll tell you," Justin snapped back.

She fell quiet, astonished: she could count on a single hand the number of times he'd dared to raise his voice to her since they'd been married.

"She asked me for a reference," he continued, "so I thought I'd better look over some of her work. Due diligence, you know? She's been processing materials expenditure for the logistics team. It's straightforward enough, and she's never been sloppy, but they're big numbers, and I didn't want it to come back to bite me if she'd slipped up anywhere."

He pressed his fingertips into his temples, as if he were nursing a headache.

"The details aren't important, but I took a month at random - last December - and ran through the outgoings... and they don't make sense. There's more than double the amount going out than there should be, and a lot of it's being paid to a supplier I've never heard of. I can't prove it, but I don't think it's a real company. I think the money's being siphoned off."

"So old Lou's had her hand in the till?" Hannah said, still smarting from the way she'd been spoken to. "I wouldn't have thought she had it in her."

"It's not her," he said, still rubbing at his head. "She's too junior - all she does is process the outgoings. She doesn't sign them off. The costs for the shipping department alone are enormous - they need C-suite approval, a Director-level signature."

She began to see where he was going with his rambling narrative, and she didn't like it.

"I checked," he added. "I checked who's been signing them off. And it's him, Han. It's Marchant. I don't know why, but he's been diverting funds from the company. Stealing from himself."

This was bad, she thought. Very bad indeed. Justin was a weakling, but he fancied himself an ethical soul - a man who lived by his principles. And as frightened as he was of his employer, he was undoubtedly more afraid by far of becoming complicit in something illegal, of the possibility of arrest - of *prison*, even. If he'd found something incriminating, something concrete, then he'd speak out. There was no doubt in her mind.

But wait.

Wait.

Was it all bad? It seemed so on the face of it, yes. But was there something else there, too - an opportunity, for herself if not for Justin? A way of turning this potential clusterfuck around to her advantage - of using it to get what she wanted, what she'd wanted for the last 10 years or more?

She thought perhaps there might be.

"What are you going to do?" she asked him.

"I don't know. What do you think I should do?"

She sat down on the couch next to him and, with a tenderness she hoped he wouldn't find suspicious, cupped his jaw in her hand and pulled his face to hers.

"I have an idea," she told him.

She'd been nearly 30 when she'd learned James Marchant was her father.

The news came via her grandmother, whom Hannah had been visiting in her nursing home. She hadn't wanted to visit; had certainly felt no compassion for the old bitch, even as the Alzheimer's ate away at her brain and muscle wastage lay claim to the rest of her. It was too late for that; *she* might not remember the beatings she'd given Hannah as a kid, the ice bath immersions and the screamed incantations masquerading as prayers, but Hannah did. Remembered them very well.

The regional paper Hannah had been working for then hadn't paid much, though, and she was struggling with her rent, so submitting to the occasional trip to bedlam had seemed a relatively small price to pay for the likelihood of a generous inheritance, when the time came. And the time was certainly near; the nurses had told her so, albeit euphemistically. She wouldn't have to wait it out much longer.

There was a television in the old bitch's room, a black and white portable. Hannah had long been grateful for its presence - with the TV on, there was no need to struggle for conversation or feign interest in any broken anecdotes about air raid shelters or the interwar years. Instead, she could use the time to sit and think, while her grandmother stared blankly at Nationwide or This Is Your Life. This particular teatime, they'd been watching the news - listening first to Mrs Thatcher on the Soviet problem in Afghanistan, then to a feel-good piece about a large donation made to a newly-opened children's hospital by a London shipping magnate.

"That's him, that is," the old woman had said, thrusting one shaking finger towards the screen. "That's your dad."

Lovely, Hannah had thought. We've reached the confabulation stage of the evening.

"That's James Marchant, Gran," she'd said, trying for soothing. "He's a businessman. In the city."

"He's your *dad*," her grandmother had insisted, sounding for a moment unexpectedly lucid. "I might not have met him, but she had pictures, your Mam did - the police gave them to me after she passed, a big stack of them. I'd remember that nose anywhere."

It had come as news to Hannah that *anything* had been salvaged from her mother's bedsit after they found her body. She'd assumed that everything of value - sentimental as well as material - had been sold, or traded directly for another bag of the heroin that had eventually killed her.

"Where?" she'd asked. "Where are the photos?"

"Wouldn't you like to know?" the old bitch had cackled with some of her former malice, her gaze never leaving the television. "Wouldn't you just like to know?"

If she hadn't needed the money so badly, Hannah would have suffocated her with a pillow then and there.

She went straight from the nursing home to her grandmother's house in Ruislip, the same three-bedroom semi she'd been raised and tormented in from the day her mother had left her in a cot in the living room to the day she'd taken herself away to college, and let herself in with the key she still kept in her purse.

There was only one place, she'd thought, that a photo album could conceivably be hidden, since she'd pawned so much of the furniture: the loft. So she'd pulled down the hatch in the ceiling of the upstairs corridor and, with the keyring torch she carried in her satchel in her hand, she'd ascended the folding stairs into the spiderwebbed darkness at the top of the house.

The photos were easy to find; the old bitch had made barely any effort to hide them, burying the album in a pile under half a dozen lengths of dusty wrapping paper.

They were *strange* photos, though. Not the posed stills she'd envisaged, with smiling faces turned to the camera in pubs, at the seaside, around the dining table, but what seemed to her like stolen snapshots - taken surreptitiously, at mid-range, without their subject's knowledge or consent.

And always the same subject. A young man, younger than she was then, well-dressed and good-looking, performing a succession of mundane activities: eating dinner, a forkful of food raised to his mouth; lighting a fire with a rolled-up newspaper; talking on the telephone, the receiver pressed to his ear. She guessed, from the quality of the film and the cut of the man's suit, that the majority had been taken in the '50s - perhaps just before or just after she was born, in '52.

She couldn't be absolutely sure, at a distance of three decades, but he'd looked very much like a younger version of James Marchant, the man she'd seen on the news earlier that day - the man the old bitch had said was her father.

It was possible, she'd conceded, that he could have been. There was no father's name on her birth certificate, and there'd been no mention - beyond what she'd heard that night - that there'd been other men on the scene for her mother around the time she was born. The story of her conception was - had always been - a void, a hole in the pattern of the world. Her mother was rarely coherent enough to recall events beyond the very immediate past, even when she *was* around, and her grandmother's go-to responses to Hannah's questions - any of her questions at all - had ranged from the lightly chastising to the irrationally violent.

Probably, then, she'd thought, there was no way of knowing for sure, one way or the other - not definitively.

But she could certainly gather enough evidence to make an educated guess.

She'd gone into work at the crack of dawn the following day, and made a point of lingering by the coffee machine until she caught the eye of one of the sub-editors, Derek Proctor - a visually unappealing man whose cluttered desk had been, she suspected deliberately, pushed into the furthest corner of the office, closer to the bank of fax machines than to his other colleagues.

Derek was short, fat, acne-scarred and ringed by a halo of body odour that the aftershave he doused himself in could never quite mitigate. He'd had a poorly-concealed crush on Hannah since the week she'd started at the Star & Echo. Just as importantly for her purposes that morning, he'd managed the Star's substantial photo archive - a vast collection of folders containing thousands of images, as he'd once boasted to her after cornering her in the stairwell, that dated back to the '30s.

Upon seeing her, and seeing her see him, he'd immediately disentangled the bulk of his enormous gut from his swivel chair and stumbled towards her, as she'd known he would.

"Hello, Derek," she'd said, in the most flirtatious voice she could muster.

His piggy eyes gleamed.

"And hello to you too!" he'd wheezed, feasting on the sight of her breasts and hips. She'd imagined him tucking into his second plate of bacon and black pudding with the same grotesque gusto in his kitchen that morning. "In a bit early, aren't you? We don't usually see you here until lunchtime!"

She'd laughed at his quip, a breathy giggle that disgusted her as much coming from her own mouth as it would have done from another woman's.

"It's funny you should ask," she'd said. "I was looking for you, actually - I wanted to catch you before you got too busy. I was rather hoping you might be able to do me a favour..."

Ten minutes later, she was at her own desk, a stack of box folders in front of her - the ones Derek had told her were most likely to yield any historical photos they had of James Marchant.

She'd worked quickly, flipping through page after page of acetate-wrapped stills showcasing some of the big-name industrialists and money-men of the 50s and early 60s, from Julian Mond to a young Robert Maxwell, until she'd found the one she thought she was looking for: a monochrome close-up of James Marchant in white tie and tails, taken (claimed its accompanying label) at a gala event at the Ritz in May 1958.

She'd opened her bag, took out the photos she'd taken from her grandmother's house the night before and compared those shots with the gala photo.

There had been no question: the man in the tie and tails was, undeniably, the man in her mother's photo albums. The man the old bitch had called her father.

And was there, she'd wondered, something else familiar about the man - about his skin and his bone structure, his aquiline nose and high cheekbones?

He looked, she'd realised, very much like her, his face and long, angular body a more masculine variation on her own - the resemblance between them not the coincidental likeness of one stranger to another of their age and race, but the genetically-determined similitude of father and daughter.

The old bitch had been right, then. He was hers; and she was his.

After that, she was obsessed - spending every hour she wasn't working scouring libraries and archives and her growing network of independent contacts for facts about Marchant, his life and business. His family.

When these seams were exhausted, she'd resolved to obtain her information more directly, through first-hand observation. She began following him, taking notes and photographs of her own: at his home, on the way to and from his multitude of businesses, in the park with his kids. And with his *other* families, too: the children she'd learned, through months of painstaking research, that he'd fathered with other women, in Harrow and Slough and Hillingdon; the ones he visited when his wife was out of town or, perhaps, so drugged-up on the sleeping pills Hannah had seen her collect from the chemist that she failed to notice when he slipped out of the house before dark.

She'd realised fairly early on in the process that Marchant - that her father - cared little for these other families; the brevity and infrequency of his visits told her so. He thought of them, she'd suspected, the same way she might think of them herself in his position: as unwise purchases made on impulse, too inconveniently cumbersome to be kept on display but too costly to be discarded altogether. As expensive but poorly-designed furniture, destined for the attic.

She'd also realised that she had no intention of becoming another of his side-progeny, his secondary children.

When they met - and they *would* meet eventually, she'd told herself - it would be as equals. And he wouldn't tolerate her, as he did the others; wouldn't consider her a cross to be borne. No; he would respect her. Admire her.

But she'd have to be smart about it - smart, and patient. It wouldn't do to rush into engineering a meeting right away. She'd have to lay the right groundwork; have to *do* something, to earn his respect.

Her entanglement with and subsequent marriage to Justin D'Amboise had come about as a consequence of her observations of her father. He'd caught her standing for two days in a row outside the Bankside HQ, pretending – poorly – to smoke Silk Cut after Silk Cut; on the third day, he'd approached her and asked what she was doing there, since she clearly wasn't as dedicated a smoker as she seemed anxious to appear.

She'd spun him a story about job-hunting, about the dearth of opportunities in regional news and her interest in the media division of

Marchant Holdings. Did he know of any openings? she'd asked him, crushing her useless, half-smoked cigarette under her heel.

He'd laughed and said he was in Accounting, so probably not the best person to advise her. And then he'd asked her out for dinner.

Ordinarily, she'd have turned him down: he was neither charismatic nor particularly handsome, with a weak chin and an albino complexion and a skinny build that not even good tailoring had improved. But then he'd looked down at his watch, sworn and, before she could open her mouth to tell him she wasn't interested and never would be, had said he was sorry, but he had to go - he had a 2 o'clock meeting, and couldn't afford to keep his boss waiting.

"He's a hell of a businessman, Marchant," he'd said, "but you don't mess him around. Not if you value your job."

She'd given him her number on the spot.

Thereafter, Justin - chinless Justin, with his ever-receding hairline - had become her primary source of day-to-day intel on her father. If he suspected that her interest in his employer - in his moods, his habits, his relationship with his colleagues - was anything other than the interest typically afforded a hard-grafting man by his devoted girlfriend at the end of the working day, then he didn't show it.

When he'd proposed, she'd said yes - encouraging him to add Marchant and his plus-one to the wedding guest list. When Marchant failed to make an appearance at the chapel, despite his RSVP, the bitterness of her disappointment caused an argument that very nearly put an end to the marriage before they'd cut the cake.

And still, she'd waited - planning for the day she'd meet her father and show him why he ought to love her. Why *she* was better than the others.

"This is what you're doing to do," she told Justin, the afternoon he came home and had his hysterics on the couch. "You're going to go to bed and get some sleep. And tomorrow, you and I are going to go to Bankside together and get those files. Then we can decide what to do with them - whether or not we take them to the police."

He didn't answer, so she poured him a glass of the Sonoma Chardonnay - a glass *she* should have been drinking - and stroked the sweaty tufts of his hair as he drained it to the dregs. Then she poured him another.

They stayed like that on the couch, the television on in the background, until 8pm, when he eventually did what he was told and went to bed, leaving her alone in the lounge to think.

She knew by then what *she* needed to do - and more than that, how she needed to do it, how the events of the following day would need to unfold.

It was perfect, really. Serendipitous.

She barely slept that night. There was too much to prepare.

She woke him at 5am, an hour before his usual alarm call, and they drove to Southwark across the empty streets of the city in pensive silence. From time to time, she placed a hand over his on the steering wheel for moral support.

It was almost 6 when they arrived at Marchant Holdings. The building was as deserted as the road outside had been, save for the security guards on the door who nodded hello to Justin as they passed.

They'll remember seeing him, she thought. Seeing both of us.

But the idea didn't trouble her. A day from now, whatever they remembered would be immaterial. They wouldn't be telling a soul what they'd seen.

They took the lift to the 13th floor, where the finance team were based, and crossed the open-plan workspace of the lower minions to Justin's office. She ushered him inside; closed the door behind them.

"Where are the files?" she asked him.

"They're on the computer," he told her, indicating the off-white IBM that dominated his desk. "I'll need to print them out, but it'll take a while."

"I'll make you a coffee," she said, as he booted up the machine.

In the small shared kitchen, she found a jar of instant granules and a mug; heaped a generous spoonful of the former into the latter, and poured hot water from the kettle on top. She added milk from the fridge and two lumps of sugar - white and refined, the kind he devoured in defiance of the damage to his teeth, justifying it as fuel for his ludicrous jogs around the park. Finally, she pulled from her purse a small freezer-bag of crushed flunitrazepam, unsealed it and shook the powder into the coffee, stirring it until it disintegrated.

She carried the mug back to his office and placed it gently on the desk beside him.

"Thank you," he said gratefully. "I don't know what I'd do without you."

He blew on the coffee to cool it, and then downed half of it in three eager gulps.

"Is it printing?" she asked, killing time until the pills kicked in.

"Not yet," he answered. "I need to..."

He hesitated, mid-sentence; pawed at his collar like a cartoon adulterer in a confessional booth.

"Is it hot in here?" he said to her.

There was something comical about the speed of change in his expression; the way his pupils unfocused and his lips parted, as if he were about to drool onto his shirt.

"Are you alright, darling?" she asked him.

He spread his palms down on the desk and lowered his head to them. And then he was unconscious - or at any rate, unconscious enough.

She opened her purse again; took out her gloves and slipped them on, and after that a second item - a long leather belt, one of his. It was black calfskin, soft and pliable; she thought it might have been one of the ones she'd given to him as a Christmas present.

She walked to the door and tied the belt in a loop around the coat hook there - then walked back to the desk, to pick up Justin.

He was still skinny, a literal lightweight, and she found she could manoeuvre him with ease. With one of his arms around her shoulders and one of hers around his waist, she walked him to the coat hook; reached for the dangling end of the belt, and tied *that*, as tightly as she could manage, around his neck.

Then she stepped around him, took his legs by the ankles and pulled, until he was half-sitting and half-lying on the floor, the calfskin belt digging into the flesh of his throat.

He choked.

It took longer than she'd hoped. When it was done, she took the mug from the desk, carried it back to the kitchen and rinsed it in the sink with soap and hot water.

There, the tap running, she reviewed the mental checklist she'd made as Justin was dying:

Switch off the computer. They could figure out what to do with the files later; she was sure there was a way they could be modified, even if they couldn't be erased altogether. Perhaps even modified to make it seem like *Justin* was his one with a hand in the till.

Wipe the surfaces - the ones she could recall touching, anyway. She doubted the police would understand Justin's unfortunate demise as anything more than a suicide, but there was no sense tempting fate.

Then call her father.

Call her father, introduce herself, and tell him what she'd done for him.

NOTTING HILL
1996

You told the police he did it," El said, looking from Hannah to Marchant. "You said he killed your husband."

"I did," Hannah agreed.

"On my instructions, I might add," Marchant said. "I was nowhere near Bankside the day poor Justin had his accident - I wasn't even in London, from memory. I had a cast-iron alibi, so there was no-one better to use as a scape-goat and a whipping-boy, if it meant drawing suspicion away from Hannah."

And it cost you nothing, El thought. It cost you nothing, but it meant you'd always have her around when you needed her, and have her on side. That she'd do whatever you wanted, whenever you wanted it, and she'd never ask questions - just let herself be used, the way you'd use a weapon. All *you* had to do was keep your mouth shut and pretend to give a shit about her.

"I couldn't *believe* it, when Rose turned up on my door," said Hannah. "Given her reputation, I thought at first she might have come to offer condolences - a little comfort to the grieving wife. You know, girl to girl?"

"You wish," spat Karen, through what El suspected were broken teeth.

"Don't pretend you know anything about me or my life," Rose said, more calmly.

"As if it were a secret!" Hannah laughed. "I'm sorry to break it to you, darling, but *everyone* knew about you and Seb. He wasn't exactly discreet. Even *Justin* knew, and I had to tell *him* about Elton John. Anyway, as I say - imagine my surprise, when you turned up like that."

"Not to say mine, when she called me to let me know," said Marchant. "Or when I realised who you were, Olivia. You've hardly changed, you know."

El glanced out of the corner of her eye at Rose, looking - not for the first time - for some physical quality in common with Marchant, some curve of the lips or twist of the head that would suggest a familial connection. But there was nothing - no similarity at all.

But he and Hannah... they were two peas in a pod.

"You've been playing us?" she said - to Hannah, or Marchant, or both. "Stringing us along?"

"What choice did you leave us?" said Marchant. "We couldn't very well let you and your cabal of caped crusaders ruin me, could we?"

"If you ask me," said Karen, "he enjoyed it. Got off on thinking he was getting one over on us. Ain't that right, Jimmy?"

Hannah was across the room before El realised she'd moved. A cracking sound bit the air as her fist connected with Karen's jaw. El winced in sympathy - but wondered, too, why Karen wasn't fighting back, wasn't resisting.

"Bastard cuffed her," Ruby said, reading El's mind again.

"Rather fitting, after her turn with Seymour Henderson," said Marchant. "But I feel I should clarify that that *wasn't* my reason for letting your little heist run its course. Although," he added to El with a wink that made her stomach turn, "my campaign certainly benefitted from your advice. I'm still very much hoping the good people of Silvertown make the right choice when they go to the ballot box."

Why bother with it, then? El thought. Why not just shut us down from the beginning? Or take us out altogether, if you were that worried? It's not like we'd have seen it coming.

Then, suddenly, she knew.

The footage, she thought. You wanted the footage – Lomax's confession.

Because you didn't know what was on it, did you? Hannah didn't tell you, because she couldn't. She knew it existed, that there were hours and hours of videotape – Rose would have told her about it. But she wouldn't have *shown* her. She cared too much about protecting everyone else's secrets. And she wouldn't have thought Hannah needed convincing you were guilty.

Which means you probably *still* don't know what's there - what Lomax said about you, how much of your dirty laundry he aired.

And that's why you want it back. Why you *need* it back.

"You're here for the tapes," she said quietly. "The tapes Rose made of Lomax."

"We are, yes," Marchant said. His grip on the handle of the gun tightened. "But sadly my other daughter is being *terribly* uncooperative. Aren't you, Olivia?"

"My name isn't Olivia," said Rose. "*Olivia* was your daughter. I'm not."

"Oh, for God's sake!" said Marchant, beginning to lose patience. "Just give me the bloody tapes. Neither of us wants me to have to hurt Sophie, do we? She *is* my granddaughter, after all."

Sophie? El thought. He's got Sophie?

"You ain't laying a hand on that girl," growled Ruby.

"I've had two men in Sussex for the last two days, standing sentry outside the house she's been staying at," said Marchant matter-of-factly. "They sleep in shifts. If I call either one of them on their mobile phones, at any time, and give them the appropriate instruction, they'll shoot her in the head. And her aunt, too - Camilla, is it?"

A strangled sound, something like a wail, escaped from Rose. But she didn't cry - didn't plead or fall to her knees, begging.

Because she knows there's no point, El realised. She's seen up close what he's capable of when someone gets in his way. Even his own children.

"Give me the tapes," Marchant repeated. "The tapes, and all the copies, and Sophie will be fine. Better than fine, with all that sea air she's been breathing."

He pressed a finger to the trigger of the gun; pointed it in Rose's direction.

"*Now*, Livvy," he said. "Do it now, please."

"Big man you are," Karen said, her words beginning to slur through a jaw that looked like it might be dislocated. "A little kid, a *defenceless* little kid, and you can't even do her yourself. You have to get some other bloke to do the job for you, like you did with Kat."

"I assure you," Marchant said, adjusting his position so that the gun was facing Karen rather than Rose, "I had nothing to do with what happened to Miss Morgan. I rather liked her - I'd been looking forward to seeing where the evening might take us."

"Bash her own head in, did she?" said Ruby.

"I wouldn't say that, no," said Hannah. "And I won't say she *made* me do it. But she certainly didn't make things easy for herself."

They'd been driving for half an hour. She was itching to move faster, to go harder on the BMW's accelerator. But she was in character, still. And cautious, docile Hannah D'Amboise would never *dream* of speeding.

Kat was a talker, she was discovering. There'd always been others around them at Ledbury Road, the drone of other people's chatter ever-present in the background, and one consequence - from Hannah's perspective, an entirely happy consequence - was the lack of one-on-one interaction with any of the women.

Her concentration was, mercifully, drifting as she drove, but she'd gathered from the parts of Kat's wittering she hadn't successfully tuned out that she was being dragged, against her will, down someone else's memory lane - that Kat had chosen this moment to reminisce about some of the darker chapters in her biography.

How she came to be a streetwalker in the arsehole of North Wales, for example.

It was to do with her father, by the sound of it - and wasn't it always?

Her father, and someone else.

"It all comes back to Marchant," Kat said, and Hannah's attention was pulled immediately back to the conversation, monologic as it was. "Just like bloody everything. He ruined my Da, see."

As she talked, Hannah realised that it wasn't the first time she'd heard the story; that her father had told her some of it himself months earlier, when he'd learned who Kat was and how Rose planned to involve her in the scheme she was plotting.

Of course, his telling had been somewhat different, with more emphasis placed on what Kat called The Protoype - but what her father had ultimately patented as TCR3, an acronym she hadn't asked him to explain - than on the saga of Mr Morgan and his wayward daughters.

But it was still, fundamentally, the same story.

"Offended your sensibilities, have I?" asked Kat, when Hannah failed to speak in what was apparently her turn.

"Not at all," she said. "I'm just so sorry you had to go through that."

"It is what it is. But I do have to wonder what sort of life I might've had, if it weren't for Marchant. Marchant and that fucking turbocharger, whatever it was."

"The TCR3?"

She'd realised her mistake almost the second she'd made it. But by then, of course, it was too late.

Kat twisted in her seat, orienting her body towards Hannah's.

"How do you know that?" she said sharply. "How do you know what it was called?"

She considered lying; fabricating a reason, a legitimate-sounding one, for knowing about the Morgans, about the TCR3 and what had become of it after it was stolen. But it would be a fool's errand, she realised; whatever story she told could be readily contradicted by Rose or one or the others, its threads very easily unpicked.

No; lying wasn't an option.

But there was other ways to handle situations like this. She'd done it before; she could do it again.

Gently, she released her foot from the accelerator and shifted the steering wheel left; the car began to slow, to veer to the side of the road.

She slid her left hand down into the side pocket of the driving seat; to the heavy steering wheel lock she knew she'd find there, calculating how easily the windows would break, if she struck them. How much force it would take to get them to shatter.

"Listen..." she began, and when Kat angled her head to look at her, she pressed down on the brake, swung her left arm over her body in a wide arc and brought the curved end of the wheel lock down on Kat's skull.

"You fucking bitch," said Karen. "You murdering fucking bitch."

She pushed herself half-upright on the sofa, her body bent at the waist and wrists cuffed behind her back, and charged forward, butting her head into Hannah's stomach and knocking her to the ground.

Two things happened then, in the chaos that followed:

Marchant, his grip still tight on the gun, stepped forward towards the two women - his aim trained on Karen as she and Hannah fought and rolled.

And Ruby, whose back had been pinned to the counter, reached behind her into the cutlery drawer, drew out one of Rose's carbon-steel cooking knives and, her eyes never leaving Marchant, closed the distance between them in three long steps – then, keeping both of her hands on the dark wood handle, drove all 6 inches of the blade into his neck.

FROM THE BRACKNELL STAR & ECHO

November 1996

JAMES MARCHANT: THE ONE THAT GOT AWAY?

He was a titan of the international business world, and one of the UK's most successful sons. Then came the murder charges. Now he's on the run.

Six months ago James Marchant, billionaire former boss of Marchant Holdings, seemed to have the world at his feet.

Happily married and rich beyond the dreams of almost all of us, he was even planning a second career - this time in politics, by contesting the seat until recently held by disgraced ex-MP Seymour Henderson in London's Silvertown district.

Until, that is, he vanished.

Many theories have circulated since about the circumstances surrounding his disappearance following the launch of his election campaign in May of this year - some plausible and some preposterous.

Police have since confirmed that Marchant was being

investigated, at the time of his vanishing, for his possible role in the £20m embezzlement scandal that has since engulfed Marchant Holdings. They have confirmed moreover that a number of Swiss bank accounts held by Marchant, their value in the tens of millions of pounds, were emptied on the same day he went missing.

Confidential sources close to that investigation have also told the Star & Echo that a *second* case is being built against Marchant by police, this time for murder - and have refused to deny that incriminating videotape evidence from one of Marchant's close associates, rumoured to have fallen into the Met's hands over the summer, would play a central role in any subsequent charges brought against him.

Continued on page 3

EPILOGUE

Leicestershire, 1997

Out in the garden, El could still see the fireworks - rockets and Roman Candles mostly, the last few released from their box before her neighbours said goodbye to their guests and retreated to bed in anticipation of the New Year's Day hangovers that would soon be upon them.

"Pretty," said Ruby, coming up behind her.

"No light pollution out here," El replied. "Makes for clearer skies - it's one of the benefits of being out of the city. You'd know that, if you were up here more."

"I'm here now, ain't I?"

To El's surprise, they all were: not just Ruby but Sita and Karen and Theo, Dexter and his new girlfriend, Kat and the motorised wheelchair she was still learning to operate. Rose had brought Sophie; even Michael had put in an appearance, though he'd spent the night sipping still mineral water and obsessively checking his work pager.

She'd laid out bedding for them in just about every room of the house - so many fold-out camp beds and air mattresses that the cottage looked like a field hospital.

"The countryside suits you," El observed, only semi-truthfully. "You should go on the run more often."

"I am *not* on the run," said Ruby, affronted. "I've just... strategically withdrawn from London. Temporarily."

She'd been staying in Rotherham, in the house Rose had bought for her foster parents before they died. El had the impression she was finding the north a struggle.

"And when will you be strategically returning?" she asked.

"Soon as I can, sweetheart," Ruby replied. "Soon as I can, that's for damn sure."

El had thought she was desensitised; that she was becoming inured to violence, even violent death, after the weeks she'd spent at Ledbury Road and the things she'd heard and seen.

But this was here, right in front of her. And there was *so much* blood - brutal arterial sprays of it, from floor to ceiling.

Marchant's throat was gone, a gaping wine-coloured hole where skin and muscle should have been. The handle of the knife projected out from the hole at an angle – an inch of blade visible below it, the rest hidden by layers of ragged flesh. The unimpressive gun lay, useless, by his side.

And over his body knelt Ruby - her clothes soaked red, her face and neck a study in scarlet. She'd been silent; fixed to the spot, her own body as still as Marchant's.

Remembering where she was, what *else* had been happening while Marchant had been dying on his daughter's kitchen floor, El had spun around on the spot, towards Karen and Hannah - expecting to find them still struggling, that she'd have to intervene in Karen's defence.

But Karen was lying on her back, eyes swollen half-shut, yet more blood cascading from her nose. And Hannah was running out of the kitchen for the front door.

El had sprung forward, ready to run after her.

"Let her go," Sita had said, with enough authority that El hadn't thought to disobey. She remembered she'd been shocked; it was usually Ruby who gave the orders, Ruby who made the decisions in a pinch.

"Go?"

This had been from Karen, the effort to speak causing her obvious pain.

"We'll find her," said Sita. "Just not now."

She'd crossed the floor to Ruby and kneeled down next to her, her knees creaking as she bent.

She's getting older, El had thought; they're both getting older.

She'd brushed a strand of grey hair from Ruby's face, pressed their heads together until they were temple to temple, and whispered to her - soft, low words that El couldn't make out.

Then she'd got to her feet, and, after a moment, Ruby had followed.

"Do you have your telephone?" Sita asked El.

El had nodded *yes*; had held up the phone in her hand as proof.

"Call the boys," Sita had said. "Not just Dexter - Michael, too. Tell them they're to come here, now. Tell them their mother and I need them."

Another burst of fireworks sprung up from across the village, showering the garden very briefly in a constellation of yellow and green.

"Is there much to do in Rotherham?" El said.

Ruby snorted disdainfully.

"About as much as you'd expect," she said. "I've been weighing up buying myself a computer, getting on that internet Karen's always banging on about."

"She'd have to teach you how to turn it on first."

She waited to be scolded; told to watch her mouth or she'd get a clip round the ear. Instead, Ruby seemed to be thinking about something.

"As it happens," she told El, "I know a thing or two already. Picked up a few bits and pieces here and there over the summer when Karen was, you know ..."

El *did* know. And she also knew why Ruby - who didn't as a rule acknowledge her own embarrassment, only other people's - sounded close to sheepish.

She and Sita and Karen, El had learned after the fact, hadn't just been running *one* con on Marchant. They'd had their own side-job going, one they hadn't disclosed to the others.

"A little insurance, darling," Sita had called it. "It's just our way. We never like to put *all* our eggs in one basket."

Karen hadn't just been bugging offices and redirecting calls at Marchant Holdings, it transpired. She'd also been picking up where Sita and Ruby left off in the '60s, sniffing out the numbers and passcodes of Marchant's Swiss bank accounts – which, they'd accurately guessed, had been swelled significantly by the money he'd been draining from the business.

And she'd found them.

The day of Marchant's death, managers at the Zurich-based banking group St Helier received instructions to transfer amounts totalling almost £97 million from four separate accounts later discovered by Interpol to have been opened by Marchant himself in 1957. The money landed on the same day in accounts held by two *other* banks headquartered in the Cayman Islands – one registered to a Martha Lazarus, and the other to an M R Chandravali. Both *these* accounts were also traced, subsequently, to James Marchant.

After that, the money vanished - directly, or so Interpol and the Metropolitan Police suspected but couldn't yet prove, into James Marchant's pockets.

Wherever he was.

The following week, while the UK media were still scratching their heads about where Marchant might have gone after his press conference, a set of videotapes was delivered by anonymous courier to the desk of DCI Laurel Duncan, one-time lead officer on Operation Hornet - the investigation into the arson deaths of Heidi Simpson and her daughter Jade. The video featured, among other things, a lengthy confession from Marchant's now-deceased head of security, and hidden-camera footage of Marchant himself ordering a hit on a former BBC journalist, now herself missing.

Immediately thereafter, Marchant's disappearance, previously considered suspicious, was reassessed and reclassified by both Interpol and the Met. Officers earlier urged to look upon Marchant as a possible victim of crime were instructed instead to regard him as a suspect - a fugitive from justice.

Meanwhile, the money - all £96,930,000 of it - was quietly washed and redistributed 6 ways: to Ruby, Sita, Karen, Kat, Rose and El.

Under the circumstances, neither El nor Rose had objected. Nor, when she'd finally been released from hospital and realised the full extent of the equipment and physiotherapy bills she'd be facing, had Kat.

"You planning on becoming a hacker, then?" El asked Ruby. "Or just looking for love over the wires?"

This time Ruby *did* clip her round the ear. But gently; affectionately.

"What am I missing?" said Michael, stepping through the back door and into the garden. He'd replaced the mineral water, El was pleased to see, with a bottle of light beer.

"You need to keep an eye on your mother," El told him. "She's been trawling the net for toyboys."

"As long as she's being safe," Michael replied.

He stooped down to kiss first his mother and then El on the cheek.

"Happy new year," he said, then added: "Let's hope this one is less eventful than the last."

El wondered how he was coping - how he'd reconciled the life he lived, the reputation he'd built, the career he'd dedicated himself to with what Sita and his mother had asked of him that summer.

Dexter, she thought, was probably just fine. She didn't know exactly what he did for his client, or exactly *how* dirty he let his hands get doing it, but she had a sense that cleaning up blood and making firearms and bodies disappear wasn't a million miles shy of it. Nor was tracking missing persons, if the way he'd taken charge of looking for Hannah was anything to go by.

For Michael, though - the straight, respectable City man who, despite everything, had folded back the sleeves of his pinstripe shirt and helped his brother lift the remains of the man his mother had killed onto a plastic sheet - it was almost certainly more of an adjustment.

"It better be," said Ruby. "It bloody better be."

El was awake by 9.30 the following morning - late by the standards of her usual routine, but early, she considered, for a New Year's Day.

She crept downstairs as quietly as she could and, stepping over the sleeping forms of Theo and Karen, tiptoed to the kitchen to put the kettle on.

Rose was up already, buttering two rounds of toast.

"Sorry," she said, in a hushed voice. "Did I wake you?"

"Not at all," El replied awkwardly. "I'm no good at lie-ins. Especially not with the dawn chorus in there."

She gestured through the kitchen door to Karen, who was snoring heavily - an unfortunate side-effect, Sita had told her, of the dental work she'd needed after her altercation with Hannah.

"Good," Rose replied, equally awkwardly. "Good."

The extra layer of awkwardness between them was new and, to El, unsettling. She couldn't speak for Rose, but she, at least, knew why it had come about - and, more to the point, who to blame for it.

Her mistake, she thought, had been asking Sita again over one of their weekly lunches why she and Ruby had been so keen to introduce her to Rose, even before they'd known about the Marchant connection.

Without Ruby there to silence her, Sita was less circumspect.

"The thing is, darling," she'd said, "we worry about you, Auntie Ruby and I. You enjoy your own company, and Lord knows we respect that, but no woman is an island. You *need* someone - someone who knows you, who *understands* you. Someone you don't have to lie to about our... escapades. Someone to bring you breakfast in bed in the morning."

It took a full minute and two more bites of baba ganoush before the penny dropped.

"You were trying to *set me up* with her?" El had demanded.

Sita had tutted.

"Honestly," she'd said. "As if we'd do anything so crass. We were only hoping to... bring you together."

"And let fate takes its course, is that it?"

The old woman had smiled and sipped at her wine.

"Really," she'd said, "is that so bad?"

In the living room, Karen let out another snore - a long, slow death-rattle that reminded El of the fireworks of the night before.

"Do you have any jam?" Rose asked.

"What?" El said, shaking off the memory of Sita and Ruby and their meddling.

"Jam. For the toast."

Rose was looking at her strangely, appraisingly, and El wondered whether she'd had her own conversation with Sita, or with Ruby up in Rotherham. And if she had, what exactly had been said.

There was a knock on the door, soft and tentative.

Rose jumped, dropping the butter knife onto her plate with a clatter. She'd been more nervous than usual since Marchant's death, El knew; nervous, and more protective than ever of Sophie. El could hardly blame her.

"It's probably just the neighbours apologising for the fireworks," she told her, trying for reassurance. "They leave a fruit basket by the gate whenever they play music past 10.30, so they're probably wracked with guilt this morning. Give me a second?"

She traversed the living room obstacle course a second time and sprinted to the front door before whoever it was could knock again.

She opened the door, and found Harriet Marchant on the doorstep.

"Hello," she said, squinting uncertainly at El as if checking she'd got the right woman, the right house. "I don't know if you'll remember me, we only met briefly and I gather you were... someone else at the time, but I thought..."

She paused; took a breath.

"I'm Harriet Marchant," she said, more calmly. "Jim Marchant's daughter. Do you think I might come in?"

El made tea. Three cups: one for her, one for Rose and one for Harriet.

"I know you killed my father," Harriet said when El joined them at the kitchen table.

Silence.

"What do you plan to do with that information?" Rose replied eventually.

"Buy you dinner?" said Harriet.

She laughed. Neither Rose nor El did.

"He was a psychopath," she said, more seriously. "And I mean that in the clinical sense, not just pejoratively. I realise I'm not telling you anything you don't already know, but I want you to know that *I* know it. I don't know what exactly prompted you to do what you did - and please, don't tell me, I'd rather *not* know - but I know what he was like, and I'm sure I could take a guess, if I were inclined. If anyone deserved to die, it was him."

Another silence.

"How?" El asked eventually. "How did you find out?"

Harriet looked at her and smiled.

"I had you followed," she said. "After the day we met in his office. He introduced you as his campaign manager once you'd left, but I had a feeling you weren't... entirely who you'd told him you were."

She's a psychologist, El remembered. She sees through people.

And she's good. Or maybe *I'm* not as good as I think I am.

"And what did you discover?" Rose said - remarkably calmly, Rose thought.

"A fair amount," said Harriet. "Who all of you are, for example. That you're... sorry, I'm not sure what the word is. Grifters?"

El shrugged.

"Works for me," she said.

"What else?" said Rose.

"I know he came to your house in Notting Hill the day he disappeared," Harriet told her. "And that he didn't come out again. I know that, that same evening, two men were seen carrying what looked like a very large rug but was probably my father's body into the back of an estate car and driving it away. And I can't say for sure, but I'm reasonably certain that if the police were to look, they'd find some of the money they say he stole from the company in your bank accounts."

Rose tensed; balled her hands into fists.

"Is that all?" she said.

She wants to know if you know the *other* thing, El thought. If you've figured out that she's your sister.

"Are you asking if I know who we are to each other?" Harriet said.

"I suppose I am," Rose answered quietly.

"Then yes," said Harriet, equally quiet. "Yes, I do know. And perhaps one day, when this has blown over completely, we could go for a coffee. See if we have anything to talk about, besides *him*. But for now," she added, "I wanted to..."

She hesitated.

"What?" said El, unsure of where the conversation would take them next - any of them.

"I wanted you to know that you're safe - from me, at least. That what I know will stay with me. I have no interest in talking to anyone about it, least of all the police."

I believe her, El realised. I believe every word she's saying.

"Why?" she asked - needing more, some confirmation that she was reading things right, that they *were* safe.

Harriet bit her lip.

"He took your mothers," she said. "Took them from you, both of them. But he *kept* mine. Kept her for almost 50 years. I won't ask you to imagine what it was like for her, or for me and my brothers. But whatever it was you did to him in that house... frankly, I wish I'd found the nerve to do it myself."

She left quickly after that, her tea untouched, letting herself out of the back door of the cottage.

El and Rose stayed at the table, lost in their respective thoughts.

"Should we tell the others?" El said, when she heard the garden gate click shut.

"Is there anything to tell, if she keeps her word?" Rose replied.

She stood up.

"I don't know about you," she said, "but I could do with another cup of tea. Can I make you one?"

El thought about Elizabeth Marchant and her children; about mothers and daughters, and losing and keeping. Finally, maddeningly, she thought that perhaps Sita was right – that it *might* be nice to have someone to bring her breakfast in bed, or at the very least a cup of tea.

"Sure," she said. "That would be great."

ABOUT THE AUTHOR

TC PARKER is a writer and researcher based in the fox-ravaged wilds of Leicestershire, where she lives with her partner and family.

The author of the El Gardener feminist heist trilogy and the horror novels *Saltblood* and *A Press of Feathers,* she's been a copywriter, a lecturer and, very briefly, an academic. Now she runs a semiotics and cultural insight agency by day and dreams up horror and crime fiction at night, when the kids are asleep.

Visit her online at www.tcparkerwrites.com and follow her on Twitter @tcparkerlives